Mitchell, David
(David Stephen)

Ghostwritten.

$24.95

DATE			

BAKER & TAYLOR

GHOSTWRITTEN

GHOSTWRITTEN

A NOVEL

DAVID MITCHELL

 RANDOM HOUSE - NEW YORK

Grateful acknowledgment is made to the following for permission to reprint
previously published material:

SIMON AND SCHUSTER: Excerpt from "The Lake Isle of Innisfree" from *The Collected
Poems of W. B. Yeats,* Revised Second Edition, edited by Richard J. Finneran.
Copyright © 1983, 1989 by Anne Yeats. Reprinted by permission of Scribner,
a division of Simon and Schuster.

WEATHERHILL, INC.: Two haiku from *Mountain Tasting* by Taneda Santoka, translated
by John Stevens. Reprinted by permission of Weatherhill, Inc.

RANDOM HOUSE and colophon are registered trademarks of Random House, Inc.

Library of Congress Cataloging-in-Publication Data

Mitchell, David (David Stephen).
Ghostwritten: a novel / David Mitchell—1st ed.
p. cm.
ISBN 0-679-46304-6 (hardcover : acid-free paper)
I. Title.

PR6063.I785 G48   2000
823'.92—dc21   99-044063

Random House website address: www.atrandom.com

Printed in the United States of America on acid-free paper

2 3 4 5 6 7 8 9

First Edition

Book design by Mercedes Everett

FOR JOHN

. . . And I, who claim to know so much more, isn't it possible that even I have missed the very spring within the spring?

Some say that we shall never know, and that to the gods we are like the flies that the boys kill on a summer day, and some say, on the contrary, that the very sparrows do not lose a feather that has not been brushed away by the finger of God.

Thornton Wilder, *The Bridge of San Luis Rey*

CONTENTS

OKINAWA

WHO WAS BLOWING on the nape of my neck?

I swung around. The tinted glass doors hissed shut. The light was bright. Synthetic ferns swayed, very gently, up and down the empty lobby. Nothing moved in the sun-smacked car park. Beyond, a row of palm trees and the deep sky.

"Sir?"

I swung around. The receptionist was still waiting, offering me her pen, her smile as ironed as her uniform. I saw the pores beneath her makeup, and heard the silence beneath the Muzak, and the rushing beneath the silence.

"Kobayashi. I called from the airport, a while ago. To reserve a room." Pinpricking in the palms of my hands. Little thorns.

"Ah, yes, Mr. Kobayashi . . ." So what if she didn't believe me? The unclean check into hotels under false names all the time. To fornicate, with strangers. "If I could just ask you to fill in your name and address here, sir . . . and your profession?"

I showed her my bandaged hand. "I'm afraid you'll have to fill the form in for me."

"Certainly . . . My, how did that happen?"

"A door closed on it."

She winced sympathetically, and turned the form around. "Your profession, Mr. Kobayashi?"

"I'm a software engineer. I develop products for different companies, on a contract-by-contract basis."

She frowned. I wasn't fitting her form. "I see, no company as such, then . . ."

"Let's use the company I'm working with at the moment."

Easy. The Fellowship's technology division will arrange corroboration.

"Fine, Mr. Kobayashi . . . Welcome to the Okinawa Garden Hotel."

"Thank you."

"Are you visiting Okinawa for business or for sightseeing, Mr. Kobayashi?"

Was there something quizzical in her smile? Suspicion in her face?

"Partly business, partly sightseeing." I deployed my alpha control voice.

"We hope you have a pleasant stay. Here's your key, sir. Room 307. If we can assist you in any way, please don't hesitate to ask."

You? Assist me? "Thank you."

Unclean, unclean. These Okinawans never were pure-blooded Japanese. Different, weaker ancestors. As I turned away and walked toward the elevator, my ESP told me she was smirking to herself. She wouldn't be smirking if she knew the caliber of mind she was dealing with. Her time will come, like all the others.

Not a soul was stirring in the giant hotel. Hushed corridors stretched into the noontime distance, empty as catacombs.

There's no air in my room. Use of air-conditioning is prohibited in Sanctuary because it impairs alpha waves. To show solidarity with my brothers and sisters, I switched it off and opened the windows. The curtains I keep drawn. You never know whose telephoto lens might be looking in.

I looked out into the eye of the sun. Naha is a cheap, ugly city. But for the background band of Pacific aquamarine this city could be any tentacle of Tokyo. The usual red-and-white TV transmitter, broadcasting the government's subliminal command frequencies. The usual department stores rising like windowless temples, dazzling the unclean into compliance. The urban districts, the factories pumping out poison into the air and water supplies. Fridges abandoned in wastegrounds of lesser trash. What grafted-on pieces of ugliness are their cities! I imagine the New Earth sweeping this festering mess away like a mighty broom, returning the land to its virginal state. Then the Fellowship will create something we deserve, which the survivors will cherish for eternity.

I cleaned myself and examined my face in the bathroom mirror. You are one such survivor, Quasar. Strong features, highlighting my samurai legacy. Ridged eyebrows. A hawkish nose. Quasar, the harbinger. His Serendipity had chosen my name prophetically. My role was to pulse at the edge of the universe of the faithful, alone in the darkness. An outrider. A herald.

The extractor fan droned. Somewhere beyond its drone I could hear a little girl, sobbing. So much sadness in this twisted world. I began shaving.

I awoke early, not remembering where I was for the first few moments. Jigsaw pieces of my dream lay dropped around. There had been Mr. Ikeda, my home-room teacher from high school, and two or three of the worst bullies. My biological father had appeared too. I remembered that day when the bullies had got everyone in the class to pretend that I was dead. By afternoon it had spread through the whole school. Everyone pretended they couldn't see me. When I spoke they pretended they couldn't hear me. Mr. Ikeda got to hear about it, and as a society-appointed guardian of young minds what did he take it upon himself to do? The bastard conducted a funeral service for me during the final home-room hour. He'd even lit some incense, and led the chanting, and everything.

Before His Serendipity lit my life I was defenseless. I sobbed and screamed at them to stop, but nobody saw me. I was dead.

After awakening, I found I was tormented with an erection. Too much gamma wave interference. I meditated under my picture of His Serendipity until it subsided.

If it's funerals the unclean want, they shall have them aplenty, during the White Nights, before His Serendipity rises to claim His kingdom. Funerals with no mourners.

I walked down the Kokusai Dori, the main street of the city, doubling back and weaving off to lose anybody who was trailing me. Unfortunately my alpha potential is still too weak to achieve invisibility, so I have to shake trailers the old-fashioned way. When I was sure nobody was following me I ducked into a games center and placed a call from a telephone booth. Public call boxes are much less likely to be bugged.

"Brother, this is Quasar. Please connect me with the minister of defense."

"Certainly, brother. The minister is expecting you. Permit me to congratulate you on the success of our recent mission."

I was put on hold for a couple of moments. The minister of defense is a favorite of His Serendipity's. He graduated from the Imperial University. He was a judge, before hearing the call of His Serendipity. He is a born leader. "Ah, Quasar. Excellent. You are in good health?"

"On His Serendipity's service, Minister, I always enjoy good health. I have overcome my allergies, and for nine months I haven't suffered from—"

"We are delighted with you. His Serendipity is mightily impressed with the depth of your faith. *Mightily* impressed. He is meditating on your anima now, in His retreat. On yours alone, for fortification and enrichment."

"Minister! I beg you to convey my deepest thanks."

"Gladly. You've earned it. This is a war against the unclean myriad, and in this war acts of courage do not go unacknowledged, nor unrewarded. Now. You'll be wondering how long you are to remain away from your family. The Cabinet believes seven days will suffice."

"I understand, Minister." I bowed deeply.

"Have you seen the television reports?"

"I avoid the lies of the unclean state, Minister. *For what snake would willingly heed the voice of the snake charmer?* Even though I am away from Sanctuary, His Serendipity's instructions are inscribed in my heart. I imagine we have caused a stir among the hornets."

"Indeed. They are talking about terrorism, showing the unclean foaming at the mouth. The poor animals are almost to be pitied—almost. As His Serendipity predicted, they are missing the point that it is *their* sins being visited on *their* heads. Be proud, Quasar, that *you* were one of the chosen ministers of justice! The

39th Sacred Revelation: *Pride in one's sacrifice is not a sin but self-respect.* Keep a low profile, nonetheless. Blend in. Do a little sight-seeing. I trust your expense account will suffice?"

"The treasurer was most generous, and my needs are simple."

"Very good. Contact us again in seven days. The Fellowship looks forward to welcoming our beloved brother home."

I returned to the hotel for my midday cleaning and meditation. I ate some crackers, seaweed snacks, and cashew nuts, and drank green tea from a vending machine outside my room. When I went out again after lunch the unclean receptionist gave me a map, and I chose a tourist spot to visit.

The Japanese naval headquarters was set in a scrubby park at the top of a hill overlooking Naha, to the north. During the war it had been so well hidden that it took the invading Americans three weeks after they had seized Okinawa to stumble across it. The Americans are not a very bright race. They miss the obvious. Their embassy had the effrontery to deny His Serendipity a residence visa ten years ago. Now, of course, His Serendipity can come and go where he pleases using subspace conversion techniques. He has visited the White House several times, unhindered.

I paid for my ticket and went down the steps. The dim coolness welcomed me. A pipe somewhere was dripping. There was one more surprise waiting for the American invaders. In order to die an honorable death, the full contingent of four thousand men had taken their own lives. Twenty days previously.

Honor. What does this frothy, idol-riddled world of the unclean know of honor? Walking through the tunnels I stroked the walls with my fingertips. I stroked the scars on the wall, made by the grenade blasts and the picks that the soldiers had used to dig their stronghold, and I felt true kinship with them. The same kinship I feel at Sanctuary. With my enhanced alpha quotient, I was picking up on their anima residue. I wandered the tunnels until I lost track of the time.

As I left that memorial to nobility a coachload of tourists arrived. I took one look at them, with their cameras and potato-chip packets and their stupid Kansai expressions and their limbless minds with less alpha capacity than a housefly, and I wished that I had one more phial of the cleansing fluid left, so that I could lob it down the stairs after them and lock them in. They would be cleansed in the same way that the money-blinded of Tokyo had been cleansed. It would have appeased the souls of the young soldiers who had died for their beliefs decades ago, as I had been ready to do only seventy-two hours ago. They were betrayed by the puppet governments that despoiled our land after the war. As have we *all* been betrayed by a society evolving into markets for Disney and McDonald's. All that sacrifice, to build what? To build an unsinkable aircraft carrier for the United States.

But I had no phials left, and so I had to endure those unclean, chattering, defecating, spawning, defiling cretins. Literally, they made me gasp for air.

I walked back down the hill under the palm trees.

In the palm of the left hand there is an alpha receptor point. When His Serendipity first granted me a personal audience He held my hand open and gently pressed this receptor point with His index finger. I felt a peculiar buzz, like a pleasant electric shock, and I was later to discover that my concentrative powers had quadrupled.

It was raining on that most precious day, three and a half years ago. Clouds marched down from Mt. Fuji, an eastern wind blew across the undulating farmland around Sanctuary. I'd enlisted on the Fellowship Welcome Program twelve weeks before, and on this morning I had completed some business with one of the undersecretaries of the Fellowship Treasury. I had signed the papers releasing me from the prison of materialism. Now the Fellowship owned my house and its contents, my savings, pension funds, my golf membership, and my car. I felt freer than I had ever believed possible. My family—my unclean, biological family, my skin family—predictably failed to understand. All my life, they had measured every last millimeter of failure and success, and here I was snapping their rule across my knee. The last letter I ever received from my mother informed me that my father had written me out of his will. But as His Serendipity writes in the 71st Sacred Revelation, *The fury of the damned is as impotent as a rat gnawing a holy mountain.*

They never loved me, anyway. They wouldn't know of the word's existence if they hadn't seen it on the TV.

His Serendipity came down the stairs, accompanied by the minister of security. The light whitened as He neared the office. I saw His sandaled feet and His purple robes first, then the rest of His beloved form came into view. He smiled at me, knowing telepathically who I was and what I had done. "I am the Guru." And He permitted me to kiss His holy ruby ring as I knelt. I could feel His alpha emanations, like a compass feels magnetic north.

"Master," I replied. "I have come home."

His Serendipity spoke cleanly and beautifully, and the words came from His very eyes. "You have freed yourself from the asylum of the unclean. Little brother. Today you have joined a new family. You have transcended your old family of the skin, and you have joined a new family of the spirit. From this day, you have ten thousand brothers and sisters. This family will grow into millions by the end of the world. And it will grow, and grow, with roots in all nations. We are finding fertile soil in foreign lands. Our family will grow until the world without is the world within. This is not a prophecy. This is inevitable, future reality. How do you feel, newest child of our nation without borders, without suffering?"

"Lucky, Your Serendipity. So very lucky to be able to drink from the fountain of truth while still in my twenties."

"My little brother, we both know that it was not luck which brought you here. Love brought you to us." Then He kissed me, and I kissed the mouth of eternal life. "Who knows," said my Master, "if you continue your alpha self-amplification as rapidly as the minister of education reports, you may be entrusted with a very special mission in the future. . . ." My heart leapt still higher. I had been discussed! Only a novice, but I had been discussed!

In the coffee bars, in shops and offices and schools, on the giant screen in the shopping mall, in every rabbit-hutch apartment, people watched news of the cleansing. The maid who came to clean my room wouldn't shut up about it. I let her babble. She asked me what I thought. I said that I was only a computer-systems engineer from Nagoya and knew nothing about such matters. Indifference was not enough for her: outrage has become compulsory. To avert suspicion, a little playacting will be necessary. The maid mentioned the Fellowship. It seems that the leprous fingers of our country's detestable media are being pointed, despite our past warnings.

I went out in the middle of the afternoon to buy some more shampoo and soap. The receptionist was sitting with her back to the lobby, glued to the set. Television is unclean lies, and it damages your alpha cortex. However, I thought just a few minutes wouldn't hurt me, so I watched it with her. Twenty-one cleansed, and many hundreds semi-cleansed. An unequivocal warning to the state of the unclean.

"I can't believe it happened in Japan," said the receptionist. "In America, yes. But here?"

A panel of "experts" was discussing the "atrocity." The experts included a nineteen-year-old pop star and a sociology professor from Tokyo University. Why do Japanese only listen to pop stars and professors? They kept playing the same footage over and over again, a scene of the uncleansed running out of the metro station, handkerchiefs smothering their mouths, retching, scratching furiously at their eyes. As His Serendipity writes in the 32nd Sacred Revelation, *If thine eye offend thee, pluck it out.* Pictures of the cleansed, lying still where their cleansing had freed them. Their skin families, sobbing in their ignorance. Cut to the prime minister, the bushiest fool of them all, swearing that he wouldn't rest until "the perpetrators of this monstrosity were brought to justice."

Is this hypocrisy not blinding? Can't they see that the real atrocity is the modern world's systematic slaughter of man's oneness with his anima? The act of the Fellowship was merely one counterattack against the true monster of our age. The first skirmish in a long war that evolution destines us to win.

And why can people not see the futility? A mere politician, one more bribe-taking, back-stabbing, under-the-table cockroach whose mind cannot even conceive of the cesspit it flounders in: How could such unclean lowlifes ever hope to coerce His Serendipity into doing anything? A boddhisatva who can make Himself invisible at will, a yogic flier, a divine being who can breathe underwater. Bring Him and His servants to "justice"? *We* are the floating ministers of justice! Of course I still lack the alpha quotient to shield myself with telepathy or telekinesis, but I am many hundreds of kilometers away from the scene of the cleansing. They'll never think of looking for me here.

I slipped out of the cool lobby.

I kept a low profile all week, but invisibility might attract attention. I invented business meetings to attend, and from Monday to Friday walked past the receptionist with a curt "Good morning" promptly at 8:30 A.M. Time dragged its heels. Naha's just another small city. The Americans from the military bases that plague these islands strut up and down the main streets, many of them with our females draped off their arms, Japanese females clad in nothing but little wraps of cloth. The Okinawan males ape the foreigners. I walked through the department stores, watching the endless chain of wanting and buying. I walked until my feet ached. I sat in shady coffee shops, where shelves sagged under the weight of magazines of mindtrash. I eavesdropped on businessmen, buying and selling what wasn't theirs. I carried on walking. Workaday idiots gaped in the rattling vacuity of pachinko machines, as I had once done in the days before His Serendipity opened my inner eyes. Tourists from the mainland toured the souvenir shops, buying boxes of tat that nobody ever really wants. The usual foreigners selling watches and cheap jewelry on the pavements, without licenses. I walked through the games arcades where the poisoned children congregate after school, gazing at screens where evil cyborgs, phantoms, and zombies do battle. The same shops as anywhere else . . . Burger King, Benetton, Nike . . . High streets are becoming the same all over the world, I suppose. I walked through backstreets, where housewives put out futons to air, living the same year sixty times. I watched a potter with a pocked face, bent over a wheel. A dying man, coughing without removing his cigarette, repaired a child's tricycle on a bottom step. A woman without any teeth put fresh flowers in a vase beneath a family shrine. I went to the old Ryukyu palace one afternoon. There were drinks machines in the courtyard, and a shop called The Holy Swordsman that sold nothing but key rings and camera film. The ancient ramparts were swarming with high school kids from Tokyo. The boys look like girls, with long hair and pierced ears and plucked eyebrows. The girls laugh like spider monkeys into their pocket phones. Hate them and you have to hate the world, Quasar.

Very well, Quasar. Let us hate the world.

The only peaceful place in Naha was the port. I watched boats, islanders, tourists, and mighty cargo ships. I've always enjoyed the sea. My biological uncle used to take me to the harbor at Yokohama. We used to take a pocket atlas to look up the ships' ports and countries of origin.

Of course, that was a lifetime ago. Before my true father called me home.

Coming out of an alpha trance one day after my noon cleansing, a spoked shadow congealed into a spider. I was going to flush it down the toilet when, to my amazement, it transmitted an alpha message! Of course, His Serendipity was using it to speak with me. The Guru has an impish sense of humor.

"Courage, Quasar, my chosen. Courage, and strength. This is your destiny."

I knelt before the spider. "I knew You wouldn't forget me, Lord," I answered, and let the spider wander over my body. Then I put him in a little jar. I resolved to buy some flypaper to catch flies, so I could feed my little brother. We are both His Serendipity's messengers.

Speculation about the "doomsday cult" continues. How it annoys me! The Fellowship stands for life, not for doom. The Fellowship is not a "cult." Cults enslave. The Fellowship liberates. Leaders of cults are fork-tongued swindlers with private harems of whores and fleets of Rolls-Royces behind the stage set. I have been privileged to glimpse life in the Guru's inner circle—not one girl in sight! His Serendipity is free of the sticky web of sex. His Serendipity's wife was chosen merely to bear His children. The younger sons of Cabinet members and favored disciples are permitted to attend to the Guru's modest domestic needs. These fortunates are clad only in meditation loincloths so they are ready to assume *zazen* alpha positioning whenever the Master condescends to bestow his blessing. And in the whole of Sanctuary there are only three Cadillacs—His Serendipity well knows when to exorcise the demons of materialism that possess the unclean, and when to exploit this obsession as a Trojan Horse, to penetrate the mire of the world outside.

To deflect suspicion from the Fellowship, His Serendipity allowed some journalists into Sanctuary to film brothers and sisters during alpha enrichment. Our chemical facilities were also inspected. The minister of science explained that we were making fertilizer. Being vegetarians, he joked, the Fellowship needs to grow a lot of cucumbers! I recognized my brothers and sisters. They gave telepathic messages of encouragement to their brother Quasar through their screen images. I laughed aloud. The unclean TV news hyenas were trying to incriminate the Fellowship, not noticing how the Fellowship was using them to transmit messages to me. The minister of security allowed himself to be interviewed. Brilliantly, he defended the Fellowship from any involvement in the cleansing. *One can only outwit demons,* His Serendipity teaches in the 13th Sacred Revelation, *if one is as cunning as the lord of Hell.*

More disturbing were the television interviews with the blind unclean. The apostates. People who are welcomed into the Fellowship's love, but who reject it and fall again into the world of shit outside Sanctuary. In his infinite mercy His Serendipity permits these maggots to live, if "living" it can be called, on condition that they do not defame the Fellowship. If they ignore this law and sow lies about Sanctuary in the press, the minister of security has to license the cleansing of them and their families.

On television the faces of the blind unclean were digitalized out, but no image-doctoring can fool a mind of my alpha quotient. One was Mayumi Aoi, who joined the Fellowship in my Welcome Program. She paid lip-service to His Serendipity, but one morning, eight weeks into the Program, we awoke to find her gone. We all suspected her of being a police agent. Hearing the lies she told about life in Sanctuary, I switched the television off and resolved never to watch it again.

A week after my first call I telephoned Sanctuary. I was answered by a voice I didn't know.

"Good morning. This is Quasar."

"Ah, Quasar. The minister of information is busy this morning. I am his undersecretary. We've been expecting your call. Have you seen the growing hysteria?"

"Indeed, sir."

"Yes. Your cleansing operation was almost *too* successful, it might appear. His Serendipity has ordered me to tell you to lie low for a couple more weeks."

"I obey His Serendipity in all things."

"In addition, you are ordered to proceed to a more remote location. Purely as a precaution. Our brothers in the unclean police have told us your details are being circulated. We must act with stealth, and guile. Officially, we are denying complicity in your gas attack. This will win us more time to strengthen the Fellowship with new brothers and sisters. This tactic worked for our cleansing experiment in Nagano Prefecture last year. How easily misled are these dung beetles!"

"Indeed, sir."

"In the event that you are arrested, you are to assume full responsibility for your attack, and claim that you had acted entirely on your own volition, after being expelled from the Fellowship for insanity. You would then be teleported out of custody by His Serendipity."

"Naturally, sir. I obey His Serendipity in all things."

"You are a great asset to the Fellowship, Quasar. Any questions?"

"I was wondering if phase two of the great cleansing has begun yet, sir? Have our yogic fliers been despatched to the parliament building to demand the integration of His Serendipity's teachings into the national curriculum? If we leave it too long, then the unclean might—"

"Quasar, you forget yourself! When was it decreed that your responsibilities included advocating Fellowship foreign policy?"

"I understand my error, sir. Forgive me, sir. I beg you."

"You are already forgiven, dear son of His Serendipity! No doubt you are lonely, away from your family?"

"Yes, sir. But I received the alpha wave messages sent from my brothers and sisters through the news broadcasts. And His Serendipity speaks to me words of comfort in my exile as I meditate."

"Excellent. Two more weeks should be sufficient, Quasar. If your funds run low, you may contact the Fellowship's Secret Service using the usual code. Otherwise maintain silence."

"One more thing, sir. The apostate Mayumi Aoi—"

"The minister of information has noticed. *The sewers of the blind unclean shall forever be sealed.* The minister of security will act, when the present scrutiny subsides. Perhaps we have shown too much mercy in the past. We are now at war."

I walked to the port in the stellar heat of mid-afternoon and collected boat schedules from a rack. I pulled open my map. I have always preferred maps to books. They don't answer you back. Never throw a map away. The islands beckoned, imperial emeralds in a sky-blue sea. I chose one labeled Kumejima. Half a day away to the west, but not so small that a visitor would stand out. There was only one boat per day, departing at 6:45 A.M. I bought a ticket for the next day's sailing.

I spent the rest of the day sitting on the quay. I recited all of His Serendipity's Sacred Revelations, oblivious to the flow of lost souls passing by.

Eventually the sun sank, crimson and wobbling. I hadn't noticed it grow dark. I walked back to my hotel, where I told the receptionist that my business was concluded and I would depart for Osaka early the next morning.

The subway train in Tokyo was as crammed as a cattle wagon. Crammed with organs, wrapped in meat, wrapped in clothes. Silent and sweaty. I was half-afraid some fool would crush the phials prematurely. Our minister of science had explained to me exactly how the package worked. When I ripped open the seal and pressed the three buttons simultaneously, I would have one minute to get clear before the solenoids shattered the phials, and the great cleansing of the world would begin.

I put the package on the baggage rack and waited for the appointed minute. I focused my alpha telepathy, and sent messages of encouragement to my co-cleansers in various metro trains throughout Tokyo.

I studied the people around me. The honored unclean, the first to be cleansed. Dumb. Sorry. Tired. Mind-rotted. Mules, in a never-ending whirlpool of lies, pain, and ignorance. I was a few inches away from a baby, in a woolly cap, strapped to its mother's back. It was asleep and dribbling and smelt of toddlers' marshiness. A girl, I guessed from the pink Minnie Mouse sewn onto the cap. Pensioners who had nothing to look forward to but senility and wheelchairs in lonely magnolia "homes." Young salarymen, supposedly in their prime, their minds conditioned for greed and bullying.

I had the life and death of those lowlifes in my hands! What would they say? How would they try to dissuade me? How would they justify their insectoid existences? Where could they start? How could a tadpole address a god?

The carriage swayed, jarred, and the lights dipped for a moment into brown.

Not well enough.

I remembered His Serendipity's words that morning. "I have seen the comet, far beyond the farthest orbit of the mundane mind. The New Earth is approaching. The judgment of the vermin is coming. By helping it along a little, we are putting them out of their misery. Sons, you are the chosen agents of the Divine."

In those last few moments, as we pulled into the station, His Serendipity fortified me with a vision of the future. Within three short years His Serendipity is going to enter Jerusalem. In the same year Mecca is going to bow down, and the Pope and the Dalai Lama will seek conversion. The presidents of Russia and the U.S. petition for His Serendipity's patronage.

Then, in July of that year, the comet is detected by observatories all over the world. Narrowly missing Neptune, it approaches Earth, eclipsing the Moon, blazing even in the midday sky over the airfields and mountain ranges and cities of the world. The unclean rush out and welcome this latest novelty. And that will be their undoing! The Earth is bathed in microwaves from the comet, and only those with high alpha quotients will be able to insulate themselves. The unclean die, retching, scratching out their eyes, stinking of their own flesh as it cooks on their bones. The survivors begin the creation of Paradise. His Serendipity will reveal himself as His Divinity. A butterfly emerging from the chrysalis of His body.

I feel into the perforated sports bag, and I rip open the seal. I have to flick the switches, and hold them down for three seconds to set the timer. One. Two. Three. The New Earth is coming. History is ticking. I zip the bag shut, let it fall to my feet, and shunt it surreptitiously under a seat with the back of my heel. The compartment is so crammed that none of the zombies notices.

The will of His Serendipity.

The train pulls into the station, and—

I hear the noises under the manhole cover, but I dare not, dare not listen to its words.

If the noises ever become words—not now, not yet. Not ever. Where would it end?

I enter the current that flows to the escalators, and away from there.

Over my shoulder, the train accelerates into the fumy darkness.

The palms of my hands were pricking and sweaty. A seagull strutted along the window ledge and peered in. It had a cruel face.

"And your name, sir?" The old lady who ran the inn grinned the grimace of a temple god. Why was she grinning? To make me nervous? She had more black gaps than stained teeth.

"My name's Tokunaga. Buntaro Tokunaga."

"Tokunaga . . . lovely name. It has a regal air."

"I've never thought about it."

"And what business are you in, Mr. Tokunaga?"

Questions and questions. Do the unclean never stop?

"I'm just an ordinary salaryman. I don't work for a famous company. I'm the department head of a small computer business in the suburbs of Tokyo."

"Tokyo? Is that so? I've never been to the mainland. We get a lot of holidaymakers from Tokyo. Though not off-season, like now. You can see for yourself, we're almost empty. I only go to the main island once a year, to visit my grandchildren. I have fourteen grandchildren, you know. Of course, when I say "main island," I mean the main island of Okinawa, not mainland Japan. I'd never dream of going there!"

"Really."

"They tell me Tokyo's very big. Bigger even than Naha. A department head? Your mother and father must be so proud! My, that's grand. I've got to ask you to fill out these dratted forms, you know. I wouldn't bother with it myself but my daughter makes me do it. It's all to do with licenses and tax. It's a real nuisance. Still. And how long will you be with us on Kumejima, Mr. Tokunaga?"

"I intend to stay a couple of weeks."

"Is that so? My, I hope you'll find enough to do. We're not a very big island, you know. You can go fishing, or go surfing, or go snorkeling, or scuba diving . . . but apart from that, life is very quiet here. Very slow. Not like Tokyo, I imagine. Won't your wife be missing you?"

"No." Time to shut her up. "The truth is, I'm here on compassionate leave. My wife passed away last month. Cancer."

The old crone's face fell, and her hand covered her mouth. Her voice fell to a whisper. "Oh, my. Is that so? Oh, my. There I go, putting my foot in it again. My daughter would be *so* ashamed. I don't know what to say—" She kept wheezing apologetically, which was doubly irksome as her breath reeked of prawns.

"Not to worry. When she passed away, she was finally released from the pain. It was a cruel release, but it was a release. Please don't be embarrassed. I am a little tired, though. Would you show me to my room?"

"Yes, of course. . . . Here are your slippers, and I'll just show you the bathroom. . . . This is the dining room. Come this way, you poor, poor, man. . . . Oh my, what you must have been through . . . But you've come to the right island. Kumejima is a wonderful place for healing. I've always believed so. . . ."

After my evening cleansing I felt fatigue that no amount of alpha refocusing could dispel. Cursing my weakness, I went to bed and sank into a sleep that was almost bottomless.

The bottom was in a tunnel. A deserted metro tunnel, with rails and service pipes. My job was to patrol it, and guard it from the evil that lived down there. A superior officer walked up to me. "What are you doing here?" he demanded.

"Obeying orders, sir."

"Which are?"

"Patrolling this tunnel, sir."

He whistled between his teeth. "As usual, a muddle at Sanctuary. There's a new threat down here. The evil can only consume you when it knows about you. If you maintain your anonymity, all will be well. Now, officer. Give me your name."

"Quasar, sir."

"And your name from your old life? Your *real* name?"

"Tanaka. Keisuke Tanaka."

"What is your alpha quotient, Keisuke Tanaka?"

"16.9."

"Place of birth?"

Suddenly, I realize that I have walked into a trap! The evil is my superior officer, ploughing me with questions so it can consume me. My last defense is not to let it know that I have caught on. I am still floundering when a new character walks down the tunnel toward us. She is carrying a viola case and some flowers, and I've seen her before somewhere. Someone from my uncleansed days. The evil that is in the guise of my superior officer turns to her and starts the same ruse. "Haven't you heard about the evil? Who authorized your presence here? Give me your name, address, occupation—immediately!"

I want to save her. Lacking a plan, I grab her arm and we run, faster than air currents.

"Why are we running?"

A foreign woman on a hill, watching a wooden pole sinking into the ground.

"I'm sorry! I didn't have time to explain! That officer wasn't a real officer. It was a disguise. It was the evil that lives in these tunnels!"

"You must be mistaken!"

"Yeah? And how would *you* know?"

As we run, our fingers lock together, I look at her face for the first time. Sidelong, she is smiling, waiting for me to get this most grisly of jokes. I am looking into the *real* face of evil.

I set off early the next morning to walk around the island. The sea was milky turquoise. The sand was white, hot, and yielding. I saw birds I'd never seen before, and salmon-pink butterflies. I saw two lovers and a husky dog walking down the beach. The boy kept whispering things to the girl, and she kept laughing. The dog wanted them to throw the stick, but was too stupid to realize that first he'd have to give the stick back to one of them. As they passed I noticed neither of them wore wedding rings. I bought a couple of riceballs for lunch in a little flyblown shop, and a can of cold tea. I ate them sitting on a grave, wondering when it was that I last belonged anywhere. I mean apart from Sanctuary. I passed an ancient camphor tree, and a field where a goat was tethered. Fieldworkers' radios played tinny pop music that drifted down to the road. They sweltered under wide, woven hats. Cars rusted away in lay-bys, vegetation growing up out of the radiators. There was a lighthouse on a lonely headland. I walked to it. It was padlocked.

A sugarcane farmer pulled up by the roadside and offered me a lift. I was footsore, so I accepted. His dialect was so heavy I could barely make out what he was trying to say. He started off talking about the weather, to which I made all the right noises. Then he started talking about me. He knew which inn I was staying at, and how long I was staying, my false name, my job. He even gave his condolences for my dead wife. Every time he used the word "computer" he sealed it in quotation marks.

. . .

Back at the inn, the gossip shop was open for business. The television flashed and blinked silently on the counter. On the coffee table five cups of green tea steamed. Seated around on low chairs were a man who I guessed was a fisherman, a woman in dungarees who sat like a man, a thin woman with thin lips, and a man with a huge wart wobbling from one eyebrow like a bunch of grapes.

The old woman who ran the inn was clearly holding court. "I still remember the television pictures on the day it happened. All those poor, poor people stumbling out, holding handkerchiefs to their mouths . . . a nightmare! Welcome back, Mr. Tokunaga. Were you in Tokyo during the attack?"

"No. I was in Yokohama on business."

I scanned their minds for suspicion. I was safe.

The fisherman lit a cigarette. "What was it like the day after?"

"It certainly took a lot of people by surprise."

Dungaree-woman nodded and folded her arms. "Looks like it's the beginning of the end for that bunch of lunatics, however."

"How do you mean?" Keeping my voice steady.

The fisherman looked surprised. "You haven't heard? The police have raided them. About time, too. The Fellowship's assets have been frozen. Their so-called minister of defense is being charged with murder of ex-cult members, and five people have been arrested in connection with the gas. Two of those five hanged themselves in their detention cells. Their suicide notes provided enough evidence for a new round of arrests. Would you like to see my newspaper?"

I flinched from the shuffling sheets of lies. "No, it's all right. But how about the Guru?" *The branches may burn in the forest fire, but new growth sprouts from the pure heart.*

"The who?" Wartman blubbulled his rubbery nose. I wanted to kneel on his neck and cut that abomination off with a sharp pair of scissors.

"The Leader of the Fellowship."

"Oh, that maggot! He's hiding, like the coward he is!" Wartman choked on the hatred in his voice! What a sick zoo the world has become, where angels are despised. "He's a true devil, is that one. A devil from hell."

"Walking evil, he is! Here you are, Mr. Tokunaga." The old woman poured me a cup of green tea. I needed to escape to my room to think, but I wanted more news. "He fleeces the poor fools who run along to him. Then he acts like their father, orders them to do his dirty work, plays out his wicked dreams, then scurries away from the consequences."

Their ignorance made me gasp! If only I could make these vermin *understand!*

"It's beyond my comprehension," said Dungaree-woman, "how such things can happen. It wasn't just him, was it? There were bright people in the Fellowship, from good universities and good families. Policemen, scientists, teachers, and lawyers. Respectable people. How could they go along with that alpha Fellowship nonsense, and choose to become killers? Is there so much evil in the world?"

"Brainwashing," said Wartman, pointing to everybody. "Brainwashing."

The thin woman examined the dragon curled around her cup. "They did not specifically choose to become killers. They had chosen to abdicate their inner selves." I didn't like her. Her voice seemed to come not from her, but from a nearby room.

"I don't altogether follow you," said Dungaree-woman.

"Society," and from the way the thin woman said the word I knew she was a teacher, "is an *outer* abdication. We abdicate certain freedoms, and in return we get civilization. We get protection from death by starvation, bandits, and cholera. It's a fair deal. Signed on our behalf by our educational system on the day we are born. However, we all have an *inner* self that decides to what degree we honor this contract. This inner self is our own responsibility. I fear that many of the young men and women in the Fellowship handed this inner responsibility to their Guru, to do with as he pleased. And that," she flicked the newspaper, "is what he did with it."

"You sound like you have fairly entrenched opinions," I remarked.

The thin woman looked at me straight in the eye. I looked straight back. Our sisters at Sanctuary are taught humility.

"But why?" The fisherman lit his pipe and bulged his cheeks in and out. "Why did his followers want to give him their will?"

The thin woman looked at me as she spoke. "You'd have to ask them yourself. Maybe there are many answers. Some get a kick out of self-abasement and servitude. Some are afraid or lonely. Some crave the camaraderie of the persecuted. Some want to be big fish in a small pond. Some want magic. Some want revenge on teachers and parents who promised success would deliver all. They need shinier myths that will never be soiled by becoming true. The handing over of one's will is a small price to pay, for the believers. They aren't going to need a will in their New Earth."

I couldn't listen to this anymore. "Maybe you're reading too much into it. Maybe they just did it because they loved him." I downed my tea in one gulp. It burned my tongue and it was too bitter. "Could I have my key now, please?"

The old woman idly passed me the key. "You must be exhausted after your long walk. My nephew's wife saw you out by the lighthouse!"

Secrets on islands are hidden from mainlanders, but never from the islanders.

I lay on my bed, and wept.

My brothers and sisters, committing self-slaughter! Which of my co-cleansers had fallen at this last hurdle, and why? We were heroes! Just a few months before the end of the unclean world! Paradise had been so near for them! I was further surprised at the minister of defense allowing himself to be captured. He has a high enough alpha quotient to displace molecules and walk through walls.

The spider in the jar had died. Why? Why, why, why?

After my evening cleansing I walked around this fishing village. Squealing children were playing some incomprehensible game. Teenagers hung around on street corners in their trendiest gear, doubtless imitating the Tokyo teenagers they see in their magazines. Mothers stood gossiping outside the supermarket. I wanted to shout at them, *The world is going to end soon, you are all going to fry in the White Nights!* Okinawan music blared out of a bar, all twinky-twanky and jangling. . . . And at the end of the street I reached the mountains, the sea, and the night.

I walked along the pebbly beach. Plastic buoys. A sea coconut, shaped like a woman's loins. Junk, washed up with the driftwood. Cans, bottles, rubber gloves, detergent containers. I heard grunts and squeals from under a peeling boat, never to float again. In the distance a shadow lit a fire.

His Serendipity speaks to me in the crashing of the waves, and the sucking of the shingle. Why telephone when telepathy is possible? His Serendipity told me that his trusted cleanser Quasar had the greatest role to play. The Days of Persecution had begun, as prophesied in the 143rd Sacred Revelation. My Master told me I shall be a shepherd for the faithful during the White Nights. And after the comet ushers in the New Earth, I shall be at the right hand of His Serendipity, administering justice and wisdom in His name. I replied to His Serendipity that I was ready to die for Him. That I loved Him as a son does his father and would protect Him as a father does a son. His Serendipity, hundreds of miles away, smiled. The comet will be here by Christmas. The New Earth is not far away now. The Fellowship of Humanity will gather together on a purer island, and the survivors will call me "Father Quasar." There will be no bullying. No victimizing. All the selfish, petty, unbelieving unclean, they will fry in the fat of their ignorance. We will eat papayas, cashew nuts, and mangos, and learn how to make traditional instruments and beautiful pottery. His Serendipity will select our mates according to our alpha quotients, and teach us advanced alpha techniques, and we will travel astrally, visiting other stars.

I knelt, and thanked my Lord for His encouragement. The moon rose over the open bay, and those same stars came on, one by one.

The baby in the woolly cap, strapped to her mother's back, opened her eyes. They were my eyes. A disembodied voice was singing a chorus over and over again. And reflected in my eyes was her face. She knew what I was going to do. And she asked me not to. But she was fated to die anyway, Quasar, when the comet comes! You shortened her suffering in the land of the unclean! The innocents, surely, will be reborn into the Fellowship of the New Earth! Cleanse yourself, and anchor your faith, deep and fast!

The radio alarm clock glowed 1:30 A.M. Bad karaoke throbbed through the walls. I was wide awake, straightjacketed by my sweaty sheets. A headache dug its thumbs into my temples. My gut pulsed with gamma interference: I lurched to the toilet. My shit was a slurry of black crude oil. I kept thinking of the thin teacher, and what I should have said to her to put her in her place. My eyes wandered around the labyrinth on the worn lino. I took a shower, as hot as the flesh could bear.

For the first time since my initiation ceremony into the Fellowship I bought some cigarettes, from a machine in the deserted lobby. I lit one, walking back up to my room. I was going to be up for a while.

My palms have become blotchy. I clean myself eight or nine times a day, but something is wrong with my skin. I have taken to watching the television every morning. Proceedings are under way to disband the Fellowship, and make membership illegal. I have been named, and my photograph shown, ransacked from Fellowship archives. Luckily it was taken with my scalp shaved and an alpha energizer on my head, so the likeness isn't close. I am the last of the Tokyo cleansers to evade capture. I saw my skin father and mother being chased into my skin sister's car by a baying pack of reporters. The whole scene was lit by flashbulbs. His Serendipity has been caught and charged with conspiracy to commit genocide, and with fraud, kidnapping, and possession of Category 1 nerve agents. The news showed the same clip of His Serendipity being bundled into a car by agents of the unclean and driven through a mob shouting for His blood. They showed it over and over again, to a sinister soundtrack, to tell the mindless that He is a villain, like Darth Vader, to be loathed and feared. The rest of the Cabinet have also been arrested. They are falling over themselves to denounce each other, hoping their death sentence will be commuted to life imprisonment. I myself was denounced by the minister of education. Even His Serendipity's wife has denounced our Master, saying that she didn't know anything about the production of the gas. She, who was so zealous about the cleansing! One television news station flew their jackals to Los Angeles, to film the elite school in Beverly Hills where His Serendipity's sons were boarded.

I telephoned Sanctuary from the port.

"State your name, business, and present location," said the cold voice. A cop. Even with the alpha quotient of a fruitfly, you could spot them a mile off. I hung up.

But this is bad. I have run out of Japan. My passport is in the possession of the Fellowship's Foreign Office, so seeking assistance with our Russian or Korean brothers and sisters is impossible. I am running out of money. Of course I have no money of my own: after my initiation every last yen was transferred to the Fellowship. My skin family has disowned me, and would turn me in. So would my skin friends from my life of blindness. This causes me no sorrow. When the White Nights come, they shall reap what they have sown. The Fellowship is my true family.

I had one final resort. The Fellowship's Secret Service. The media had mentioned nothing about their arrest, so perhaps they had gone to ground in time. I dialed the secret number, and gave the encoded message: *"The dog needs to be fed."*

I kept on the line, saying nothing, as instructed during my cleansing training sessions at Sanctuary. The Secret Serviceman on the other end hung up when enough time for my call to be traced had elapsed. Help would be on its way. A levitator would be dispatched, bearing a wallet of crisp ten-thousand yen notes. He will scan for my alpha signature, and find me during one of my rambles around the island, when I am alone, or asleep in a grove of palm trees. He will be there when I awake, glowing, perhaps, like Buddha or Gabriel.

. . .

Kumejima is a squalid, incestuous prison. To think, this lump of rock was once the main trading center of the Ryuku Empire with China. Boats laden with spices, slaves, coral, ivory, silk. Swords, coconuts, hemp. The shouts of men would have filled the bustling harbor, old women would have knelt in the marketplace, with their scales and piles of fruit and dried fish. Girls with obedient breasts lean out of the dusky windows, over the flower boxes, promising, murmuring. . . .

Now it's all gone. Long gone. Okinawa became a squalid apology for a fiefdom, squabbled over by masters far beyond its curved horizons. Nobody admits it, but the islands are dying now. The young people are moving to the mainland. Without subsidies and price-fixing the agriculture would collapse. When the mainland peaceniks get the American military rapists off the islands the economy will slow, splutter, and expire. The fish are all being fished out by factory trawlers. Tracks lead nowhere. Building projects have been started, but end in patches of concrete, piles of gravel, and tall, thorny weeds. Such a place would be ripe for His Serendipity's Mission! I long to awaken people, to tell people about the White Nights and the New Earth, but I daren't risk bringing attention to myself. My last defense is my ordinariness. When that wears out, I have nothing but my novice's alpha potential to protect me.

The island's bewhiskered policeman spoke to me yesterday. I passed him outside a snorkel shop while he was bent over tying up his shoelaces.

"How's your holiday, Mr. Tokunaga?"

"Very restful, officer. Thank you."

"I was sorry to hear about your wife. It must have been terribly traumatic."

"Kind of you to say so, officer." I tried to focus my alpha coercion faculty to make him go away.

"So you'll be off tomorrow, Mr. Tokunaga? Mrs. Mori at the guest house said you were staying for a couple of weeks."

"I'm thinking of extending, actually, just a few more days."

"Is that a fact? Won't your company be missing you?"

"Actually, I'm working on a new computer system. I can do it here just as well as in Tokyo. In fact, the peace and quiet is more conducive to inspiration."

The policeman nodded thoughtfully. "I wonder . . . At the junior high school the youngsters have recently started up a computer club. My sister-in-law's the headmistress there. Mrs. Oe. You've met already, I believe, at Mrs. Mori's. I wonder . . . Mrs. Oe is far too polite to dream of imposing upon your time herself, I know, but . . ."

I waited.

"It would be a great honor for the school if you could go along some time and tell the computer class about life in a real computer company. . . ."

I sensed a trap. But it would be safer to get out of it later than refuse now. "Sure."

"That would be very kind of you. I'll mention it when I see my brother next. . . ."

I met the husky dog on the beach. His Serendipity chose to address me in its barks.

"What did you expect, Quasar? Did you think raising the curtain on the age of *Homo serendipitous* was going to be easy?"

"No, my Lord. But when are the yogic fliers going to be dispatched to the White House and the European parliament, to demand your release?"

"Eat eggs, my faithful one."

"Eggs, my Lord?"

"Eggs are a symbol of rebirth, Quasar. And eat Orange Rocket ice lollies."

"What do they symbolize, Guru?"

"Nothing. They contain vitamin C in abundance."

"It shall be so, my Lord. But the yogic fliers, my Father—"

My only reply was a barking dog, and a puzzled look from the two lovers, jumping up suddenly from behind a stack of rusty oil drums. The three of us looked at each other in confusion. The dog cocked its leg and pissed against a tractor tire. The ocean boomed its indifference.

.   .   .

The little baby girl in the woolly cap, she had liked me. How could she have liked me? It was just some facial reflex, no doubt. She gurgled at me, smiling. Her mother looked at whom she was smiling, and she smiled at me too. Her eyes were warm. I didn't smile back. I looked away. I wish I had smiled back. But I wish they hadn't smiled at me. Would they have survived? Or would the gas have got them? If they hadn't moved, it would have leaked out of the package and straight into their noses, eyes, and lungs. . . .

Mom. Dad.

But we were only defending ourselves! There was one day, during my assignment to the ministry of information. One of our sister's skin relatives, her unclean uncle, had taken court action to stop her selling their family's farmhouse and land. He was a property lawyer. The Secret Service had brought this flesh brother in for questioning. His Serendipity instantly knew he was a spy sent by the unclean. An assassination plot was being engineered, it seemed. Laughable! All of us in Sanctuary knew how, thirty years ago, while traveling in Tibet, a being of pure consciousness named Arupadhatu transmigrated into His Serendipity, and revealed the secrets of freeing the mind from its physical shackles. This had been the beginning of His Serendipity's path up the holy mountain. Even if the body of His Serendipity were harmed, He could leave His old body and transmigrate into another, as easily as I change hotels and islands. He could transmigrate into His own assassin.

Anyway, this lawyer was injected with truth serum and confessed to everything. His mission had been to put an odorless poison into the refectory rice cookers. His Serendipity's wife conducted the interview herself, I heard.

You see! We were only defending ourselves.

My fingernails are coming loose.

I spent the afternoon walking to the lighthouse. I sat on a rock and watched the waves and the birds. A typhoon was moving up

the coast of China, skirting Taiwan, and looming over the Okinawan horizon. Clouds were piling up in the west, winds were un-
raveling. I was being discussed, and decisions were being taken.
What had gone wrong? A few more months, and my alpha quotient would have been 25, putting me in the top two hundred on
Earth—His Serendipity had assured me, in person. I had in-
gested some of His Serendipity's eyelashes. After winning converts on the Welcome Program I was rewarded with a test tube of
the Guru's sperm to imbibe. It boosted my gamma resistance. I
had been taken off the lavatory docket and been made a cleanser.
For the first time in my life, I was becoming a name.

The corrugated iron roof of an abandoned shed clattered to
and fro in the wind.

Nothing has gone wrong. Nothing has gone wrong, Quasar. It
was your faith that brought you to His Serendipity's notice. It is
your faith that will guide you through the Days of Persecution,
through the terrible days of the White Nights to the New Earth. It
is your faith that will nourish you now.

Everything around me on this godforsaken island is crumbling. I should have stayed in Naha. I should have hidden in snow
country, or deep-frozen Hokkaido, or lost myself amid a metrop-
olis of my own kind. What happened, I wonder, to Mr. Ikeda?
Where do people who drop off the edge of your world end up?

Typhoon weather.

The curtains I keep drawn. Our minister of defense received
some reports that the government of the unclean had developed
microcameras which they implanted in the craniums of seagulls,
which were then trained to spy. Not to mention the Americans' secret satellites, scrolling over the globe, scanning for the Fellowship
at the behest of the politicians and the Jews, who long ago had set
up the Freemasons, and funded Chinese efforts to pollute the well
of history.

I was sitting with my back to the lighthouse on the lonely headland. Headlights approached, seeking me out. I looked for a place
to hide. There was none. A seagull watched me. It had a cruel

face. A blue and white car pulled up. Too late, I looked for a place to hide. A door opened, and a dim light lit up the interior.

They've found me! The rest of forever in a cell . . .

And then, so strangely, I'm relieved it's all over. At least I can stop running.

A hand was already clearing stuff from the front seat. Its owner leaned forward. "Mr. Tokunaga, I presume?"

Grimly, I nodded, and walked toward my captor.

"I've been searching for you. The name's Ota. I'm the harbormaster. You spoke with my brother just the other day, about giving a lecture at my wife's school. How about a lift back to town? You must be tired, after walking all the way out here, all on your own?"

I obeyed, and still trembling I climbed in and put on my seat belt.

"Lucky I was passing . . . there's a typhoon warning, you know. I saw a figure, all hunched like it was the end of the world, and I thought to myself, I wonder if that's Mr. Tokunaga? Not feeling too chipper, this evening?"

"No."

"Maybe you've been overdoing it. The island air is good for clearing the head, but at the rate you've been tramping around . . . Terribly sorry to hear about your wife."

"Death is a part of life."

"That's a sound philosophy, but it can't be easy to keep your thoughts focused."

"I can. I'm a good focuser."

He braked and beeped a couple of times at a goat standing in the middle of the road. Magisterially, the goat sniffed at us, and wandered into a field.

"Must tell Mrs. Bessho that Caligula's escaped again. You name it, goats eat it! So, you're a good focuser, you were saying. Splendid, splendid. It would be a crime not to try diving while you're here, you know. We have the finest Pacific reefs north of the equator, I'm told. By the way, the youngsters are delighted at the prospect of a real computer man coming to talk to them. No great scholars, I'm afraid, but they're keen. My wife would like you to join us for dinner tomorrow, if you're free. So, Mr. Toku-naga. Tell me a little about yourself. . . ."

The road looped back around to the port, as all the roads on this island eventually do.

Clouds began to ink out the stars, one by one.

TOKYO

SPRING WAS LATE, and so was I. The commuters streamed to work with their collars and umbrellas up. The cherry trees lining the backstreets were still winter trees, craggy, pocked, and dripping with morning rain. I fished around for my keys, rattled up the shutters, and opened the shop.

I looked through the post while the water was boiling. Some mail orders—good. Bills, bills—bad. A couple of inquiries from a regular customer in Nagano about rare discs that I'd never heard of. Bumf. An entirely ordinary morning. Time for oolong tea. I put on a very rare Miles Davis recording that Takeshi had discovered in a box of mixed-quality discs that he'd picked up at an auction last month out in Shinagawa.

It was a gem. "You Never Entered My Mind" was blissful and forlorn. Some faultless mute-work, the trumpet filtered down to a single ray of sound. The brassy sun lost behind the clouds.

The first customer of the week was a foreigner, either American or European or Australian, you can never tell because they all look the same. A lanky, zitty foreigner. He was a real collector, though, not just a browser. He had that manic glint in his eyes, and his fingers were adept at flicking through meters of discs at high speed, like a bank teller counting notes. He bought a virgin copy of "Stormy Sunday" by Kenny Burrell, and "Flight to Denmark" by Duke Jordan, recorded in 1973. He had a cool T-shirt, too. A bat flying around a skyscraper, leaving a trail of stars. I asked him where he was from. He said thank you very much. Westerners can't learn Japanese.

. . .

Takeshi phoned a bit later.

"Satoru! Have a good day off yesterday?"

"Pretty quiet. Sax lesson in the afternoon. Hung around with Koji for a bit afterwards. Helped Taro with the delivery from the brewery."

"Any vast checks for me in the post?"

"Sorry, nothing that vast. Some nice bills, though. How was your weekend?"

This was what he had been waiting for. "Funny you ask me that! I met this *gorgeous* creature of the night last Friday at a club in Roppongi." I could almost hear his saliva glands juicing. "Get this. Twenty-five," which for Takeshi is the perfect age, making him ten years her senior. "Engaged," which for Takeshi adds the thrill of adultery while subtracting any responsibility. "Only shag women who have more to lose than you do" was a motto of his. "Clubbed until four in the morning. Woke up Saturday afternoon, with my clothes on back-to-front, in a hotel somewhere in Chiyoda ward. No idea how I got there. She came out of the shower, naked, brown, and dripping, and damn if she wasn't *still* gasping for it!"

"It must have been heaven. Are you seeing her again?"

"Of course we're seeing each other again. This is love at first sight! We're having dinner tonight at a French restaurant in Ichigaya," meaning they were having each other in an Ichigaya love hotel. "Seriously, you should see her ass! Two overripe nectarines squeezed together in a paper bag. One prod and they explode! Juice everywhere!"

Rather more than I needed to know. "She's engaged, you say?"

"Yeah. To a Fujitsu photocopier ink cartridge research-and-development division salaryman who knew the go-between who knew her father's section head."

"Some guys get all the luck."

"Ah, it's okay. What the eyes don't see, eh? She'll make a good little wifey, I'm sure. She's after a few nights of lust and sin before she becomes a housewife forever."

She sounded a right slapper to me. Takeshi seemed to have

forgotten that only two weeks ago he'd been trying to get back with his estranged wife.

The rain carried on falling, keeping customers away. The rain fell softly, then heavily, then softly. Static hisses on telephone lines. Jimmy Cobb's percussion on "Blue in Green."

Takeshi was still on the telephone. It seemed to be my turn to say something.

"What's she like? Her personality, I mean."

Takeshi said, "Oh, fine," like I'd asked about a new brand of rice cracker. "Well. I've got to go and sort out my estate agent's office. Business has been a bit slack there, too. I'd better put the shits up the manager a bit. Sell lots of discs and make me lots of money. Phone me on my cell phone if you need anything—" I never do. He rang off.

Twenty million people live and work in Tokyo. It's so big that nobody really knows where it stops. It's long since filled up the plain, and now it's creeping up the mountains to the west and reclaiming land from the bay in the east. The city never stops rewriting itself. In the time one street guide is produced, it has already become out of date. It's a tall city, and a deep one, as well as a spread-out one. Things are always moving below you, and above your head. All these people, flyovers, cars, walkways, subways, offices, tower blocks, power cables, pipes, apartments, it all adds up to a lot of weight. You have to do something to stop yourself caving in, or you just become a piece of flotsam or an ant in a tunnel. In smaller cities people can use the space around them to insulate themselves, to remind themselves of who they are. Not in Tokyo. You just don't have the space, not unless you're a company president, a gangster, a politician, or the emperor. You're pressed against people body to body in the metro, several hands gripping each strap on the trains. Apartment windows have no view but other apartment windows.

No, in Tokyo you have to make your place *inside* your head.

There are different ways people make this place. Sweat, exercise, and pain is one way. You can see them in the gyms, in the well-ordered swimming pools. You can see them jogging in the small, worn parks. Another way to make your place is TV. A bright, brash place, always well lit, full of fun and jokes that tell you when to laugh so you never miss them. World news carefully edited so that it's not *too* disturbing, but disturbing enough to make you glad that you weren't born in a foreign country. News with music to tell you who to hate, who to feel sorry for, and who to laugh at.

Takeshi's place is the nightlife. Clubs, and bars, and the women who live there.

There are many other places. There's an invisible Tokyo built of them, existing in the minds of us, its citizens. Internet, manga, Hollywood, doomsday cults, they are all places where you go and where you matter as an individual. Some people will tell you about their places straight off, and won't shut up about it all night. Others keep it hidden like a garden in a mountain forest.

People with no place are those who end up throwing themselves onto the tracks.

My place comes into existence through jazz. Jazz makes a fine place. The colors and feelings there come not from the eye but from sounds. It's like being blind but seeing more. This is why I work here in Takeshi's shop. Not that I could ever put that into words.

The phone rang. Mama-san.

"Sato-kun, Akiko and Tomomi have got this dreadful flu that's doing the rounds, and Ayaka's still feeling a mite delicate." Ayaka had an abortion last week. "So I'll have to open the bar and start early. Any chance you could get your own dinner tonight?"

"I'm nineteen! Of course I can get my own dinner tonight!"

She did her croaky laugh. "You're a good lad." She rang off.

I felt in a Billie Holiday mood. "Lady in Satin," recorded at night with heroin and a bottle of gin the year before she died. A doomed, Octoberish oboe of a voice.

I wondered about my real mother. Not longingly. It's pointless to long. Mama-san said she'd been deported back to the Philippines afterwards, and would never be allowed back into Japan. I can't help but wonder, just sometimes, who she is now, what she's doing, and whether she ever thinks about me.

Mama-san told me my father was eighteen when I was born. That makes me old enough to be my father. Of course, my father was cast as the victim. The innocent violated by the foreign seductress who sank her teeth into him to get a visa. I'll probably never know the truth, unless I get rich enough to hire a private detective. I guess there must be money in his family, for him to be patronizing hostess bars at my tender age, and to pay to clean up the stink of such a scandal so thoroughly. I'd like to ask him what he and my mother felt for each other, if anything.

One time I was sure he had come. A cool guy in his late thirties. He wore desert boots and a dark-tan suede jacket. One ear was pierced. I knew I recognized him from somewhere, but I thought he was a musician. He looked around the shop, and asked for a Chick Corea recording that we happened to have. He bought it, I wrapped it for him, and he left. Only afterwards did I realize that he reminded me of me.

Then I tried calculating what the odds against a random meeting like that were in a city the size of Tokyo, but the calculator ran out of decimal places. So I thought perhaps he'd come to see me incognito, that he was as curious about me as I was about him. Us orphans spend so much time having to be level-headed about things that when we have the time and space to romanticize, wow, can we romanticize. Not that I'm a real orphan, in an orphanage. Mama-san has always looked after me.

I went outside for a moment, to feel the rain on my skin. It was like being breathed on. A delivery van braked sharply and beeped at an old lady pushing a trolley who glared back and wove her hands in the air as if she was casting a spell. The van beeped again like an irritated muppet. A mink-coated leggy woman who considered herself extremely attractive and who obviously kept a rich husband strode past with a flopsy dog. A huge tongue lolled between its white teeth. Her eyes and mine touched for a moment, and she saw a high school graduate spending his youth holed up in a poky shop that obviously nobody ever spent much in, and then she was gone.

This is my place. Another Billie Holiday disc. She sang "Some Other Spring," and the audience clapped until they too faded into the heat of a long-lost Chicago summer night.

. . .

The phone.

"Hi, Satoru. It's only Koji."

"I can hardly hear you! What's that racket in the background?"

"I'm phoning from the college canteen."

"How did the engineering exam go?"

"Well, I worked really hard for it. . . ." He'd walked it.

"Congratulations! So your visit to the shrine paid off, hey? When are the results out?"

"Three or four weeks. I'm just glad they're over. It's too early to congratulate me, though. . . . Hey, Mom's doing a sukiyaki party tonight. My dad's back in Tokyo this week. They thought you might like to help us eat it. Can you? You could sleep over in my sister's room if it gets too late. She's on a school trip to Okinawa."

I ummed and ahhed inwardly. Koji's parents are nice, straight people, but they feel it's their responsibility to sort my life out. They can't believe that I'm already content where I am, with my discs and my saxophone and my place. Underlying their concern is pity, and I'd rather take shit about my lack of parents than pity.

But Koji's my friend, probably my only one. "I'd love to come. What should I bring?"

"Nothing, just bring yourself." So, flowers for his mom and booze for his dad.

"I'll come around after work then."

"Okay. See you."

"See you."

It was a Mal Waldron time of day. The afternoon was shutting up shop early. The owner of the greengrocery across the street took in his crates of white radishes, carrots, and lotus roots. He rolled down his shutter, saw me, and nodded gravely. He never smiles. Some pigeons scattered as a truck shuddered by. Every note of "Left Alone" fell, drops of lead into a deep well. Jackie McLean's saxophone circled in the air, so sad it could barely leave the ground.

The door opened, and I smelled air rainwashed clean. Four

high school girls came in, but one of them was completely, completely different. She pulsed, invisibly, like a quasar. I know that sounds stupid, but she did.

The three bubbleheads flounced up to the counter. They were pretty, I guess, but they were all clones of the same ova. Their hair was the same length, their lipstick the same color, their bodies curving in the same way beneath their same uniform. Their leader demanded in a voice cutesy and spoiled the newest hit by the latest teen dwoob.

But I didn't bother hearing them. I can't describe women, not like Takeshi or Koji. But if you know Duke Pearson's "After the Rain," well, she was as beautiful and pure as that.

Standing by the window, and looking out. What was out there? She was embarrassed by her classmates. And so she should have been! She was so real, the others were cardboard cutouts beside her. Real things had happened to her to make her how she was, and I wanted to know them, and read them, like a book. It was the strangest feeling. I just kept thinking—well, I'm not sure what I was thinking. I'm not sure if I was thinking of anything.

She was listening to the music! She was afraid she'd scare the music away if she moved.

"Well, have you got it or haven't you?" One of the cutout girls squawked. It must take a long time to train your voice to be so annoying.

Another giggled.

Another's pocket phone trilled and she got it out.

I was angry with them for making me look away from her.

"This is a disc collector's shop. There's a toy shop in the shopping mall by the metro station that sells the kind of thing you're looking for."

Rich Shibuya girls are truffle-fed pooches. The girls at Mama-san's, they have all had to learn how to survive. They have to keep their patrons, keep their looks, keep their integrity, and they get scarred. But they respect themselves, and they let it show. They respect each other. I respect them. They are real people.

But these magazine girls have nothing real about them. They have magazine expressions, speak magazine words, and carry magazine fashion accessories. They've chosen to become this. I don't know whether or not to blame them. Getting scarred isn't nice. But look! As shallow, and glossy, and identical, and throwaway, as magazines.

"You're a bit uptight aren't you? Been dumped by your girlfriend?" The leader leaned on the counter and swayed, just a few inches away from my face. I imagined her using that face in bars, in cars, in love hotels.

Her friend shrieked with laughter and pulled her away before I could think of a witty retort. They flocked back toward the door. "Told you!" one of them said. The third was still speaking into her pocket phone. "I dunno where we are. Some crappy place behind some crappy building. Where are you?"

"You coming?" the leader said to the one still staring into space, listening to Mal.

No, I thought with all my might. *Say no, and stay with me in my space.*

"I said," said the leader, "are—you—coming?"

Was she deaf?

"I guess so," she said, in a real voice. A beautiful, real voice.

Look at me, I willed. *Look at me. Please. Just once, look straight at me.*

As she left, she looked at me over her shoulder, my heart trampolined, and she followed the others into the street.

———————

The cherry trees were budding. Maroon tips sprouted and swelled through the sealed bark. Pigeons ruffled and prilled. I wish I knew more about pigeons. Were they strutting about like that for mating purposes, or just because they were strutty birds? That would be useful knowledge for school syllabuses. None of this capital of Mongolia stuff. The air outside was warmer and damp. Being outside was like being in a tent. A jackhammer was pounding into concrete a few doors down. Takeshi said that yet another surf and ski shop was opening up. How many surfers and skiers are there in Tokyo?

I put on a Charlie Parker anthology, with the volume up loud to drown out the ringing of metal. Charlie Parker, molten and twisting, no stranger to cruelty. "Relaxin' at Camarillo," "How Deep is the Ocean?," "All the Things You Are," "Out of Nowhere," "A Night in Tunisia."

I dressed the girl in calico, and she slipped away through a North African doorway.

Here, being as different as I am is punishable.

I was in Roppongi one time with Koji. He was on the pull and got talking to a couple of girls from Scotland. I just assumed they were English teachers at some crappy English school, but they turned out to be "exotic dancers." Koji's English is really good— he was always in the top class at school. English being a girl's subject, I didn't study it much, but when I found jazz I studied at home because I wanted to read the interviews with the great musicians, who are all American. Of course reading is one thing, but speaking is quite another. So Koji was mostly doing the translating. Anyway, these girls said that everyone where they come from actually *tries* to be different. They'll dye their hair a color nobody else has, buy clothes nobody else is wearing, get into music nobody else knows. Weird. Then they asked why all girls here want to look the same. Koji answered, "Because they are girls! Why do all cops look the same? Because they're cops, of course." Then one of them asked why Japanese kids try to ape American kids. The clothes, the rap music, the skateboards, the hair. I wanted to say that it's not America they're aping, it's the Japan of their parents that they're rejecting. And since there's no homegrown counterculture, they just take hold of the nearest one to hand, which happens to be American. But it's not American culture exploiting us. It's us exploiting it.

Koji got lost trying to translate the last bit.

I tried asking them about their inner places, because it seemed relevant. But I just got answers about how tiny the apartments were here, and how houses in Britain all have central heating. Then their boyfriends turned up. Two bloody great U.S. marine gorillas. They looked down at us, unimpressed, and Koji and I decided it was time for another drink at the bar.

. . .

But yeah, it's certainly different here. All through my junior high school days people hassled me about my parents. Finding part-time jobs was never easy, either: it was as tough as having Korean parents. People find out. It would have been easier to say they'd died in an accident, but I wasn't going to lie for those knob-heads. Plus if you say someone's dead, then it tempts fate to kill them off early. Gossip works telepathically in Tokyo. The city *is* vast, but there's always someone who knows someone whom someone knows. Anonymity doesn't muffle coincidence: it makes the coincidences more outlandish. That's why I still think one of these days my father might wander into the shop.

So, from elementary school onwards I used to be in fights. I often lost, but that didn't matter. Taro, Mama-san's bouncer, always told me it's better to fight and lose than not fight and suffer, because even if you fight and lose your spirit emerges intact. Taro taught me that people respect spirit, but even cowards don't respect cowards. Taro also told me how to headbutt taller adversaries, how to knee in the balls, and how to dislocate a man's hand, so that by high school nobody much bothered me. One time a gang of junior yakuza were waiting outside school for me, because I'd given one of their kid brothers a nosebleed. I still don't know who tipped Mama-san off—Koji, most probably—but Mama-san sent Taro along that day to pick me up. He waited until they had formed a ring around me down an alley, and then he strolled along and scared seven shades of shit out of them. Now I think about it, Taro's been more like a dad to me than anyone else.

A leathery man in a blood-red jacket came in, ignoring me. He found the Charles Mingus section and bought about two thirds of the stock, including the collectors' items, peeling off ten-thousand yen notes like toilet paper. His eyeballs seemed to pulse to the bass rhythm. He left, carrying his purchases in a cardboard box that he assembled himself on the counter. He hadn't asked for a discount, though I would have gladly given him one, and I was left with a wad of money. I phoned Takeshi to tell him the good news, and that it might be best if he came to pick the money up himself that night. I knew he had a cash-flow problem.

"Ah," gasped Takeshi. "Baby! That's the way. That is very, very, very good!"

There was hallucinogenic music on in the background that sounded like a migraine, and a woman being tortured by tickling.

Feeling I'd phoned at a bad time I said goodbye and hung up.

And still only eleven in the morning.

Koji was the class egghead at high school, which made him an outsider, too. He should have gone to a much better high school, but until he was fifteen his dad was always being transferred, so it was never that easy for him to keep up. Koji was also diabolically bad at sports. I swear, in three years I never saw him manage to hit a baseball once. There was one time when he took an almighty swing, the bat flew out of his hands and hurtled through the air like a missile, straight into Mr. Ikeda, our games master, who idolized Yukio Mishima even though I doubted he'd ever got through a whole book by anybody in his entire life.

I was doubled up laughing, so I didn't realize nobody else was. That cost me school toilet-cleaning duty for the whole term, with Koji. That's when I learned Koji loved the piano. I play the tenor saxophone. That's how I got to know Koji. A winded games teacher and the foulest toilets in the Tokyo educational system.

One of our regulars, Mr. Fujimoto, came in during the lunch hour. The bell rang and a gust of air rustled papers all around the shop. He was laughing as usual. He laughed because he was pleased to see me. He put a little parcel of books down on the counter for me. I always try to pay for them, but he never lets me. He says it's a jazz disc consultancy fee.

"Mr. Fujimoto! How's work today?"

"Terrible!" Mr. Fujimoto only has one voice, and that is very loud. It's as though his greatest fear is to not be heard. And when he really laughs the noise almost pushes you backwards.

The shop is smack bang between the business district of Otemachi and the publishing district around Ochanomizu, so our

salaryman customers usually work in one or the other. You can always tell the difference. There's a certain look that megamoney
bestows on its handlers. A sort of beadiness, and hunger. Hard to
put your finger on, but it's there all right. Money is another of
those inner places, by the way. It's a way to measure yourself.

The publishing salarymen, however, often have a streak of
manic jollity. Mr. Fujimoto is a prime specimen. He puns regu-
larly and appallingly. For example:

"Afternoon, Satoru-kun! Say, couldn't you get Takeshi to give
this place a new coat of paint? It's looking kind of run-down."

"Do you think so?" I can smell the payoff approaching.

"Definitely! It's positively seedy!"

Uh?

"Seedy! CD! See-Dee!"

I wince in genuine pain and Mr. Fujimoto gurgles apprecia-
tively. The worse the better.

This lunchtime Mr. Fujimoto was looking for something Lee
Morgan-ish. I recommended Hank Mobley's "A Caddy for
Daddy," which he promptly bought. I know his tastes. Anything
on the loony side of funky. As I handed over his change he suddenly became serious. He switched to a more formal mode of
speech, took off his heavy glasses, and started cleaning the lenses.

"I was wondering whether you might be planning to apply for
college next year?"

"Not really, no . . ."

"So, would you be thinking about entering a particular profession?"

He'd rehearsed this beforehand. I guessed what was coming.

"I don't really have any plans at the moment. I guess I'll just
wait and see."

"Of course, Satoru, it's absolutely none of my business, and
please forgive me for interfering in your plans, but the only reason I'm asking is that a couple of positions in my office have just
become available. Very humble. Just glorified editorial assistants,
basically, but if you were interested in applying then I'd be happy
to recommend you for one of them. Certainly I could get you to
the interview stage. And it would be a foot in the door. I started

out myself this way, you know. Everybody needs a step up, occasionally."

I looked around the shop.

"That's a very generous offer, Mr. Fujimoto. I'm not sure how to answer."

"Think it over, Satoru. I'm going to Kyoto for a few days on business. We won't start interviewing until I get back. I'd be happy to have a word with your present employer on your behalf, if that's what's worrying you. . . . I know Takeshi has a lot of respect for you, so he wouldn't stand in your way."

"No, it's not really that. Thank you. I'll think seriously about it. Thank you . . . How much are the books?"

"Nothing. Your consultancy fee. They're just a few samples, we give 'em out free to people in the trade. These pocket paperback classics, they walk off the shelves. I remember you said you enjoyed *The Great Gatsby*—there's a new Murakami translation of Fitzgerald's short stories we've just brought out, *Lord of the Flies*, that's a laugh a minute, and a new García Márquez."

"It's very kind of you."

"Nonsense! Just give the idea of publishing a serious think. There are worse ways to make a living."

I'd thought about the girl every day since. Twenty or thirty or forty times a day. I'd find myself thinking of her and then not want to stop, like not wanting to get out of a hot shower on a winter morning. I ran my fingers through my hair and contemplated my face, using a Fats Navarro CD as a hand mirror. Could she ever feel the same way back? I couldn't even remember accurately what she looked like. Smooth skin, highish cheekbones, narrowish eyes. Like a Chinese empress. I didn't really think of her face when I thought of her. She was just there, a color that didn't have a name yet. The idea of her.

I got angry with myself. It's not as if I'm ever going to see her again. This is Tokyo. And besides, even if I did see her again, why should she be in the least bit interested in me? My mind can only hold one thought at a time. I may as well make it a worthwhile thought.

I thought about Mr. Fujimoto's offer. What *am* I doing here? Koji's getting on with his life. All my high school classmates are in college or in a company. I am unfailingly updated on their progress by Koji's mom. What am I doing?

A guy in a wheelchair flashed by outside.

Hey, hey, this is my place, remember. Time for jazz.

"Undercurrent" by Jim Hall and Bill Evans. An album of water, choppy and brushed by the wind, at other times silent and slow under trees. On other songs, chords glinting on inland seas.

The girl was there, too, swimming naked on her back, buoyed along by the currents.

I made myself some green tea and watched the steam rise into the disturbed afternoon. Koji was knocking on the window, grinning at me goonishly, and pressing his face up against the glass so he looked like a poison dwarf.

I had to grin back. He came in, walking his loping bumpy walk.

"You were miles away. I came via Mister Donuts. Vanilla Angel donuts okay?"

"Thanks. Let me make you some tea. This great Keith Jarrett record came in yesterday, you must give it a listen. I can't believe he makes it up as he goes along."

"A hallmark of genius. Fancy a couple of drinks later?"

"Where?"

"Dunno. Somewhere frequented by nubile girls on the prowl for young male flesh. The Student's Union bar perhaps. But if you're busy sorting out the meaning of existence we could make it another night. Smoke?"

"Sure. Pull up a chair."

Koji likes to think of himself as a ruthless womanizer like Takeshi, but really his emotions are as ruthless as a Vanilla Angel donut. That's one reason I like him.

We lit up. "Koji, do you believe in love at first sight?"

He rocked back on his chair and smiled like a wolf. "Who is she?"

"No no no no. No one. I was just asking."

Koji the philosopher gazed upwards. At length he blew a smoke ring. "I believe in lust at first sight. You gotta keep a certain hardness, or you just turn to goo. And goo isn't attractive. And whatever you do, don't let her know how you feel. Or you're lost." Koji went into Humphrey Bogart mode. "Stay enigmatic, kid. Stay tough. You hear?"

"Yeah, yeah, like you, for example. You were as tough as Bambi when you were last in love. But seriously?"

Another smoke ring. "But seriously . . . well, love has got to be based on knowledge, hasn't it? You have to know someone intimately to be able to love them. So love at *first* sight is a contradiction in terms. Unless in that first sight there's some sort of mystical gigabyte downloading of information from one mind into the other. That doesn't sound too likely, does it?"

"Mmm. Dunno."

I poured my friend's tea.

The cherry blossoms were suddenly there. Magic, frothing and bubbling and there just above our heads filling the air with color too delicate for words like "pink" or "white." How had such grim trees created something so otherworldly in a backstreet with no agreed-upon name? An annual miracle, beyond my understanding.

It was a morning for Ella Fitzgerald. There are fine things in the world, after all. Dignity, refinement, warmth, and humor, where you'd never expect to find them. Even as an old woman, an amputee in a wheelchair, Ella sang like a girl who could still be in high school, falling in love for the first time.

The phone rang. "It's Takeshi."

"Hi, boss. Are you having a good day?"

"I am not having a good day. I'm having a very bad day."

"I'm sorry to hear that."

"I am a fool. A bloody fool. A bloody, bloody fool. Why do men do this?" He was drunk, and me still on my morning tea. "Where does this impulse come from, Satoru? Tell me!" Like I knew but was refusing to grant him enlightenment. "A sticky wrestle in an anonymous bedroom, a few bite marks, about three seconds' worth of orgasm if you're lucky, a pleasant drowse for thirty minutes, and when you come to you suddenly realize you've become a lecherous, lying sleazebag who's flushing several million sperm and six years of marriage down the toilet. Why are we programmed to do this? Why?"

I couldn't think of an answer that was both honest and consoling. So I went for honesty. "No idea."

Takeshi told the same story three times in a loop. "My wife dropped by to pick me up for lunch. We were going to go out, talk things over, maybe sort things out. . . . I'd bought her some flowers, she'd bought me a new striped jacket she'd seen somewhere. Hopelessly uncool, of course, but she remembered my size. It was a peace pipe. We were just leaving when she went to the bathroom and what did she find?"

I almost said "a nurse's corpse," but thought better of it. "What?"

"Her bag. And dressing gown. The nurse's. And the message she'd written to me, in lipstick. On the inside of the mirror."

"What was the message?"

I heard ice cubes crack as Takeshi poured himself another drink. "None of your business. But when my wife read it she calmly walked back into the living room, poured vodka on the jacket, set it alight, and left. The jacket shriveled up and melted."

"The power of the written word."

"Damn it, Satoru, I wish I was your age again. It was all so bloody simple back then! What have I done? Where does this myth come from?"

"What myth?"

"The one that plagues all men. The one that says a life without darkness and sex and mystery is only half a life. Why? And it was hardly like I'd been rooting Miss Celestial Beauty Incarnate. She was just some stupid slag of a nurse. . . . Why?"

I'm only nineteen. Graduated from high school last year. I don't know.

It was all pretty pathetic to listen to. Luckily at that moment Mama-san and Taro came in so I could leave Takeshi's unanswerable questions unanswered.

. . .

If Mama-san were a bird she would be a kind, white crow.

Taro would not be a bird. Taro would be a tank. For decades, long before I was on the scene, he has escorted Mama-san everywhere. Their relationship has depths to it that I've certainly never sussed. I've seen old photos of them from the sixties and seventies. They were a beautiful couple, in their way. Now they make me think of a frail mistress and a faithful bulldog. Taro, the rumors go, used to do odd jobs for the yakuza in his youth. Debt collection, and suchlike. He still has some versatile friends in that world, which is very useful when it comes to paying protection money on The Wild Orchid. Mama-san gets a sixty percent discount. Another of those friends with connections at city hall managed to obtain my full Japanese citizenship.

Mama-san brought me my lunch box. "I know you overslept this morning," she crackled, "because of all the bloody racket."

"Sorry. What time did the last guests leave last night?"

"The Mitsubishi men: 3:30 A.M., or so . . . One of them has a real thing for Yumi-chan. He insisted on a date next Saturday."

"What did Yumi-chan say?"

"The Mitsubishi men pay on time. They have a whacking entertainment budget they need to use up every month. I promised her a new outfit from somewhere plush if she said yes. Besides, the man's married, so it won't get complicated."

"Go out with Koji last night?" Taro cased the joint like a bodyguard looking for escape routes.

"Yes. I drank a bit too much. That's why I overslept."

Taro guffawed. "He's a good lad, that Koji. He's got his shit together. Meet any chicks?"

"Only ones who want to know whether your sports car has tinted windows."

Taro harrumphed. "Brains aren't everything in a woman. Ayaka was saying only this morning, a lad your age should be stoking the poker more, it's not healthy to—"

"Taro, put Satoru down." Mama-san smiled at me contentedly. "Aren't the cherry blossoms outside a picture? Taro's taking me on a shopping expedition, and then we're going to see the blossoms in Ueno Park. Mrs. Nakamori's girls have invited ours along to a cherry-blossom party this afternoon, so we're going along to make sure they don't get up to too much mischief. Oh yes. That reminds me. Mrs. Nakamori asked if you and Koji might be free to play in their cocktail lounge next Sunday. Apparently the trombonist in their regular band was involved in some sort of accident involving a bent pipe and some zoo animals. I thought it best not to pry. The poor man isn't going to be able to unbend his arm until June, so the band has had to cancel their fixtures. I told Mrs. Nakamori that I wasn't sure when Koji started back at college. Maybe you could give her a ring today or tomorrow? Come along now, Taro. We must be off."

Taro picked up the book I was reading. "What's this? *Madame Bovary*, eh? That French geezer? Wouldn't you credit it, Mamasan? We couldn't get him to study for six years of education, now he's reading on the job." He read out a bit I'd underlined: " *'One should be wary of touching one's idols, for the gilt comes off on one's fingers.'* " He thought about it for a moment. "Funny things, books. Yes, Mama-san. We'd better go."

"Thanks for bringing my lunch."

Mama-san nodded. "Ayaka made it. It's broiled eel. She knows how much you like it. Remember to thank her later. Good-bye now."

The sky was brightening up. I ate my boxed lunch, wishing I was in Ueno Park too. Mama-san's girls are fun. They treat me like a kid brother. They would have spread out a big blanket under a tree and would be singing old tunes with made-up words. I've seen foreigners get drunk in bars out in Shibuya and places, and they turn into animals. Japanese people never do that. The men might get friskier, but never violent. Alcohol lets off steam for Japanese. For foreigners, alcohol just seems to build steam up. And they kiss in public, too! I've seen them stick their tongues in and grope the girl's breasts. In bars, where everyone can see! I can never get over that. Mama-san always tells Taro to tell them we're full, or else she stings them for such a whopping cover charge that they never come back.

·   ·   ·

The disc finished. I ate the last morsel of broiled eel, rice, and pickle. Ayaka knew how to make a good boxed lunch.

My back hurt. I'm too young for my back to hurt. This chair has become really uncomfortable lately; I can't sit still. When Takeshi gets over his present financial crisis I'll ask him about getting a new one. Looks like I'll have to wait a long time, though. I wondered what to play next. I burrowed through a box full of unsorted discs that Takeshi had left on the floor behind the counter, but there was nothing I didn't already know. Surely I could find something. We have twelve thousand discs in stock. I realized I was scared of not needing music any more.

It turned out to be quite a busy afternoon. A lot of browsers, but a lot of buyers too. Seven o'clock came round quickly. I cashed up, put the takings in the safe in the tiny office, set the alarm and locked the office door. Put my lunch box and *Madame Bovary* in my bag, a Benny Goodman CD that I was going to borrow that night—a perk of the job—flicked off the lights, and locked the door.

I was outside rolling down the shutter when I heard the phone ringing inside. Damn! My first impulse was to pretend I hadn't heard it, but then I knew that I'd be spending the whole evening wondering who had been trying to ring. I'd probably have to start phoning around to people just to see if they'd phoned *me,* and if I did that I'd have to explain why I hadn't answered in the first place. . . . Damn it. It would be easier just to open up the shop again and answer it.

I've thought about it many times since: if that phone hadn't rung at that moment, and if I hadn't taken the decision to go back and answer it, then everything that happened afterwards wouldn't have happened.

An unknown voice. Soft, worried. *"It's Quasar. The dog needs to be fed!"*

Excuse me? I listened for more. The static hiss sounded like the crashing of waves, or could it be the noise of a pachinko arcade? I didn't say anything—it's best not to encourage these crank callers. There was nothing more. As though he was waiting for something. So I waited a little longer, and then I hung up, puzzled. Oh well.

I had my back to the door when it opened. The bell jingled, and I thought, "Oh no, let me out of here!" I turned around, and when I looked up I almost fell backwards over a limited edition box set of Lester Young. The floor of Takeshi's Jazz Hole swelled.

It's you! Peering into the dimness of my place.

She was speaking to me. She was actually here. She'd come back alone. I'd imagined this scene so many times in my head, but each time it was *I* who started things. I almost didn't catch what she was saying. She'd actually come back!

"Are you still open?"

"—yes!"

"You don't seem very open. The lights are off."

"—yes! Erm, I was getting ready to close, but until I close, I'm very completely open. Here!" I switched the lights on again. "There." Wishing I sounded cooler. I must look like a junior high school kid.

"Don't let me stop you going home."

"Don't let—no, you're not. Erm, I. Take your time. Please. Come in."

"Thank you." The her that lived in her looked out through her eyes, through my eyes, and at the me that lives in me.

"I—" I began.

"This—" she began.

"Go on," we both said.

"No," I said. "You go on. You're the lady."

"You're going to think I'm a nutcase, but I came in about ten days ago, and—" She was unconsciously rolling on the balls of her heels. "And there was this piece of music you were playing. . . . I can't get it out of my head. A piano and a saxophone. I mean, there's no reason why you should have remembered it or me or anything. . . ." She trailed off. There was something odd about the way she spoke. Her accent swung this way and that. I loved it.

"It was two weeks ago. Exactly. Plus a couple of hours."

She was pleased. "You remember me?"

I didn't quite recognize my own laugh. "Sure I do."

"I was with my revolting cousin and her friends. They treat me like an imbecile because I'm half-Chinese. My mother was Japanese, you see. Dad's Hong Kong Chinese. My home's in Hong Kong." Nothing apologetic about the way she spoke. *I'm not pure Japanese and if you don't like that you can stick it.*

I thought of Tony Williams's drumming in "In a Silent Way." No, I didn't *think* of it. I felt it, somewhere inside.

"Hey, that's nothing! I'm half-Filipino. The music was 'Left Alone' by Mal Waldron. Would you like to hear it again?"

"Would you mind?"

"'Course I wouldn't mind. . . . Mal Waldron's one of my gods. I kneel down to him every time I go to the temple. What's Hong Kong like, compared to Tokyo?"

"Foreigners say it's dirty, noisy, and poky, but really, there's nowhere like it. Not anywhere. And when Kowloon gets too much you can escape to the islands. On Lantau Island there's a big Buddha sitting on a hill . . ."

For a moment I had an odd sensation of being in a story that someone was writing, but soon that sensation too was being swallowed up.

―――――――

The cherry blossoms had come and almost gone. New green leaves, still silky and floppy, were drying on the trees lining the back street. Living and light as mandolins and zithers. The commuters streamed by. Not a coat in sight. Some had come out without their jackets. No denying it, spring was old news.

The phone rang. Koji, calling from the college canteen. "So. Who is she?"

"Who?"

"Stop it! You know perfectly well who! The girl at Mrs. Nakamori's last night who sat there swooning on your every note! Let me see . . . Her name began with 'Tomo' and ended with 'yo.' What was she called I wonder? Oh yes, that's right. Tomoyo."

"Oh, *her* . . ."

"Don't give me that! I saw you two making eyes at each other."

"You imagined it."

"You *were* making eyes at each other! The whole bar saw. A sea cucumber would have noticed. Her father definitely did. Taro noticed. He came up to me afterwards and asked me who she was. I'd hoped that he could tell me. He said to grill you. And what Taro wants he gets, so I'm grilling you."

"There's not much to tell. She came into the shop four weeks ago. Then she came in again last week. We got talking, just about music, and we went out on a date or two last week. That's all."

"A date or seven you mean."

"Well, you know how it goes."

"Not that I want to be nosy or anything, it's just that I didn't get the chance to interrogate her last night. But, er, so have you, y'know, snipped her ribbons and unwrapped her packaging yet?"

"The girl's a lady!"

"Ah, yes, but every lady is a woman."

"No. We haven't."

"You always were a slow worker, Satoru. Why not?"

"Because . . ." I remember her body wrapped inside my duffle coat as we walked along, sharing the same umbrella. I remember spending the whole movie holding her hand. I remember her eyes scrunched up in laughter as we watched a street performer who stood motionless on a pedestal until you left a coin in his urn, when he changed his expression and pose until the next coin was dropped in. I remember her trying not to laugh at my bowling alley disasters. I remember lying on the blanket in Ueno Park as the cherry blossoms fell onto our faces. I remember her in this room, in this chair, listening to my favorite music as she did her homework. I remember her face as she concentrated, and that strand of hair that fell down, almost touching her notebook. I remember kissing the nape of her neck in elevators between floors, and springing apart when the doors suddenly opened. I remember her telling me about her goldfish, and her mother, and life in Hong Kong. I remember her asleep on my shoulder on the night bus. I remember looking at her across the table. I remember her telling me about the ancient Jomon people who buried their kings in mounds, on the Tokyo plain. I remember her face at Mrs. Nakamori's when Koji and I did "Round Midnight" better than we've ever played it before. I remember.... "I dunno, Koji. Maybe we didn't do it because we could have done it." Was that true? It would have been easy, just to slip into a love hotel. My body certainly wanted to. But . . . but what? "I really can't say. Not because I'm being coy. I don't know."

Koji made the sage noise that he always does on the rare occasions when he doesn't understand something. "So, when do I get to see her again?"

I swallowed. "Never, probably. She's going back to international school in Hong Kong. She only comes to Tokyo every couple of years with her father to visit relatives for a few weeks. We have to be realistic."

Koji sounded more depressed about it than I did. "That's terrible! When's she going back this time?"

I looked at my watch. "In about thirty minutes."

"Satoru! Stop her!"

"I really think . . . I mean, I think that—"

"Don't *think*! Do something!"

"What do you suggest? Kidnap her? She's got her life to get on with. She's going to study archaeology at university in Hong Kong. We met, we enjoyed each other's company, very much, and now we've parted. It happens all the time. We can write. Anyway, it's not like we've fallen longingly in love with each other, or anything like that—"

"Beep beep beep."

"What's that supposed to mean?"

"Oh, I'm sorry, that was my bullshit alarm going off."

I dug out some old big band Duke Ellington. It reminds me of wind-up gramophones, silly moustaches, and Hollywood musicals from before the war. It usually cheers me up. "Take the 'A' Train," rattling along on goofy optimism.

I looked gloomily into the murky lake at the bottom of my teacup, and I thought about Tomoyo for the fiftieth time that day.

The phone rang. I knew it was going to be Tomoyo. It was Tomoyo. I could hear airplanes and boarding announcements in the background.

"Hello," she said.

"Hello."

"I'm phoning from the airport."

"I can hear airplanes taking off in the background."

"Sorry I couldn't say 'good-bye' properly last night. I wanted to kiss you."

"So did I, but with everyone there, and everything . . .'"

"Thanks for inviting me and Dad to Mrs. Nakamori's last night. My dad says thanks too. I haven't seen him nattering away like he did with your Mama-san and Taro for *ages*."

"I haven't seen them nattering away like that for ages, either. What were they talking about?"

"Business, I guess. You know Dad has a small stake in a night-club. We both loved the show."

"It wasn't a show! It was just me and Koji."

"You're both really good musicians. Dad didn't shut up about you."

"Nah . . . Koji's good, he makes me sound passable. He phoned about twenty minutes ago. I hope we weren't too gooey at the bar last night. Koji thought we were a bit obvious."

"Don't worry about it. And hey! Dad even implied, in his roundabout way, you could visit during your holidays. He might manage to find a bar for you to play sax in, if you wanted to."

"Does he know? About us?"

"I don't know."

"Takeshi doesn't exactly give me holidays. . . . At least, I've never asked for one."

"Oh . . ." She changed the subject. "How long did it take you to get so good?"

"I'm not good. John Coltrane is *good*! Wait a sec—" I grabbed a copy of John Coltrane and Duke Ellington playing "In a Sentimental Mood." Smoky and genuflective. We listened to it together for a while. So many things I wanted to say to her.

There was a series of urgent rings. "I'm running out of money—there's something—Oh, damn, 'bye!"

"'Bye!"

"When I get back I'll—"

A lonely hum.

. . .

At lunchtime Mr. Fujimoto came in, saw me, and laughed. "Good afternoon, Satoru-kun!" he jubilated. "Blue skies, just you wait and see! Tell me, what do you think of this little beaut?" He put a little package of books on the counter, and straightened out his bow tie, arching his eyebrows and acting proud.

A grotesque polka-dot frog-green bow tie. "Absolutely unique."

His whole body wobbled with mirth. "We're having a disgusting tie competition in the office. I've got 'em licked, I think."

"How was Kyoto?"

"Oh, Kyoto was Kyoto. Temples and shrines, meetings with printers. Uppity shopkeepers who think they have a monopoly on manners. It's good to be back. Once a Tokyoite, always a Tokyoite."

I started my rehearsed speech. "Mr. Fujimoto, when I told Mama-san about your kind offer to help me get an interview at your office she gave me this to give you. She thought you and your co-workers might enjoy it at a cherry-blossom party." I heaved the huge bottle of rice wine onto the counter.

"*Sake!* My word, that *is* a big boy! This will last awhile, even in an office full of publishers! How extraordinarily kind."

"No, it was kind of you. I'm sorry I'm too ignorant to accept your generous offer."

"Not at all, not at all. No umbrage taken, I promise you. . . . It was just a passing . . ." Mr. Fujimoto looked for the right word, blinking hard, and laughed when he couldn't find it. "I don't blame you in the least. You wouldn't want to end up being like me, would you?" He found that a lot funnier than I did.

"It's not my place to say this, but I wouldn't mind ending up being like you at all. You've got a good job. Unforgettable bow ties. A great taste in the world's finest jazz discs."

He stopped smiling for once and gazed out. "The last of the cherry blossom. On the tree, it turns ever more perfect. And when it's perfect, it falls. And then of course once it hits the ground it gets all mushed up. So it's only *absolutely* perfect when it's falling through the air, this way and that, for the briefest time. . . . I think that only we Japanese can really understand that, don't you?"

A van roaring the message *Vote for Shimizu, the only candidate who really has the guts to fight corruption* screeched past like a drunken batmobile. *Shimizu never betrays, Shimizu never betrays, Shimizu never betrays.*

Mr. Fujimoto trailed his fingers through the air. "Why do things happen the way they do? Since the gas attack on the subway, watching those pictures on TV, watching the police investigate like a crack squad of blind tortoises, I've been trying to understand. . . . Why do things *happen* at all? What is it that stops the world simply . . . seizing up?"

I'm never sure whether Mr. Fujimoto's questions are questions. "Do you know?"

He shrugged. "I don't know the answer, no. Sometimes I think it's the only question, and that all other questions are tributaries that flow into it." He ran his hand through his thinning hair. "Might the answer be 'love'?"

I tried to think, but I kept seeing pictures. I imagined my father—that man who I had imagined was my father—looking out through the rear window of a car. I thought of butterfly knives, and a time once three or four years ago when I was walking out of McDonald's and a businessman slammed down onto the pavement from a ninth floor window of the same building. He lay three meters away from where I stood. His mouth was gaping open in astonishment. A dark stain was trickling from it, over the pavement, between the bits of broken teeth and glasses.

I thought about Tomoyo's eyebrows, her nose, her jokes, her accent. Tomoyo on an airplane to Hong Kong. "I'd rather be too young to have that kind of wisdom."

Mr. Fujimoto's face turned into a smile that hid his eyes. "How wise of you." He ended up buying an old Johnny Hartman disc with a beautiful version of "I Let a Song Go Out of My Heart."

A mosquito blundered its way into my ear, suddenly there, loud as an electric blender. I pulled my head away and swatted the little bugger. Mosquito season. I was scraping its fuselage onto a bit of paper when Takeshi's estranged wife marched in, pushing her sunglasses up into her bountiful hair. She was accompanied by a sharp-dressed man who I immediately sensed was a lawyer. They have a look about them. When Takeshi offered me this job I'd spent a whole evening over at their apartment in Chiyoda, but now apart from the curtest of nods Takeshi's wife ignored me. The lawyer did not acknowledge my existence.

"*He*," Takeshi's wife pronounced the pronoun with the unique bitterness of the ex-wife, "only leases the property, but the stock is worth quite a lot. At least, *he* was always boasting that it is. The real money's in the hair salons, though. This is just a hobby, really. One of *his* many hobbies."

The lawyer demurred.

They turned to go. Takeshi's wife looked at me as she was stepping through the door. "You can learn something from this, Satoru. *Never* make a big decision which will alter the shape of your life on the basis of a relationship! You may as well take out a mortgage on a house made of sponge cake. Remember that." And she was gone.

I thought about what she had said as I put on a Chet Baker disc. A trumpet with nowhere urgent to be and all day to get there. And his voice, zennish murmurings in the soft void. *My funny valentine, you don't know what love is, I get along without you very well.*

The phone rang. A hysterical Takeshi. Drunk again.

"Don't let them in! Don't let that mad cow in!"

"Who?"

"Her! Her and her backstabbing-scumbag-bloodsucking law-yer, who *should* be representing *me*! They're going after my testi-cles with a meat cleaver! Don't let them look at the stock—*don't* let them look at the accounts—it's illegal—and hide the limited edi-tion original Louis Armstrong. And the gold disc of "Maiden Voy-age." Stick it down your boxer shorts or something—and—"

"Takeshi!"

"What?"

"It's a bit late, I'm afraid."

"What?"

"They've already been. Just to look around for a few seconds, so the lawyer could see the place. They didn't look at the accounts, they didn't evaluate anything."

"Oh. Great. Just great. Great. What an *utter,* pigging mess.

That woman is mad cow disease on two legs. . . . And what legs they are. . . ." He hung up.

The sunlight hummed and was soft. Shadows of twigs and branches swayed ever so slightly against the back wall. I thought of a time many years ago when two or three of Mama-san's girls had taken me boating on a lake. One of my earliest memories.

Your place does keep you sane, but can also keep you lonely.

What was I going to do? I rolled up my shirt and looked on my forearm. There was a snake which Tomoyo had drawn on with a blue pen yesterday afternoon. I asked her, why a *snake*? She'd laughed at me like she was in on a joke that I wasn't in on.

Two thoughts walked into my place.

The first thought said that we hadn't slept together because sex would have closed an entrance behind us and opened an exit ahead of us.

The second thought told me quite clearly what to do.

Maybe Takeshi's wife was right—maybe it is unsafe to base an important decision on your feelings for a person. Takeshi says the same thing often enough. Every bonk, he says, quadruples in price by the morning after. But who are Takeshi or his wife to lecture anybody? If not love, then what?

I looked at the time. Three o'clock. She was how many thousand kilometers and one time zone away. I could leave some money to cover the cost of the call.

"Good timing," Tomoyo answered, like I was calling from the cigarette machine around the corner. "I'm unpacking."

"Missing me?"

"A tiny little bit, maybe."

"Liar! You don't sound surprised to hear me."

I could hear the smile in her voice. "I'm not. When are you coming?"

And so we talked about what flight I could catch, where we would go, how she would level things with her father, what I could do to avoid eating into my meager savings too much. I felt as near to Paradise as I have ever been.

HONG KONG

THE MOON, THE moon, in the after . . .

There's a mechanism in my alarm clock connected to a switch in my head that sends a message to my arm which extends itself and commands my thumb to punch the OFF button a moment before the thing beeps me awake. Every morning, without fail, no matter how much whisky I drank the night before or what time I finally got to bed. I've forgotten.

Fuck. That was a horrible, horrible dream. I can't remember all the details, and I don't think I want to. The office was being raided. Huw Llewellyn had stormed in, with the Chinese police and my old scoutmaster whose Volvo I once shat on, they were all on rollerblades, and in my haste to erase the suddenly numerous files relating to Account 1390931 I kept mistyping my password. K-A-T-Y-F-R-B, no, K-T-Y, no, K-A-T-Y-F-O-R-B-W—no, and I'd have to start over. They work their way up the building, floor by floor, coffee cups were spilling in their wake, the electric fan swings its eye this way again, and unpaid telephone bills flutter through the air, bats at dusk. . . . There's a window open, and forty days and nights up the wind is vicious. The mouse on my computer sits there frozen, refusing to double-click. Was it any of this? Was what any of this? I've forgotten.

How many times have I dreamed of computers? I'd keep a dream diary, but even that might be used to help nail me one day. I imagine reporters printing the screwier ones, and prison analysts discussing the porn ones in supermarket aisles. I wonder who had the first computer dream, where, and when? I wonder if computers ever dream of humans.

Horn-rimmed Llewellyn. I'd only met him yesterday, and here the cunt was already gate-crashing my subconscious.

Fuck. The minute hand clicks again. The second hand glides around, reeling in my life surely as a kite string when it's time to go home. Fuck. I'm eating into my morning time safety margin. Another morning feeling as shattered as I felt the night before. My face feels cracked and ready to fall off in Easter-egg bits. And to cap it all I'm going down with another bout of flu, I swear it. Hong fucking Kong and I spend half my life walking around feeling like a steamed dumpling. Easter must be around now. Come on, Neal, you can make it as far as the shower. A hot shower will do the trick. Bollocks. Some speed would do the trick, but it's all snorted away.

I haul myself out of bed, stepping on a cold waffle and a plate. Fuck! She's coming today, I think, she'll clean it up. At least there'll be some food waiting when I get back. Something Chinese, but at least I won't have to face another waffle.

Into the living room. There is a message for me on the answering machine. Luckily I remembered to switch on the Sleepeasy mode before I went to bed, otherwise I'd have got even less sleep than I did. I swipe all the crap on the sofa onto the floor, jab the PLAY button, and lie on the sofa. . . .

"Rise and shine, Neal! This is Avril. Thanks for disappearing last night. Remember you've got the meeting with Mr. Wae's lawyers at 9:30, and Theo wants a full briefing beforehand, so you'd better get here by 8:45 sharp. Get the coffee perkin'. See you soon."

Avril. Nice name, silly slag.

Don't get too comfortable there, Neal. One, two, three, up! I said, "Up!" Into the kitchen, chuck the old filter into the overflowing bin, fuck, it's gone everywhere, ho-hum, sorry, maid, fresh filter, fresh coffee, more than the recommended dosage thank you very much, click ON. Trickle your thickest juice there for your Uncle Neal my baby, that's the way. I've forgotten. Open the fridge. Half a lemon, three bottles of gin, a pint of milk that expired over a month ago, dried kidney beans, and . . . waffles. God is still in heaven, I still have some waffles left. Waffle in toaster. Back to bedroom, Neal. There'll be a white shirt hanging in the closet, where she hangs them up every Sunday, every one the skin of a *gwai lo,* shagged and fleeced. I'll be so fucking angry if she's yanked them off the hangers again. . . . She'll do anything for attention.

No, it's okay. Hanging in a neat row. Boxer shorts, trousers, slung over the chair where you left them last night. The cheap, tubular chair. I miss the Queen Anne one. It was the one thing in this apartment older than me. One more bit of Katy gone. Grab a vest, a shirt, your jacket, something's missing—belt. Where's my belt?

"Okay. Very fucking funny. Where's my belt?"

The air conditioner drones from the living room.

"I'm going into the living room right now. Unless I find my belt on the arm of the sofa, I am going to go fucking ballistic."

I go into the living room. I find my belt on the arm of the sofa.

"Just as fucking well."

I remember that I got dressed without my shower. I stink, and there is a meeting with what's-his-face from the Taiwan Consortium this morning.

"You plonker, Neal," and nobody disagrees. When you call yourself a plonker nobody ever disagrees with you. The shower will cost me the rest of my safety margin. Unless the morning routine—"routine"—goes like clockwork, I will miss that crucial ferry, and have to start fabulating some impressive excuses.

I click off the air conditioner. "It's only fucking May. You want to freeze me to death? Who would you have to drive round the bend then, hey?"

In the bathroom I find she's been up to her usual tricks with the soap bottle. Katy always bought those pump-action containers of liquid soap, and so does the maid, which was all well and good until she discovered what fun it was to hammer the pump up and down. It is all over the walls, in the toilet bowl, on the floor of the shower cubicle, probably—yes—under where I just laid my shirt. Smeared trails everywhere like jerked-off semen.

"Very fucking amusing. Are you going to clean up this mess?"

Funny, she never touches any of the toiletries that Katy left behind. It's only ever my stuff. Why don't I just chuck that woman-stuff out? I still have a box of tampons in the cabinet. Two boxes. Heavy flow, light flow. The maid never touches the tampons—I can't understand why. Maybe it's a Chinese thing, like the babies not wearing nappies, and just crapping through that bum-flap wherever and whenever. The maid suffers no qualms about working through the talcum powder, skin moisturizers, and bath pearls, though. Why should she feel any qualms, if she doesn't about anything else?

The shower deluges my head. Soak, shampoo, rub, rinse, conditioner, finger up a smearage of the pumped-out body soap, lather, rinse. I give myself a full two minutes. Bathe now, pay later.

Toweling myself dry, I suck in my gut, but it doesn't make much difference these days. Neal, when did that thing start growing on you? Stress is supposed to make you lose weight. Doubtless it does, but a dietary credit of ninety percent waffles, fruit pastilles, cigarettes, and whisky must outweigh the stress debit. You look pregnant. "Ow!" I flinch. If Katy had got pregnant . . . would anything be different? Would you have got out while you could, or would you have more to worry about? Is it possible to worry more than I do and not . . . not just die from it? I don't know.

Something is burning! Fuck, the iron!

No, I hadn't switched the iron on. That's waffle smoke. Fucking great. No fucking breakfast. Take your time, Neal, it's a waffle past redemption. A Waffle Too Far. When is a waffle not a waffle? When it's a piece of fucking charcoal, that's when. I'll just have to heap the sugar into the coffee, I suppose. Liquid breakfast. Into the living room. A trickle of black is coming under the door, and I think it is blood. Whose blood? Her blood? Nothing would surprise me in this apartment anymore. Then I see it is dark brown. Fucking great. I used two filters instead of one, and we know what happens when you do that, don't we, Neal?

Into the kitchen. Off with the coffee machine, off with the toaster, off with his head. Fancy a nice glass of water for breakfast, Neal? Why thank you, Neal. No clean glasses. Okay, a bowl of water. Splendid. "Bon appetit, Neal." I survey my culinary empire. It looks like Keith Moon has been a houseguest for a month. No it doesn't. Keith Moon would leave it cleaner than this. Sorry, Maidie. I'll make it up to you later. "You'll fucking well make sure I will, won't you?"

Put on your tie and get to work, Neal. Mustn't keep the slitty-eyed moneymakers waiting any longer than you probably will. What a morning, I haven't even looked out of the window to see what the weather is doing. I look on my pager: dry and cloudy. No umbrella, then. That Asian non-weather. I've forgotten. I already know the view: bare hillside, dulled by mist, and the lethargic sea.

I click off the air conditioner. Again. I leave the alarm clock radio on for her, like my mum used to for the dog. From the bedroom I hear the business news in Cantonese. I don't know if she likes it. Sometimes she switches it off, sometimes she doesn't, sometimes she retunes it.

"Try to behave," I say, squeezing into my laced-up shoes, grabbing my briefcase and picking up my clutch of keys.

Katy always answered, "I hear and obey, oh hunter-gatherer."

She never answers.

Going, going, gone.

The elevator was on its way down. Thank God. Otherwise I'd miss the bus to the ferry. The doors opened. I squeezed into the all-male space, half-yellow, half-pinko-gray, but all the same Financial Zone tribe. We couldn't afford to live here if we weren't. The space smelt of suits, aftershave, leather, and hair-mousse, and something lingering. Maybe badly ducted testosterone. Nobody said a word. Nobody breathed. I turned around, so that my dick wasn't facing another moneymaker's dick, and saw the door to my apartment: 144.

"Not good," Mrs. Feng had said. " 'Four' in Chinese means 'Death.' "

"You can't spend all of your life avoiding four," Katy had protested.

"True," said Mrs. Feng, closing her sad eyes. "But there is another problem."

"Which is?" said Katy, giving me a half-smile.

"The elevator," said Mrs. Feng, opening her sharp eyes.

"We're on the fourteenth floor," I said. "Don't tell me we can't use the elevator."

"But it's directly opposite your own door!"

"So?" Katy was no longer smiling.

"The elevator doors are jaws! They eat up good luck. In this place you shall have none."

I looked up, and saw myself looking down through smoked glass, from among the tops of the unmoving heads. Like I was spirit-walking.

"You're also on Lantau Island," she had added as an afterthought.

Ping, went the bell.

"What's wrong with Lantau Island? It's the one place in Hong Kong where you can pretend the world was once beautiful."

"We don't like the currents. Too much north, too much east."

Ping, went the bell, ping, ping, ping. First floor. Ground floor. Whatever. The bus was waiting. We all ran across the road and boarded it, the James Bond music blaring in my head. I thought of little boys boarding a pretend troop transporter in a game of war.

Standing room only on the bus, but I don't mind. It reminds me of being crushed on the Dear Old Circle Line back in Dear Old Blighty. The cricket season will be starting now. That's why I like this bus. From the moment I get on it until the moment I enter the office, everything is out of my hands. I don't have to decide anything. I can zombify.

Until, that is, some fucker's cell phone drills through my eardrum. That is so annoying! Answer it. Answer it! Deaf-o, answer your fucking telephone! What are you all looking at me like that for?

Right, my phone. When these things first appeared, they were so cool. Only when it was too late did people realize they are as cool as electronic tags on remand prisoners.

I answer it, allowing the electrons of irrelevance to finish their journey along wires, into space, and back into my ear.

"Yeah? Brose speaking."

So, now every last jackass on this bus knows my name is Brose.

"Neal, this is Avril."

"Avril." Who else? She had probably slept over in the office. She was still hard at work on the Taiwan Portfolio when I left last night stroke this morning stroke whenever it was. Jardine-Pearl had a posse of lawyers working on this one. Cavendish had me, Avril, and Ming, who couldn't manage the lease on our—I mean my—apartment without fucking it up and getting me right royally rogered on the deposit. The Chinese are bad enough, estate agents are even worse, but Chinese Estate Agents are Satan's Secret Servicemen. They should be lawyers, but they probably make more cash doing what they do. Fuck, the Taiwan Portfolio! On top of everything else I had to worry about, I had this maze of details, small print, traps. It was probably good Avril was on this case, but fuck, she got on my tits sometimes. London had sent her in January, and she was so piously keen. Me, three years ago.

"Sleep well?"

"No."

Avril probably wanted me to apologize for leaving early last night. This morning. One A.M. Early, right. She could fucking forget it.

"I'm phoning about the Mickey Kwan File."

"What about it?"

"I can't find it."

"Oh."

"So where is it? You had it last night. Before you went home."

Fuck you, Avril. "I had it yesterday evening. Six hours before I went home."

"It's not on your desk now. And it's nowhere in Guilan's office. So it must be in your office somewhere, because I haven't touched it since yesterday afternoon. Might you—might it have been misfiled? Could it have been put under something, again? In a drawer somewhere?"

"I am on a bus on Lantau Island, Avril. I can't quite see my office from here."

I thought I heard somebody sniggering behind the wall of

suits, ties, and faces pretending not to listen. Sniggering like a loooooooooony. Maybe it was just a sneeze.

Avril was a walking experiment in humorlessness. I should nickname her "Spock." "I don't understand you sometimes. Yes, I know you can't see your office from there, Neal. I know that very well. But in case you've forgotten—again—Horace Cheung and Theo want a progress report on the Wae Folio in fifty-two—no, fifty-one—minutes. You are not here, because you are still on a bus on Lantau Island. You will not get here for another thirty-eight minutes, forty-one minutes if you haven't had breakfast and have to stop for donuts. Mr. Cheung is always ten minutes early. This means I have to complete said progress report by the time you waltz in through that door. As I need the Mickey Kwan File to do this, I need it now."

I sighed, and tried to think of a withering response, but I was all out of wither. I must be going down with this flu that's doing the rounds. "What you say is all true, Avril. But I honestly, really, truly, madly, deeply don't know where the file has got to."

The bus lurched to and fro. I caught a glimpse of tennis courts, the international school, the curve of a bay, and a fishing junk in the tepid Asian white.

"You have a copy on hard disk, don't you?"

I was suddenly very awake. "Yes, but—"

"I'll download the file off your hard disk, and whip off a copy on my printer. It's only about twenty pages, yeah? So just tell me your password."

"I'm afraid I can't do that, Avril."

A pause while Avril thought. "I'm afraid you can, Neal."

I remembered watching a rabbit being skinned, where or when I couldn't remember. The knife seemed to unzip it. One moment a dozing Mr. Bunny, the next a long rip of blood, from buck teeth to rabbity penis.

"But—"

"If you've downloaded any Swedish dominatrix hard porn pix from the Internet, I promise your secret is safe with me."

No matter how quietly I tried to speak, ten people would hear me. "I can't tell you my password like this. It's a security breach."

"Neal, you probably haven't noticed, in fact I know you

haven't, otherwise you wouldn't have gone home last night, but we are on the verge of losing this account. The Dae Folio is worth $82 million. Dutch Barings and Citibank are both singing under their balcony every night, and they sing more sweetly than we do. If we don't have the Mickey Kwan gains to offset the upsets in Bangkok and Tokyo, we're history. And D.C. is going to know exactly why—I'm not going to take the rap for this. You might be happy spending the rest of your life managing a McDonald's in Birmingham, but I want a little more out of life. Now tell me your password! You can change it when you get to work. Your 'security breach' is going to last forty-nine minutes. Come on! If you can't trust me, who can you trust?"

Absolutely Fucking Nobody, that's who I can trust. I pulled my jacket over my head and held the phone in my armpit. Quasimodo Brose. "K-A-T-Y-F-O-R-B-E-S." Don't tell her not to snoop. That would make her snoop. "There. Happy?"

To her credit, Avril didn't take the piss. I'd have been happier if she had. Have I reached the stage where people feel sorry for me?

"Got it. See you in Theo's office. I won't let anyone else touch your PC."

The bus pulled into Discovery Bay harbor. The turbo ferry was waiting, as always. Nobody needs to hurry—the first bell is ringing now. The second bell will ring in one minute. The third in two minutes. The boat wouldn't leave for three minutes, and bus to boat took less than sixty seconds, if you have your pass ready, which we all do. That's a wide enough safety margin to drive a Toyota Landcruiser up. The bus doors hissed open, and the troops filed off, the bus rocking as they jumped, one by one.

Was she here, among us? Holding my hand? Why had I always assumed she stayed in the apartment all day? It's more logical she roams around the place. She likes attention.

Leave it, Neal. That's your apartment. Your "home" life. You go there because you have nowhere else to live. Don't bring her to Hong Kong Island. She probably can't cross water. Don't the Chinese say something like that? They can't jump—that's why there are steps into the holy places—and they can't cross water. No?

Twenty paces to the ticket barrier. Well, I think the morning's crisis is lowering its revolver. The really incriminating stuff is locked lower down in the bowels of my hard disk, and Avril simply doesn't have the time to go prodding around at random. She doesn't have the motive. And she is too stupid. As the comings and goings of Account 1390931 became ever more complex, my security arrangements became ever more intricate, my lies more incredible as one near miss lurched to another. The truth is that Denholme Cavendish's yes-men don't want to know the truth that even people handicapped by an Etonian education must dimly be able to smell by now. Don't worry, Neal. Avril will be printing off her precious Mickey Kwan File. Guilan will be making a pot of coffee so thick you could fill cracks in the road with it. I'll fob Theo off with some bollocks about overzealous auditors, and, like most superiors, he'll be too proud to ask me the simplest questions. Theo will fob the Cavendish Compliancy Body off with some bollocks about capital tied up in double-hedging Japanese banks. They'll fob Jim Hersch off with some bollocks about the house being told in no uncertain terms that it needs to put itself in order during the next financial quarter, and he'll fob Llewellyn's master off by swearing that he is totally and completely confident that Cavendish Holdings is absolutely clean in regard to these rumors smeared by—and here I have to be frank with you old boy— by the Chinese, and we don't need degrees in police detection to know who's pulling the strings of the Hong Kong People's Police these days, do we, Comrade, eh? Eh? And hey presto, we'll all get our six-figure bonuses, five figures of which have already been spent and the rest of which will vanish into cars, property, and the entertainment sector during the next eighteen months. You've done it again, Neal. Back from the brink. Nine lives? Nine hundred and ninety-fucking-nine more like.

Everything is in order, that's the second bell, Neal. That gives you sixty seconds.

"Neal? Why aren't you getting on this ferry?"

That feeling when vomiting is a certainty, and you wonder what you've eaten.

I don't have enough inside me to vomit.

What's the matter? Is she making me stay? Tugging my arm?

No. It's nothing to do with her. I know when she's here, and she's not here now. And she can't make me do anything. I choose. I'm the master. That's one of the rules.

There was something more remarkable than her altogether.

Last night, Avril and I were preparing a briefing for Mr. Wae the shipping magnate. The computer was fucking up my eyes, I hadn't eaten since a BLT at lunch, I'd gone through hunger and numbness several times as my stomach downsized. Around midnight I started feeling dizzy. I came down to this coffee bar just across the street from Cavendish Tower, and ordered the biggest fuckoff triple shitburger they did, two of them, and put ten sugar cubes into my coffee. I drank it through my tongue, and my blood sang like the Archangel Gabriel as the sugar flooded in. That can't be natural, Neal. Fuck Natural.

I watched the cars, people, and stories trundle up and down the street. In the distance a giant bicycle pump was cranking itself up and hissing itself down. I watched the neon signs intone their messages, over and over. There was a song playing, that Lionel Richie hit from years ago, about the blind girl. A real weepie. I'd lost my virginity to that song under a mountain of coats at a friend's party in Telford. Fuck knows what I was doing in Telford. Fuck knows what anybody is doing in Telford.

This kid and his girl came in. He ordered a burger and cola. She had a vanilla shake. He picked up the tray, looked around for a seat which wasn't there, and caught me watching him. He came over, and in nervous English asked me if they could share my table. It wasn't Chinese English. Chinks would normally die rather than sit with one of us. Either that or they'll just pile in without acknowledging that you're even there. So I nodded, tapping the ash from my cigarette. He thanked me gravely, in English. "Sankyou very mochi," he said.

She was Chinese, I could tell that, but they spoke in Japanese. He had a saxophone case, and a small backpack with airline tags still attached. They could barely have been out of high school. He needed a good long sleep. They didn't hug or cloy over each other like a lot of Chinese kids do these days. They just held hands over the table. Of course, I didn't understand a word, but I guessed they were discussing possibilities. They were so happy. Sex twitched in the air between them, which made me think that they hadn't done it yet. None of that lazy proprietorship which settles in after the first few times.

Right at that moment, if Mephistopheles had genied his way from the greasy ketchup bottle and said, "Neal, if I let you be that kid, would you pledge your soul to the Lord of Hell for all eternity?" I'd have answered, "Like a fucking shot I will." Nipkid or no Nipkid.

I looked at my Rolex: a quarter past midnight. What life is this?

I was wrong about the sky. It's not dreary white. . . . When you look you see ivory. You can see a glow, there, above the mountain where the sun polishes it pearly and wafer thin.

And the sea isn't blank; there are islands out there, right at the edge.

Soft brush strokes on a fresh scroll hanging in Mrs. Feng's room, four floors above us.

Ahem. May I remind you, Neal, that you have credit card bills that would make Bill Gates twitch? That your divorce settlement will gouge out most of the money you thought was yours? That lawyers with fingers in the kinds of pies yours are in simply do not miss appointments with Mr. Wae. These Taiwanese shipping magnates eat breakfast with politicians powerful enough to make skyscrapers appear and disappear.

Ten seconds before the third bell and the barriers come down! Worry about your existentialist dilemmas during your lunch hour—right, when did I last have a lunch hour?—whenever, but get on that *fucking* boat right now! I am not telling you again.

A man gallops down the walkway from the shops. Andy Somebody, I know his face slightly from my Lantau polo club period. Not that you can find a single fucking pony on the whole fucking island. His Ralph Lauren tie is flapping like a live snake, his shoelaces are undone, my, Andy Somebody needs to be careful. He might fall and break his crown, and ill Jill'll hill crumbling after.

"Stop that boat! Wait!" My, my, Andy Somebody is Lawrence of Olivier.

Is this how she observes me? This indifference, laced with mockery?

The Chinese barrier guard, most likely the bus driver's brother's half-twin stepcousin-in-law, flicks his switch and the turnstiles close. Andy Somebody's flight through the air ends gripping the bars, and he represses the howl of a demented prisoner. "Please!"

The Chinese barrier guard makes the faintest gesture with his head at the "Boat Departures" board.

"Let me through!"

Barrier Guard swishes his head, and he goes back to his coffee booth.

Andy Somebody whinnies, fumbles for his mobile phone, and manages to drop it. He walks away speaking into it to Larry, inventing excuses, and pretending to laugh.

The turbo ferry pulls away from the jetty, and buzzes away into the distance.

I don't understand you sometimes.

Katy insisted that I didn't see her off at the airport. Her flight was in the afternoon, it was a manic Friday. My desk at work had become a canyon floor between two unstable formations of contracts. And so the day she left we had taken the bus before my usual one and drank a cup of coffee at the jetty café. That café, there. In the window seat Andy Somebody has pulled out his laptop computer and is hammering the keyboard as though he's trying to avert a thermonuclear war. Sitting hunched like that is going to knacker his back. Nope, he doesn't know it, but Andy's sitting at the very table where Katy and I staged our Grand Farewell.

It was not a Noël Coward Grand Farewell. Neal Brose and Katy Forbes brought you a much unlovelier performance. Neither of us had anything to say, or rather we had everything to say, but after all those nights of not saying a word, we suddenly found we had not one dollar of time left between us. I suppose we talked about airport layouts, watering plants, what Katy was looking forward to once she got back to London. It was like we'd met the night before, fucked in a Kowloon hotel, and had just woken up. In fact, we hadn't had sex for five months, not since finding out.

Fuck, it was horrible, horrible. She was leaving me.

It is what we didn't say that I remember best. We didn't mention Mrs. Feng, or her. We didn't mention whose "fault"—fuck, haven't thousands of years of infertility come up with a better word than "fault"—it was. Katy was always capable of mercy. We had never discussed therapy, clinics, adoption, procedures, that umbrella of "ways around it," because neither of us had the will, and we didn't now. I guess. If nature couldn't be fucked to knit us together, we sure as hell weren't going to be. We didn't mention the word "divorce," because it was as real and near as that mountain there. We didn't mention the word "love." That hurt way too much. I was waiting for her to say it first. Maybe she was waiting for me. Or maybe it was that we had left those days and nights for the starry-eyed beepy muppets born seven or eight years after us. Those kids in the coffee bar last night. They were who love was for. Not us old fucks over thirty. Forget it.

The bell for the ferry had rung. On this spot, right here, this pinkish paving slab I'm standing on right now. I know it well because I walk around it every day. Here was where I thought I should embrace her and maybe kiss her good-bye.

"You'd better get on your ferry," she said.

Okay, if that was how she wanted it.

"Good-bye," I said. "Nice being married to you."

I instantly regretted those words, and I still do. It sounded like a parting shot. She turned and walked away, and I sometimes wonder, had I run back to her, could we have found ourselves pinballed into an altogether different universe, or would I have just got my nose broken? I never found out. I obeyed the ferry bell. Ashamed, I didn't look for her on the shore as the ferry pulled away, so I don't know if she waved. Knowing Katy, I doubted it. It took me about forty-five seconds to forget her, anyway. On page five of *South China Business News,* ten lines of newsprint mugged my attention. A new Sino-American-British investigative body, the Capital Transfer Inspectorate, had just raided the offices of a trading company called Silk Road Group. It was not well known to the general public, but it was very well known to me. I, personally, as per instructions received, had ordered the transfer of $115 million, the Friday before, from Account 1390931, to the Silk Road Group.

Oh . . . fuck.

There was nobody but me.

The road from the jetty and the harbor village led to the Polo Club. Flags hanging limp today. After the Polo Club the road became a track. The track led to the beach. At the beach the track turned into a path, winding along the shore. I'd never taken the path any further, so I had no idea where it might lead. A fisherman looked up, his gnarled fingers knotting a net, and our eyes met for a moment. I forget, outside my Village of the Short Lease Damned, people actually live out their whole lives on Lantau Island.

Dad used to take me fishing at weekends. A gloomy reservoir, lost in Snowdonia. He was an electrician. It's honest work, real work. You install people's switchboards for them, connect their lighting, tidy up cowboy and DIY botch jobs so they don't burn their houses down. Dad was full of a tradesman's aphorisms. "Give a man a fish, Neal, and you feed him for a day. Teach him to fish, and you feed him for life." We were at the reservoir when I told him I was going to do Business Studies at Polytechnic. He just nodded, said, "That could lead to a good job in a bank," and cast off. Was that the beginning of the path I'm still on? The last time we went fishing was when I told him I'd got the job with Cavendish Hong Kong, and a salary three times that of my ex-headmaster. "That's grand, Neal," he said. "Your mother will be proud as punch." I had hoped for more of a reaction from him, but he had retired by that time.

Truth be told, fishing bored me. I'd rather be watching the footy on the box. But Mum insisted that I went with him, so I did, and now I'm glad I went. Even today, the word "Wales" brings back the taste of tuna and egg sandwiches and weak, milky tea, and the memory of my dad looking out over a murky lake walled in by cold mountains.

Her coming was the hum of a fridge. A sound you grow accustomed to before you hear it. I didn't know how long cupboards had been left open, air conditioners switched on, curtains twitched open, before I became conscious of her. Living with Katy postponed it. Katy thought I was doing what she was doing, I thought Katy was doing what she was doing. She didn't come in the dramatic way they do in the movies. Nothing was hurled across the room, no ghosts in the machine, no silly messages typed on my computer or spelled out with the fridge magnet letters. Nothing like *Poltergeist* or *The Exorcist*. More like a medical condition, that, while terminal, grows in such small increments that it is impossible to diagnose until too late. Little things: hidden objects. The honey left on top of the wardrobe. Books turning up in the dishwasher. That kind of thing. Keys. She had a penchant for keys. No, she's never been an in-your-face houseguest. Katy and I joked about her even before we believed in her: Oh, it's only the ghost again.

In the end, however, I think she affected the three of us deeper than any amount of smashed vases.

I do remember the day that hum became a noise. It was a Sunday afternoon, last autumn. I was at home for once. Katy had gone shopping at the supermarket down in the village. I was vegging out on the sofa, one eye on the newspaper and one on *Die Hard 3* dubbed into Cantonese. I realized there was a little girl playing on the carpet in front of me, lying on her belly, and pretending to swim.

I knew she was there, and I knew there was no such child.

The conclusion was obvious.

Fear breathed on the nape of my neck.

Half a building blew up. "We'd better get some more FBI agents," said the stupid deputy who didn't trust Bruce Willis.

Reason entered, brandishing its warrant. It ordered that I behave as though nothing untoward was happening. What was I going to do? Go screaming from the apartment to—where? I'd have to come back at some point. There was Katy to think about, too. Was I to tell her that a ghost was watching us morning, noon, and night? If this drawbridge was lowered, what else would come in? I forced myself to pretend to finish the article, though it could have been written in Mongolian.

Fear was handcuffed, but it could still yell at the top of its lungs, *There's a fucking ghost in your apartment! A fucking ghost, you hear me?*

She was still there, swimming. She was on her back now.

I had to lower the paper. Would it mean I was mad if she was there, or if she wasn't?

What did I know about her?

Only that she wasn't threatening me.

I folded the newspaper and looked at where I had thought she was.

Nobody, and nothing. *See?* said Reason, smugly.

Neal, said Neal, *you're cracking up.*

I walked resolutely towards the kitchen.

Behind my back I heard her giggle.

Fuck you, said Fear to Reason.

I heard the lock being jiggled, and Katy's keys echoing in the hallway outside. She dropped them. I walked over to the door and opened it for her. She was bending down, so she couldn't see my expression, which I'm glad about.

"Phew!" said Katy, smiling and straightening up.

"Welcome home," I said. "I say. Is that champagne?"

"Champagne, lobster, and lamb, my hunter-gatherer. You've been asleep, haven't you? You're all groggy."

"Uh . . . yeah. Don't tell me I've missed your birthday again?"

"No."

"Then what?"

"I want to feed you up, so you make lots of sperm and get frisky. I've decided that I want a baby. What do you think?"

How Katy.

I was in a ramshackle yard, walled in by falling-down fisherman's cottages. Paths forked off and forked off some more. A black dog eyed me with its one eye, looking at what I am. I wished it were on a chain. What are the odds of that dog having rabies? Enough of their masters certainly seem to. A woman stood up from behind a cabbage the size of a small hut. She said, "You going to the Big Buddha, yes?"

I saw myself, blundering in her yard. A foreign devil with mud round his ankles, shoes from Pennsylvania, a silk tie made in Milan, a briefcase full of Japanese and American gadgetry worth more money than she saw in three years. What must she think?

"Yes," I said.

She pointed with a blunt vegetable down one of the paths.

"Thank you."

At first the path was clear, but as it went deeper into the wood it grew more ambiguous. Leaves, stems, shoots, nodules, thorns, thicket. A common dirt-colored bird that sang in emerald and opal. Dry grass. Soil, stones, loose rocks, worms moving underground.

I'm not thinking about it. The day was just beginning to warm up.

I heard a helicopter, and imagined Avril and Guilan leaning out with a headset and binoculars. Avril would be speaking into a camera like a radio station's traffic reporter. I giggled. Something jumped and thumped in the undergrowth. I froze, but heard nothing more. There's a thought. Are there snakes on Lantau Island?

> *Thirty-two days hath September,*
> *April, June, and November.*
> *And fuck the rest . . .*

Insects buzzed around my head, thirsty for sweat to drink.

It's time to bring in the maid.

Fair's fair, she was Katy's idea from the start. I never wanted one, didn't choose her, and for the first six months—until this winter—I didn't even see her. I never even met the maid until Katy was back in Britain. There was a circle of men at Cavendish who were into hiring maids willing to do more than fluff pillows and take the kids to school and back. Most of the men at Cavendish's hired Filipinos, because they had no permanent residency, and so had to be more compliant. They also know that the more accommodating they were, the more likely they'd be handed on when their master left Hong Kong.

Maybe Katy had heard these tales in the wives' club. Maybe that was why she chose a Chinese maid. I was surprised when Katy told me she wanted one. Katy came from an upper-middle-class Cambridge family, but from a firmly lower-middle-class income bracket where you traded on your family's name and tightened your belt to put the kids through good schools. We met at a law firm in London, for fuck's sake, not the House of Lords.

But here we were, out in the colonies. Well, the ex-colonies. I was disappointed that she'd been swayed by the wives' club. But then, as Katy pointed out, I wasn't the one who had to clean up my mess. I couldn't argue when Katy pointed out that after she got pregnant, she'd have to take it easy. I suspected Katy was on a culture-bridging kick, and had chosen penetrating the Chinese psyche as a hobby.

If that suspicion had been correct, then for Katy it badly backfired. All Katy got from her hobby was grief, which she then passed on to me, the moment I was through the door. Katy gave her presents, but she took them without saying a word. Katy said she was surly, inscrutable, and kept dropping mile-wide hints about how her starving family in the mainland needed more money. Katy suspected she was working at a hostess bar for more money at night. Katy couldn't be sure, but she thought a pair of gold earrings had gone missing. Looking back, I wonder if that was the work of our host daughter?

"If you're not happy with her, sack her."

"But how about her starving family?"

"It's not your problem! You're not Lady Bountiful."

"Spoken like a true lawyer."

"You're the one who's whinging about her morning, noon, and night."

"I want you to speak to her, Neal."

"Why me?"

"I've tried, but women only respect men in this culture. Just be assertive. I'll give her this Saturday off, and ask her to come on Sunday. Make sure you're here."

"But they're your earrings."

That had been the wrong thing to say.

When I managed to calm Katy down I asked her what I was supposed to say.

"Tell her that there are certain standards we wish her to meet. Say that perhaps we weren't clear enough when we first hired her."

"Maybe she's just a lazy bitch. What makes you think I'll have any effect?"

"The Chinese psyche: if you let her know who the master is, they listen. She looks at me like I'm a piece of dog shit. Theo's wife was telling me about it, she had the same problem. It doesn't even matter if she doesn't understand everything. They can tell from the tone of your voice."

And the next Sunday I met the maid. So you see, Katy brought us together.

I had expected a cleaning lady. Maid meant maid. I guessed she was twenty-eight or twenty-nine. She was in a black and white uniform and black tights. The material must make her skin sweat. She listened insouciantly, while I ran through my patter, avoiding eye contact for most of the time. Her hair was luscious, her skin dusky. After thirty seconds of being in the same room, I knew that she and I would end up fucking each other, and I knew that she knew it too.

And from then on, even on the nights when Katy and I had sex three times to get her pregnant, I would close my eyes and see the maid underneath me.

The path rose sharply behind the Trappist Monastery, up into the purplish morning. Soon the tree line was far below. I never knew there was so much sky here! I took my jacket off and slung it over my shoulder. I was still carrying my briefcase.

I got to an outcrop and sat down. My heart was twanging like a double bass. Should I take some of those tablets? The doctor who does the Cavendish people, a Chinese quack, just said, "Take three of these every day and you'll be all right." I said, "What are you giving me?" He said, "A bottle of pink ones, a bottle of green ones, and a bottle of blue ones." Cheers, Doc. Maybe I'll give the medicine a miss.

Alchemy was changing the sky. The sun was burnishing the leaden dullness to silver. In turn the silver was shrouding blue. It was going to be a nice day after all.

A nearby furry rock lifted its head, blinking. It looked at me sorrowfully and mooed. I hadn't been this close to a cow I wasn't eating since . . . who knows? Wales, for all I knew. Hong Kong glistened in the distance, through the haze. Skyscrapers, construction, clamoring upwards like trees in a jungle.

My cellular telephone rang and triggered an instant relapse.

Fuck, what *have* I done! Please God let me wake up! *Please!*

The cow mooed dolefully. Fuck. Fuck. Double Fuck to the power of Fuck squared. I am a lawyer living in a world where "thirteen" means "thirteen million bucks" and I am bunking off work like a schoolboy skipping double maths! The Taiwanese! Think! What excuse is serious enough, plausible enough, and yet too implausible for it to be a lie? Kidnapping? No, a heart attack? Avril knows I'm on medication. A seizure? Think! Serious, violent, incapacitating vomiting, then why aren't I on the boat, I'd need to pay a doctor, I'd need a receipt, and a reliable witness—

Answer me! Answer me!

I clicked ANSWER, and said, er . . .

Neal, isn't it about time that *you* decided what constitutes a crisis?

Er . . . Nothing. I listened to Neal's heart. It sounded like a percussion grenade in a neighboring valley.

"Neal? Neal?" Avril, sure enough. "Neal, where are you?"

A large fly landed on my knee. A gothic tricycle. My relapse was over.

"Neal? Can you hear me? Chiang Yun's here. He's being very polite, but he's wondering what is so important that you are late for this meeting. And so am I. And so will Jim Hersch. And if Chiang Yun isn't important enough to warrant your valuable time,

Mr. Gregorski from St. Petersburg has already phoned you twice, and it's not even 9 A.M."

I looked at my Rolex. My, my, how time had flown. The cow frowned. I smelt its shit near by.

"I know you're there, Neal. I can hear you breathing. This had better be good. This had better be jolly good. Because nothing short of a capsized ferry is going to save you this time. Neal? You hear me, Neal? Okay, look Neal, if you're unable to speak, then tap the phone twice now, all right?"

Aha! Doubt was creeping into her contempt! I chuckled. Avril the ever-resourceful. Avril will go far will Avril.

"Neal! This is not funny! You are *royally* messing up one of the biggest contracts we've ever seen! One of the biggest that has ever been heard of! I'm going to have to tell D.C. You can't seriously expect me to take the flack for this!"

Ah, shut the fuck up. I clicked the thing off and placed it on the warm rock.

A buzzard circled, and there was an anvil-shaped cloud.

You never see them coming. They lurk in the overlooked and un-dusted places. They grow to huge proportions, and all along you don't even dream about them, not in their true form. And then one day a chance meeting happens, a glimpse of what you didn't know you wanted, and a latch is raised . . .

Avril tried my beeper. Jesus, I was armed to the teeth with telecommunications devices. Like John Wayne unholstering him-self after a hard day slaughtering Hispanic bandits with bad teeth, I unclipped it. I clicked open my briefcase. There was the Mickey Kwan File—whoops—and Huw Llewellyn's business card. I put in my beeper and cell phone. I stood up, took a big underarm swing, and hurled it into the void. It drew an elegant parabola; I could still hear my beeper, a costly, mewling kitten. The briefcase hit the mountainside running, and spun down the slope in terminal leaps . . . in big beautiful wheels, fast enough to kill on impact, like Mama Lion, like a tumbler, like a lemming, like Piggy from *Lord of the Flies.*

My briefcase hung for a moment in the morning sun, weight-less.

Then it plummeted like a gannet into the sea.

———————

It seemed Katy had forgotten to cancel the maid.

The first week after Katy's departure I came home one night to find my washing done, the dishes washed up and neatly stacked, the toilet and the bathroom cleaned, and the windows polished. She'd even ironed my shirts, bless her sour-plum little Chinese nipples.

I certainly wasn't going to cancel that. Weekdays, I had to plan in my Filofax when I was going to shit. Seriously.

The maid didn't take long to work out that Katy had gone.

She came one Sunday morning. I was lying on the sofa watch-ing *Sesame Street*. I heard the keys, and she entered as if she owned the place. She was not wearing her apron.

She locked the door behind her, walked over to me as though I was inanimate, knelt on me, and started massaging my cock with one hand. Big Bird, Ernie, and Bert were singing a song about the magic "E" that makes the "A" say its name. I tried to kiss her but she shoved my face back with her hand, and kept it there, her hand coiling me tighter and tighter. She pulled off my T-shirt, and pushed my trousers down with her foot. Athletic girl. She pinched the skin between my balls, like a ring through the nose of an ox, led me to the bedroom, and laid me down on Katy's side of the bed. She slid out of her pants and knelt on my rib cage. I started unbuttoning her, but she made a tsu-tsuuuu noise, slapped me, and dug her fingernails into my scrotum until I capitulated. Then she spoke, for the first, and almost the last, time.

"Say: you want me, you don't want Katty Bitch."

"Yeah, I do."

"Say!"

"I want you, I don't want her."

"Say: Katty Bitch is bitch trash, I am real woman."

I can't say that.

Still keeping my testicles hostage, she pulled off her top with one hand, and unclipped her bra. I heard her giggling in the other room. Her nipples rose and darkened like something in a tale.

"She was a bitch. Trash. You are a real woman."

"You would give money. You would give her stuff. All of it. A present."

"She took a lot back with her."

"She left much things. Mine now. Say it." Her hand slid up my shaft, tighter and tighter.

"It's yours now."

She put my hand onto her breast. "Say: You stronger than me."

"You are stronger than me."

Formalities, rituals, and contract signing over, she lunged down on me. For a fraction of a second I thought about contraception, but the warmth and wetness and rhythm nudged me further and further away.

Once I tried to get on top, but she bit me and elbowed me and rolled me back over.

Afterwards the fan droned on our bodies. Nothing left of all that fire but the smell of low tide. I felt . . . I don't know what I felt. Maybe I felt nothing. The theme music of *Sesame Street* played itself out.

She got up, and sat down at Katy's dressing table. She opened the drawer, and took out a coral necklace, and fastened it around her neck. Slenderer than Katy's.

I wanted her again. This was costing me more than money, so I may as well push for maximum value and damn myself properly. I got up and fucked her from behind, on the dressing table. We broke the mirror.

Sex with the maid became a drug. Once pricked, I was addicted. I thought about her at work. When I got back in the evening, my erection would start even as I inserted my key. If I could smell Katy's cologne in the entrance hall, it would mean she was waiting. If not, well, if not, I'd have to make do with whisky. Hugo Hamish and Theo at the office tried to persuade me to go drinking at Mad Dogs a few times, thinking I was cut up about

Katy, but the truth is, she didn't cross my mind that often. She was living in another compartment, and I didn't have to encounter her unless I went looking for her. The maid was different: she came looking for me.

When I got home one night and saw Mrs. Feng's shoes in the entrance I realized trouble had come visiting. Mrs. Feng and Katy were sitting at our dining-room table. They had that speak-of-the-devil look. The final verdict on Neal Brose had just been handed down.

"Neal," Katy said in her headmistress voice, which came out when she was nervous as fuck but wanted to seem in control. "Mrs. Feng's been telling me about our visitor. Sit down."

I wanted a beer, I wanted a shower, I wanted steak and chips, I wanted Manchester United versus Liverpool on satellite TV.

"Listen to Mrs. Feng! Before you do anything."

The sooner this was over, the sooner I could get on with my evening.

Mrs. Feng waited for me to sit down and stop fidgeting. The way she looked at me made me feel a suspect at an identity parade. "You are not alone in this apartment."

"We know."

"She is hiding now. She is a little girl, and is afraid of me."

I could quite see why. Mrs. Feng's eyes were smoked glass. When she blinked I swear I heard doors hiss.

"There are three possibilities. For centuries, unwanted childrens were left on Lantau by night, to the mercy of the winter nights and the wild animals. She could be one such ancient. But these rarely reside in modern buildings. A second possibility is, she was one of the undesirables rounded up by the Japanese when they occupied Hong Kong during the war. They were brought to Discovery Bay, ordered to dig their graves, up where Phase 1 was built in the seventies, and shot so they fell back into the holes. Perhaps she had stolen some bauble. The third possibility is that she is a . . . I don't know the English word. She is the child of a *gwai lo* man and a maid. The man would have left, and the maid flung the girl off one of these buildings."

"Modern mothercare."

"Neal, shut up!"

"A boy would bring disgrace, but a baby girl, worse than that. It often happens, even when the parents are married and both Chinese, if they are not rich. The dowries can cripple a couple's married life. I believe that she is one of these."

Why were they both looking at me? Was it my fault?

"There's something else," Katy said. "Mrs. Feng says she's drawn to men. You."

"Do you know what you're sounding like?"

"Mrs. Feng says she sees me as a rival, and for as long as we're here, I'll never be able to have a baby. We'll have to leave Lantau. It can't follow you over water."

"Dr. Chan forwarded a slightly more plausible reason for the nonappearance of a Brose-Forbes junior, don't you think?" Fuck, that came out wrongly.

"So, you're saying it's all a figment of my imagination."

"No. Occasionally, there is a presence here. But stratospheric rents on Central and Victoria Peak are a rather more concrete reality. The Chinese are the first to forget their sacred fucking *feng shui* when money's making the suggestion. Forget it, Katy. We can't afford to move. And there is no way we're moving in with the Triad and the Plebs and the Immigrants down in Kowloon. You'd have a baby there and they'd chop it up and desiccate it for medicine."

Mrs. Feng watched us. I could swear she was enjoying this.

"Mrs. Feng," I said. "You know everything there is to know. What should we do? Call an exorcist?"

My sarcasm was dead on arrival. Mrs. Feng nodded slightly. "In ordinary circumstances, yes, there are a number of specialist geomancers I could recommend. But this apartment is so very unlucky, I believe it is beyond redemption. You must move."

"We're not moving. We can't move."

Mrs. Feng stood up. "Then you will excuse me."

Katy stood and made "won't you stay and have some more tea" noises, but she was already passing through the doorway. "Beware," she warned without turning around, "of what is at the other end of the door."

While I was trying to work out what the fuck that was supposed to mean, Katy stood up and went into the spare bedroom.
I heard her lock it.

Madness, fucking madness. I got myself a beer, and lay on the
sofa, too tired to make myself some food. Thanks, Katy. You've
had all fucking day to make something. So what if there is a fucking ghost?

I never knew there were so many fucking locks in this place.

The boy and the girl in the café last night, I keep seeing them.

Katy and me. What happened to Love?

Well, Love went to bed. It fucked, over and over, until it got
sore-knob bored, quite frankly. Then Love looked around for
something else to do, and it saw its lovely friends all having lovely
babies. So Love decided to do the same, but Love kept having its
periods, same as ever, however much it inseminated itself. So
Love went to an infertility clinic, and discovered the truth. As far
as I know Love's stiff is there to this very day. And that, boys and
girls, is the Story of What Happened to Love.

I want to go back to the coffee bar and tell them. "Listen to me,
both of you, you are ill. You're not seeing things how they are."

Who are you to tell anyone they are ill, Neal?

Katy had phoned that evening. The maid had left two minutes before. I was just climbing into the shower, still sticky. How do
women manage to time these things? She spoke to my answering
machine. She was drunk. I let her speak to it, listening in, standing stark bollock naked in the living room, smelling of multiple
sex with the maid Katy had hated.

"Neal, I know you're there. I can tell. It's five in the afternoon
here, dunno what that makes it there, eleven I suppose." I didn't
know what the time was either. "I've been watching the Brits get
slaughtered at Wimbledon. . . . Wanted to say hello I s'pose,
dunno why I'm phoning really, I'm well, thanks, how are you? I'm
well. I'm flat-hunting. I should be closing on a little flat in Islington this time next week. The pipes are noisy but at least there
aren't any ghosts. Sorry, that's not funny. I'm doing a lot of P.A.ing

for Cecile's Temp Agency, just to keep my hand in. Vernwood's left for Wall Street. Some hotshot fresh from the London School of Economics has been given his desk. I was wondering if you could get the Queen Anne chair shipped back sometime, it's worth a bob or two, you know. Spoke with your sister last week, bumped into her in Harvey Nic's funnily enough, quite by chance. . . . She said you'd just extended your contract by another eighteen months. . . . Will you be coming back at Christmas? Might be nice to meet up, I just thought, y'know, but then again you'll probably have people to meet and all that. . . . And some of my jewelry is still in your apartment. We wouldn't want that maid getting her hands on it and running back to China, eh? I don't think I ever got those keys back from her. You'd better change the locks. I'm okay, but I need a holiday. About forty years would do me. Well, if you're not too tired when you get in give me a call, I'll be watching the doubles finals for the next couple of hours. . . . Oh, and your sister said to tell you to call your mother. . . . Your dad's pancreatic thingy has come back. . . . 'Bye then . . ."

I never got round to returning that call. What would I say?

A grave. Its back to the mountain, its face to the sea. The sun was high and pestilent. I took off my tie and hung it on a thorny tree. No point trying to read the name of the grave's occupant. There are thousands of these Chinese hieroglyphs making up the world's clonkiest writing system. I knew five: alcohol, mountain, river, love, exit. I sometimes think, these hieroglyphs *are* the real Chinese, living down through the centuries, hiding their meanings in their similarities to outwit the foreigner, by and large immune to tampering. Mao himself failed to modernize his language.

I'd followed the path down from the last peak. There'd been a brackish stream, a bush of birds, a butterfly with zebra stripes on wings wide as side-plates. I'd lost the path once or twice, and it had come back to find me once or twice. It reminded me of the Brecon Beacons. I grew up when I realized that everywhere was basically the same, and so were the women.

This time there was no way on. A false trail. I'd have to backtrack, through the maze of thorn bushes and couch grass. I sat down and looked at the view. Another extension to the new airport was being built out there on reclaimed land. Little bulldozers played in the glistening silt flats. Sweat trickled down my wrists, my chest, down the crack between my buttocks. My trousers clung to my thighs. I should be taking my medication about now, but all that was in a briefcase in the bottom of a bay somewhere.

I wondered if anyone had been sent to come and get me. Ming, probably. Avril was no doubt busy probing deeper into my hard disk, with Theo Fraser at her shoulder. Where might that lead? All those e-mails from Petersburg, all those see-no-evil-hear-no-evil seven- and eight-figure transfers of funds to out-of-the-way places?

Unless you've lived with a ghost, you can't know the truth of it. You assume that morning, noon, and night, you're walking around obsessed, fearful, and waiting for the exorcist to call. It's not really like that. It's more like living with a very particular cat.

For the last few months I've been living with three women. One was a ghost, who is now a woman. One was a woman, who is now a ghost. One is a ghost, and always will be. But this isn't a ghost story: the ghost is in the background, where she has to be. If she was in the foreground she'd be a person.

Katy and I had come back from some stupid Cavendish party. We'd come into the lobby together, I checked our mailbox, putting down my briefcase. There were some letters. We got in the elevator, ripping open the envelopes. Halfway up I realized I'd left my briefcase down in the lobby next to the mailbox. When we got to the fourteenth floor, Katy got out, and I went back down, got my briefcase, and returned to our floor. When the elevator doors opened I saw Katy still outside the apartment, and I knew something was very wrong.

She was white and trembling. "It's locked. It's bolted. From the inside."

Burglars. On the fourteenth floor? They must still be in there.

It's not burglars, and we both knew it.

She had come back.

I don't know how I knew what to do, but I took out my own keys, and rattled them a few times. Then I tried the door.

It swung open into the darkness.

Katy didn't speak to me, even though I know she was awake for most of the night. Looking back, that was the beginning of the end.

So I backtracked.

A bus full of curious people drove past, packed as usual. Fuck, the way that the Chinese will just stare at you! *So* rude! Have they never seen a sunburning foreigner in a suit out for a midday walk before?

The sun! The smack of a boxing glove. I was parched. The helicopter came back. The sides of the valley hummed and swished. I should have come here months ago. It was waiting, and I'd done nothing but truck to and fro from the office, on that turbo ferry across the River Styx.

What kind of place did the maid live in? In Kowloon, or the New Territories somewhere? She'd get a bus or a streetcar from the port, and get off far beyond where the decent shops finished. The same sort of place Ming lives in, I suppose. Down a backstreet, its walls crowded up to fifteen floors with dirty signs for sweatshops and strip clubs and money changers and restaurants and God knows what. Nothing more than a rafter of mucky sky. The noise, of course, would never stop. The Chinese brain must be equipped with a noise-filtration device, that allows them to only listen to the one band of racket that they want to hear. Taxis, cheap little ghetto blasters, chanting from the temple, satellite TV, sales pitches floating aloft through megaphones. You'd go down an alley, there'd be the smell of grime and piss and *dim sum*. People would be hanging about in doorways needing new shirts and a shave, selling drugs. Upstairs—the elevators in those kinds of places never work—and into a tiny apartment where a family of seven bicker and watch TV and drink. Strange to think I work in the same city. Strange to think of the little palaces up on Victoria Peak. That's probably where the Japanese kid is getting over his jet lag now. His girl bringing him lemon tea on a silver tray. Or more likely, her maid bringing in the lemon tea. I wonder how they met. I wonder.

There are so many cities in every single city.

When I first came to Hong Kong, before Katy joined me, I was given one day's holiday to get over jet lag. I felt fine, so I decided to use it exploring the city. I traveled the trams, jolted by the poverty I saw, and walked the overhead walkways, feeling safe only among the business suits and briefcases. I took the cable car up to Victoria Peak, and walked around. Rich wives were strolling in groups, and maids with the children, and teenage couples walking arm-in-arm looking at all the other teenage couples. There were a couple of stalls mounted on wheels, the sort of setup my father used to call market barrows. They sold maps, peanuts in their shells, and the bland salty snack things that Chinese and Indians are so fond of. One of them sold maps in English, and postcards, so I bought a few. Suddenly a pile of cans next to the stall moved and barked something in Chinese. A face caked in grease and creased with age emerged and looked at me with loathing. I jumped out of my skin. The stall-holder laughed, and said, "Don't worry. He's harmless."

The garbage man growled, and repeated the same words, slowly, and louder, at me.

"What's he saying?"

"He's begging."

"How much does he want?" A stupid question.

"He's not begging for money."

"What's he begging for?"

"He's begging for time."

"Why does he do that?"

"He thinks you're wasting yours, so you must have plenty to spare."

My tongue was parched. I hadn't drunk for hours . . . since that bowl of water at breakfast. Usually, I only ever drank coffee and whisky. An old farmer was burning something that popped like firecrackers. Bamboo? Grainy mauve smoke drifted across the road. My eyes were watering. I was under a vast tree that fanned out across the sky and hid it incompletely as words will hide whatever is behind them.

Red roses grew wild up the brick wall crumbling back to sand. A roped-up dog went hysterical as I walked past. A flurry of fangs and barks. It thought I was a ghost. Futons, airing. A Chinese pop song. God-awful and tinny. Two old people in a room devoid of furniture, steam rising from their teacups. They were motionless and expressionless. Waiting for something. I wish I could go into their room and sit down with them. I'd give them my Rolex for that. I wish they would smile, and pour me a cup of jasmine tea. I wish the world was like that.

I watched the cars, people, and stories trundle up and down the night road. In the distance a giant bicycle pump was cranking itself up and hissing itself down. I watched the neon signs intone their messages, over and over. The Japanese kid and his girl had disappeared fuck knows where, and Lionel Richie had dissolved in his own saccharine bathtub. My second burger had gone cold and greasy; I couldn't finish it. A version of "Bohemian Rhapsody" was playing, unbelievably sung in Cantonese. I should be getting back to Mr. Wae's briefings or Avril will start the Sacred Martyr Act. One more song; and one more megasugar coffee, then I'll go back like a good boy. It was "Blackbird" by the Beatles. I never listened to this one properly before. It's beautiful.

"Neal Brose?"

A Welsh voice, unknown and familiar. A short, Mr. Mole-ish bloke, with horn-rimmed glasses.

"Yeah?"

"My name's Huw Llewellyn. We met at Theo and Penny Fraser's New Year party."

"Ah, yeah, Huw . . . Sure, sure . . ." I didn't know him from Adam.

"Mind if I pull up a pew?"

"Sure . . . If you can say that about molded plastic seats bolted onto cast-iron frames. You'll have to forgive my frazzled memory, Huw. Who are you with?"

"I used to be with Jardine-Pearl. Now I'm at the Capital Transfer Inspectorate."

Fuck. Now I remember. We'd talked about rugby, then business. I'd dismissed him as a born compromise candidate. "Poacher turned gamekeeper, eh?"

Huw Llewellyn smiled as he unloaded his tray, and wriggled out of his corduroy jacket, with leather pads on the elbows. So fucking Welsh. A veggieburger and a styrofoam cup of hot water, with tea bleeding out of its bag. "People usually say, 'It takes a thief to catch a thief.'"

Dad used to say that. "I've read about your raids on—who was it? Silk Road Group?"

"Yep. Would you pass me a sachet of ketchup, please?"

"I've heard some interesting rumors about them money laundering for Kabul's biggest drug exporter. Is it true? Go on, I won't tell a soul."

Huw bit into his veggieburger, chomped a few times, smiling, and swallowed. "I've heard some interesting rumors about Account 1390931."

Fuck. I suddenly wanted to vomit my shitburger. I laughed lightly. "I don't know what you're talking about."

Fuck. That's exactly what liars say.

Huw squeezed the tea bag with a plastic fork. "Go on, I won't tell a soul."

"Is it a bicycle combination lock?"

"No, it's a Cavendish Holdings account that only you have the keys to."

He had upped the stakes. "Is this a fishing expedition, or do you have a warrant for my arrest?"

"I prefer to see this as a friendly chat."

"Mr. Llewellyn, you don't know who you're dealing with."

"Mr. Brose, I know far more about Andrei Gregorski than you. Believe me. You're being set up. I've watched him do it before. Why do you think neither his name—nor Denholme Cavendish's name—appears on not one single document, not one single computer file? Because they like you? Trust you? You are their bulletproof vest."

How much did he know? "It's just a hush-hush hedge fund for—"

"I don't want to watch you zip yourself up in lies, Mr. Brose. I know your personal life is in tatters. But unless you cooperate with me, by the weekend things are going to take a sharp turn for the worse. I am your last way out."

"I don't need a way out."

He shrugged, and swallowed the last morsel. He'd put that away without me noticing. "Then our friendly chat has come to an end. Here is my business card. I strongly recommend a change of mind, by tomorrow noon. Good night."

The door swung. I was left looking at the wreckage of my shit-burger.

I went back into Cavendish Tower, but changed my mind in the lobby. I asked the night watchman to wait five minutes, then tell Avril I'd gone home. I waited twenty minutes at the harbor for the next ferry, looking across the black water at all the shining sky-scrapers. Back on Lantau Island—just as a precaution—I emptied three quarters of my account from the bank's cash machine, in case my cards got frozen. There wasn't another bus for thirty minutes, so I walked back to Phase 1 through the chilly night.

She was waiting in the apartment. The air conditioner was belting out frigid air.

"For fuck's sake, I'm sorry! I had a lot of work!"

Resentful silence.

"I've got a lot on my mind! Okay? I'm going to bed."

I hid the money in a shoe box at the bottom of Katy's dressing table. I'd think of a better hiding place before the maid came. She might be a necessary drug, but she was still a thieving bitch.

————————

I came to a shrine, and the sound of running water. There was a fountain guarded by two dragons. Hygiene be fucked, I was thirsty. I drank until I heard the water sloshing about in my belly. At least I wasn't going to die of dehydration. I wanted to dunk my arms and face into this cool, clear water, so I unstrapped my Rolex, perched it on the nose of a dragon, stripped off my shirt, and immersed as much of my torso in the fountain as I could. I opened my eyes under the water, and saw the underbellies of wavelets, with the sun beneath.

Where now? There was an easy path and a steep path. I took the easy one, and twenty meters later arrived at the cesspit. I came back to the dragons and started climbing sharply. I was feeling much, much better. As though my body had stopped fighting the flu, and was submitting to its will.

The path steepened. At times I had to use my hands to scramble up. The trees were growing dense, scaly, and damp, the pinpricks of light that got to the path sharp and bright as lasers. I took off my jacket and gave it to a blackberry bush. It was already ripped. Maybe a passing monk or escaped refugee will take a shine to it. The air was busy with out-of-tune birds and their eyes.

Time lost me.

I looked at my Rolex, and remembered that I'd left it on a dragon's nose.

Grabbing a root to pull myself up, it came off in my hand and I tumbled down the path a few yards. I heard a crack, but stood up right as rain. I felt fabulous. I felt immortal.

Higher up loomed a rock as big as a house, but I scaled it like a teenager, and was soon surveying my domain from the top. A slow-moving 747 made its stately descent, skinning the afternoon with its jagged blade of noise. I waved at the people. The sun glints off the tail. She is with me, waving too, jumping up and down. It's good to make somebody feel good, even if she doesn't exactly exist.

"She likes me."

The maid was standing in front of the mirror, naked, holding up Katy's summer frocks against her body. If she liked one she'd try it on. If it fit, she'd put it into Katy's Louis Vuitton bag. If she didn't, it joined the others on the reject pile.

I was floating, anchored to the bed by the deadweight of my groin. "Who likes you?"

"The little girl."

"What little girl?"

"Your little girl. Who lived here. She liked me. She wanted sister to play with."

The wind blew the curtains gently. These Chinese are fucking crazy.

The last time Katy called, she wasn't drunk. I took that as a bad sign.

"Hello, Neal's Answerphone. This is Katy Forbes, Neal's separated wife. How are you? You must be rushed off your feet, considering how Neal has forgotten how to pick up receivers and dial. I want you to tell Neal that I am now the proud owner of a palatial residence in northeast London, that we're having the rainiest summer since a very long time ago, and all the cricket is being rained off. Tell him that I'm having sessions with Dr. Clune twice a week, and that they are working wonders. Tell him that Archie Goode is going to be my lawyer, and that the divorce papers should get to him by the end of the week. Tell him I'm not going for his jugular, I just want what's rightfully mine. Lastly, tell him it would prepare the ground for an amicable settlement if he gets off his lazy arse and ships me home my Queen Anne chair. He knows it's the one heirloom I give a damn about. Good night."

The key to understanding Neal Brose is that he is a man of departments, compartments, apartments. The maid is in one, Katy is in another, my little visitor in another, Cavendish Hong Kong in another, Account 1390931 in another. In each one lives a Neal Brose who operates quite independently of the neighboring Neal Broses. That's how I do it. My future is in another compartment, but I'm not looking into that one. I don't think I'll like what I'll see.

Weird thing was, the maid was right. When I came back and the maid was there, the atmosphere in my apartment was palpably different. Muted Sibelius rather than thunderous Wagner. If she'd been real, I imagined her sitting under the table, chattering away to her dolls. She'd leave us alone, and the curtains would stay where I left them. Maybe I'd hear the kiss kiss kiss of her feet running across the marble floor in the living room.

If the maid wasn't there, there'd be this air of reproachment and neglect. It was the same when I went away on business—I went to Canton once, a right fucking shithole it is too—and when I got back she was so pissed off with me that I had to stand there apologizing to the thin air.

The path stopped climbing, and crested the ridge. I saw Buddha's head above the camphor trees, almost close enough to touch. That was one Big Buddha. Platinum, spun on a wheel of deep blue. The trees were dream trees, now. A shadow cat, a cat shadow.

My skin buzzed. My immortality was ebbing away. In this sun it must be turning to bacon. I think I had broken a toenail, I could feel something wet and warm in my shoe. I could feel my organs sag against each other, still functioning, but slowing like tired swimmers.

Why is the moon up there, up above you, Lord Buddha? White, blue, roaring in its silent furnace of sunlight. The moon, the moon, in the afternoon.

I stepped into a once and future century. People, coach tours, a car park, souvenir stands, advertisement hoardings, people crowding around ticket booths—only the British and the Slavs know how to queue—motorbikes . . . Here and not here. They were on the wrong side of a wall of bright liquid. A babble of languages from the room next door.

Lord Buddha's lips were full and proud. Always on the verge of words, yet never quite speaking. His lidded eyes, hooding a secret the world needs.

The moon was in on the joke. New, old, new, old. If I met the old garbage man now, I'd say, I'm sorry, but I don't have any spare time to give you. Not even a minute. Not even a spare ten fucking seconds.

I wondered if that Japanese kid was playing his saxophone in a bar somewhere, over in a bar in Central or Kowloon. I would like to hear him. I'd like to watch his girl watching him. I would like that very much. I don't think it's going to happen now. I'd like to talk with them, and find out how they met. I'd like to ask him about jazz, and why John Coltrane is so famous. So many things to know. I'd like to ask him why I married Katy, and whether I was right to sign and return those divorce papers. Was Katy happy at last, now? Had she met someone who loved her, someone with a respectable sperm count? Would she be a tender, wise mother, or would she turn out to be a booze-soaked saggy fuck in her middle age? Would Huw Llewellyn nail Andrei Gregorski, or would Andrei Gregorski nail Huw Llewellyn? Would Mr. Wae the shipping magnate take his business elsewhere? Would Manchester United win the premiership? Would the Cookie Monster's teeth fall out? Would the world be over by Christmas?

She brushed nearby, and blew on the back of my neck, and a million leaves moved with the wind. My skin was so hot it no longer seemed my own. A new Neal inside the old opened his eyes. Platinum in the sun, blue in the shade. He was waiting for my old skin to flake off so he could climb out and walk abroad. My liver squirmed impatiently. My heart was going through its options. What's that organ: the one that processes the sugar?

What led me here?

My dad would describe Denholme Cavendish—Sir Denholme Cavendish—as a man educated beyond his intellect. "Now, Nile." D.C. pursed his lips together in the manner of the old general he believed himself to be. The traffic of Barbican, twenty floors below us, punctuated the pompous old fuck's dramatic pauses. "A key question to understanding the role we're projecting for you in Hong Kong is this: what is Cavendish Holdings?"

No, D.C., the key question is: what answer do you want to hear?

Play it safe, Neal. Let him feel intellectually on top. And don't tell him he's too fucking stupid to get my name right. "A top-line legal and investment corporation, Sir Denholme."

Good. He had an insight coming on. "We're a corporation. A

top-line corporation. But that's not all we are, Nile, my word no. We are a family! Isn't that so, Jim?"

Jim Hersch smiled his "you've put your finger on it!" smile.

"Sure, we have our family squabbles. Jim and I have had some fine old catfights in our time, haven't we, eh, Jim, eh?"

Same smile. "Sure have, Sir D." You smooth American fuck, Hersch.

"You see, Nile? No quarter given to yes-men at Cavendish! But we pull through in the end, Nile, and let me tell you how! Because we understand the value of cooperation. Mutual reliance. Mutual trust. Mutual assistance." He lit his cigar like Winston Churchill and gazed at the portrait of his grandfather, who gazed back. I wanted to snigger. The man was a walking cliché. How could this fuck-for-brains run a law firm with offices in five continents? The answer was obvious: he only thought he ran it. "Playing the Asian markets requires a certain . . . how did I put it to Grainger, Jim, the other day?"

"I believe you said 'flair and verve in the strategizing stages,' Sir D."

"Flair! And verve! That's it, you see. *Flair!* And *verve!* In the *strategizing stages!* Now in London, New York, everyone knows what's what. The playing field is even, the goalposts are fixed. But Asia is the last wild frontier, eh? The bandits of corruption live in the Chinese hills, and make lightning raids! Regulators? Forget 'em! Paid off. Every last man. No, for our townships to prosper in Asia, we have to play by their rules, but play better! I'm talking about originality in capital manipulation! About reinterpretation! You have to recognize the real but invisible goalposts when you see them! And use whatever means are at your disposal to score. You with me, Nile?"

"One hundred percent, Sir Denholme."

What was the old fuck on about?

"I want to add a special account to your Hong Kong portfolio. It's for an ally of mine. A Russian chap, based in Petersburg, you'll meet him one day. You'll be hearing from him soon enough. A splendid fellow. Chap by the name of Andrei Gregorski. A real mover and shaker. He's done a few favors for us in the past." He leaned forward over the desk, tapping his cigar into an intricate ashtray inlaid with jade and amber, and etched with lotus flowers and orchids.

"He's asked me to set up an account for his operation with our Hong Kong branch. I want to put you in charge of it."

"What do I do with it?"

"Whatever he tells you to. However much, wherever, whenever. Child's play for a trooper of your experience."

We'd come to the clincher.

"I think I can manage that, Mr. Cavendish."

"Keep it hush-hush. Just between you, me, Jim, and grandfather here, eh?"

I get it. The old fuck's asking me to bend the law.

"One thing matters and one thing only." I'd always assumed it was his leather chair that creaked, but now I wondered whether or not it was really him. He prodded each word at me with his cigar. "Do—you—have—the—balls?" The blackheads on the tip of his nose urgently needed squeezing. "Eh? Eh?"

I'm a financial lawyer. I bend the law every day.

"They were firmly attached when I last used them, Sir Denholme."

D.C. was deciding whether or not he liked my answer. Then his laughter ignited, sending a projectile of saliva hurtling between my eyebrows. Jim Hersch smiled too, a photo smile of a manager in a local newspaper. And I was smiling the same smile, too.

Do I go back further?

How about this? Hong Kong had been appropriated by British drug pushers in the 1840s. We wanted Chinese silk, porcelain, and spices. The Chinese didn't want our clothes, tools, or salted herring, and who can blame them? They had no demand. Our solution was to make a demand, by getting large sections of the populace addicted to opium, a drug which the Chinese government had outlawed. When the Chinese understandably objected to this arrangement, we kicked the fuck out of them, set up a puppet government in Peking that hung signs on parks saying

NO DOGS OR CHINESE, and occupied this corner of their country as an import base. Fucking godawful behavior, when you think about it. And we accuse *them* of xenophobia. It would be like the Colombians invading Washington in the early twenty-first century and forcing the White House to legalize heroin. And saying, "Don't worry, we'll show ourselves out, and take Florida while we're at it, okay? Thanks very much." Hong Kong became the trading hub of the biggest, most populated continent in the world. This led to one big burping appetite for bent financial lawyers.

Or is it not a question of cause and effect, but a question of wholeness?

I'm this person, I'm this person, I'm that person, I'm that person too.

No wonder it's all such a fucking mess. I divided up my possible futures, put them into separate accounts, and now they're all spent.

Big thoughts for a bent little lawyer.

My forehead kissed the tarmac, soft as a sleeping daughter. I keeled over into a fetal position. A lurching tide of voices sloshed the hull of my hearing. What the fuck is going on?

Now I understand what this insane fucking day has been about!

Hilarious!

I am fucking dying!

No doubt about it. Now that I'm dying again I recognize the signs.

Thirty-one years old, and I am fucking dying!

Avril's going to be so fucked off with me. And when D.C. hears, well, I think I can safely kiss my six-figure bonus goodbye. How will Katy take it? That's the clincher. Dad?

Hilarious . . .

She comes through the wall of legs and torsos. She looks down at me, and she smiles. She has my eyes, and the maid's body, in miniature. She gives me her hand, and we pick our way through the crowd of gawkers, the shocked, the titillated, and the gum-chewing. What can have happened to fascinate them so on such an afternoon?

Hand in hand we walk up the steps of the Big Bright Buddha, brighter and brighter, into a snowstorm of silent light.

HOLY MOUNTAIN

UP, UP, AND up, and down, maybe.

The Holy Mountain has no other directions. Your left and right, your south, north, west, east, leave them at the Village. You won't be needing them. You have ten thousand steps to go before you reach the summit.

There is a road, now. I saw it. Buses and trucks go up and down. Fat people from Chengdu and further drive up in their own cars. I watched them. Fumes, beeps, noise, oil. Or they drive up in taxis, sitting in the back like Lady Muck Duck. They deserve all the fleecing they get. Engine-powered pilgrimages? Even Lord Buddha doesn't give a shovelful of chickenshit for engine-powered pilgrimages. How do I know? He told me Himself.

On the Holy Mountain, all the yesterdays and tomorrows spin around again sooner or later. The world has long forgotten, but we mountain-dwellers live on the prayer wheel of time.

I am a girl. I was hanging out the washing on a line I had suspended from the upstairs-room window ledge and the Tree. The height of our Tea Shack above the path, it was safe from thieves, and the Tree tells the monkeys not to steal our things. I was singing to myself. It was spring and the mist was thick and warm. Upbound, a strange procession marched out of the whiteness.

The procession was ten men long. The first carried a pennant, the second, a kind of lute I'd never seen, the third, a rifle. The fourth was a footman. The fifth was dressed in silken robes the color of sunset. The sixth was an older man in a khaki uniform. Seven to ten were baggage carriers.

I ran to get my father, who was planting sweet potatoes behind our house. The chickens fussed like my old aunts in the Village. When my father and I got around to the front, the strangers had reached our Tea Shack.

My father's eyes popped open. He hurled himself onto the ground, and yanked me down into the dirt with him. "Silly little bitch," he hissed. "It's the Warlord's Son. Kowtow!" We knelt, pressing our foreheads into the ground, until one of the men clapped.

We looked up. Which one was the Warlord's Son?

The man in silk was looking at me, smiling from the corner of his mouth.

Footman spoke. "Sire, is it your wish to rest awhile?"

The Warlord's Son nodded, not taking his eyes off me.

Footman barked at my father. "Tea! The best you have in your pit of roaches, or the crows will dine on your eyeballs tonight!"

My father leapt to his feet and pulled me with him behind the table. My father told me to polish the best tea bowls, while he loaded fresh charcoal onto the brazier. I had never seen a Warlord's Son before. "But which one is he?" I asked.

My father slapped me with the back of his hand. "It's none of your concern." He glanced over his shoulder nervously at the men, who were laughing at me. My ear began to throb. "The striking gentleman, in the beautiful robes," muttered my father, loud enough to be overheard.

The Warlord's Son—I guessed he was twenty—removed his hat and sleeked back his hair. Footman took one look at our best bowls and rolled his eyeballs. "How dare you even think it?" A baggage carrier unpacked some silver bowls, decorated with golden dragons with emerald scales and ruby eyes. Another servant unfolded a table. A third spread a perfectly white cloth. I thought I was dreaming.

"The girl may serve the tea," said the Warlord's Son.

I felt his eyes touch my body as I poured the tea. Nobody spoke. I didn't spill a drop.

I looked to my father for approval, or at least for reassurance. He was too busy worrying about his own skin. I didn't understand.

The men spoke in crisp, shiny Mandarin. Their magnificent, strange words paraded past. Words about somebody called Sun Yat-sen, somebody called Russia, somebody else called Europe. Firepower, taxes, appointments. What world had these men come from?

My father took my shawl off and told me to tie back my hair and wash my face. He made me serve some more tea. He was picking his teeth with a splintered chopstick, and watching the men carefully from the shadows.

Silence thickened the air. The mist had closed in. The mountainside was dark with white. The afternoon became so sluggish that it stopped altogether.

The Warlord's Son stretched his legs and arched his back. He picked at his teeth with a bejeweled toothpick. "After drinking tea as bitter as that, I want sherbet. You, rat-in-the-shadows, you may serve me a bowl of lemon sherbet."

My father fell to his knees and spoke to the dirt. "We have no such sherbet, Lord."

He looked around at his men. "How tiresome! Then tangerine sherbet will have to suffice."

"We have no sherbet at all, Lord. I'm very sorry."

"Sorry? I can't eat your 'sorry.' You wreck my palate with your brew of nettles and foxshit. What kind of stomach do you think I have? A cow's?"

His look told his entourage to laugh, which they did.

"Oh well. There's nothing for it. I'll have to eat your daughter for dessert."

A poison thorn slid in, bent, and snapped.

My father looked up. The Khaki Man coughed.

"What's that cough supposed to mean? My father told me to come on this accursed pilgrimage. He didn't say I couldn't have any fun."

Footman inspected my father like shit on his boot. "Get your upstairs room as ready as you can for His Lordship."

My father made a gurgling noise. "Sir . . . Lord. I—I mean—"

The Warlord's Son imitated the buzzing of a horsefly. "These wormholes! Can you believe it? Give him one of the bowls. They were a wedding present from my ogre-in-law, I never liked them. As a dowry. More than a fair exchange for sluicing out a peasant girl's cunt. They're from Siam. She'd better be a virgin for workmanship like that!"

"She is, Lord. Untouched. I promise it. But I've had some genuine marriage proposals, from suitors in high places. . . ."

Footman unsheathed his sword, and looked at his master. The Warlord's Son thought for a while. "Suitors in high places? Carpenters' cocks. Very well, give him two bowls. But no more haggling, Mr. Wormhole. You've tried your luck enough for one morning."

"My Lord's reputation for generosity is just! No wonder all who hear of My Lord's grace weep with love at the very mention—"

"Oh, shut up."

My father looked around at me. "You heard His Lordship, girl! Ready yourself!"

I could smell their sweat. Something unspeakable was going to happen. I knew where babies came from. My aunts down in the Village had told me about why my bad blood leaked out every month. But . . .

Lord Buddha was watching me from his shrine beside the Tree. I asked him for it not to hurt as much as I feared.

"Up." Footman jabbed towards the stairs with his sword. "Up!"

The silences after his last gasp were sung together by a blackbird. I lay there, my eyes unable to close. His were unable to open. I listed the places where I hurt, and how much. My loins felt ripped. Something inside had torn. There were seven places on my body where he had sunk his fangs into my skin and bitten. He'd dug his nails into my neck, and twisted my head to one side, and clawed my face. I hadn't made a noise. He had made all the noise for both of us. Had it hurt him?

I could feel him shrinking inside me, at last. He finally stirred to pick his nose. He pulled himself out of me, and a few seconds later something slid out of me and down my thighs. I looked.

Gummy blood and something white was staining our only sheet. He wiped himself on my dress, and looked down at me critically. "Dear me," he said, "we're no Goddess of Beauty, are we?"

He got dressed. He dug his big toe into my navel, and looked down at me from the dimness. A spoonful of saliva splashed onto the bridge of my nose. "Skinned little bunny."

A spider spun the dimness between the rafters.

"Mr. Wormhole," I heard him say as he descended the creaking stairs. "You should be paying me. For breaking in your foal."

A flutter of laughter.

If I were a man, I would have flown down the stairs and shoved a dagger into his back. That afternoon, without a word to me, my father went to sell the bowls.

In the misty dusk an old woman came. She labored slowly up the stairs to where I lay, wondering how I could defend myself if the Warlord's Son called again on his way down. "Don't worry," she said. "The Tree will protect you. The Tree will tell you when to run, and when to hide." I knew she was a spirit because I only heard her words after her lips had finished moving, because the lamplight shone through her, and because she had no feet. I knew she was a good spirit because she sat on the chest at the end of the bed and sang a lullaby about a coracle, a cat, and the river running round.

Ten or twenty days later, my father returned, penniless. I asked him about the money, and he threatened to whip me. When we wintered with my cousins I was told the whole story: he'd gone to Leshan and spent half my dowry on opium and brothels. The other half he had spent on a scabby horse that died before he got back to the Village.

I was airing my bedding from the upstairs room's window ledge when I heard their voices. A boy and a girl had arrived without me noticing—my hearing is drawing in. Through a spyhole in the planking I watch them for some moments. Her face is made-up like the daughter of a merchant, or else a whore. Her breasts are budding, and the boy has that look men get when they want something. And not a chaperone in sight! She was leaning against her hands, against the skin of my Tree on the hidden side, where a hollow will cup a young girl's body perfectly. Above it, a bunch of violets grow every spring, but she cannot see it.

The boy swallows hard. "I swear I will love you forever. Truly."

He rests his hands on her hips, but she swats them away. "Did you bring your radio to give me?" The girl has a voice used to getting its way.

"I brought you my life to give you."

"Did you bring your radio? The little silver one that can pick up Hong Kong?"

I hobbled downstairs, the stairs and my ankles creaking. So intent are they on getting what they both want, they didn't notice me until I was at the chicken coop. "Tea?"

They spring apart. Big Ears blushes like a tomato. Does she thank me for guarding her honor? No. She looks at me, arms folded, quite unabashed, though her legs are as wide apart as a man's. "Yes. Tea."

They come around to the entrance to the Tea Shack. She sits down, crosses her legs, and pulls lipstick and a mirror from her shoulder bag. He sits opposite her, and just stares, like a dog at the moon. "Radio," she orders. He gets a shiny little box out of his bag, and slides out a long wire. She takes it, touches the side, and suddenly a woman's voice is on the path, singing about love, the southern breeze, and pussy willows.

"Where's she coming from?"

The girl deigns to notice me. "It's the latest hit from Macau." She looks at the boy. "Haven't you heard it?"

"'Course I have," he says, gruffly.

There are things I will never understand.

My father shrieked at me and the chickens squawked. "You little slut! You little fool! After everything I've done for you, after the sacrifices I've made, this is how you thank me! If it had been a boy, the Warlord's Son would have showered us with gifts! Showered us! We could have lived in his castle! I would have been appointed a dignitary with servants! Fruits from the islands! But why would anyone want to acknowledge that!"

He jabbed his fingernail into my baby's loins. My baby howled. Only five minutes old, and already learning. "You've sold your chances of a decent marriage for a nightpot of watery shit!"

One of my aunts led him out.

The Tree was looking in, and smiling. "Isn't she beautiful?" I asked.

The shadows and light on my baby's face were leafy and green.

A few days later, it was agreed that my daughter would be raised with relatives living three days' ride downstream. A large landowning household, one more daughter could be slipped in without much fuss. An uncle told me that the distance would conceal the shame I'd inflicted on our family's honor. My chastity was gone forever, of course. Perhaps in a few years some widower pig farmer might be persuaded to take me in as a mistress and nurse for his old age. If I was lucky.

I resolved then and there not to be lucky.

These same uncles all agreed that the Japanese would never get this far down the Yangtze, nor this far into the mountains. And supposing they did? Everyone knows how Japanese soldiers need more oxygen than humans, so they could never get up the Holy Mountain. The war had nothing to do with us. Many of the village sons were conscripted by the Warlord, and sent to fight on the side of some kind of alliance, but that was beyond the Valley, where the world is less real. Places called Manchuria, Mongolia, and further.

My uncles never knew truth from chickenshit. I dreamed of a clay jar of rice in the cave. When I asked a monk what it meant, he told me it was a suggestion from Lord Buddha.

When the Holy Mountain is windy, sounds from afar are blown near, and nearby sounds are blown away. The Tea Shack creaks— my lazy father never lifted a hammer in his life—and the Tree creaks. That's why we didn't hear them until they had kicked the windows in.

My father was climbing into the cupboard. I listened, nervous, but already resigned to whatever fate Lord Buddha had laid out for me. I wrapped my shawl around me. They didn't speak Valley language. They didn't even speak Cantonese, or Mandarin. They made animal noises. I spied through the cracks in the planking. It was difficult to see in the lamp light, but they looked almost human. My village cousins had told me that foreigners had elephant noses and hair like dying monkeys, but these ones looked a lot like us. On their uniforms was sewn insignia that looked like a headache—a red dot with red stripes of pain flashing out.

Lights were shone into our faces, and rough hands hauled us downstairs. The room was full of beams of lantern light, men, pots and pans being overturned. Our money box was found and smashed open. That headache insignia. A thing with wings swung above. The smell of men, men, always men. We were brought before a man with spectacles and a waxy mustache.

I was the breadwinner, but I looked at the floor.

"A nice cup of green tea, perhaps," my father wrestled through a stammer, "sir?"

This one could speak. Strange Cantonese, squeezed through a mangler. "We are your liberators. We are requisitioning this wayside inn in the name of His Imperial Egg of Japan. The Holy Mountain now belongs to the Asian Sphere of Co-prosperity. We are here to percolate our Sick Mother China from the evil of the European imperialists. Except the Germans, who are a tribe of honor and racial purity."

"Oh," said my father. "That's good. I like honor. And I'm a sick father."

The door banged open—I thought it was a gunshot—and a soldier wearing a gallery of medals came in. Waxy Mustache saluted Medal Man, and shouted animal noises. Medal Man peered at my father, then at me. He smiled from the corner of his mouth. He made some quiet animal noises to the other soldiers.

Waxy Mustache barked at my father. "You have harbored fugitives in your inn!"

"No, sir, we hate that goat-fucking Warlord! His son raped my daughter here!"

Waxy Mustache translated this into animal noises to Medal Man. Medal Man raised his eyebrows in surprise, and grunted back.

"My men are pleased to hear your daughter provides comfort to passers-by. But we are displeased to hear your slur of our ally, the Warlord. He is working with us to purge the Valley of communism."

"Of course, when I said—"

"Silence!"

Medal Man forced the mouth of his gun into my father's mouth. "Bite," he said.

Medal Man looked into my father's eyes. "Harder."

Medal Man uppercutted my father's chin. My father spat out bits of tooth. Medal Man chortled. My father's blood dripped to the floor in flower-splashes. He staggered back into a tub of water, as though he had rehearsed it.

The soldier holding me relaxed his grip as he laughed. I staved in his kneecap with a bottle of oil and sent the lamp in my face flying across the room. Whoever it hit screamed and dropped something that smashed. I ducked and ran for the door. Lord Buddha slipped a brass chopstick into my hand, and opened the door for me as my fingertips touched it, and shut it behind me. There were three men outside—one got a good grip, but I stuck the brass chopstick through the side of his mouth and he let go. The Japanese soldiers followed me up the path, but it was a moonless night, and I knew every rock, curve, bear path, and fox trail. I slipped off the path, and heard them vanish into the distance.

My heart had slowed by the time I reached the cave. The Holy Mountain fell away below me, and the windy forest moved like the ocean in my dreams. I wrapped myself in my shawl, and watched the light of heaven shine through the holes in the night until I fell asleep.

My father was black with bruises, but he was up and limping through the wreckage of the Tea Shack. His mouth looked like a rotting potato. "You caused this," he scowled by way of greeting, "you fix it. I'm going to stay with my brother. I'll be back in two or three days." My father hobbled off down the path. When he returned he had become an old man waiting to die. That was weeks later.

My daughter was blossoming into a local beauty, my aunts told me. Her guardian had already turned down two proposals of marriage, and she was still only twelve. The guardian was setting his sights high: if the Kuomintang forces took over the Valley soon, he could possibly arrange a union with a Nationalist administrator. He might even get himself a fat appointment as a clause in the marriage negotiations. A photographer had been paid to take her picture, which was being circulated among possible suitors in high places. When I wintered in the Village an aunt brought me one of these photographs. She had a lily in her hair, and a chaste, invisible smile. My heart glowed with pride, and never stopped.

My daughter's father, the Warlord's Son, never lived to see her blossom. This causes me no sorrow. He got butchered by a neighboring Warlord in alliance with the Kuomintang. He, his father, and the rest of his clan were captured, roped and bound, slung onto a pile at a crossroads down in the Valley, doused in oil, and burnt alive. The crows and dogs fought over the cooked meat.

Lord Buddha promised to protect my daughter from the demons, and my Tree promised that I would see her again.

Far, far below, a temple bell gongs, the surface of the dawn ripples, and turtledoves fly from the wall of forest, up, and up. Always up.

———————

A government official strutted downbound out of the mist. I guessed he'd been driven to the summit. I recognized his face from his grandfather's. His grandfather had scraped a living from the roads and marketplaces in the Valley, shoveling up manure and selling it to local farmers. An honest, if lowly, way to get by.

His grandson sat down at my table, and slung his leather bag onto the table. Out of his bag he produced a notebook, an account book, a metal strongbox, and a bamboo stamp. He started writing in his notebook, looking up at the Tea Shack from time to time, as though he was thinking about buying it.

"Tea," he said presently, "and noodles."

I began preparing his order.

"This," he said, showing me a card with his picture and name on it, "is my Party ID. My identification. It never leaves my person."

"Why do you need to carry a picture of yourself around? People can see what you look like. You're in front of them."

"It says I am a Local Cadre Party Leader."

"I daresay people work that out for themselves."

"This mountain has been incorporated into a State Tourism Designation Area."

"What's that in plain Chinese?"

"Turnpikes will be placed around the approach routes to charge people to climb."

"But the Holy Mountain has been here since the beginning of time!"

"It's now a state asset. It has to earn its keep. We charge people one yuan to climb it, and thirty yuan for the foreign bastards. Traders on state asset property need a trading license. That includes you."

I tipped his noodles into a bowl, and poured boiling water onto the tea-leaves.

"Then give me one of these licenses."

"Gladly. That will be two hundred yuan, please."

"What? My Tea Shack has stood here for thousands of years!"

He leafed through his account book. "Then perhaps I should consider charging you back rent."

I bent behind the counter and spat into his noodles, stirring them around so my phlegm was good and mixed. I straightened up, chopped some green onions, and sprinkled them on. I put them in front of him.

"I've never heard such nonsense."

"Old woman, I don't make the rules. This order is direct from

Beijing. Tourism is a prime thrust of socialist modernization. We earn dollars from tourists. I know you don't even know what a dollar is, and don't even try to understand economics, because you can't. But understand this: the Party orders you to pay."

"I've heard all about the Party from my cousins in the Village! Your bubbling baths and your flash cars and your queue-jumping and stupid conferences and—"

"Shut your ignorant mouth now if you want to make a living from the People's Mountain! The Party has developed our Motherland for half a century and more! Everyone else has paid! Even the monasteries have paid! Who are you, or your chicken-fucking country cousins, to dare think you know best? Two hundred yuan, now, or I'll be back in the morning with the Party's police officers to close you down and throw you in jail for non-payment! We'll truss you up like a pig, and carry you down the mountain! Think of the shame! Or, pay what you owe. Well? I'm waiting!"

"You're in for a long wait then! I don't have two hundred yuan! I only make fifty yuan in a season! What am I supposed to live on?"

The official slurped up his noodles. "You'll have to shut up shop and ask your country cousins to let you pick fleas from their sows in the corner. And if your noodles weren't so salty you might sell more."

If I'd been a man I'd have thrown him into my cesspit, Party official or no Party official. But he had the upper hand here, and he knew it.

I unfolded a ten-yuan note from my apron pocket. "It must be a difficult job, keeping track of all the tea shacks up and down the Mountain, who's paid what . . ."

He swished out his mouth with green tea, and sluiced out a jet that spattered against my window. "Bribery? Corruption? Cancer in the breasts of our Motherland! If you think I'm going to agree to postpone the victory of socialism, to smear the bright new age that is our nation's glorious destiny—"

I unfolded another twenty yuan. "That's all I have."

He pocketed the money. "Boil those eggs, and pack them with those tomatoes."

I had to do as he said. Once a shit shoveler, always a shit shoveler.

Two monks ran out of the mist, upbound, gasping.

Running monks are as unusual as honest officials. "Rest," I said, unfolding a fresh cloth for them. "Rest."

They nodded gratefully and sat down. I always serve Lord Buddha's servants the best tea for free. The younger monk wiped the sweat from his eyes. "The Kuomintang are coming! Two thousand of them. The Village was being abandoned when we left. Your father was climbing into his cousin's cart—they were going into the hills."

"I've seen it all before. The Japanese wrecked my Tea Shack."

"The Kuomintang make the Japanese look civilized," said the elder monk. "They are wolves. They loot what food and treasure they can carry, and burn or poison what they can't. In a village down the Valley they cut off a boy's head just to poison a well!"

"Why?"

"The communists are gaining momentum all over China now, despite the American bombs. The Kuomintang have nothing to lose. I've heard they're heading to Taiwan to join Chiang Kai-shek, and have orders to bring what they can. They scraped the gold leaf off the temple Buddhas at Leshan."

"It's true!" The younger monk shook some grit from his sandal. "Don't let them get you! You have about five hours. Hide everything deep in the forest, and be careful when you come back. There might be some stragglers. Please! We'd hate to see anything happen to you!"

I gave the monks some money to burn incense for my daughter's safety, and they left, running up through the mist. I hid my best cooking utensils high in my Tree, and, asking His pardon, hid Lord Buddha up above where the violets grew.

The mist cleared, and it was suddenly autumn. When the wind blew the leaves streamed up the path like rats before a sorcerer.

The trees grew as tall as the Holy Mountain itself. Their canopy was the lawn of heaven. *Follow*, said the unicorn's eyes. *Lay your hand on my shoulder.* Corridors of bark and darkness led to further corridors of bark and darkness. My guide had hooves of ivory. I was lost, and happy to be lost. We came to a garden at the bottom of a well of light and silence. Over an intricate bridge inlaid with jade and amber, lotus flowers and orchids swayed gently. Bronze and silver carp swam with the dark owls around my head. *This is a peaceful place,* I thought to the unicorn. *Will you stay awhile?*

Mother, thought the unicorn, a tear growing bigger and bigger in her human eye. *Mother, don't you recognize me?*

I awoke with the saddest feeling.

Hiding in my cave, watching the rain, I wished I could change into a bird, or a pebble, or a fern, or a deer, like lovers in old stories. On the third day the sky cleared. The smoke from the Village had stopped. I cautiously returned to my Tea Shack. Wrecked again. Always, it is the poor people who pay. And always, it is the poor people's women who pay the most. I set about clearing up the mess. What choice is there?

The communists came with early summer. There were only four of them—two men, two women. They were young, and wore neat uniforms and pistols. My Tree told me they were coming. I warned my father, who, as usual, was asleep in his hammock. He opened one eye: "Fuck 'em, they're all the same. Only the badges and medals change." My father was dying as he had lived. With the minimum effort possible.

The communists asked if they could sit down in my Tea Shack and talk with me. They called each other "Comrade" and addressed me respectfully and gently. One of the men was the lover of one of the women—I could see that immediately. I wanted to trust them, but they kept smiling while I talked. I've always been wronged by smilers.

The communists listened to my complaints. They didn't seem to want anything, except for green tea. They just wanted to give things. They wanted to give things, like education, even to girls. Health care, so that the ancient plague of China would be vanquished. They wanted an end to exploitation in factories and on the land. An end to hunger. They wanted to restore dignity to motherhood. China, they said, was no longer the sick old man of

Asia. A New China was emerging from somewhere called Feudalism, and the New China would lead the New Earth. It would be here in five years' time, because the international revolution of the proletariat was a historical inevitability. Everybody would have their own car in the future, they said. Our children's children would go to work by flying machine. Because everyone would have enough for their needs, and so crime would naturally die out.

"Your leaders must know powerful magic."

"Yes," said one of the women. "The magic is called Marx, Stalin, Lenin, and Class Dialectics."

It didn't sound like very convincing magic to me.

My father rolled out of his hammock. "Tea," he told me. "We're very glad to see the communists bring a bit of order to our Valley and Mountain," he said, looking at the girls and picking his teeth with his thumbnail. "The Nationalists raped her." He jerked his head at me. "Must have been desperate."

I felt hot shame rising. Had he really forgotten it was the Warlord's Son? The girl who was in love came over and held my hand. Such a young hand, it was, so pure that I was afraid for it.

"The old regimes violated plenty of women. That was their way of life. In Korea the Japanese army herded up all the girls in a township, gave them Japanese names, and they spent the whole war on their backs. But those days are gone now."

"Yes," said one of the men. "China has been raped by capitalists and imperialists for centuries. Feudalism relegated women to cattle. Capitalism bought and sold women like cattle."

I wanted to tell him he didn't know anything about being violated, but the woman was being so kind to me, I could barely speak. Other than my Tree and Lord Buddha, nobody had ever shown me such kindness. She promised to bring me medicine, if I needed any. They were kind, bright, and brave. They addressed my father as "sir," and even paid for their tea.

"Are you going up the Holy Mountain on a pilgrimage?"

The boys smiled. "The Party will free the Chinese race from the fetters of religion. Soon there will be no more pilgrims."

"No more pilgrims? So isn't the Holy Mountain going to be holy?"

"Not 'holy,' " they agreed. "But still very impressive, for a mountain." And I knew right then that even though their intentions were true their words were chickenshit.

When I wintered in the Village that year, distressing news reached me from Leshan. My daughter, her guardian, and his wife had fled to Hong Kong, after the communists had ordered their arrests as enemies of the revolution. Everybody knew that nobody ever returned from Hong Kong. A tribe of foreign bandits called the British spread lies about Hong Kong being Paradise, but the moment anybody arrived there they were put in chains and forced to work in poison gas factories and diamond mines until they died.

That evening my Tree had promised I would see my daughter again. I didn't understand. But I have learned that my Tree tells truths that don't make sense until the light of morning.

The fat girl wore stripy clothes that made her look fatter. She looked at the noodles, steaming and delicious, and looked at me. She slurped up a mouthful, held them in her mouth for a moment, shook her head, and spat them onto the table.

"Foul."

Her witchy friend took a long drag on her cigarette. "That bad, huh?"

"I wouldn't feed it to a pig."

"Old woman, don't you have any chocolate?"

Nothing was wrong with my noodles. "Any what?"

Fat Girl sighed, bent down, scooped up some dirt, and sprinkled it onto the noodles. "That might improve the taste. I'm not paying a yuan for it. I wanted food. Not pig swill."

Witchy Friend snickered, and looked in her bag. "I've got cookies somewhere. . . ."

Anger is pointless on the Holy Mountain. I rarely feel it. But when I see food being wasted so wantonly, I feel such rage that I can't control myself.

The noodles—and dirt—slid down Fat Girl's face. Her skin shone under the grease. Her wet shirt clung to her neck. Her mouth was an "O" of shock. She gasped like a surfacer, flapped her arms, and fell backwards. Witchy Friend had leapt up and stepped back, flapping her wings.

Fat Girl climbed to her feet, red and heaving. She started charging at me, but changed her mind when she saw I had a pot of boiling water ready to douse her. I would have done it, too. She retreated to a safe distance, and yelled. "I'm going to report you you you you *bitch*! You wait! Just you wait! My brother-in-law knows an undersecretary at the Party office and I'm going to have your flea-infested Tea Shack *bulldozed*! With you under it!"

Even when they were out of sight around the bend their threats floated downwards through the trees. "Bitch! Your daughters fuck donkeys! Your sons are sterile! Bitch!"

"I can't abide bad manners," said my Tree. "That's why I left the Village."

"I didn't want to get angry, but she shouldn't have wasted the food!"

"Shall I ask the monkeys to ambush them and remove their hair?"

"That would be a very petty revenge."

"Then consider it done."

The time that famine came up the Valley was the worst of all times.

The communists had organized all the farms in the Valley into communes. Nobody owned the land. There were no landowners anymore. The landowners had been hounded into their graves, had donated their land to the people's revolution, or were in the capitalists' prisons with their families.

All the peasants ate in the commune canteen. The food was free! For the first time in history every peasant in the Valley knew he would get a square meal in his stomach at the end of the day. This was the New China, the New Earth.

Nobody owned the land, so nobody made sure it was respected. The offerings to the spirits of the rice paddies were neglected, and at harvest time rice was allowed to rot on the stalk. And it seemed to me that the less the peasants worked, the more they lied about how much they worked. When pilgrim-peasants from different communes in the Valley sat in my Tea Shack and argued agriculture, I watched their stories get taller. Cucumbers big as pigs, pigs big as cows, cows big as my Tea Shack. Forests of cabbages! You could get lost in them! Apparently Mao Tse Dong Thought had revolutionized production techniques, and was even spreading to the woods. The commune planner had found a mushroom as big as an umbrella on the southern slopes.

Most worrying of all, they believed their own chickenshit, and attacked anyone who dared used the word "exaggerate." I was just a woman growing old on a Holy Mountain, but no radish of mine got bigger.

That winter, the Village was bleaker, muddier, madder than I ever knew it.

I lived with my cousin's family. Rice farmers for generations. I asked my cousin's husband, why had they all become so lazy? The men got drunk most evenings, and didn't stir from their beds until the middle of the next morning. Of course, the women ended up doing most of the things the men were too hungover to manage.

It was all wrong. Bad spirits sat with the crows on the rooftops, incubating ill-intent. In the streets, alleyways, and the market square, nobody was walking. Days passed without a kind word. The main monastery in the Village had been closed. I wandered through it sometimes, through its moon gates and ponds choked with duckweed. It reminded me of somewhere else. The Village was suffering from a plague that nobody had noticed.

I went to speak to the village elders. "What are you going to eat next winter?"

"The fruits of Mother China!"

"You're not growing anything."

"You don't understand. You haven't seen the changes."

"I'm seeing them now. It's not tallying up—"

"China will provide for her sons. Mao Tse Dong will provide!"

"When things don't tally up, it's the peasants who pay! However clever this Mao's thoughts are, they don't fill bellies."

"Woman, if the communists hear you talk that way, you'll be

sent away for reeducation. Go back up your mountain if you don't like it here. We're playing mah jong."

That same winter Mao decreed his Great Leap Forward. New China faced a new crisis: a shortage of steel. Steel for bridges, steel for ploughshares, steel for bullets to stop the Russians invading from Mongolia. And so all the communes were issued with furnaces and a quota.

Nobody in the Village knew what to do with a kiln—the blacksmith had been hanged from his roof as a capitalist—but everyone knew what happened to you if the kiln went out on your watch. My cousins, nieces, and nephews now had to work scavenging for wood. The school was closed, and the teachers and students mobilized into firewood crews to keep the kilns fed. Were my nephews to grow up with empty heads? Who would teach them to write? When the supply of desks and planking was used up, virgin forests at the foot of the Holy Mountain were chopped. Healthy trees! News came up the Valley, where trees were scarcer, that the communists organized lotteries amongst the non-Party villagers. The "winners" had their houses dismantled and burned to keep the furnaces fed.

The steel was useless. The black, brittle ingots came to be called "turds," but at least you can use real turds for manure. Every week the women loaded the ingots onto the truck from the city, wondering why the Party wasn't sending soldiers to the Village to mete out punishment.

We discovered the answer by late winter, when the rumors of food shortages traveled up the Valley.

The first reaction among the men was typical. They didn't want to believe it was true, so they didn't.

When the village rice warehouse stood empty, they started to believe it. Still, Mao would send the trucks. He might even lead the convoy personally.

The Party officials said the convoy had been hijacked down the Valley by counterrevolutionary spies, and that more rice would be on its way very soon. In the meantime, we would have to tighten our belts. Peasants from the surrounding countryside started arriving in the Village to beg. They were as scrawny as chickens' feet.

Goats disappeared, then dogs, then people started bolting their gates from dusk until dawn. By the time the snows were melting, all the seed for the next year's harvest had been eaten. New seed would be coming very soon, promised the Party officials.

"Very soon" still hadn't arrived when I set off back up the path to my Tea Shack, four weeks earlier than my usual departure. It would still be bitterly cold at night, but I knew Lord Buddha and my Tree would look after me. There would be birds' eggs, roots, nuts. I could snare birds and rabbits. I'd survive.

Once or twice I thought of my father. He wouldn't survive another year, even down in the comfort of the Village, and we both knew it. "Good-bye," I'd said, across my cousin's back room. He never stirred from the bed except to shit and piss.

His skin had less life in it than a husk in a spider's web. Sometimes his lidded eyes closed, and his cigarette shortened. Was anything under those lids? Remorse, resentment, even indifference? Or was there only nothing? Nothing often poses in men as wisdom.

Spring came late, winter dripping off the twigs and buds, but no pilgrims walked out of the mist. A mountain cat liked to stretch herself out on a branch of my Tree, and guard the path. Swallows built a nest under my eaves: a good omen. An occasional monk passed by. Glad of the company, I invited them into my Tea Shack. They said that my stews of roots and pigeon meat were the best thing they had eaten for weeks.

"Whole families are dying now. People are eating hay, leather, bits of cloth. Anything to fill their bellies. When they die, there's nobody left to bury them, or perform the funeral rites, so they can't go to heaven, or even be reborn."

When I opened my shutters one morning the roof of the forest was bright and hushed with blossom. The Holy Mountain didn't care about the stupid world of men. A monk called that day. His skin wrapped his hungry face tightly. "According to Mao's latest decree, the new enemies of the proletariat are sparrows, because they devour China's seeds. All the children have to chase the birds with clanging things until the birds drop out of the sky from exhaustion. The problem is, nothing's eating the insects, so the Village is overrun by crickets and caterpillars and bluebottles. There are locust clouds in Sichuan. This is what happens when men play at gods and do away with sparrows."

The days lengthened, the year swung around the hot sun and deep skies. Near the cave I found a source of wild honey.

"Your family are surviving," a monk from the Village told me, "but only because of money sent by your daughter's people in Hong Kong. A husband was found for your daughter after New Year. He works in a restaurant near the harbor. And a baby is already coming. You are to become a grandmother."

My heart swelled. My family had done nothing but heap shame onto my daughter since her birth, and now she was saving their skins.

Autumn breathed dying colors into the shabby greens. I prepared firewood, nuts, dried sweet potatoes, and berries and fruit, stored up jars of wild rice, and strengthened my Tea Shack against blizzards, patching together clothes made of rabbit fur. When I went foraging, I carried a bell to warn away the bears. I had decided in the summer that I was going to winter on the mountain. I sent word down to my village cousins. They didn't try to persuade me. When the first snows fell, I was ready.

The Tea Shack creaked under the weight of icicles.

A family of deer moved into the glade nearby.

I was no longer a young woman. My bones would ache, my breath would freeze. And when the deep midwinter snows came, I would be trapped in my Tea Shack for days on end with nobody except Lord Buddha for company. But I was going to live through this winter to see the icicles melt in the sun, and to kiss my daughter.

When I saw my first foreigner, I didn't know what to feel! He—I guessed it was a he—loomed big as an ogre, and his hair was yellow! Yellow as healthy piss! He was with a Chinese guide, and after a minute I realized that he was speaking in real language! My nephews and nieces had been taught about foreigners in the new village school. They had enslaved our people for hundreds of years until the communists, under the leadership of Mao Tse Dong, had freed us. They still enslave their own kind, and are always fighting each other. They believe evil is good. They eat their own babies and love the taste of shit, and only wash every two months. Their language sounds like farting pigs. They rut each other on impulse, like dogs and bitches in season, even in alleyways.

Yet here was a real, living foreign devil, talking in real Chinese with a real Chinese man. He even complimented my green tea on its freshness. I was too astonished to reply. After a few minutes my curiosity overcame my natural revulsion. "Are you from this world? My nephew told me there are many different places outside China."

He smiled, and unfolded a beautiful picture. "This," he said, "is a map of the world." I'd never seen such a thing.

I looked in the middle for the Holy Mountain. "Where is it?" I asked him.

"Here. This is where we are now. The mountain is here."

"I can't even see it."

"It's too small."

"Impossible!"

He shrugged, just like real people shrug. He was good at mimicry. "This is China, you can see that, right?"

"Yes," I said dubiously, "but it still doesn't look big enough. I think someone sold you a broken map."

His guide laughed, but I don't think being ripped off is anything to laugh about. "And this is the country I'm from. A place called 'Italia.'"

Italia. I tried to say this place, but my mouth couldn't form such absurd sounds so I gave up. "Your country looks like a boot." He nodded, agreeing. He said that he came from the heel. It was all too strange. His guide asked me to prepare some food.

While I was cooking the foreign devil and his guide carried on speaking. Here was another shock—they seemed to be friends! The way they were sharing their food and tea . . . How could a real person possibly be friends with a foreign devil? But they seemed to be. Maybe he was hoping to rob the devil when he was sleeping. That would make sense.

"So how come you never talk about the Cultural Revolution?" the devil was saying. "Are you afraid of police retaliation? Or do you have wind of an official revision of history proving that the Cultural Revolution never actually happened?"

"Neither," said the guide. "I don't discuss it because it was too evil."

My Tree had been nervous for weeks, but I hadn't known why. A comet was in the northeast, and I dreamed of hogs digging in the roof of my Tea Shack. The mist rolled down the Holy Mountain, and stayed for days. Dark owls hooted through the daylight hours. Then the Red Guard appeared.

Twenty or thirty of them. Three quarters were boys, few of whom had started shaving. They wore red arm bands, and marched up the path, carrying clubs and homemade weapons. I didn't need Lord Buddha to tell me they were bringing trouble. They chanted as they marched near.

"What can be smashed—" chanted half . . .

"Must be smashed!" answered the other. Over and over.

I recognized the leader, from the winter before the Great Famine. He was a dunce at school, who rarely moved a muscle except to do occasional bricklaying work. Now he swaggered up to my Tea Shack like the Lord of Creation. "We are the Red Guard! We are here in the name of the Revolutionary Committee!" He yelled as if hoping to knock me over by the power of volume.

"I know exactly who you are, Brain." "Brain" was his Village nickname, because he didn't have any. "When you were a little boy your mother used to bring you to my cousin's house. I cleaned your ass when you shat yourself."

I thought these children were like bears: if you show fear they attack. If you act as if they're not really there, they carry on up the path.

Brain slapped me across my face!

It stung, my eyes watered, and my nose felt caved-in, but it wasn't the pain that shocked me—it was the thought of an elder being slapped by a youth! It ran against the laws of nature!

"Don't call me that again," he said, casually. "I really don't like it." He turned around. "Lieutenants! Find the hoard that this capitalist roader has leeched out of the masses! Start looking in the upstairs room. Mind you search thoroughly! She's a devious old leech!"

"What?" I touched my nose and my fingers came away scarlet.

Boots thumped up the stairs. Banging, ripping, laughing, smashing, splintering.

"Help yourself," Brain told the other Red Guards, pointing to my kitchen. "This saggy corpse stole it from you in the first place, remember. Destroy that religious relic first, though. Smash it to atoms!"

"You'll do nothing of the sort—"

Another blow felled me, and Brain stood on my face, pushing my head down into the mud. He stamped on my windpipe. I thought he was trying to kill me. I could feel the imprint of his boot. "Just you wait until I tell your mother and father about this." I barely recognized my voice, it sounded so strangled and weak.

Brain tossed his head back and barked a short laugh. "You're going to report me to my mommy and daddy? I'm pissing my pants at the prospect. Let me tell you what Mao says about your parents: 'Your mother may love you, your father may love you, but Chairman Mao loves you more!' "

I heard Lord Buddha being smashed.

"You're going to be in trouble when the real communists hear about this!"

"Those revisionists are being liquidated. The Village Party Females have been found guilty of whoring with a Trotskyite splinter group." He dug his big toe into my navel, and looked down at me from the dimness. A spoonful of saliva splashed onto the bridge of my nose. "Whoring, a subject you're no stranger to, I've heard."

I was still strong enough to feel anger. "What do you mean?"

"Spreading your thighs for that feudalist! The Warlord's Son! Runs in the family, no doubt! We know all about your mongrel whelp sucking the imperialists' cocks in Hong Kong! Conspiring to overthrow our glorious revolution! Don't look so shocked! The villagers were falling over each other to denounce class traitors! Don't tell me you've forgotten how good it felt to have a man up you!" He bent down to whisper in my ear. "Maybe you need a lit-

tle reminder?" He squeezed my breast. "That hairy pouch between your legs still has a splash of oil in it, has it? Maybe—"

"We found her money, General!"

That probably saved me. The Red Guard certainly wouldn't.
He stood up again, and opened my strongbox. In the background
the destruction of my Tea Shack was continuing. The youths were
stripping my Tea Shack of food like locusts.

"I'm appropriating your stolen goods in the name of the People's Republic of China. Do you wish to lodge an appeal with the
People's Revolutionary Tribunal?"

He knelt on my shoulder blades and peered into my face. My
face was still pressed sidewards into the dirt, but I stared straight
back. I could see right up his nose.

"I'll take that as a no. And what is this? Speak of the devil?
Your suckling runt, unless I'm very much mistaken." He twirled
the photograph of my daughter between finger and thumb. Brain
clicked open his lighter and watched for my reaction as he fed a
corner to the flame. Not my daughter! The lily in her hair! Grief
was rattling in me, but I suffered in silence. I wasn't going to give
Brain the pleasure of a single tear. He flicked my blackening treasure away before it burnt his fingers.

"We're all done here, General," a girl said. A girl!

Brain freed my windpipe at last. "Yeah. We should be pushing
on. There are more dangerous enemies of the revolution than
this abomination higher up the mountain."

I leaned against my Tree and looked at the wreckage of my Tea
Shack.

"The world's gone mad," I said. "Again."

"And it will right itself," said my Tree. "Again. Don't grieve too
much. It was only a photograph. You will see her before you die."

Something in the wreckage gave way, and the roof thumped
down.

"I live here quietly, minding my own business. I don't bother
anybody. Why are men forever marching up the path to destroy
my Tea Shack? Why do events have this life of their own?"

"That," answered my Tree, "is a very good question."

·   ·   ·

I was one of the lucky ones. The following day I went down the path to the Village to borrow supplies. The monastery had been looted and smashed, and many of the monks shot where they knelt in the meditation hall. In the courtyard of the moon gate I saw a hundred monks kneeling around a bonfire. They were burning the scrolls from the library, stored since the days Lord Buddha and his disciples wandered the Valley. The monks' ankles were tied to their stretched-back heads. They were shouting "Long Live Mao Tse Dong Thought! Long Live Mao Tse Dong Thought!" over and over. Gangs of Red Guard patrolled the rows, and stoned any monk who flagged. Outside the school the teachers were tied to the camphor tree. Around their necks hung signs: THE MORE BOOKS YOU READ, THE MORE STUPID YOU BECOME.

Posters of Mao were everywhere. I counted fifty before I gave up counting.

My cousin was in her kitchen. Her face was as blank as the wall.

"What happened to your tapestries?"

"Tapestries are dangerous and bourgeois. I had to burn them in the front yard before the neighbors denounced me."

"Why is everybody carrying a red book around with them? Is it to ward off evil?"

"It's Mao's red book. Everyone has to own one. It's the law."

"How could one bald lard-blob control all of China like this? It's—"

"Don't let anyone hear you say such things! They'll stone you! Sit down, Cousin. I suppose the Red Guard dropped by on their way up to burn the temples at the summit? You must drink some rice wine. Here you are. One cup. Drink it all down, now. I've got some bad news. Your remaining relatives in Leshan have gone."

"Where? To Hong Kong?"

"To Correction Camps. Your daughter's presents aroused their neighbors' envy. The whole household has been denounced as class traitors."

"What's a Correction Camp? Do people survive?"

My cousin sighed and waved her hands. "Nobody knows . . ." No more words.

Three sharp knocks and my cousin cringed like a mantrap had snapped on her gut.

"It's only me, Mother!"

My cousin lifted the latch, and my nephew came in, nodding a greeting at me. "I came back from a Self-Criticism Meeting in the marketplace. The cow farmer got denounced by the butcher."

"What for?"

"Who cares? Any crap will do! Truth is, the butcher owed him money. This is a handy way to wipe clean the slate. That's nothing, though. Three villages down the Valley a tinker got his knob cut off, just because his grandfather served with the Kuomintang against the Japanese."

"I thought the communists fought alongside the Kuomintang against the Japanese?"

"That's true. But the tinker's grandfather chose the wrong uniform. Chop! And outside Leshan, there's a village where a pig roast was held two days ago."

"So?" said my cousin.

My nephew swallowed. "They haven't had pigs there since the famine."

"So?" I croaked.

"Three days ago the commune committee was shot for embezzling the people's butter cream. Guess what—guess who—they put in the pot. . . . Attendance at the pig roast was compulsory on pain of execution, so everyone shares in the guilt. Pot or shot."

"It must be quiet down in hell," I thought aloud. "All the demons have come to the Holy Mountain. Is it the comet, do you think? Could it be bathing the world in evil?"

My nephew stared at the bottle of rice wine. He had always supported the communists. "It's Comrade Mao's wife's doing! She was just an actress, but now all this power has gone to her head! You can't trust people who lie for a living."

"I'm going back to my Tea Shack," I said. "And I'm never coming down from the Holy Mountain again. Visit me sometimes, Cousin, when your ankles let you climb the path. You'll know where to find me."

.   .   .

The eye was high above. It disguised itself as a shooting star, but it didn't fool me, for what shooting star travels in a straight line and never burns itself out? It was not a blind lens, no: it was a man's eye, looking down at me from the cobwebbed dimness, the way they do. Who were they, and what did they want of me?

I can hear the smile in my Tree's voice. "Extraordinary! How do you tune yourself in to these things?"

"What do you mean?"

"It hasn't even been launched yet!"

Once again, I rebuilt my Tea Shack. I glued Lord Buddha back together with sticky sap. The world didn't end, but hell did empty itself into China and the world was bathed in evil that year. Stories came up the path, from time to time, brought by refugees with relatives at the summit. Stories of children denouncing their parents, and becoming short-lived national celebrities. Truckloads of doctors, lawyers, and teachers being trucked to the countryside to be reeducated by peasants in Correction Camps. The peasants didn't know what they were supposed to teach, the Correction Camps were never built in time for the class enemies' arrival, and the Red Guard sent to guard them slowly grew desperate as they realized that they had been sent into exile along with their captives. These Red Guard were children from Beijing and Shanghai, soft with city living. Brain had been denounced as a Dutch spy, and sent to an Inner Mongolian prison. Even Mao's architects of his Cultural Revolution were denounced, their names reviled in the next wave of official news from Beijing. What kind of a place was the capital, where such things were loosed from their cages? The cruelest of the ancient emperors were kittens alongside this madman.

No monks prayed, no temple bells rang, not for many seasons.

As the guide told his foreign devil, it was all too evil.

Summers, autumns, winters, and springs swung round and around. I never went down to the Village. The winters were sharp-fanged, to be sure, but the summers were bountiful. Clouds of purple butterflies visited my upstairs room during the mornings, when I hung out the washing. The mountain cat had kittens. They became semitame.

A handful of monks returned to live at the summit of the Holy Mountain, and the Party authorities didn't seem to notice. One morning I awoke to find a letter pushed under the door of my Tea Shack. It was from my daughter—a *letter*, and a photograph, in color! I had to wait until a monk came by, because I can't read, but this is what it said:

> Dear Mother,
>
> I've heard that some short letters are being allowed through at the moment, so I'm trying my luck. As you can see from the photograph, I'm almost a middle-aged woman now. The young woman to my left is your granddaughter, and do you see the baby she is holding? She is your great-granddaughter! We are not rich, and since my husband died we lost the lease on his restaurant, but my daughter cleans foreigners' apartments and we manage to live well enough. I hope one day we can meet on the Holy Mountain. Who knows? The world is changing. If not, we will meet in heaven. My stepfather told me stories about your mountain when he was alive. Have you ever been to the top? Perhaps you can see Hong Kong from there! Please look after yourself. I shall pray for you. Please pray for me.

A trickle of pilgrims slowly grew to a steady flow. I could afford to buy chickens, and a copper pan, and a sack of rice to see me through the winter. More and more foreigners came up the path: hairy ones, puke-colored ones, black ones, pinko-gray ones. Surely they're letting too many in? Foreigners mean money, though. They have so much of it. You tell them a bottle of water is twenty yuan, and often they'll pay up without even doing us the courtesy of haggling! That's downright rude!

A day passed nearby, not long ago. In summer, I hire out the upstairs room for people to sleep in. I set up my father's hammock in the kitchen downstairs and sleep in that. I don't like doing it, but I have to save money for my funeral, or in case a famine returns. I can make more money from a foreigner this way than in a whole week of selling noodles and tea to real people. This night a foreigner was staying, and a real man and his wife and son from Kunming. The foreigner couldn't speak. He communicated in gestures like a monkey. Night had come. I'd boarded up the Tea Shack, and lay in the hammock waiting for sleep to come. My visitors' son couldn't sleep, so the mother was telling him a story. It was a pretty story, about three animals who think about the fate of the world.

Suddenly, the foreigner speaks! In real words! "Excuse me, where did you hear that story first? Please try to remember!"

The mother is as surprised as me. "My mother told it to me when I was a little girl. Her mother told it to her. She was born in Mongolia."

"Where in Mongolia?"

"I only know she was born in Mongolia. I don't know where."

"I see. I'm sorry for troubling you."

He clunks around. He comes downstairs and asks me to let him out.

"I'm not giving you a refund, you know," I warn him.

"That doesn't matter. Good-bye. I wish you well."

Strange words! But he is determined to leave, so I slide the bolts and swing open the door. The night is starry, without a moon. The foreigner was upbound, but he leaves downbound. "Where are you going?" I blurt out.

The mountain, forest, and darkness close their doors on him.

"What's up with him?" I ask my Tree.

My Tree has nothing to say, either.

———————

"Mao is dead!"

My Tree told me first, one morning of bright showers. Later an upbound monk burst into my Tea Shack, his face brimming over with joy, and confirmed the news.

"I tried to buy some rice wine to celebrate, but everybody had the same idea, and not a drop could be bought anywhere. Some people spent the night sobbing. Some spent the night telling everybody to prepare for the invasion from the Soviet Union. The Party people spent the night hiding behind closed shutters. But most of the villagers spent the night celebrating, and setting off fireworks."

I climbed to the upstairs room, where a young girl was sleepless with fear. I knew she was a spirit, because the moonlight shone through her, and she couldn't hear me properly. "Don't worry," I told her. "The Tree will protect you. The Tree will tell you when to run and when to hide." She looked at me. I sat on the chest at the end of my bed and sang her the only lullaby I know, about a cat, a coracle, and a river running around.

It was a kind year. One by one, the temples were rebuilt, and their bells rehung, so the sun and the moon could be properly greeted, and Lord Buddha's birthday celebrated. Monks became commonplace visitors again, and the flow of pilgrims increased to dozens in a single day. Fat people were whisked by on stretchers, carried by teams of two or three men. A pilgrimage by stretcher? As pointless as a pilgrimage by car! Chicken-brains who still believed in politics talked in excited voices about the Four Modernizations, the trial of the Gang of Four, and a benign spirit come to save China called Deng Xiaoping. He could have as many modernizations as he wanted as long as he left my Tea Shack alone. The slogan of Deng Xiaoping was this: "To Become Rich is Glorious!"

The eye of Lord Buddha opened at the summit of the Holy Mountain on several occasions, and the monks lucky enough to witness this miracle leapt off the precipice, through the double rainbow, and landed on their feet in Paradise. Another miracle happened above my head. My Tree decided to have children. One autumn morning, I found it growing almonds. Higher up, hazelnuts. I could scarcely believe this miracle, but I was seeing it with my own eyes! A branch rustled higher up still, and a persimmon dropped at my feet. A week later I found windfallen quinces, and lastly, wrinkled, tart apples. As I slept the Tree creaked, and the music of dulcimers lit the path of dreams.

. . .

I dreamed of my father in the dark place where it hurt. I looked into the dripping pond near the cave, and he was looking back up at me, forlornly, with his hands tied behind his head. Sometimes when I was preparing tea for guests I could hear him in the upstairs room, shuffling around, looking for cigarettes and coughing. Lord Buddha explained that he was wracked with guilt, and that his soul was locked in a cage of unfinished business, down in the dim places. There it would stay until I went on a pilgrimage of my own up to the summit.

Make no mistake, I think my father was Emperor Chickenshit. Finding virtue in him was harder than finding a needle in the Yangtze River. He never spoke a word of kindness or thanks to me, and he sold my chastity for two tea bowls. But, he was my father, and the souls of the ancestors are the responsibility of the descendants. Besides, I wanted a good night's sleep without his self-pity whining its way into my dreams. Lastly, it would be discourteous of me to spend this life working on the Holy Mountain without once making the pilgrimage to the summit. I was of the age when old women wake up bedbound, to discover their last day of moving around as they wished had been the day before, and they hadn't even known it.

It was a fine morning before the rainy season. I rose with the sun. My Tree gave me some food. I boarded up the Tea Shack, hid my strongbox under a pile of rocks at the back of the cave, and set off upbound. Fifty years before I could have reached the summit before dark. At my age, I wouldn't arrive before the afternoon of the following day.

Steps, gulleys, steps, mighty trees, steps, paths clinging to the rim of the world.

Steps in sunlight, steps in shadow.

When evening fell I lit a fire in the porch of a ruined monastery. I slept under my winter shawl. Lord Buddha sat at the end of my bed, smoking, and watching over me, as he does all pilgrims. When I awoke I found a bowl of rice, and a bowl of oolong tea, still steaming.

. . .

I stumbled into a future lifetime. There were hotels, five and six floors high! Shops sold glittery things that nobody could ever use, want, or need. Restaurants sold food that smelt of things I'd never smelt before. There were rows of huge buses with colored glass, and every last person on board was a foreign devil! Cars crowded and honked their horns like herds of swine. A box with people in it flew through air, but nobody seemed surprised. It breathed like the wind in the cave. I passed by a crowded doorway and looked in. A man was on a stage kissing a silver mushroom. Behind him was a screen with pictures of lovers and words. Somewhere in the room a monster hog was having its bollocks lopped off. Then I realized the man was singing! Singing about love, the southern breeze, and pussy willows.

I was nearly knocked over by a stretcher-bearer, carrying a foreign woman who wore sunglasses even though there wasn't any sun.

"Watch where you're standing," he gasped.

"Which way is the summit of the Holy Mountain?" I asked.

"You're standing on it!"

"Here?"

"Here!"

"Where's the temple? You see, I need to offer prayers for the repose of—"

"There!" He pointed with a nod.

The temple was smothered in bamboo scaffolding. Workmen teemed up and down ladders, along platforms. A group of them were playing football in the forecourt, using statues of ancient monks as goals. I walked up close to the goalkeeper to make sure my eyes weren't deceiving me again.

"My, my, it's General Brain of the Red Guard!"

"Who the fuck are you, old woman?"

"The last time we met you were standing on my throat and getting quite turned on, I remember. You smashed up my Tea Shack and stole my money."

He recognized me but pretended not to, and turned away, muttering darkly. At that moment the ball shot past him and a shout of victory rang out through the mist.

"This is a pleasant coincidence, isn't it, General Brain? You're a cunning one, I'll give you that. First, you're the head of a team to smash the temples to bits. Then, you're the foreman of a team sent to restore them! Is this socialist modernization?"

"How do you know I'm the foreman?"

"Because even when you're shirking off work you give yourself the easiest job."

Brain's face couldn't decide what to do. It kept flitting from one expression to another. Some of the workers had overheard me, and were looking at their foreman askance. I left him, picking my way through the sawing and hammering at the temple gate. Grudges are demons that gnaw away your bone marrow. Time was already doing a good enough job of that. Lord Buddha has often told me that forgiveness is vital to life. I agree. Not for the well-being of the forgiven, though, but for the well-being of the forgiver.

I passed through the great doorway, and stood in the cloisters, wondering what to do next. An elderly monk with a misshaped nose walked up to me. "You're the lady who owns the Tea Shack, aren't you?"

"Yes, I am."

"Then you shall be my guest! Come to the Sanctuary for a bowl of tea."

I hesitated.

"Please. Don't be nervous. You are very welcome here."

An apprentice monk in his saffron robe was dabbing gold leaf onto Lord Buddha's eyebrow. He looked at me, and smiled. I smiled back. Somewhere, a jackhammer was pounding the pavement and an electric drill buzzed up and down.

I followed the monk through a maze of cloisters smelling of incense and cement dust. We came to a quiet place. There were some statues of Lord Buddha, and some hanging scrolls. The tea was waiting for us in the empty room. "What do the scrolls say?"

The monk smiled modestly. "Calligraphy. It's an idle hobby of mine. The one on the left:

In the sunlight on my desk,
I write a long, long letter.

and on the right:

> *Mountains I'll never see again*
> *Fade in the distance.*

Forgive the shoddy workmanship. I'm an amateur. Now, let me pour the tea."

"Thank you. You must be delighted. All these pilgrims come to visit your temple."

The monk sighed. "Very few of them are pilgrims. Most don't even bother entering the temple."

"Then why do they come all the way to the Holy Mountain?"

"Because it's somewhere to drive their cars. Because lots of other people come here. Because the government has designated us a National Treasure."

"At least the Party has stopped persecuting you."

"Only because it pays better to tax us."

A passerby whistled a song that was both happy and sad. I heard a brush sweeping.

"I've come here about my father," I began.

The monk listened gravely, nodding from time to time as I told my story. "You were right to come. Your father's soul is still too burdened to leave this world. Come with me into the temple. There's a quiet altar to one side, safe from the tourists' flashbulbs. We shall light some incense together, and I shall perform the necessary rites. Then I shall see about finding you a bed for the night. Our hospitality is spartan, but sincere. Like yours."

The monk showed me back to the great doorway the morning after. Another day lost in fog.

"How much?" I felt inside my shawl for my money bag.

"Nothing." He touched my arm respectfully. "All your life you've filled the bellies of errant monks when their only food was pebbles. When the time comes, I'll see to it that your funeral rites are taken care of."

Kindness always makes me weep. I don't know why. "But even monks have to eat."

He gestured into the noisy fog. Lights blinked on and off. Dim buses growled. "Let them feed us."

I bowed deeply, and when I looked up again he had gone. Only his smile remained. Walking away to the downbound path, I caught sight of Brain, lugging a bucket of gravel up a ladder. His face was bruised and cut. Men, honestly. A group of girls ran screaming and laughing across the square, barely avoiding me. The monk was right: there was nothing holy here any more. The holy places were having to hide deeper, and higher.

A man came to see me, at my Tea Shack. He said he was from the Party newspaper, and that he wanted to write a story about me. I asked him the name of his story.

" 'Seventy Years of Socialist Entrepreneurialism.' "

"Seventy Years of What?"

His camera flashed in my face. I saw phoenix feathers, even when I closed my eyes.

"Socialist Entrepreneurialism."

"Those are young 'uns' words. Ask the young 'uns about it."

"No, madam," he pushed on, standing back a few yards and aiming his camera at my Tea Shack. Flash! "I've done my home-work. You were a pioneer, really. There's money to be made out of the Holy Mountain, but you were among the first to see the op-portunity, and you're still here. Remarkable, really. You are the Granny That Lays the Golden Eggs. That would be a good subtitle!"

It was true that during the summer months the path had be-come crowded with climbers. Every few steps was a Tea Shack, a Noodle Stall, or a Hamburger Stand—I tasted one once, foreign muck! I was hungry again less than an hour afterwards. Clustered around every shrine was a crowd of tables selling plastic bags and bottles that littered the path higher up.

"I'm not a pioneer," I insisted. "I lived here because I never had any choice. As for making money, the Party sent people to smash my Tea Shack because I made money."

"No they didn't. You're old, and you're quite mistaken. The Party has always encouraged fair trade. Now, I know you have sto-ries that will interest my readers."

"It's not my job to interest your readers! It's my job to serve noodles and tea! If you really want something interesting to write about, write about my Tree! It's five trees in one, you know. Almonds, hazelnuts, persimmons, quinces, and apples. 'The Bountiful Tree.' That's a better name for your story, don't you think?"

"Five trees in one," repeated the newspaper man.

"I admit, the apples are tart. But that's nothing. The Tree talks!"

"Really?"

He left soon afterwards. He wrote his stupid story, anyway, inventing my every word. A monk read it out to me. Apparently I had always admired Deng Xiaoping's enlightened leadership. I'd never even heard of Tiananmen Square, but apparently I believed the authorities responded in the only possible way.

I added "writers" to my list of people not to trust. They make everything up.

"Do you know who I am?"

I open my eyes.

The leaf shadows of my Tree dapple her beautiful face.

"The lilies in your hair, my darling, they suited you. Thank you for your letter. It came just the other day. A monk read it to me."

She smiled the way she does in the photograph.

"This is your *great*-granddaughter," says my niece, as though I'm making a mistake.

My niece is the mistaken one, but I'm too tired to explain the nature of yesterdays.

"Have you returned to China for good, my darling?"

"Yes. Hong Kong is China now, anyway. But yes."

There is pride in my niece's voice. "Your great-granddaughter has done very well for herself, Aunt. She's bought a hotel and restaurant in the Village. There's a spotlight on the roof that turns around and around, all through the night. All the rich people from the city come there to stay. A film star stayed only last week. She's had a lot of good offers of marriage—even the local Party Chief wants her hand."

My heart curls up, warm, like a tame mountain cat in the sun.

My daughter will honor me as an ancestor, and bury me on the Holy Mountain, facing the sea. "I've never seen the sea, but they say Hong Kong is paved with gold."

She laughs, a pretty laugh. I laugh, too, to see her laughing, even though it makes my ribs ache and ache.

"You can find a lot of things on Hong Kong's pavements, but not much gold. My employer died. A foreigner, a lawyer with a big company, he was extremely wealthy. He was very generous to me in his will."

With the intuition of an old dying woman, I know she isn't telling the whole truth.

With the certainty of an old dying woman, I know it's not the truth that much matters.

I hear my daughter and niece making tea downstairs. I close my eyes, and hear ivory hooves.

A ribbon of smoke uncoils as it disappears, up, up, and up.

MONGOLIA

THE GRASSLANDS ROSE and fell past the train, years upon years of them.

Sometimes the train passed settlements of the round tents that Caspar's guidebook called *gers*. Horses grazed, old men squatted on their haunches, smoking pipes. Vicious-looking dogs barked at the train, and children watched as we passed. They never returned Caspar's wave, they just looked on, like their grandfathers. Telegraph poles lined the track, forking off to vanish over the restless horizon. The large sky made Caspar think of the land where he had grown up, somewhere called Zetland. Caspar was feeling lonely and homesick. I felt no anticipation, just endlessness.

The Great Wall was many hours behind us now.

A far-flung, trackless country in which to hunt myself.

Sharing our compartment was a pair of giant belchers from Austria who drank vodka by the pint and told flatulent jokes to one another in German, a language I had learned from Caspar two weeks before. They were betting sheaves of Mongolian currency—togrugs—on a card game called cribbage one of them had learned from a Welshman in Shanghai, and swearing multicolored oaths. In the top bunk sat an Australian girl called Sherry, immersed in *War and Peace*. Caspar had been an agronomist at university before dropping out and had never read any Tolstoy. I caught him wishing he had, though not for literary reasons. A Swede from the next compartment invited himself in from time to time to regale Caspar with stories of being ripped off in China. He bored us both, and even Caspar's sympathies were with the Chinese. Also in the Swede's compartment was a middle-aged Irish woman who either gazed out of the window or wrote numbers in a black notebook. In the other neighboring compartment was a team of four Israelis—two girlfriends and their boyfriends. Other than chatting politely with Caspar about hostel prices in Xi'an and Beijing, and the new bursts of violence in Palestine, they kept themselves to themselves.

Night stole over the land again, dissolving it in shadows and blue. Every ten or twenty miles tongues of campfire licked the darkness.

Caspar's mental clock was several hours out, so he decided to turn in. I could have adjusted it for him, but I decided to let him sleep. He went to the toilet, splashed water over his face, and cleaned his teeth with water he disinfected in a bottle with iodine. Sherry was outside our compartment when he came back, her face pressed against the glass. Caspar thought, How beautiful. "Hello," he said.

"Hello." Sherry's eyes turned towards my host.

"How's the *War and Peace*? I have to admit, I've never read any Russians."

"Long."

"What's it about?"

"Why things happen the way they do."

"And why do things happen the way they do?"

"I don't know, yet. It's *very* long." She watched her breath mist up the window. "Look at it. All this space, and almost no people in it. It almost reminds me of home."

Caspar joined her at the window. After a mile had passed: "Why are you here?"

She thought for a while. "It's the last place, y'know? Lost in the middle of Asia, not in the east, not in the west. 'Lost as Mongolia,' it could be an expression. How about you?"

Some drunk Russians up the corridor groaned with laughter.

"I don't really know. I was on my way to Laos, when this impulse just came over me. I told myself there was nothing here, but I couldn't fight it. Mongolia! I've never even thought about the place. Maybe I smoked too much pot at Lake Dal."

A half-naked Chinese toddler ran up the corridor, making a zun-zun noise which may have been a helicopter, or maybe a horse.

"How long have you been traveling?" asked Caspar, not wanting the conversation to lag.

"Ten months. You?"

"Three years, this May."

"Three years! Oath, you *are* a terminal case!" Sherry's face turned into a huge yawn. "Sorry, I'm bushed. Being cooped up doing nothing is exhausting work. Do you think our Austrian friends have shut up the casino for the night?"

"I only hope they have shut up the joke factory. You don't know how lucky you are, not speaking German."

Back in their compartment, the Austrians were snoring in stereo. Sherry bolted the door. The gentle sway of the train lulled Caspar towards sleep. He was thinking about Sherry.

Sherry peered over the bunk above him. "Do you know a good bedtime story?"

Caspar was not a natural storyteller, so I stepped in. "I know one story. It's a Mongolian story. Well, not so much a story as a sort of legend."

"I'd love to hear it," Sherry smiled, and Caspar's heart missed a gear.

There are three who think about the fate of the world.

First there is the crane. See how lightly he treads, picking his way between the rocks in the river? Tossing and tilting back his head. The crane believes that if he takes just one heavy step, the mountains will collapse and the ground will quiver and trees that have stood for a thousand years will tumble.

Second, the locust. All day the locust sits on a pebble, thinking that one day the flood will come and deluge the world, and all living things will be lost in the churn and the froth and black waves. That is why the locust keeps such a watchful eye on the high peaks, and the rain clouds that might be gathering there.

Third, the bat. The bat believes that the sky may fall and shatter, and all living things die. Thus the bat dangles from a high place, fluttering up to the sky, and down to the ground, and up to the sky again, checking that all is well.

That was the story, way back at the beginning.

Sherry had fallen asleep, and Caspar wondered for a moment where this story had come from. I closed his mind and nudged it towards sleep. I watched his dreams come and go for a little while. There was a dream about defending a gothic palace built on sand flats with pool cues, and one about his sister and niece. His father entered the dream, pushing a motorbike down the corridor of the Trans-Siberian express with a sidecar full of money that kept blowing away. Drunk and demanding as ever, he asked Caspar what the devil he thought he was playing at, and insisted that Caspar still had some very important videotapes. Caspar had become a half-naked little boy and knew nothing about them.

My own infancy was spent at the foot of the Holy Mountain. There was a dimness, which I later learned lasted many years. It took me that long to learn how to remember. I imagine a bird beginning as an "I." Slowly, the bird understands that it is a thing different from the "It" of its shell. The bird perceives its containment, and as its sensory organs begin to function it becomes aware of light and dark, cold and heat. As sensation sharpens, it seeks to break out. Then one day, it starts to struggle against the gluey gel and brittle walls, and cannot stop until it is out and alone in the vertiginous world, made of wonder, and fear, and colors, made of unknown things.

But even back then, I was wondering: why am I alone?

The sun woke Caspar. He had dried tears in his eyes and his mouth tasted of watch straps. He badly wished he had some fresh fruit to eat. And the Austrians had already beaten him to the bathroom. He slid out of bed, and we saw Sherry was meditating. Caspar pulled on his jeans and tried to slip out of the compartment without disturbing her.

"Good morning, and welcome to Sunny Mongolia," Sherry murmured. "We get there in three hours."

"Sorry I disturbed you," said Caspar.

"You didn't. And if you look in that plastic bag hanging off the coat hook, you should find some pears. Have one for breakfast."

"So," said Sherry, four hours later. "Grand Central Station, Ulan Bator."

"Strange," said Caspar, wanting to express himself in Danish.

The whitewash was bright in the pristine noon sun. The never-silent wind blew on over the plains, into the vanishing point where the rails led. The signs were in the Cyrillic alphabet, which neither Caspar nor any of my previous hosts knew. Chinese hawkers barged off the train, heaving bags of goods to sell, shouting to one another in familiar Mandarin. A couple of listless young Mongolians on military service fingered their rifles, thinking of where they would rather be. A group of steely old women were waiting to get on the train, bound for Irkutsk. Their families had come to see them off. Two figures hovered in the wings, in black suits and sunglasses. Some youths sat on a wall, looking at the girls.

"I feel like I've climbed out of a dark box into a carnival of aliens," said Sherry.

"Sherry, I know, erm, as a young lady, you have to be careful of whom you trust when you're traveling, but, I was wondering—"

"Stop sounding like a Pom. Yes, sure. I won't jump you if you don't jump me. Now. Your *Lonely Planet* says there's a halfway decent hotel in the Sansar district, at the eastern end of Sambuu Street. . . . Follow me. . . ."

I let Sherry take care of my host. One less thing for me to worry about. The Austrians said good-bye and headed off to the Kublai Khan Holiday Inn, no longer laughing. The Israeli team nodded at us and marched off in another direction. Caspar had already forgotten about the Swede.

Backpackers are strange. I have a lot in common with them. We live nowhere, and we are strangers everywhere. We drift, often on a whim, searching for something to search for. We are both parasites: I live in my hosts' minds, and sift through their memories to understand the world. Caspar's breed live in a host country that is never their own, and use its culture and landscape to learn, or to stave off boredom. To the world at large we are both immaterial and invisible. We chew the secretions of solitude. My incredulous Chinese hosts who saw the first backpackers regarded them as quite alien entities. Which is exactly how humans would regard me.

All minds pulse in a unique way, just as every lighthouse in the world has a unique signature. Some minds pulse consistently, some erratically. Some are lukewarm, some are hot. Some flare out, some are very nearly not there. Some stay on the fringe, like quasars. For me, a roomful of animals and humans is like a roomful of suns, of differing magnitudes and colors, and gravities.

Caspar, too, has come to regard most people as blips on a radar. Caspar is as lonely as me.

"Did I blink?" remarked Sherry. "Where's the city? Beijing was a city, Shanghai was a city. This is a ghost town."

"It's like East Germany in the Iron Curtain days."

Ranks and files of faceless apartment blocks, with cracks in the walls and boards for windows. A large pipeline mounted on concrete stilts. Cratered roads, with only a few dilapidated cars trundling up and down. Goats eating weeds in a city square. Silent factories. Statues of horses and little toy tanks. A woman with a basket of eggs stepping carefully between the broken flagstones and smashed bottles and wobbling drunks. Streetlights, ready to topple. A once-mighty power station spewing out a black cloud over the city. On the far side of the city was a gigantic fairground wheel that Caspar and I doubted would ever turn again. Three westerners in black suits walked by. Caspar thought they were in the wrong place and time.

Ulan Bator was much bigger than the village at the foot of the Holy Mountain, but the people we saw here lacked any sense of purpose. They just seemed to be waiting. Waiting for something to open, for the end of the day, for their city to be switched on, or just waiting to be fed.

Caspar readjusted the straps on his backpack. "My *Secret History of Genghis Khan* did not prepare me for this."

That night Caspar dug into his mutton and onion stew with relish. He and Sherry were the only diners in the hotel, which was actually the sixth and seventh floors of a crumbling apartment building.

The woman who had brought the food from the kitchen looked at him blankly. Caspar pointed at it, gave her a thumbs-up sign, smiled, and grunted approvingly.

The woman looked at Caspar as though he were a madman, and left.

Sherry snorted. "She's about as welcoming as the customs woman at the border."

"One of the things that my years of wandering have taught me is, the more impotent the country, the more dangerous its customs officials."

"When she showed us the room she gave me a look like I'd run over her baby with a bulldozer."

Caspar picked out a bit of fleece from a meatball. "Service-sector communism. It's quite a legacy. She's stuck here, remember. We can get out whenever we want."

He had some instant lemon tea from Beijing. There was a flask of hot water on the sideboard, so he made a cup for himself and Sherry, and they watched the waxy moon rise over the suburb of *ger*s and campfires. "So," began Caspar. "Tell me more about that Hong Kong pub you worked in. What was the name? Mad Dogs?"

"I'd rather hear more stories of the weirdos you met during your jewelry-selling days in Okinawa. Go on, Vikingman, it's your turn."

So many times in a lifetime do my hosts feel the beginnings of friendship. All I can do is watch.

As my infancy progressed, I became aware of another presence in "my" body. Stringy mists of color and emotion condensed into droplets of understanding. I saw, and slowly came to recognize, gardens, paths, barking dogs, rice fields, sunlit washing drying in warm town breezes. I had no idea why these images came when they did. Like being plugged into a plotless movie. Slowly I walked down the path trodden by all humans, from the mythic to the prosaic. Unlike humans, I remember the path.

Something was happening on *my* side of the screen of perception, too. Like a radio slowly being turned up, so slowly that at first you cannot be sure of it being there. Slowly, I felt an entity that was not me generating sensations, which only later could I label loyalty, love, anger, ill-will. I watched this other clarify, and pull into focus. I began to be afraid. I thought *it* was the intruder! I thought the mind of my first host was the cuckoo's egg that would hatch and drive me out. So one night, while my host was asleep, I tried to penetrate this other presence.

My host tried to scream but I would not let him wake. Instinctively, his mind made itself rigid and tight. I prised my way through, clumsily, not knowing how strong I had become, ripping my way through memories and neural control, gouging out great chunks. Fear of losing the fight made me more violent than I ever intended. I had sought to subdue, not to lay waste.

When the morning brought the doctor he found my first host unresponsive to any form of stimulus. Naturally, the doctor could find no injury on the patient's body, but he knew a coma when he saw one. In southwest China in the 1950s there were no facilities for people with comas. My host died a few weeks later, taking any clues of my origin that may have been buried in his memories with him. They were hellish weeks. I discovered my mistake—*I* had been the intruder. I tried to undo some of the damage, and piece back together some of the vital functions and memories, but it is so much easier to destroy than it is to re-create, and back then I knew nothing. I learned that my victim had fought as a brigand in bad times or a soldier in good ones in northern China. I found fragments of spoken languages which I would later know as Mongolian and Korean, but he had been illiterate. That was all. I couldn't ascertain how long I had been embryonic.

I assumed that if my host died, I would share his death. I turned all my energies to learning how to perform what I now call transmigration. Two days before he died, I succeeded. My second host was the doctor of my first. I looked back at the soldier. A middle-aged man lay on his soiled bed, stretched out on his frame of bones. I felt guilt, relief, and I felt power.

I stayed in the doctor for two years, learning about humans

and inhumanity. I learned how to read my hosts' memories, to erase them, and replace them. I learned how to control my hosts. Humanity was my toy. But I also learned caution. One day I announced to my host that a disembodied entity had been living in his mind for two years, and would he like to ask me anything?

The poor man went quite mad, and I had to transmigrate again. The human mind is so fragile a toy. So puny!

Three nights later the waitress slammed a bowl of mutton down in front of Caspar. She had turned and gone before he had a chance to groan.

"Mutton fat for dinner," beamed Sherry. "There's a surprise."

The waitress cleared the other tables. Caspar was experimenting at using mind control to make his mutton taste like turkey. I resisted the temptation to help him succeed. Sherry was reading. "Get this for Soviet doublespeak. From the nineteen-forties, during Choilbalsan's presidency. It says, 'In the final analysis, life demonstrated the expediency of using the Russian alphabet.' What the author says this means, is that if you used Mongolian they shot you. Oath, how did people *live* under a master race like that, and why—"

The next moment all the lights in the building died.

Dim light came from the window of smoke stars, and a glowing red sign in Cyrillic beyond the wasteland. We had wondered what the sign meant, and we did again now.

Sherry chuckled and lit a cigarette. Her eyes reflected little flames. "I suppose you paid the power station ten dollars to stage this blackout, just to get me alone in a dark room with the manly smell of mutton."

Caspar smiled in the darkness, and I recognized love. It forms like a weather pattern. "Sherry, let's hire the jeep for tomorrow. We've seen the temple, seen the old palace. I'm feeling like a moody tourist. I hate feeling like a moody tourist. The Fräulein at the German embassy reckoned there would be a delivery of gas in the morning."

"Why the rush?"

"The place is going backwards in time. I feel the end of the world is waiting in those mountains, somewhere . . . We should get out before the nineteenth century comes around again."

"That's a part of U.B.'s charm. Its ramshackleness."

"I don't know what 'ramshackleness' means, but there is nothing charming about this place. Ulan Bator proves that Mongolians cannot do cities. You could set a movie about a doomed colony of germ-warfare survivors here. Let's get out. I don't even know why I'm here. I don't think the people who live here know either."

The waitress walked in and put a candle on our table. Caspar thanked her in Mongolian. She walked out. "Come the revolution, darling . . ." thought Caspar.

Sherry started shuffling a pack of cards. "You mean Mongolians are *designed* for arduous lifetimes of flock-tending, child-bearing, frostbite, illiteracy, *Giardia lamblia,* and *ger*-dwelling?"

"I don't want to argue. I want to drive to the Khangai mountains, climb mountains, ride horses, bathe naked in lakes, and discover what I am doing on Earth."

"Okay, Vikingman, we'll move on tomorrow. Let's play cribbage. I believe I'm winning, thirty-seven games to nine."

I would need to move on soon, too. Hosted by a Mongolian, my quest in this country was formidable. Hosted by a foreigner, my quest was plainly impossible.

I was here to find the source of the story that was already there, right at the beginning of "I," sixty years ago. The story began, *There are three who think about the fate of the world . . .*

———

Once or twice I've tried to describe transmigration to the more imaginative of my human hosts. It's impossible. I know eleven languages, but there are some tunes that language cannot play.

When another human touches my host, I can transmigrate. The ease of the transfer depends on the mind I am transmigrating into, and whether negative emotions are blocking me. The fact that touch is a requisite provides a clue that I exist on some physical plane, however subcellular or bioelectrical. There are limits. For example, I cannot transmigrate into animals, even primates: if I try the animal dies. It is like an adult's inability to climb into children's clothes. I've never tried a whale.

But how it *feels,* this transmigration, how to describe that! Imagine a trapeze artist in a circus, spinning in emptiness. Or a snooker ball lurching around the table. Arriving in a strange town after a journey through turbid weather.

Sometimes language can't even read the music of meaning.

The morning wind blew cold from the mountains. Gunga stooped through the door of her *ger,* slapping the chilly morning air into her neck and face. The hillside of *gers* was slowly coming to life. In the city an ambulance siren rose and fell. The River Tuul glowed gray, the color of lead. The big red neon sign flicked off: LET'S MAKE OUR CITY A GREAT SOCIALIST COMMUNITY.

"Camelshit," thought Gunga. "When are they going to dismantle that?"

Gunga wondered where her daughter had got to. She had her suspicions.

A neighbor nodded to her, wishing her good morning. Gunga nodded back. Her eyes were becoming weaker, rheumatism had begun to gnaw at her hips, and a poorly set broken femur from three winters ago ached. Gunga's dog padded over to be scratched behind the ears. Something else was wrong, too, today.

She ducked back into the warmth of the *ger.*

"Shut the bloody door!" bawled her husband.

It was good to transmigrate out of a westernized head. However much I learn from the nonstop highways of minds like Caspar's, they make me giddy. It would be the euro's exchange rate one minute, a film he'd once seen about art thieves in Petersburg the next, a memory of fishing with his uncle between islets the next, some pop song or a friend's Internet home page the next. No stopping.

Gunga's mind patrols a more intimate neighborhood. She constantly thinks about getting enough food and money. She worries about her daughter, and ailing relatives. Most of the days of her life have been very much alike. The assured dreariness of the Soviet days, the struggle for survival since independence. Gunga's mind was a lot harder for me to hide in than Caspar's, however. It's like trying to make yourself invisible in a prying village as opposed to a sprawling conurbation. Some hosts are more perceptive about movements in their own mental landscape than others, and Gunga was very perceptive indeed. While she had been sleeping I acquired her language, but her dreams kept trying to smoke me out.

Gunga set about lighting the stove. "Something's wrong," she said, to herself, looking around the *ger*, half expecting something to be missing. The beds, the table, the cabinet, the family tableware, the rugs, the silver teapot that she had refused to sell, even when times were at their hardest.

"Not your mysterious sixth sense again?" Buyant stirred under his pile of blankets. Gunga's cataracts and the gloom of the *ger* made it difficult to see. Buyant coughed a smoker's cough. "What is it this time? A message from your bladder, we're going to inherit a camel? Your earwax telling you a giant leech is going to come and molest your innocence?"

"A giant leech did that years ago. It was called Buyant."

"Very funny. What's for breakfast?"

I may as well start somewhere. "Husband, do you know anything about the three who think about the fate of the world?"

A long pause in which I thought he hadn't heard me. "What the devil are you talking about now?"

At that moment Oyuun, Gunga's daughter, came in. Her cheeks were flushed red and you could see her breath. "The shop had some bread! And I found some onions, too."

"Good girl!" Gunga embraced her. "You were gone early. You didn't wake me."

"Shut the bloody door!" bawled Buyant.

"I knew you had to work late at the hotel, so I didn't want to wake you." Gunga suspected Oyuun wasn't telling the whole truth. "Was the hotel busy last night, Mom?" Oyuun was an adept subject-changer.

"No. Just the two blondies."

"I found Australia in the atlas at school. But I couldn't find— what was it? Danemark, or somewhere?"

"Who cares?" Buyant rolled out of bed, wearing a blanket as a shawl. He would have been handsome once, and he still thought he was. "It's not as if *you'll* ever be going there."

Gunga bit her tongue, and Oyuun didn't look up.

"The blondies are checking out today, and I'll be glad to see the back of them. I just can't understand it, her mother letting her daughter wander off like that. I'm sure they're not married, but they're in the same bed! No ring, or anything. And there's something weird about him, too." Gunga was looking at Oyuun, but Oyuun was looking away.

" 'Course there is, they're foreigners." Buyant burped and slurped his tea.

"What do you mean, Mom?" Oyuun started chopping the onions.

"Well, for one thing, he smells of yogurt. But there's something else too. . . . It's in his eyes. . . . It's like they're not his own."

"They can't be as weird as those Hungarian trade unionists who used to come. The ones they flew in the orchids from Vietnam for."

Gunga knew how to blot out her husband's presence. "That Danemark man, he tips all the time, and he keeps smiling like he's touched in the head. But last night, he touched my hand."

Buyant spat. "If he touches you again I'll twist his head off and ram it up his asshole. You tell him that from me."

Gunga shook her head. "No, it was like a kid playing tag. He just touched my hand with his thumb, and was gone, out of the kitchen. Or like he was casting a spell. And please don't spit inside the *ger*."

Buyant ripped off a gobbet of bread. "A *spell*, ah yes, that must be it! He was probably trying to bewitch you. Woman, sometimes I feel it was your grandmother I married, not you!"

The women carried on preparing food in silence.

Buyant scratched his groin. "Speaking of marriage, Old Gombo's eldest boy came around asking for Oyuun last night."

Oyuun stared steadily into the noodles she was stirring. "Oh?"

"Yep. Brought me a bottle of vodka. Good stuff. Old Gombo's a buffoon horseman who can't hold his drink, but his brother-in-law has a good government job, and the younger son is turning into quite a wrestler, they say. He was the champion two years running at school. That's not to be sniffed at."

Gunga chopped, and the onions made her nostrils sting. Oyuun said nothing.

"It's a thought, isn't it? The older son is obviously quite taken with Oyuun. . . . If she gets Old Gombo's grandson in the oven it'll show she can deliver the goods *and* force Old Gombo's hand. . . . I can think of worse matches."

"I can think of better ones," said Gunga, stirring some noodles into the mutton soup. A memory passed through of Buyant visiting her in her parents' *ger*, through a flap in the roof, just a few feet away from where her parents were sleeping. "Someone she loves, for example. Anyway, we've already agreed. Oyuun will finish school and, fate willing, get into the university. We want Oyuun to do well in the world. Maybe she'll get a car. Or at least a motorbike, from China."

"I don't see the point. It's not like there are any jobs waiting afterwards, especially not for girls. The Russians took all the jobs with them when they left. And the ones that they left the Chinese grabbed. Another way foreigners rip us Mongolians off."

"Camelshit! The vodka took all the jobs. The vodka rips us off."

Buyant glared. "Women don't understand politics."

Gunga glared back. "And I suppose men do? The economy would die of a common cold if it were healthy enough to catch one."

"I tell you, it's the Russians—"

"Nothing's ever going to get better until we stop blaming the Russians and start blaming ourselves! The Chinese are able to make money here. Why can't we?" Some fat in a pan began to hiss. Gunga caught a glimpse of her reflection in her cup of milk, frowning. Her hand trembled minutely, and the image rippled away. "Today is all wrong. I'm going to see the shaman."

Buyant thumped the table. "I'm not having you throwing away our togrugs on—"

Gunga snapped back at him. "I'll throw my togrugs anywhere I please, you soak!"

Buyant backed down from this fight he couldn't win. He didn't want the neighbors overhearing, and saying he couldn't control his woman.

Why am I the way I am? I have no genetic blueprint. I have had no parents to teach me right from wrong. I have had no teachers. I had no nurture, and I possess no nature. But I am discreet and conscientious, a nonhuman humanist.

I wasn't always this way. After the doctor went mad, I transmigrated around the villagers. I was their lord. I knew their secrets, the bends of the village's streams and the names of its dogs. I knew their rare pleasures that burned out as quickly as they flared up, and of the memories that kept them from freezing. I studied extremes. I would drive my hosts almost to destruction in pursuit of the pleasure which fizzed along their neural bridges. I inflicted pain on those unlucky enough to cross my path, just to understand pain. I amused myself by implanting memories from one host into another, or by incessantly singing to them. I'd coerce monks to rob, devoted lovers to be unfaithful, misers to spend. The only thing I can say for myself is that after my first host, I never killed again. I cannot say I did this out of love for humanity. I have only one fear: to be inhabiting a human at the moment of death. I still don't know what would happen.

I have no story of a blinding conversion to humanism. It just didn't happen that way. During the Cultural Revolution, and when I transmigrated into hosts in Tibet, in Vietnam, in Korea, in El Salvador, I experienced humans fighting, usually from the safety of the general's office. In the Falkland Islands I watched them fight over rocks. "Two bald men fighting over a comb," an ex-host commented. In Rio I saw a tourist killed for a watch. Humans live in a pit of cheating, exploiting, hurting, incarcerating. Every time, the species wastes some part of what it could be. This waste is poisonous. That is why I no longer harm my hosts. There's already too much of this poison.

.   .   .

Gunga spent the morning at the hotel, sweeping and boiling some water to wash sheets. Seeing Caspar and Sherry again from the outside was like revisiting an old house with a new tenant. They paid and waited until their rented jeep turned up. I bade Caspar good-bye in Danish as he slung his backpack in, but he just assumed Gunga was saying something in Mongolian.

As Gunga made the beds, she imagined Caspar and Sherry lying here, and then thought about Oyuun, and Gombo's youngest son. She thought about the rumors of child prostitution spreading through the city, and how the police were being paid off in foreign money. Mrs. Enchbat, the widow who owned the hotel, stopped by to do some bookkeeping. Mrs. Enchbat was in a good mood—Caspar had paid in dollars, and Mrs. Enchbat needed to raise a dowry. While Gunga was boiling water for washing they sat down and shared some salty tea.

"Now Gunga, you *know* that I'm not a one for gossip," began Mrs. Enchbat, a little woman with a mouth wise as a lizard's, "but our Sonjoodoi saw your Oyuun walking out with Old Gombo's youngest again yesterday evening. People's tongues will start wagging. They were seen at the Naadam festival together. Sonjoodoi also said Gombo's eldest has got a crush on her."

Gunga chose counterattack. "Is it true your Sonjoodoi's become a Christian?"

Mrs. Enchbat considered her reply coolly. "He's been seen going to the American missionary's apartment once or twice."

"What does his grandmother have to say about that?"

"Only that it proves what suckers Americans are. They think they're making converts to their weird cult, they're just making converts to powdered milk—whatever's the matter, Gunga?"

A riot of doubt had broken out in my host. Gunga knew I was here. Quickly, I tried to calm her. "No. Something's wrong. I'm going to see the shaman."

The bus was crowded and stuck in first gear. At the end of the line was a derelict factory from the Soviet days. Gunga had already forgotten what it had once manufactured. I had to look in her unconscious: bullets. Wildflowers were capitalizing on the brief summer, and wild dogs picked at the body of something. The afternoon was weak and thin. People from the bus trudged their way past where the road ran out to a hillside of *gers*. Gunga walked with them. The giant pipe ran along on its stilts. It had been a part of a public-heating system, but the boilers needed Russian coal. Mongolian coal burned at temperatures too cool to make it work. Most of the locals had gone back to burning dung.

Gunga's cousin had gone to this shaman when she couldn't get pregnant. Nine months later she gave birth to boy twins, born with cauls, an omen of great fortune. The shaman was an adviser to the president, and he had a reputation as a horse-healer. It was said he had lived for twenty years as a hermit on the slopes of Tavanbogd in the far-west province of Bayan Olgii. During the Soviet occupation, the local officials had tried to arrest him for vagrancy, but anyone who went to get him returned empty-handed and empty-headed. He was two centuries old.

I was looking forward to meeting the shaman.

I have my gifts: I am apparently immune to age and forgetfulness. I possess freedom beyond any human understanding of the world. But my cage is all my own, too. I am trapped in one waking state of consciousness. I have never found any way to sleep, or dream. And the knowledge I most desire eludes me: I have never found the source of the story I was born with, and I have never discovered whether others of my kind exist.

When I finally left the village at the foot of the Holy Mountain I traveled all over southeast Asia, searching the attics and cellars of old people's minds for other minds without bodies. I found legends of beings who might be my kindred, but of tangible knowledge—I found not one footprint. I crossed the Pacific in the 1960s.

Remembering my insane doctor, I mostly maintained a vow of silence. I had no wish to leave behind me a trail of mystics, lunatics, and writers. On the other hand, if I came across a mystic, lunatic, or writer I would sometimes talk with him. One writer in Buenos Aires even suggested a name for what I am: *noncorpum*, and *noncorpa*, if ever the day dawns when the singular becomes a plural. I spent a pleasant few months debating metaphysics with him, and we wrote some stories together. But the "I" never became a "We." During the 1970s I placed an advertisement in the *National Enquirer.* The U.S.A. is even crazier than the rest of humanity. I followed up each of the nineteen replies I received: mystics, lunatics, or writers, every one. I even looked for clues in the Pentagon. I found a lot of things that surprised even me, but nothing related to *noncorpa.* I never went to Europe. It seemed a dead place, cold in the shadows of nuclear missiles.

I returned to my Holy Mountain, possessing knowledge from over a hundred hosts, but still knowing nothing about my origins. I had tired of wandering. The Holy Mountain was the only place on Earth I felt any tie to. For a decade I inhabited the monks who lived on its mountainsides. I led a tranquil enough life. I found companionship with an old woman who lived in a tea shack and believed I was a speaking tree. That was the last time I spoke with a human.

"Come in, daughter," said the shaman's voice from inside the *ger.*

Sun-bleached jawbones hung over the door. Gunga looked over her shoulder, suddenly afraid. A boy was playing with a red ball. He threw it high into the hazy blue, and watched it, and caught it when it fell. There was an *Ovoo,* a holy pile of stones and bones. Gunga asked for its blessing and entered the smoky darkness.

"Come in, daughter." The shaman was meditating on a mat. A lamp hung from the roof frame. A tallow candle spluttered in a copper dish. The rear of the *ger* was walled off by hanging animal skins. The air was grainy with incense.

There was a carved box by the entrance. Gunga opened it, and put in most of the togrugs that Caspar had tipped her the day before. She slipped off her shoes, and knelt in front of the shaman, on the right-hand side of the *ger,* the female half. A wrinkled face, impossible to guess the age of. Gray, matted hair, and closed eyes that suddenly opened wide. He indicated a cracked teapot on a low table.

Gunga poured the dark, odorless liquid into a cup of bone.

"Drink, Gunga," said the shaman.

My host drank, and began to speak—the shaman halted her with his hand.

"You have come because a spirit is living within you."

"Yes," both Gunga and I answered. Gunga felt me again, and dropped the cup. The stain of the undrunk liquid spread through the rug.

"Then we must find out what it wants," said the shaman.

Gunga's heart pounded like a boxed bat. Gently, I shut down her consciousness.

The shaman saw the change. He picked up a feather and drew a symbol in the air.

"To whom am I speaking?" asked the shaman. "An ancestor of this woman?"

"I don't know who I am." My words, Gunga's voice, dry and croaky. "I want to discover who I am." Strange, to be uttering the word "I" once again.

The shaman was calm. "What is your name, spirit?"

"I've never needed a name."

"Are you an ancestor of this woman's?"

"You already asked that. I'm not. Not as far as I know."

The shaman struck a bone against another bone, muttering words in a language I didn't know. He sprang to his feet and flexed his fingers like claws.

"In the name of Khukdei Mergen Khan art thou cast hence from the body of this woman!"

Human males. "And then what do you suggest?"

The shaman shouted. "Be gone! In the name of Erkhii Mergen who divided night from day, I command it!" The shaman shook a rattling sack over Gunga. He blew some incense smoke over my host, and sprinkled some water in her face.

The shaman gazed at my host, waiting for a reaction. "Shaman, I'd hoped for something more intelligent. This is my first proper conversation for a very long time. And you'd be doing Gunga more good if you used that water to wash her. She believes that the Mongolian body doesn't sweat, so she doesn't wash and she has lice."

The shaman frowned, and looked into Gunga's eyes, searching for something that wasn't Gunga. "Your words are perplexing, spirit, and your magic is strong. Do you wish this woman ill? Are you evil?"

"Well, I've had my moments, but I wouldn't describe myself as evil. Would you?"

"What do you want of this woman? What ails you?"

"One memory. And the lack of all others."

The shaman sat back down and resumed his initial repose. "Who were your people when you walked as a living body?"

"Why do you think I was once human?"

"What else would you have been?"

"That's a fair question."

The shaman frowned. "You are a strange one, even for one of your kind. You speak like a child, not one waiting to pass over."

"What do you mean, 'my kind'?"

"I am a shaman. It is my calling to communicate with spirits. As it was with my master, and his master before him."

"Let me explore your mind. I need to see what you have seen."

"The spirits do not commune with one another?"

"Not with me, they don't. Please. Let me in. It's safer for you if you don't resist."

"If I allow you to possess me for a short time, you will leave this woman?"

"Shaman, we have a deal. If you touch Gunga, I will leave her now."

I experience memories like a network of tunnels. Some are serviced and brightly lit, others are catacombs. Some are guarded, yet others are bricked up. Tunnels lead to tunnels, deeper down. So it is with memories.

But access to memories does not guarantee access to truth. Many minds redirect memories along revised maps. In the tunnels of the shaman's memory I met what may have been spirits of the dead, or delusions on the part of either the shaman or his customers or both. Or *noncorpa*! Maybe there were many footprints, or maybe there were none. Or maybe evidence was there in forms I couldn't recognize. I deepened my search.

I found this story, told twenty summers earlier on a firelit desert night.

Many years ago, the red plague stalked the land. Thousands of people died. The healthy fled in its face, leaving behind the infected, saying simply, "Fate will sift the living from the dead." Among the abandoned in the land of birds was Tarvaa, a fifteen-year-old boy. His spirit left his body and walked south between the dunes of the dead.

When he appeared in the *ger* of the Khan of Hell, the Khan was surprised. "Why have you left your body behind while it is still breathing?"

Tarvaa replied, "My Lord, the living considered my body gone. I came here without delay to pledge my allegiance."

The Khan of Hell was impressed with the obedience shown by Tarvaa. "I decree that your time has not yet come. You may take my fastest horse and return to your master in the land of birds. But before you go you may choose one thing from my *ger* to take with you. Behold! Here you may find wealth, good fortune, comeliness, ecstasy, grief and woe, wisdom, lust, and gratification. . . . Come now, what will you have?"

"My Lord," spoke Tarvaa, "I choose the stories."

Tarvaa put the stories in his leather pouch, mounted the fastest horse of the Khan of Hell, and returned to the land of birds in the south. When he got there, a crow had already pecked out Tarvaa's body's eyes. But Tarvaa dared not return to the dunes of the dead, fearing that to do so would be ungracious to the Khan. So Tarvaa took possession of his body, and rose up, and though he was blind he lived for a hundred years, traveling Mongolia on the Khan of Hell's horse, from the Altai mountains in the far west, to the Gobi desert in the south, to the rivers of Hentii Nuruu, telling stories and foreseeing the future, and teaching the tribesmen the legends of the making of their land. And from that time, the Mongols have told each other tales.

· · ·

I decided to go south, like Tarvaa. If I lacked clues in reality, I would have to find them in legends.

———————

Jargal Chinzoreg is as strong as a camel. He trusts only his family and his truck. As a boy, Jargal longed to be a pilot for the Mongolian air force, but his family lacked the bribes to get him into the Party school in the capital, so he became a truck driver. This was probably lucky, in the long run: nobody knows what would happen if the handful of rusting aeroplanes that constitutes the Mongolian Air Force were started up again. There's talk in the parliament of scrapping the Air Force altogether, given Mongolia's glaring inability to defend itself against any of its neighbors, even lowly Kazakhstan. Since the economic collapse, Jargal has worked for whoever has access to fuel: the black marketeers, the theoretically privatized iron works, timber companies, meat merchants. Jargal will do anything to make his wife laugh, even put socks up his nose and chase her around the *ger* making a noise like a horny yak.

The road we are traveling, from Ulan Bator to Dalanzagad, is the least worst in the country. It's usually passable, even in rainy weather. The road is 293 kilometers long, and Jargal knows its every pothole, bend, ditch, checkpoint, and checkpoint guard. He knows which petrol pumps are likely to have petrol when, how much life is left in each of the parts of his thirty-year-old Russian truck, and possible sources for spares.

The horizon widens, the mountains toss and turn and then lie down until the grasslands begin. There's a lonely tree. A signpost. A dusty café that hasn't been open since 1990. A barracks where the Soviet army once did maneuvers, desolate now with the plumbing and wiring ripped out.

The sun changes position. A cloud shaped like a marmot. Jargal wipes the sweat from his eyes, and lights a Chinese cigarette. He remembers a Marlboro a Canadian hitchhiker gave him last year.

A chestnut horse stands on a ridge, looking down at the road.

There's a settlement beyond those rocks. The great sky marmot has become a cylinder valve. There's a rock shaped like a giant's head seventy kilometers outside of Dalanzagad. Many years ago a wrestler used it to crush the head of a monstrous serpent. The sky turns clear jade in the evening cold. Jargal lights another cigarette. Five years ago, around here—just off this incline—a truck rolled over with its cargo of propane gas. They say you can still see the burning driver running towards the road screaming for help that will forever be too late. Jargal knew him. They used to drink together at the truckers' hotels.

Jargal sees the town lights in the distance, and he thinks of his wife on the day their first son was born. He thinks about the toy goat that his aunt, Mrs. Enchbat, made for his baby daughter out of old scraps of cloth and string. She is still too young to talk well, but already she rides as if she were born in the saddle.

Pride is something I have never felt.

"You've never been interested in the old stories before." The wizened man in an army jacket frowned. "They were prohibited when the Russians were here. All we had was goatshit about the heroes of the revolution. I was a teacher then. Did I ever tell you about the time Horloyn Choibalsan came to our school? The president himself?"

"About fifteen minutes ago, you senile fart," muttered a greasy listener. A radio in the bar played pop songs in Japanese and English. Three or four men were playing chess, but had become too drunk to remember the rules.

"If I told any of the old stories in the classroom," the old man continued, "I'd have been a candidate for 'reeducation.' Even Gingghis Khan, the Russians said he was a feudal character. Now every bunch of *gers* with a covered pisspool is rushing to prove Gingghis was born by *their* bend in the river. . . ."

"That's very interesting," I said. Jargal was bored. It was uphill work for me to keep him here, polite. "Do you know one about the three animals who think about the fate of the world?"

"I could tell you a few stories of my own, though. Did I ever tell you about the time Horloyn Choibalsan came to my school? In a big, black car. A black Zil. I want another dumpling. How come you're so interested in the old stories all of a sudden anyway?"

"I'll get you another dumpling. Look, a nice big one . . . lots of lard. It's my son. He complains if I tell the same one twice. You know what kids are like, always demanding new things. . . . I remember when I was a kid, about three animals who think about the fate of the world. . . ."

The wizened man burped. "There's no future in stories. . . . Stories are things of the past, things for museums. No place for stories in these market-democracy days."

Suddenly a shouting match broke out. Chessmen whistled past. A window cracked. "He came in a big, black car. There were bodyguards and advisers and KGB men. Trained in Moscow." The drunk was standing on a table, shouting down into the foray. A man with a birthmark like a mask was smashing the board down on his rival's head. I gave up and let Jargal get us out of here.

The man in the museum looked at Jargal and me in astonishment. "Stories?"

"Yes," I began.

He started laughing, and I had to stop Jargal taking a swipe at him. "Why would anyone be interested in stories about Mongolia?"

"Because they are our culture," I suggested. "And I don't want you to tell me stories. I want information about the origin of the stories."

Silence. I noticed the wall clock had stopped.

"Jargal Chinzoreg," said the curator, "you are spending too long in your truck, or with your family. You always were a weird one, but now you're sounding like a crazy old man, or a tourist. . . ."

A man wearing the smartest suit in Mongolia walked out of an office. The director was laughing the laugh of a man of no importance. The suit was carrying a briefcase, and chewing gum.

"We've got our stuffed birds," continued the curator, "our Mongolian-Russian eternal friendship display. Our dinosaur bones, our scrolls, and the Zanabazar bronzes we could hide from the departing Russians. But if it's information you want, you've got no business here. I ask you!"

The suit drew level. Even though it was a dull day, he had already slipped on a pair of sunglasses. "You know," he said, suddenly addressing us, "what's-his-face down in Dalanzagad is putting together an anthology of Mongolian folk stories. It's a quaint idea. He's hoping to get it translated into English and flog them to tourists. He put a proposal to the state printing press last year. It was turned down—no paper. But he's been doing some lobbying, and at the next meeting he might pull it off."

The suit went. I thanked him.

"Now, Jargal Chinzoreg," said the curator, "will you please get lost? It's lunchtime."

The manager shut his office door with a loud sigh of relief.

Jargal looked at the curator's watch. "But it's only ten-thirty."

"Exactly. We'll reopen at about three."

The moon was in the morning sky, a globe of cobweb.

"Sir!" Jargal ran across the empty road in front of the museum. The suit was getting into a Japanese-made four-wheel drive. Jargal was nervous: the owner of such a car must be a powerful man. "Sir!"

The suit turned, his hand twitching inside his jacket. "What?"

"I'm sorry to bother you, sir, but would you try to remember the name of the gentleman you just mentioned? The folklorist? It might be very important to me."

The suit's guard went up. I had used the wrong register of speech for a truck driver. The suit touched his forehead, and dropped his keys. Jargal picked them up and handed them to him. I made sure they touched, and I transmigrated. Like Gunga's, it was a hard mind to penetrate. Unusually viscous, like jumping through a wall of cold butter.

I didn't need to scan my new host's memory for long. "His name is Bodoo."

Some passersby were staring at the immobile government man. My new host regained control. "Now, you'll excuse me, I have important business that won't wait."

Oh yes it will. Here's a picture. Bodoo is a short, balding man with glasses, sideburns, and a tufty mustache. We are going to meet, you and I, Bodoo. You are going to direct me to my birthright.

I watched Jargal walk away, a man awakening from a strange dream.

My new host was Punsalmaagiyn Suhbataar, a senior agent of the Mongolian KGB with a disdain of vulnerable things. We sped south, his four-wheel drive spewing up clouds of dust. He chewed gum. The grass grew sparser, the camels scraggier, the air drier. The road to Dalanzagad wasn't signposted, but there was no other road. The checkpoint guards saluted.

I would feel guilty for using my host so selfishly, but as I read Suhbataar's past I felt vindicated. During his career he had killed over twenty times, and supervised the mutilation or torture of ten times that number of prisoners. He had accrued a medium-sized fortune in a vault in Geneva at the expense of his old overlords in Moscow, and his new ones in Petersburg. Even I couldn't see into the hole where his conscience should be. Outside this hole, his mind was cold, clear, and cruel.

As night fell I let Suhbataar stop to stretch his legs and drink some coffee. It was good to see the stars again, the whole deep lake of them. Humans thicken the skies above their cities into a broth. But Suhbataar is not a man given to astral contemplation. For the fiftieth time he wondered what he was doing there, and I had to snuff out the thought. We spent the night at a truck drivers' boardinghouse, scarcely bothering to talk to the owner, whom Suhbataar didn't intend to pay. I made enquiries about Bodoo, the folklorist curator of Dalanzagad museum, but nobody knew him. While my host slept I broadened the Russian I acquired from Gunga.

The following day the hills flattened to a gravel plain, and the Gobi desert began. I was getting weary of it all. Another day of horses and clouds and mountains nobody names. Suhbataar's mind didn't help. Most humans are constantly writing in their heads, editing conversations and mixing images and telling themselves jokes or replaying music. But not Suhbataar. I may as well have transmigrated into a cyborg.

Suhbataar drove over the body of a dog and into the dusty regional capital of Dalanzagad. An unpainted place that dropped from nowhere onto a flat plot of dust devils. Doomed strips of turfless park where women in headscarves sold eggs and dried goods. A few three- or four-floor buildings, with suburbs spilling around the edges. A dirt-strip runway, a flyblown hospital, a corrupt post office, a derelict department store. Beyond stories of black-market dinosaur eggs fetching $500 and snow-leopard pelts from the Gov'-Altai mountains to the south fetching up to $20,000, Suhbataar knew less about the southernmost province of Mongolia than he cared about it.

There's a police office he could go and scare, but I took Suhbataar straight to the museum to enquire after Bodoo. The door was locked, but Suhbataar can open any door in Mongolia. Inside was similar to the last museum, booming with silence. Suhbataar found the curator's office empty. A large, stuffed buzzard incorrectly labeled as a condor hung down from the ceiling. One of its glass eyes had dropped out and rolled away somewhere.

There was a middle-aged woman knitting in the empty bookshop. She didn't seem surprised to see a visitor in the locked-up museum. I doubted she had been surprised by anything for years.

"I'm looking for a 'Bodoo,' " Suhbataar announced.

She didn't bother looking up. "He didn't come in yesterday. He didn't come in today. I don't know if he'll come in tomorrow."

Suhbataar's voice fell to a whisper. "And may I ask where the esteemed curator is vacationing?"

"You can ask, but I dunno if I'll remember."

For the first time since I transmigrated into Suhbataar, he felt pleasure. He slipped his gun onto the counter, and clicked off the safety catch. He aimed at the hook suspending the buzzard.

BANG!

The thing crashed to the floor, disintegrating on impact into a cloud of plaster, powder, and feathers. The noise of the gunshot chased its own tail through all the empty rooms.

The woman threw her knitting high into the air. As her mouth hung open I saw how bad her teeth were.

Suhbataar whispered. "Look, you tapeworm-infested dung-puddle peasant bitch—with bad teeth—here is how our little interview works. I ask the questions, and then you answer them. If I feel you are being just the least bit evasive, you will spend the next ten years in a shit-smeared prison, in a distant part of our glorious Motherland. Do you understand?"

The woman blanched and tried to swallow.

Suhbataar admired his gun. "I don't believe I heard you."

She whimpered yes.

"Good. Where is Bodoo?"

"He heard that the KGB man was coming. He did a runner. I swear, he didn't say where. Sir, I didn't know you were the KGB man. I swear, I didn't."

"And where does Bodoo reside in your fine township?"

The woman hesitated.

Suhbataar sighed, and from his jacket pocket pulled out a gold lighter. He set fire to the card NO SMOKING sign on the counter. The quivering woman, Suhbataar and I watched it shrivel and burn up into a flapping black flap. "Maybe you want to be locked up and maimed in prison? Maybe you want me to castrate your husband? Maybe you want your children to be taken into care by a Muslim-run orphanage in Bayan Olgii with a nasty reputation for child abuse?"

Beads of sweat sprang up through her mascara. Idly, Suhbataar considered ramming her head through the glass counter, but I interceded. She scribbled an address on the margin of her newspaper and handed it over. "He lives there with his daughter, sir."

"Thank you." Suhbataar yanked the phone line out of the wall. "Have a nice day."

Suhbataar circled the house. A prefabricated little place on the edge of town with only one door. There was a barrel for rainwater, which falls ten times in a good year, and an optimistic herb garden. The wind was loud and dusty. My host pulled out his gun and knocked. I clicked the safety catch on without Suhbataar noticing.

The door was opened by Bodoo's daughter. A boyish-looking girl in her late teens. We noted that my host was expected. Suhbataar guessed that she was alone in the house.

"Let's keep this painless," said Suhbataar. "You know who I am and what I want. Where is your father?"

This girl had attitude. "You don't really expect me just to turn in my own father? We don't even know the charge."

Suhbataar smiled. Something in the dark hole was humming. His eyes ran over the girl's body, and imagined slashing it. He stepped forward, gripping her forearm.

But for once Suhbataar was not going to get what he wanted.

I implanted an overwhelming desire to drive to Copenhagen via Baghdad into Suhbataar's mind, and made him throw his wallet containing several hundred dollars at Bodoo's daughter's feet. I transmigrated through the young woman's forearm. It was difficult—the girl's defenses were high and thick, and she was about to scream.

I was in. I clamped the scream shut. We watched the dreaded KGB agent throw money at her feet, spring into his Toyota, and drive west at breakneck speed. My order might not get Suhbataar quite as far as Caspar's flowerbeds, but it should take him well clear of Dalanzagad, and into a displeased border patrol in a volatile country where nobody spoke Russian or Mongolian.

My new host watched Suhbataar's car disappear. The screeching tires flung ribbons of dust to the desert wind.

I saw her name, Baljin. A dead mother. There! *The three who think about the fate of the world.* A different version, but the same story. Her mother is weaving by firelight, on the far side of the room. Baljin is safe and warm. The loom clanks.

Now all I had to do was find out where the story is from. I overrode Baljin's relief and took us into her father's study, which was also his bedroom and the dining room. Baljin was her father's amanuensis and accompanied him on fieldwork. The notes for his book were in the drawer. Not good! Bodoo had taken them with him when he fled.

I laid Baljin down on the bed and closed down her consciousness while I searched her memory for information on the origin of the tale. In what town is it still known and told? I spent half the afternoon searching, even for after-memories, but Baljin's only certainty is that her father knows.

So where was Bodoo? Yesterday he left for his brother's *ger*, two hours' ride west of Dalanzagad. Unless he received an all-clear message from Baljin by noon that day he would depart for Bayanhongoor, five hundred kilometers northwest across the desert. I woke Baljin, and looked at her watch. It was already three. I assured her the danger had passed, that the KGB do not want to question her father about anything, and that he can be contacted safely and told to come home. I waited for Baljin to choose the next logical step.

We needed to borrow a horse, or maybe a motorbike.

Two hours later we were thirty kilometers west of Dalanzagad in a sketchy village known in the local dialect only as "the bend in the river." Baljin found her uncle, Bodoo's brother, repairing his jeep. I had missed Bodoo by five hours. He left before noon, believing that the KGB must have reopened the file on his part in the democracy demonstrations. Baljin told her uncle about the wallet thrown at her feet. I had erased the memories of Suhbataar's aggression. Bodoo's brother, a tough herder who can wrestle rams to the ground and slit their throats in ten seconds, laughed. He stopped laughing when Baljin gave him half the money. This would feed his family for a year.

We could go after his brother in the jeep, if we could get it working. I transmigrated, and with Jargal Chinzoreg's automotive knowledge started reassembling the engine.

Evening came before I got the engine working. My host considered it dangerous to leave after nightfall, so we decided to wait until dawn of the following day. Baljin brought her uncle a cup of *airag*. In the cold river children were swimming and women were washing clothes. The river flowed from springs at the feet of the Gov'-Altai mountains, born of winter snow. The sunset smelt of cooking. Baljin's niece was practicing the *shudraga*, a long-necked lute. An old man was summoning goats. How I envy these humans their sense of belonging.

Men arrived on horseback from the town, hungry for news.

They had learned of Suhbataar's visit two days ago from the truck drivers' grapevine. They sat around the fire as Baljin told the story yet again, and an impromptu party got going. The younger men showed off their horsemanship to Baljin. Baljin was respected as one of the finest archers in all Dalanzagad, male or female, and she was unbetrothed, and the daughter of a government employee. Baljin's aunt made some fresh *airag*, stirring mare's milk into fermented milk. The mares were grazed on the previous autumn's *taana* grass, which makes the best *airag*. It grew dark, and fires were lit.

"Tell us a story, Aunt Baljin," said my host's eight-year-old. "You know the best ones."

"How come?" said a little snotty boy.

"Because of Grandpa Bodoo's book, stupid. My Aunt Baljin helped him write it, didn't you, Aunt Baljin?"

"What book?" said Snotty.

"The book of stories, stupid."

"What stories?"

"You are so facile!" The girl exhibited her recent acquisition. "Aunt Baljin, tell us 'The Camel and the Deer.'"

Baljin smiled. She had a lovely smile.

Now: long, long ago, the camel had antlers. Beautiful twelve-pronged antlers. And not only antlers! The camel also had a long, thick tail, lustrous as your hair, my darling.

["What's 'lustous'?" asked Snotty.]

["Shut up, stupid, or Aunt Baljin will stop, won't you, Aunt Baljin?"]

At that time the deer had no antlers. It was bald, and to be truthful rather ugly. And as for the horse, the horse had no lovely tail, either. Just a short little stumpy thing.

One day the camel went to drink at the lake. He was charmed by the beauty of his reflection. "How magnificent!" thought the camel. "What a gorgeous beast am I!"

Just then, who should come wandering out of the forest, but the deer? The deer was sighing.

"What's the matter with you?" asked the camel. "You've got a face on you like a wet sun."

"I was invited to the animals' feast, as the guest of honor."

"You can't beat a free nosh-up," said the camel.

"How can I go with a forehead as bare and ugly as mine? The tiger will be there, with her beautiful coat. And the eagle, with her swanky feathers. Please, camel, just for two or three hours, lend me your antlers. I promise I'll give them back. First thing tomorrow morning."

"Well," said the camel, magnanimously. "You do look pretty dreadful the way you are, I agree. I'll take pity on you. Here you are." And the camel took off the antlers and gave them to the deer, who pranced off. "And mind you don't spill any, erm, berry juice on them or whatever it is you forest animals drink at these dos."

The deer met the horse.

"Hey," said the horse. "Nice antlers."

"Yes, they are, aren't they?" replied the deer. "The camel gave them to me."

"Mmmn," mused the horse. "Maybe the camel will give me something, too, if I ask nicely."

The camel was still at the lake, drinking, and looking at the desert moon.

"Good evening, my dear camel. I was wondering, would you swap your beautiful tail with me for the evening? I'm going to see this finely built young filly I know, and she's long been an admirer of yours. I know she'd simply melt if I turned up in her paddock wearing your tail."

The camel was flattered. "Really? An admirer? Very well, let's swap tails. But be sure to bring it back first thing tomorrow morning. And be sure you don't spill any, erm, never mind, just look after it, all right? It's the most beautiful tail in the whole world, you know."

Since then many days and years have passed, but the deer still hasn't given back the camel's antlers, and you can see for yourself that the horse still gallops over the plains with the camel's tail streaming in the wind. And some people say, when the camel comes to drink at the lake he sees his bare, ugly reflection, and snorts, and forgets his thirst. And have you noticed how the camel stretches his neck and gazes into the distance, to a far-off sand dune or a distant mountain top? That's when he's thinking, "When is the horse going to give me back my tail?" And that is why he is always so sad.

Dust devils bounced off the shell of the jeep like kangaroos. Nothing among these rocks but scorpions and mirages, for the length and breadth of the morning.

Bodoo's brother stopped in an isolated *ger*. A camel was tethered outside, but there was no one around. As Gobi etiquette permits, my host entered the *ger*, prepared some food, and drank some water. The owner's camel snorted like a human. A warning flared up from my host's unconscious, but it went before I could locate its source. The wind was strong but the world was silent. There was nothing to blow against, or in, or through.

We got back in the jeep. Gazelles darted through the distance, flocks of them turning like minnows in a river. Bodoo's brother drove down the Valley of the Vulture's Mouth, where we stopped at a store for enough provisions and petrol to get us to Bayanhongoor. Bodoo had passed through early that morning. We were catching up with him.

Hawks circled high. One of the last Gobi bears shambled along the fringe of forest. There are less than a hundred left. Bodoo's brother slept in the jeep, under several blankets. It gets cold at night, even in summer. Dreams came, of bones and stones with holes.

The next day, the dunes, the longest running for eighty miles, swelling and rolling, grain by grain. Bodoo's brother sang songs that lasted for miles, with no beginning and no end. The dunes of the dead. There were bones, and stones with holes.

There was a stationary jeep in the shimmering distance. Bodoo's brother pulled up to it and cut his engine. A figure was asleep under a makeshift canopy in the back.

"Are you all right, stranger? Are you in need of any help? Any water?"

"Yes," said the figure, suddenly sitting up and showing his

face, chewing gum. "I need your jeep. Mine seems to have broken down." At point-blank range Punsalmaagiyn Suhbataar fired his handgun twice, a bullet for each of my host's eyes.

Nobody replies. Firelight without color. Outside must be night, if there is an outside. I am hostless and naked. The faces all stare in the same direction, all of them all of their ages. One of them coughs. It is Bodoo's brother, his eye wounds already healed. I try to transmigrate into him, but I cannot inhabit a shadow. I've never known silence so deep. By being what I am, I thought I understood almost everything. But I understand almost nothing.

A figure rises, and leaves the *ger* through a curtain. So simple? I follow the figure. "I'm sorry, I'm afraid you can't come through here," says a girl I hadn't noticed, no older than eight, delicate and tiny as an ancient woman.

"Will you stop me?"

"No. If there is a door for you, you are free to pass through." Wrens flutter.

I touch the wall. There is no door. "Where is it?"

She shrugs, biting her lip.

"Then what shall I do?"

A swan inspects the ground. She shrugs.

Tallow candles spit and hiss. These few guests are many multitudes. Thousands of angels swim in a thimble. From time to time one of the guests stands up, and walks through the way out that is not there. The wall of the *ger* yields, and reseals behind them, like a wall of water. I try to leave with them, but for me it never even bends.

The monk in a saffron robe sighs. He wears a yellow hat that arcs forward. "I'm having some problems with my teeth."

"I'm sorry to hear that," I say. The little girl talks to her twitchy marmot.

Horses galloping by, or thunder? The swan spreads its wings and flies up through the roof. Bodoo's brother has gone through the door.

"But why can't I pass through? The others have."

The little girl is playing cat's cradle with a length of twine, knitting her brow. "You chose not to!"

"I chose nothing."

"All your tribe leave your body while it still breathes."

"What do you mean, my tribe?"

The monk with the yellow hat is here, humming through his broken mouth. He whispers in her ear; she stares at me distrustfully. "Very well," she concurs. "The circumstances are uncommon. But what can I do?"

The monk turns to me. "I'm sorry—my teeth." A prophet's nod. "Time has gone around, the years are cold and far away. . . . I kept my promise." And he, too, passes through the wall of the *ger.*

Last to leave is the little girl, carrying her marmot. She feels sorry for me, and I don't want her to go. I'm all alone.

I was in a human host again, and the walls of the *ger* were living, pulsing with viscera and worry and nearby voices. I explored the higher rooms, but found nothing! No memories, no experiences. Not even a name. Barely an "I." Where were those voices coming from? I looked deeper. There were whispers, and a suffusion of purposeful well-being. I tried to open my host's eyes to see where I was, but the eyes would not open. I checked that there were eyes—yes, but my host had never learned to open them, and couldn't respond. I was in a place unlike any other, yet my host didn't know where. Or rather, my host didn't know anywhere else. A blind mute? The mind was pure. So very pure that I was afraid for it.

The well-being transformed into palpitating fear. Had I been detected? A knot of pain was being pulled tight. Panic, such panic I had never known since I butchered the mind of my first host. The curtain was ripped, and my host emerged into the world between her mother's legs, screaming indignantly at this rude wrenching. The cold air flooded in! The light, even through my eyelids, made my host's tender brain chime.

I transferred into my host's mother along the umbilical cord, and the depth of emotion was sheer and giddy. I forgot to insulate and I was swept away by joy, and relief, and loss, and gain, and emptiness, and fulfillment, a memory of swimming, and the claw-sharp, bloodied love, and the conviction that she would never again put herself through this agony.

But I have work to do.

Another *ger*. Firelight, warmth, and the shadows of antlers. I searched for our location. Well. Good news and bad. My new host was a Mongolian in Mongolia. But I was far to the north of where Bodoo was last heading, not far from the Russian border. I was in the province of Renchinhumbe, near the lake of Tsagaan Nuur and the town of Zoolon. It was September now and the snows would be coming soon. The midwife was the grandmother of the baby I just left; she was smiling down at her daughter, anesthetizing the umbilical cord with a lump of ice. Her hair cobwebby, her face round like the moon. An aunt bustled about in the background with pans of warm water and squares of cloth and fur, chanting. This flat and quiet song was the only sound.

It was the early hours of the morning. The mother's labor had been long and hard. I dulled her pain, put her into a deep sleep, and set about helping her unstitched body repair itself. As my host slept I had time to wonder where I had been since Suhbataar shot my previous host. Had I hallucinated the strange *ger*? But how could I have? I *am* my mind—do I have a mind I don't know about within my mind, like humans? And how was I reborn in Mongolia? Why, and by whom? Who was the monk in the yellow hat?

How do I know that there aren't *noncorpa* living within me, controlling my actions? Like a virus within a bacteria? Surely I would know.

But that's exactly what humans think.

The door opened and an autumn sunrise came in, with the baby's father, grandparents, cousins and friends and aunts and uncles. They had slept in a neighboring *ger* and now crowded into their home, excited and eager to welcome their newest relative. When they spoke I had great difficulty understanding—I had a new dialect of Mongolian to learn. The mother was glowing with tired happiness. The baby bawled, and the elders looked on.

I left the mother and transmigrated into her husband as they kissed. His tribe was known to Baljin as the reindeer people. Reindeer are their food, currency, and clothing. They are seminomadic. A few of the men visit Zoolon several times a year to exchange meat and hides for supplies, and to sell powdered reindeer antler to Chinese merchants who market it in their country as an aphrodisiac. Other than this there is little contact with the rest of the world. When the Russians were busy making a proletariat in this nonindustrial country to justify a socialist revolution, the reindeer people had proved impossible even to conduct a census among. They had survived when the local Buddhist clergy was being liquidated.

My host was only twenty, and his heart was brimming over with pride. I'm rarely envious of humans, but I was now. I am, and always shall be, wholly sterile. I have no genes to pass on. For my new host, the birth of his offspring was the last bridge into true manhood, and would increase his status with his peers and his ancestors. A son would have been preferable, but there would be other births.

I noticed his name, Beebee. He lit a cigarette and left the *ger*. I envied the simplicity of his expectations. He knows how to ride reindeer, and how to skin them, and which of their organs, eaten raw, assist which aspect of human physiology. Beebee knows many legends, but not three who think about the fate of the world.

The night ebbed away, the dawn dripped into a pool of light, and the shadows in the pine trees around the village murmured with gray. An early riser's footfalls crunched in the heavy frost. His head was hooded, and his teeth shone. A shooting star crossed the sky.

Well, what now?

Nothing about my quest had changed. Bodoo was still the only lead I had. I had to get back south, to the town of Bayanhongoor. If I could access the museum network, it should be fairly easy to track him down. Three months had passed since he had fled Suhbataar. This setback would cost me time, but immortals don't lack time.

I told Beebee's grandmother-midwife that Beebee had some business in town that day. I hated to separate the young father from his baby daughter, but the grandmother gladly shooed us out. Men get in the way.

Beebee and his eldest brother rode through forests, between hewn mountains, along narrow lakes. Fishing boats, willows, and wild geese flying up and down the morning. An ibex stood on a hillcrest. I learned from Beebee about the moose, elk, and lynx, about the argali sheep, wolves, and how to trap wild boars. We saw a bear fishing in a river thrashing with salmon. Sharp rainbows, misty sunshine. There are no roads here, but the cold weather had firmed the mud and so the going was easy.

Beebee and his brother discussed the new baby, and how she should be named. I wondered about kinship. For all my Mongolian hosts, the family is the *ger,* to be protected in, to be healed in, to be born in, to make love in, and to die in. A parasite, I could experience all of these, secondhand, but I could never be *of* these.

Unless, perhaps . . . This hope kept me going.

Zoolon was another decrepit town of wooden buildings, concrete blocks, and dead lorries rusting in shallow pools where dogs drank. A power station churned smoke into the perfect sky. Another ghost factory with saplings growing from the chimney stack. A few squat apartment blocks. A crowd gathered around the small corrugated shack that served as the town's only restaurant. Beebee usually drank there after seeing the owner of the tannery.

"Some foreigners in town," a bearded hunter told Beebee. "Round-eyes."

"Russians from over the border? Anything new to trade?"

"Nah. Others."

Beebee walked into the restaurant, and I saw Caspar poking at something on his plate with a fork, and Sherry poring over a map with a compass.

"It's good to see you!" I spoke before I thought. Townsmen in the restaurant stared, amazed. Nobody knew this nomadic herder could speak any language other than a reindeer-flavored dialect of Mongolian.

"G'day," replied Sherry, looking up. Caspar's eyes were more guarded.

"How are you enjoying their country?" This was very indulgent. I had to dampen and then erase Beebee's shock at hearing himself speak in a language he'd never learned.

"It's beautiful," Caspar and Sherry said at exactly the same time.

"Full of surprises. Anyway. Enjoy the rest of your stay. But I'd advise you to get somewhere warmer before winter sets in. . . . Somewhere nearer the ocean. Vietnam can be beautiful in November, up in the hill country, at least it was. . . ."

Beebee sat down and ordered a plate of food while waiting for his brother. His tribe exchanges reindeer meat for credit with the restaurant owner. I picked up the three-week-old newspaper from Ulan Bator. Beebee was illiterate: his dialect has no written form, and his tribe has no schools. There was little news, much whitewashing, and a belated report on the national-day festival. None of it meant much to Beebee, who rarely left his tribe, never left the province, and never wished to.

I was turning past the obituary page when an article caught my eye: DOUBLE TRAGEDY FOR MONGOLIAN CULTURE.

Bodoo was dead.

I rarely feel despair; I forget how it gouges.

Both brothers had died in the same week of a heart attack, which I knew from Suhbataar was one of the Mongolian KGB's favorite ways to dispose of political liabilities.

This tragedy was made all the more poignant by the imminent publication of the late professor's lifework, a comprehensive anthology of Mongolian folk stories. Out of deference to this anthropological giant, we include one story below, retold by the late professor.

I should have sent Suhbataar over a cliff. Damn him. And damn me.

A hand slapped down on Beebee's shoulder. My host's hand slid to the hilt of his hunting knife. The drunk man swayed. His breath made Beebee flinch. "What are you pretending to read the newspaper for, Reindeer Man? And what's this about you speaking arsey foreign languages? Where were you when *I* was fighting for democracy? That's what I want to know." His pupils were huge, and his eyelids red. "You can't read Cyrillic. You can't read Mongolian. And it sure ain't written in reindeer. Where were you when I was fighting for communism? That's what I want to know. Go on, read for me, then, antler-head." Then he bellowed: "Oy! Bring me some frigging vodka! It's story time. . . ."

I was back to where I had started. I was frustrated enough to transmigrate into this wino and hurl him through the wall, but what would be the point? I read the story. I owed it to Bodoo.

In a lost spring of the Buriat nation, Khori Tumed, a young hunter, was roaming the southernmost shore of Lake Baikal. Winter was melting from the silver birches, drip by drip, and Khori Tumed gazed at the turquoise mountains beyond the lake.

As he rested, the hunter saw nine swans flying from the northeast, low over the water. Khori Tumed grew uneasy—they flew in a circle, and silently. Fearing enchantment he hid in the hollow of a gnarled willow. And sure enough, as the swans alighted on the strand, each transformed into a beautiful girl, each with pale skin, slender limbs, and jet-black hair, and each more radiant than the last. The swan-girls disrobed and draped their garments on the very willow tree that concealed Khori Tumed. The hunter's limbs grew heavy—not from fear, but desire and love. Very carefully, when the girls were swimming a little way from the shore, he stole one of the robes.

The swan-girls returned from their bathing to the willow tree. One by one they slipped into their robes, and rose as silent swans, circling out and away over Lake Baikal. The ninth swan-girl—and the most beautiful—searched frantically for her missing robe, and called out to her sisters, but the swans were already vanishing towards the northeast.

With a thump, Khori Tumed jumped down from the tree, gripping her robe.

"Please! Give me back my dress! I must follow my sisters!"

"Marry me," said Khori Tumed. "I will dress you in emerald silk when the summer comes, and the fur of black bears will keep you warm when the snows fall."

"Let's talk about it—but please give me back my robe for now."

The hunter smiled gently. "That I will not do."

The swan-girl watched her sisters disappear from sight. She knew that she had no choice—either accept the stranger's hand in marriage, or freeze to death that very night. "Then I must go with you, mortal, but be warned—when our sons are born I shall not name them. And without names, never shall they cross the threshold into manhood."

So the swan-girl returned to Khori Tumed's *ger* and became a woman of his tribe. In time, she even learned to love the precocious young hunter, and they lived in happiness together. Eleven fine sons were born to them, but the swan-girl was bound by her oath, and Khori Tumed's sons were never blessed with names. And in the evening, she looked longingly to the northeast, and Khori Tumed knew she was thinking of her homeland beyond the winter dawn.

Years arrived, years saddled up and rode away.

One day at the end of autumn when the forests were dancing and dying, Khori Tumed was gutting a ewe while his wife sat embroidering a quilt. Their eleven sons were away, hunting.

"Husband, do you still have my swan's robe?"

"You know I do," replied Khori Tumed, carving the sheep's midriff.

"I would so like to see if I can still fit into it."

He smiled. "What do you take me for? Some kind of marmot brain?"

"My love, if I wanted to leave you now, I could use the door." The swan-girl got up and kissed his neck. "Let me."

Khori Tumed's resolve melted. "Very well, but I'm going to bolt the door." He washed his hands, unlocked his iron-bound chest, and gave the robe to his wife. He sat in the bed, watching her undress and wrap herself in the magical garment.

A wild beating of wings filled the *ger,* and the swan flew up through the gap in the roof, the chimney-flap which Khori Tumed had forgotten to seal! In despair Khori Tumed lunged upwards at the swan with a ladle, and just managed to hook the swan's foot with its handle. "Please! My wife! Don't leave me here without you!"

"My time here is over, mortal. Love you I always shall, but my sisters are calling for me now, and I must obey their call!"

"Then at least tell me the names of our sons, so that they may become men of the tribe!"

And the swan-girl named their sons, as she hovered above the tent: Caragana, Bodonguud, Sharaid, Tsagaan, Gushid, Khudai, Batnai, Khalbin, Khuaitsai, Galzut, Khovduud. And the swan-girl circled the encampment of *gers* three times to bless all who lived there. And it is said that the tribe of Khori Tumed were such people, and that the eleven sons became eleven fathers.

The drunk's eyes had closed, and his face had drooped into his plate of lukewarm meatballs. Everyone in the place was silent. Three young children sat on the other side of the table, entranced by the story. Beebee remembered his new daughter. I looked at Bodoo's picture in the newspaper, and wondered who he really had been, this man I had only known through the memories of others.

The restaurant was emptying out, and the conversation reverted to recent wrestling matches. The sight of two round-eyes eating was only gossipworthy for so long. I watched the way Sherry whispered something to Caspar, and I watched the smile spread over Caspar's face, and I knew they were lovers.

This venture was futile. To look for the source of a story is to look for a needle in a sea. I should transmigrate into Sherry or Caspar, and resume my search for *noncorpa* in other lands.

The bearded hunter walked in with his gun. The memory of being shot flashed back, but the hunter leaned the rifle against the wall, and sat down next to Beebee. He started dismantling it, and cleaning the parts one by one with an oily rag.

"Beebee, right? Of the Reindeer Tribe of Lake Tsagaan Nuur?"

"Yes."

"With a new baby daughter?"

"Arrived last night."

"You'd better return to your tribe," said the hunter. "I met your sister at the market just now. She's looking for you, with your brother. Your wife's hysterical and your daughter's dying."

Beebee cursed himself for coming to town. I wanted to beg his forgiveness. I thought about transmigrating into the hunter, and from him back into Caspar or Sherry, but my guilt made me stay. Maybe I could help with his baby's illness if we got back in time.

I've often thought about that moment. Had I transmigrated at that time, everything would have been different. But I stayed, and Beebee ran to the marketplace.

Dusk was sluggish with cold when we reached Beebee's encampment. The breath of the yaks hung white in the twilight. From far up the valley we heard the wind. It sounded to me like a wolf, but all reindeer people know the difference.

Beebee's *ger* was full of dark shapes, lamps, steam, and worry. A bitter oil was burning in a silver dish. The grandmother was preparing a ritual. Beebee's wife was pale in her bed, cradling the baby, both with wide unblinking eyes. She looked at Beebee. "Our baby hasn't spoken."

The grandmother spoke in hushed tones. "Your daughter's soul has gone. It was born loose. Unless I can summon it back she will be dead by midnight."

"At the hospital back in Zoolon, there's a doctor there, trained in East Germany in the old days—"

"Don't be a fool, Beebee! I've seen it happen too often before. You and that mumbo-jumbo medicine. It's not a matter of medicine! Her soul's been untethered. It's a matter of magic!"

He looked at his limp daughter, and began to despair. "What do you intend to do?"

"I shall perform the rites. Hold this dish. I need your blood."

The grandmother pulled out a curved hunting knife. Beebee was not afraid of knives or blood. As the grandmother washed his palm I transmigrated into the old woman, intending to transfer into the baby to see the problem for myself.

I got no further.

I found something I had never seen in any human mind: a canyon of another's memories, running across her mind. I saw it straightaway, like a satellite passing over. I entered it, and as I did so I entered my own past.

There are three, says the monk in the yellow hat, *who think about the fate of the world.* I am a boy aged eight. I have my own body! We are in a prison cell, smaller than a wardrobe, lit by light from a tiny grill in one corner, the size of a hand. Even though my height is not yet four feet, I cannot stand up. I've been in here a week and I haven't eaten for two days. I have become used to the stink of our own excrement. A man in a nearby box has lost his mind and wails through a broken throat. The only thing I can see through the grill is another grill in a neighboring coffin.

It is 1937. Comrade Choibalsan's social engineering policies, a carbon copy of Josef Stalin's in distant Moscow, are in full swing. There are show trials staged every week in Ulan Bator. Several thousand agents of the impending Japanese invasion from Manchuria have been executed. Nobody is safe. The minister for transport has been sentenced to death for conspiring to cause traffic accidents. The dismantling of the monasteries is well under way. First the taxes were sent skywards, and then began "reeducation." I and my master have been found guilty of feudal indoctrination. We were told this yesterday by the hand that brought us some water. I think it was yesterday. The lids of nearby coffin-cells have been pried off and their helpless occupants hauled off.

"I'm afraid, master," I say.

"Then I shall tell you a story," says the monk.

"Will they shoot us?"

"Yes." It hurts my master to speak. His teeth were rifle-butted into spiky fragments.

"I don't want to die." I think of my mother and father. I can see their faces. My mother and father! Lowly herders, who worked their knuckles to the bone to bribe their son's way into a monastery: five years later their ambition signed his death warrant.

"You won't die. I promised your father you wouldn't die, and you won't."

"But they killed the others."

"They won't kill *you*. Now listen! There are three who think about the fate of the world. . . ."

The sky is thick with crows. Their noise is deafening. Stones are being broken. I, my master, and about forty other monks and their novices are taken over a field littered with naked corpses. The ground is blotched with crimson. Those who cannot walk are dragged. Beside a copse of trees the firing squad is waiting. The soldiers are a roughshod band: this is not the regular Red Army. Many of them are brigands from the Chinese border, who become soldiers when times are lean. There are some children, brought here to dig mass graves, and to watch the executions of us counterrevolutionaries as part of their socialist education. My own brothers and sisters have already been dispersed all over Mongolia.

Wild dogs look on from a pile of rocks.

We wait while the Soviet officer walks over to the mercenaries who will do the killing. They discuss the logistics of the execution as though they are talking about planting a field. They actually laugh.

The master is intoning a mantra. I wish he would stop. I am numb with fear.

There is a girl standing in the mouth of a *ger,* making tea. Domesticity, here and now, is dreamlike. My master abruptly breaks off his mantra and summons her over. She hesitates, but she comes. No one is looking. Her eyes are big, and her face is round. My master touches me with his left hand, and touches her with his right hand, and I feel my memories drawn away on the current.

My master knew how to transmigrate me! My mind is untethered and begins to follow my memories—but at that moment a soldier slams my master's arm away from the girl, and the connection is broken, and the girl kicked away.

This girl's own memories piece together my last minute of life. We watch the boy—myself—and we watch the master chanting. Even as the barrels of the guns are leveled—

Everything moves so slowly. The air thickens, and sets, hard. Every gleam is polished. An order is given in Russian. The rifles go off like firecrackers. The row of men and boys folds and topples.

There is one more thing. This the girl cannot see, but I know how to look. The boy's body is in the mud, too, its small cranium shattered, but with an unmoored mind. I can see it! Adrift, pulsing. One of the mercenaries strolls over to the pile of bodies, lifting the bodies on top with his foot to ensure the ones underneath are dead. He touches the boy, and in that instant my soul pulses into its new home.

Many years before it would stir, unable to identify itself, long after the mercenary had returned to his native corner of China, at the foot of the Holy Mountain.

That is the end.

The present. The grandmother is motionless. I would like to read her life, how she was sent away to another corner of her country, how she was married into a tribe of strangers. But there is no time.

"I am here."

"Well, I didn't think it was Leonid Brezhnev poking around in there," says the grandmother. "It's about time! I saw the comet."

"You know about me?"

"Of course I know about you! I've been carrying your early memories around with me for all these decades! Rumors about the Sect of the Yellow Hat were common currency in my tribe. When your master linked us on your execution day, I knew what he was doing. . . . I've been waiting."

"It was a long journey. The only clues were in my memories, and you had those."

"My body should have ground to a halt winters ago. I've tried to die several times, but I was never allowed through. . . ."

I looked down at the baby. "Is she going to die?"

"That depends on you."

"I don't understand."

"My granddaughter's body is *your* body. She was born with *you* as her soul and mind. She is a shell. Her body will be dead within three hours if you don't return to her. If you want her to survive, you have to choose to be shackled by flesh and bones once more."

I considered my future as a *noncorpum*. Nowhere in the world would be closed to me. I could try to seek out other *noncorpa,* the company of immortals. I could transmigrate into presidents, astronauts, messiahs. I could plant a garden on a mountainside under camphor trees. I would never grow old, get sick, fear death, die.

I looked down at the feeble day-old body in front of me, her metabolism dimming, minute by minute. Life expectancy in Central Asia is forty-three, and falling.

"Touch her."

Outside, bats dangle from the high places, fluttering up to the sky, and down to the ground, and up to the sky again, checking that all is well. Inside, my wail, screamed from the hollows of my eighteen-hour-old lungs, fills the *ger.*

PETERSBURG

IT'S A LASHING bitch of a day out. Rain, rain, rain, the sky splits and spills. God Almighty, give me a cigarette.

Jerome was explaining the other day that, believe it or not, glass is actually a liquid that thickens at the bottom as the years pass. Glass is a thick syrup. But you never know where you are with Jerome. Rudi said that my bottom is getting thicker as the years go past, too, and he laughed for a whole minute.

I yawn a yawn so wide that my body shudders. Nobody notices. Nobody even recognizes me. If my presence intrudes on their grazing at all, they assume I'm a loin of lamb who slept her way into this meager sinecure on a plastic chair in a tiny gallery in the Large Hermitage. I don't mind. In fact that is precisely how I want it. I can bide my time. We have a lot of time, us Russians.

So then, ladies and gentlemen. Let us begin our safari of the more common gallery visitors. May I first introduce the shufflers. You will observe how this tribe shuffle in packs, from picture to picture, allotting each an equal period of time. Passing by are the big game hunters, for whom only the Cézannes, the Picassos, and the Monets will do. Watch out for their flashbulbs and pounce! You can fine 'em $5—hard currency—and who'll know a thing about it? The shamblers are less systematic. Usually lone hunters, they shamble zigzag through the halls, pausing for a long time when something catches their eyes. Over there! See him? A peeping Tom! There! Lurking behind the pedestals. Beware, ladies! Our friends of the weaker sex are here not to observe the ladies in the gilt frames, but the ones in the black fishnets. A few of the bolder ones steal glances at me. I outstare them. Margarita Latunsky has nothing to fear from any of them. Where were we? Ah yes, the sheep. You will hear them bleating in the background, herded by their guide and being told what to admire and why. Who is he, you ask, holding forth in a loud voice about what Agnolo Bronzino really meant to say half a millennium ago in Florence? He is a lecturer, exposing his erudition like a flasher in Smolnogo Park. I've been accosted myself on many occasions, beside the duck pond. "Bit small, isn't it?" They wither on the vine! Back to the gallery. A few times a day we get a visit from Lord God Almighty: one of the directors, strutting about like they own the place, which I suppose in a way they do. Or they think they do. Only I, and a chosen few, know what it is that they really own. Occasionally Jerome comes in with his notebook to study the next picture, but we pretend not to notice one another. We are professionals. Lastly there are the other gallery attendants, peroxided and lank, each on a chair for their fat butts. My butt isn't really fat, by the way. I made Rudi admit he was joking. The other attendants are slags and trollops, each and every one. Cave cranny-clammy. Oh, they scowl at me, and gossip about my understanding with the director of acquisitions, Head Curator Rogorshev. It isn't simply the jealousy of the jilted that makes them hate me. And I told them this. It's the jealousy that any menopausal frump feels towards a real woman.

None of them matters. None of them. I have higher things to consider.

Yes, it's been a cold, rainy summer in our cold, rainy city. Jerome said the only way Peter could get people to come and live in this marsh of frost and mud was to make it illegal for any builder to work anywhere else in his empire, from the Baltic to the Pacific. That, I can believe.

There's no one in my gallery now—the marble statue of Poseidon and these five pictures are no big crowd-pullers, even if one of them is a Delacroix—so I stand up and walk over to the window, to stretch my legs. You don't think Margarita Latunsky is going to sit still for seven hours flat, do you? The cold glass kisses the tip of my nose. Wall after wall of rain, driven up the Neva from the Baltic. Past the new oil refinery built by deutsche marks, past the docks, past the rusting naval station, past the Peter and Paul Fortress over on Zayachy Island where I first met Rudi, over the Leytenanta Schmidta bridge, where many years ago I used to drive with my politburo minister, sipping cocktails in the back of his big black Zil with the flags mounted above the headlamps. Come now, there's no need to act surprised. Remember who I am! There was no harm done; his wife was happy enough lying on a Black Sea beach with her limpid children. She probably had young goaty Cossack masseurs queueing up to ply her below the shoulder blades.

I turn my back to all that, spinning on my heel, and do a mazurka across the slippery wooden floor. I wonder, did they do that when Empress Catherine was in charge here? I can imagine her, maybe in this very room, dancing a few steps with the young Napoléon, or cavorting with the dashing composer Tolstoy, or tit-illating Gingghis Khan with a glimpse of the royal calf. I feel an affinity with any woman who has powerful and violent men suck-ing olives from between her toes. Empress Catherine started life as a lowly outsider, too, Jerome told me. I whirl, and spin, and I remember the applause I used to get at the Pushkin Theater.

I gaze into my next conquest. Our next conquest, I should say. *Eve and the Serpent* by Delacroix. Loot brought back from Berlin in 1945. Head Curator Rogorshev was saying how the Krauts want it all back now! What a nerve! We spend forty million lives getting rid of their nasty little Nazis for them, and all we get out of it is a few oil paintings. I've always had a soft spot for this one. It was I who proposed *Eve* be our next heist. Rudi wanted to go for something bigger, like an El Greco or one of the van Goghs, but Jerome thought we shouldn't get greedy.

"Go on, my dear," urges the snake. "Take one. Hear it? 'Pluck me,' it's saying. That big, shiny red one. 'Pluck me, pluck me now and pluck me hard.' You know you want to."

"But God," quotes Eve, putting out feelers for an *agent provo-cateur,* clever girl, "expressly forbids us to eat the fruit from the Tree of Knowledge."

"Ah yessssss, God . . . But God gave us life, did He not? And God gave us desire, did He not? And God gave us taste, did He not? And who else but God made the damned apples in the first place? So what else is *life* for but to *tassste* the *fruit* we *desire*?"

Eve folds her arms schoolgirlishly. "God expressly forbade it. Adam said."

The snake grins through his fangs, admiring Eve's playacting. "God is a nice enough chap in His way. I daresay He means well. But between me, you and the Tree of Knowledge, He is terribly insecure."

"Insecure? He made the entire bloody universe! He's omnipotent."

"Exactly! Almost neurotic, isn't it? All this worshiping, morning, noon, and night. It's 'Oh Praise Him, Oh Praise Him, Oh Praise the Everlassssting Lord.' I don't call that omnipotent. I call it pathetic. Most independent authorities agree that God has never sufficiently credited the work of virtual particles in the creation of the universsssse. He raises you and Adam on this diet of myths while all the really interesting information is locked up in these juicy apples. Seven days? Give me a break."

"Well, I see your point. But Adam will hit the frigging roof."

"Ah yess . . . your hairless, naked hubby. I saw him frolicking with a fleecy little lamb in a meadow just this morning. He looked so content. But how about you, Eve? Do you want to spend the rest of eternity noncing around with a family of docile animals and a supreme being who insists on choosing a name like 'Jehovah' to keep you company? I don't think so. Adam might be pissed off for a little while, but he'll change his tune when I show him bronze-tipped arrows, crocodile-skin luggage, and virtual-reality helmets. I think that you, Eve, are destined for higher thingsss."

Eve looks at the apple, a big cider apple hanging in the golden afternoon. She gulps. "Higher things? You mean, Forbidden Knowledge?"

The snake's tongue flickers. "No, Eve, my dear one. That's just a smoke screen. What we're really talking about here is *Desire*. Care for a cigarette while you think my proposal over?"

.   .   .

Footsteps echo down the stairs. I sit down, resuming my sentinel posture. I would die for that cigarette.

In walks Head Curator Rogorshev and the head of security, a troll with a face that always seems about to pop and splatter bystanders with gobbets of cranium.

"I thought we could approach the Great Hall by way of the Delacroix. Such an underrated little treasure!" Head Curator Rogorshev turns to me, tracing the inside of his lips with the tip of his tongue.

I simper like the virgin he likes me to be.

"I'll have to have all these fittings sniffed for explosives." The head of security snorts in once and out once, wiping his nose on his sleeve.

"Whatever. I know how the French ambassador loves to point at things with his stick." They walk on. At the door the head curator turns, blows me a kiss, points to his watch, and mouths "six o'clock." Then he flexes his index finger like his itty-bitty hard-on.

I flash him a look that says "Oh yes, oh *yes*! Stop before I *explode*!"

He trots after the security man, thinking, "Ooh, Head Curator Rogorshev, you cunning rogue, you master of seduction, another female of the species caught in your web." The truth is, Head Curator Rogorshev is a master of only one thing, and that is the art of kidding himself. Look at him! That shock of shiny black hair? I glue it on myself every Monday. There will come a time, not long from now, when he will see whose web he has been stuck in during the last year. And so will the Serious Crime Police Squad.

My birthday is coming soon. Another one. That explains why Rudi has been too busy to see me recently. He knows how I love surprises.

Gutbucket Petrovich comes to take my place while I go for a tea break. They dropped me off the rota once, and left me sitting in my gallery for a whole day. I made Rogorshev sack the ringleader.

None of them ever speaks to me now, but they never forget my tea break.

The staff canteen is empty. The catering workers have already gone home by the time my break comes around, so I am all alone in the echoing hall. The Gutbucket crew considers this ostracism a victory, but it suits me. I make myself a cup of my own American coffee and smoke my favorite French cigarettes. The soft flame ignites the tinder-dry tip and I suck and—Ah! As exquisite as being shot! I know how much my dear co-workers would adore the merest puff of this cigarette, so I like to leave the room perfumed.

I can see Dvortsovaya Square from here. A whirlpool of wet cobbles. It takes two minutes just to walk across. A dwarf is running after his umbrella; he'll cover it in one.

How dare those dairy cows come on so pious with me? The fact is they are stewing with jealousy that I possess the basic female skills to net my men, while they do not. They can't net their hair. I admit that my little understanding with Head Curator Rogorshev brings me my privileges, quite beside its place in the grander plan, but if they could, any of those warty hags would die for these privileges quicker than you could say "knickers around your ankles." Yes, even Gutbucket Petrovich, with her frothy new pan-scrubber hairstyle and lardy thighs.

When Petersburg was Leningrad, I could have had the whole ruddy lot posted to the middle of fucking nowhere! Further than nowhere! They'd have been shipped out wholesale to mind a museum in the Gobi desert and live in *gerts!*

I was the concubine of two powerful men, you see. First, a politician. I'm not going to tell you his name: he was as high as you could get in the Politburo without being knocked off as a potential threat. High enough to know the codes to nuclear warheads. He could have ended the world if he'd wanted to, virtually. He pulled some strings at the Party Office for me and got me a lovely little apartment overlooking Alexandra Nevskogo Square. When he died suddenly of a heart attack, I selected for my next lover an admiral in the Pacific Fleet. Of course, I was given a new apartment—and the lifelong lease—that befitted an admiral's station. I still live there now, near Anichkov Bridge, down Fontanki Embankment. He was very affectionate, my admiral. Just between you and me, I think he used to try a little too hard. He'd try to outdo the presents that the politician had bought for me. He was terribly possessive. My men always are.

My God, were those ever the days.

"Lymko," I'd say, "I'm a little cold when we go to the ballet at night. . . ." And the very next morning a mink coat would be delivered. "Lymko, I need a little sparkle in my life. . . ." I'd show you the diamond brooch that came, but I had to sell it to set up a business venture of Rudi's, back in our early days, you understand. It would have made Gutbucket Petrovich's jaw drop so far that she wouldn't be able to shut her mouth for a week. "Lymko, so-and-so at the Party department store was quite beastly last week. Quite improper. I wouldn't want to get anyone into trouble, but he said things about your professional integrity that hurt me deeply. . . ." And the next morning so-and-so would discover that he had been promoted to junior cleaner in the public shit-houses around Lake Baikal. Everyone knew about me, but everyone played along to keep the peace. Even his wife, kept out in the naval base at Vladivostok with her clutch of admiral brats.

Another cigarette. The ashtray is already half-full. The dwarf never caught his umbrella.

Back on my plastic chair. I'm almost groaning with boredom. I'm forced to play this game of patience, dying of a lack of interest, day after day after day. The end of the afternoon staggers into view. I'm hungry and I need a vodka. Rogorshev has his own secret bottle. I count the seconds. Forty minutes times sixty seconds, that's twenty-four thousand seconds to go. There's no point looking outside to relieve the boredom. I already know the view. The Dvortsovaya embankment, the Neva, the Petrograd side. I'd get Head Curator Rogorshev to change my gallery, but Rudi says no, not now that we're so close to the big night. Jerome agrees with him for once, so I'm stuck here.

Strange to think, us Russians once mattered in the world. Now *we* have to go begging for handouts. I'm not a political woman—thinking about politics was too damned dangerous when I was growing up. Besides, what was this Union of Soviet Socialist Republics, really? "Republics" need real elections and I never saw any of those, I damn well never heard of any "Soviets"—I'm not even sure what one is. "Socialism" means the common people own the country, and all my mother ever owned was her intestinal parasites. And where was the "union"? Us Russians pouring roubles into these pointless little countries full of people eating snakes and babies all over Asia just to stop the Chinks or the Arabs getting their hands on them? That's not what I call a *union*. That's what I call buying up the neighbors. An empire by default. But could we ever kick ass in those days! Jerome told me that some schoolkids in Europe have never even *heard* of the USSR! "Listen, *meine kinder*," I'd tell 'em, "about this country you've never heard of, we used to have enough nuclear bombs to make your side of the Berlin Wall glow beet-red for the next ten thousand years. Just be grateful. You could have been born with the arms of a mushroom and a bag of pus for a head, if you'd been born at all. Think about it."

But sometimes, I wonder if much has changed at all, since Scumbag Gorbachev. Sure, for the common people, their floorboards rotted through and down they fell. At the top, I mean. The same people who shredded their Party membership cards now wheel out the democracy bullshit slogans by the steaming cartload—"flair and verve in the strategizing stages," "originality in capital manipulation," "streamlining and restructuring." The letters I type out for Head Curator Rogorshev are full of it. But really, where's the difference? It is now what it's always been. Recognizing the real but invisible goalposts, and using whatever means are at your disposal to score. These means might be in a bank vault in Geneva, in a hard disk in Hong Kong, encased in your skull or in the cups of your bra. No, nothing's changed. You used to pay off your local Party thug, now you pay off your local mafia thug. The old Party used to lie, and lie, and lie some more. Now our democratically elected government lies, and lies, and lies some more. The people used to want things, and were told, work and wait for twenty years, and then maybe it'll be your turn. The people still want things, and are told, work, and wait for twenty years, and then maybe it'll be your turn. Where's the difference?

I'm going to tell you a secret. Everything is about wanting. Everything. Things happen because of people wanting. Watch closely, and you'll see what I mean.

But like I said, I'm not a political woman. The things you think of, sitting here.

I recognized Head Curator Rogorshev's footsteps striding down the corridor outside—with the footsteps of a woman. I heard him telling her the same jokes he had told me months before while I was seducing him, and I heard her laughter flutter, just like mine had. It's a very special talent that men have, to possess seeing eyes yet be so blind.

"And here," Head Curator Rogorshev said, wheeling a tall leggy woman into my gallery, "you'll doubtless recognize *Eve and the Serpent* by Lemuel Delacroix." He winked clumsily at me, like I couldn't see what was going on.

She was repulsed by the head curator—a sign of good taste—but she hid it well. Western clothing, French boots, an Italian handbag. Dark, a touch of Arabia in the shape of her eyes. Thirty or thirty-one, but to men like Rogorshev she would look younger. No eyeshadow, rouge, or foundation, but well-chosen mulberry lipstick. Interesting. I had a rival. Good.

"Ms. Latunsky, this is Tatyana Makuch. Tatyana will be with us on release from the Stanislow Art Museum in Warsaw for the next six weeks. We're very lucky to have her."

Tatyana walked over to me, her boots creaking slightly. I stood up. We were the same height. We looked into one another's eyes, and shook hands slowly. Blue.

"Charmed," I said. "Truly."

"Delighted," she replied. "Sincerely." What a rich voice. Polish-flavored Russian. Coffee with chocolate in it.

"Head Curator Rogorshev," I said without looking at him, "shall I still come to your office at the usual time this evening? Or will Miss Makuch be taking over your personal dictations from now on?"

Tatyana spoke first, with just the right half-smile. "It's *Mrs.*
Makuch. And I'm afraid my talents don't extend to secretarial
skills."

She was good. She was very good.

"It's all right, Ms. Latunsky," Head Curator Rogorshev was
saying to me, as if he had any say in the matter. "Please come at
the usual hour. I have some important dispatches I wish to
make—" God, he spreads it on thick—"and I know only you can
perform to my satisfaction." He got his lines from lunchtime dra-
mas. "Please come along now, Mrs. Makuch, we must complete
our whirlwind tour before the clock strikes six and I turn into a
werewolf!"

"We'll be seeing each other," Tatyana said.

"We will be."

A quarter to six. We were shooing out the lingerers. The rain
won't stop and the minutes won't leave. Head Curator Rogorshev
will be prettying himself up in his private washroom now. Not
many men get to manicure their own corpse. A cigarette would be
nice. Jesus Christ, the sooner Rudi and I get out of this damned
place the better. I say to Rudi, "Look! Let's just bag ten whoppers
in one night! Some Picassos, some Cézannes, some El Grecos, and
in seventy-two hours we could be shopping for chalets in Switzerland on the money we've already got, and sell off pieces of the
golden goose year by year." Lakes, yachts, waterskiing in the summer. I've already designed my boudoir. I'm going to have a full-
length leopard-skin coat. The locals will call me the White Russian
Lady, and all the women will be jealous and warn their cheese-
making financier husbands against me. But they won't need to
worry. I'll have Rudi. Away from all the distractions of the lowlife
here, I know he'll straighten out. When the weather is warm, he'll
teach our children to swim, and when it's cold we'll all go skiing.
As a family.

"Let's do it! Gregorski can get the visas ready," I say. "It's so
simple!"

"It's not simple at all!" he says. "Forget the fact you're a
woman and use your brain! The reason it's worked so far is that

we haven't been greedy. If we lift pictures at a faster rate than Jerome can replace them, people notice they are missing! And for every single picture that is missing, multiply by ten the number of pigs Interpol puts on the case! Multiply by twenty the payoffs I have to dish out! Multiply by thirty the difficulty I have in finding buyers! And multiply by fifty the years we'll get in the slammer!"

"It's all very well for you to lecture me in arithmetic; it's not you who has to get skewered by that bald porker every week!"

Then Rudi really bawls me out and, if he's been drinking, slaps me about a bit, just a bit, because of the drink, and he storms out and goes for a drive and I might not see him for a couple of days. He's under a lot of pressure.

"I love you!" yells Head Curator Rogorshev, jockeying up and down with my bra strap wrapped around his windpipe. "Rabbit's coming! Oh, gobble me and be spliced, my fairy cake. I gobble you and devour you! Bunny's coming! Destroy me, my whore, my master, I love you!"

I know he's imagining I'm Tatyana. That's fine. I make it tolerable by imagining he is Rudi. I hope he'll finish soon so I can have a cigarette. I'll steal some of his Cuban cigars for Rudi, to impress his business contacts. I wrap my legs around his hippo girth to hasten the end. He groans like a kid on an out-of-control go-cart hurtling down a hill, and mercifully soon comes the hanged-man gasp and the legs on his eighteenth-century chaise longue stop squeaking.

"God, my God, I love you." He kisses the flat bone between my breasts. For a moment I wonder if he means it, whether there is an alchemy that turns lust to love. "You're not jealous of Tatyana, are you? She could never replace you, you know, Margarita, my love. . . ."

I blow a smoke ring and watch it spinning into the corners of his office, where the evening is thickening. I imagine a circle of wild swans and pat his toupee-less pate. He doesn't even bother to take his socks off these days. His portrait—farcically flattering— stares down from behind the desk. Quite the man of destiny.

All alchemists were frauds and liars, but it doesn't matter. I'll work on Rudi. He doesn't know it yet but we'll be spending Christmas in Zurich.

Head Curator Rogorshev always leaves first. He showers in his private office bathroom so his wife can pretend nothing is happening, and I might do a little paperwork for the sake of appearances. I hear him, singing and shampooing me down the plug hole. He puts on a new shirt, kisses me to show me he cares, and goes off. I might do some invoicing for Rudi's cleaning company, or make Jerome out a new pass, or some free passes for Rudi's clients. Or I might just stare out of the window at the cupolas of St. Andrew's Cathedral. I usually leave around 7:30. Jerome wants the guards to stay used to seeing me around after hours.

"Nothing to declare tonight?" The head of security at the staff exit grins his buttery grin. I wish I could be around to see it dribble off his chin when the shit explodes. He knows about my affair with Rogorshev, and has the hots for me himself. Of course, it's a part of the plan for everyone to know. He body-searches me! Me, Margarita Latunsky! Him, an ex-army malingerer who thinks shiny badges and a walkie-talkie make him Rambo. I feel his hands lingering longer than they should. I think of ways I could incriminate him from Zurich.

"No, Chief," I demur, a wary little stray, "no stolen masterpieces tonight."

"Good girl. The floor polishers are due. . . ."

"Not for three weeks. Three weeks today. 9:30 P.M."

"Three weeks today." He ticks a clipboard and waves me through. I feel his eyes pucker my body as I walk away. He is repulsive, but I can't blame him. I've always had this mystical allure to men.

In the winter, I take the metro. Otherwise, I prefer to walk. If the weather's fine I walk up to the Troisky Bridge, and then cross the Mars Fields, where the women wait. But if it's raining I walk down Nevsky Prospect, a street of ghosts if there ever was one. Jerome says that every city has its street of ghosts. Past the

Stroganov Palace and the Kazan Cathedral. Past the Aeroflot offices, and the scrubby Armenian Café. Past the flat where I made love to my Politburo member. It's been turned into an American Express office now. All these new shops, Benetton, the Häagen-Dazs shop, Nike, Burger King, a shop that sells nothing but camera film and key-rings, another that sells Swatches and Rolexes. High streets are becoming the same all over the world, I suppose. In the subway is an orderly row of beggars and buskers. I buy a pack of cigarettes from a kiosk, and a little bottle of vodka. Surely buskers in no other city on Earth can hold a candle to ours. A saxophonist, a string quartet, a wisp of a woman playing a didgeridoo, and a Ukrainian choir all competing for spare roubles. Sometimes I give money to the priests. I don't know why, they've never given anything to me. The beggars often hold cards on which is written their own particular sob story, often with translations in different languages. Only visitors to the city bother to read them. Petersburg is built of sob stories, pile-driven down into the mud.

Go over the Anchikov Bridge and turn left. Mine is four down. Through the heavy iron door, past the cabin where the porter is sleeping—a quick look in my mailbox where, to my surprise, there's a letter from my dear, ailing sister—across the weedy courtyard and up three flights of stairs. If Rudi's at home the TV is turned up loud. Rudi can't abide silence. Tonight it's all quiet. We had the little disagreement about our leaving date yesterday evening, so he's decided to concentrate on business for a little, I suppose. That's fine. I cook the fish that I bought for our dinner, and leave him half in the pot in case he comes home later. He's never away for more than one or two nights. Not usually.

The White Nights are here. Bluish midnight dims to indigo at about two. The sun will rise again a little later without pomp. I stay in my living room and think about the past and about Switzerland. This is where my admiral and I made love. Under this very window. He used to tell me stories of the ocean, Sakhalin, the White Sea, submarines under the ice. We watched the stars come out. I pile the washing-up in the sink and light a mosquito coil. I put the Cuban cigars in Rudi's coat pocket so he'll find them and think about me. I can hear jazz playing some-where. There was a time when I would have gone and found it and danced and been admired, desired. Men's faces shone. They vied for the next dance.

I light another cigarette and pour myself a brandy. Just a small one, and not the best bottle. Rudi needs that for when his business partners come over for meetings. I set fire to my sister's letter, unopened, and lay it in the ashtray. That'll teach her. Sipping my brandy I watch the front of flame turn the bitch's words into a ribbon of smoke. Rise, spiral, and disappear, up, and up, and up.

The jazz has stopped. Rudi still isn't home. Little Nemya, fed and happy, comes and curls up on my lap, falling asleep as I tell her my troubles.

Jerome is making tea. His movements are clockwork, like a but-ler's. Rudi is late again. Rudi is usually late by three quarters of an hour. It's a beautiful summer's day around lunchtime, and the streets and parks of Vasilevsky Island are shimmering in the heat as though underwater.

"What gives the tea that smell?"

Jerome thinks for a moment. "I don't know the Russian for it. In English it's called 'bergamot.' It's the rind of a species of cit-rus."

I just say, "I see. Nice teacup."

Jerome hands me a cup, on a saucer, and sits down. His Rus-sian is fluent, but I never know what to say to him. "This bone china is a last surviving luxury," he says, "real Wedgwood. It should be worth a lot, but since your civilization fell into its own basement bin I probably couldn't even get a tin of tuna for it. Don't drop it."

"I've never broken a beautiful thing in my life," I tell him.

"I'm sure that might be true. Anyway," Jerome stands up again, "since our *nouveau riche* Robert De Niro has better things to do, allow me to give you a private view of my handiwork." He goes into the next room, his studio, and I hear things being shunted across the floorboards. A camphor tree swims in the sun in the little park next to St. Andrew's Cathedral. Over the Ley-tenanta Bridge on Angliyaskaya Embankment a new Holiday Inn is being constructed. Today is Heroes' Day, so nobody is on the scaffolding. I hear a sports car being revved to a roar and a sudden screech of brakes.

"Ah," Jerome calls through. "Sounds like Rudi."

Jerome's apartment is sparse, in a not unpleasant part of the city. Not as well situated as mine, of course. On stuffy days when the wind is from the north you can smell the chemical factory, but other than that it's not so bad. It's bigger than my apartment, if you include his studio—though he never lets anyone into his studio. The living room is dominated by the largest liquor cabinet I've ever heard of. It dominates the room like a cathedral altar in a country chapel. Apparently it was a present from Leonid Brezhnev. Jerome keeps the place tidier than a woman would. But Jerome has never had a woman here, or anywhere else, I imagine. I wonder if all English men are so orderly, or whether it's only English queers. Jerome was a spy in the Cold War. He used to lecture in art history at Cambridge University. Moscow hasn't paid his war pension for six or seven years now, and he's wanted for treason in Britain, so he's scuppered. He always talks about selling his memoirs, but ex-spies trying to flog their stories are two-a-rouble these days. His only marketable talent is his ability to paint copies of masterpieces. That's why he's a member of our circle. I notice a shiny, maroon flying jacket that could not possibly belong to tall, spindly Jerome. I need a cigarette, so I light one. There's nothing to use as an ashtray, so I have to use the saucer. From a nearby room I can hear a piano.

Jerome returns, unveiling the picture, tutting at my cigarette.

Eve and the Serpent, not by Lemuel Delacroix, but by Jerome . . . I don't know his family name. Smith or Churchill, probably. I've never much liked Jerome, but I have to admire his craftsmanship. "I can't see how anyone could tell them apart. Even the way the gilt on the frame is worn away on the bottom."

"I can't quite get the cracks in the glaze right, not quite. And there are secrets in the blue pigment that got lost in the nineteenth century, and not even Gregorski's money can procure them. No, it's not perfect. But it will do. Nobody is going to be looking for a difference until it's too late."

"You've spent twice as long on this one, compared to the last."

"Well, my dear, that's Russian Constructivism for you! Kandinsky's an absolute cinch, from a copyist's point of view. Just measure the proportions of the stripes, get the tone right, slap on the paint, and bingo! No, Delacroix deserves more than that. . . . You could call it a labor of love, this one. I would have liked a fortnight more, just to tamper, but Gregorski's chomping at the bit for another sting this month. I could *die* to get my hands on the original, though, even if it's only to look after it overnight. Moreover, the Delacroix is worth enough to let me raise the *Titanic* and buy up Bermuda."

"A quarter of Bermuda," I reminded him. "Split four ways."

"Did you know that Delacroix was a friend of Nicholas I? He was employed by the tsar several summers running to help decorate the Cathedral of Our Savior. A westerner in service to the Russian state. Maybe that helps to explain the empathy I feel with the man." When Jerome rattles on like this, I feel I'm no longer in the room with him.

A coded knock at the door. I wait for the sequence to finish, rolling my eyeballs at this pantomime. The code is correct, but Jerome waves me through into the kitchen anyway, his finger on his lips. I suppose old habits die hard. "Open up!" says Rudi, just like he always does. "It's drafty out here." Jerome relaxes. The word "drafty" indicates that Rudi is alone and hasn't got a gun pointed in the small of his back. "Cold" means "get away." Exactly how you would get out of a sixth-floor apartment with one entrance and no fire escape is another matter. But boys will be boys.

"Babe," Rudi greets me, breezing in and handing Jerome a pizza he picked up from one of his restaurants. His new suede jacket is the color of black currant juice. He likes to call me "babe," even though he is younger than me by eight or nine years. He's smiling. A good sign. He takes off his wraparound sunglasses, and whoops at the picture. "Jerome, even better than your normal high standard!"

Jerome mock-bows. "How good of you to drop by!" Rudi never sees Jerome's irony, leaving it to me to feel offended for him. "Yes, thank you. I am rather pleased with my production. How did the meeting with our public guardian friend at the City Hall go?"

"Gregorski's cool. He'll send someone over to pick up the Delacroix here the morning after."

Right then, it felt wrong. "Why aren't you meeting the buyers directly this time?"

Rudi lifted his hand like the Pope. "Helsinki's a long way to go, babe. . . . Why not let them come here? It's a sign we're moving up. It also means I don't have to risk my neck at the border. . . . Oh, kitten, I missed you last night. . . ." There was a silliness to Rudi's grin. A landslipped cocaine silliness. A bad sign. He tried to grab my breasts, but I didn't let myself be grabbed, and Rudi fell onto the sofa laughing. "Tell her, Jerome!"

"Tell her what?" Jerome came through with plates and a knife for the pizza.

"Gregorski's on the level."

Jerome frowned. "If he's not, and chooses to sell us up the river, we will be royally butt-fucked from here to Windsor."

Rudi's smile shriveled up like a burning page. "Jesus Christ, what's the matter with you two today? The sun's shining, in two weeks—and forty-eight hours—we're going to be two hundred thousand dollars richer, and here you two are looking like you've had to sell your mother to a body-donor peddler! The point is for Mr. High-and-fucking-Mighty Gregorski, if we're not on the level, *he* is the butt-fucked. He's not dealing with tadpoles anymore. I have muscle in this city. I have muscle outside this city. I have muscle."

"Oh, St. Ciaran above, nobody's disputing that—" began Jerome, making the mistake of sounding martyred.

Rudi's eyes began to shine. "Dead, damned, fucking right nobody is disputing that! *Kirsch* is not disputing that! *Shirliker* and his associates are not disputing that! Arturo fucking *Kopeck* is not disputing that! You know who Arturo Kopeck is? Only the *biggest— fucking*—crack dealer east of Berlin and west of the Urals! So why are my own *partners* disputing the notion that *I* have more *muscle* than Boris fucking *Frankenstein?*"

Jerome's owl gaze. "Nobody's disputing that. Are we, Margarita?"

My poor, dear baby. Bad cocaine. "No, Rudi. Nobody's doing any disputing."

Rudi seemed to suddenly forget what we'd been talking about. "Any tabasco sauce, Jerome? That dumb Georgian bitch forgot to put any on. Big tits, gives a good blow job, but dippy as horseshit. Remind me to sack her before she gets too far behind on her rent."

"I'll get the tabasco," I said, smiling at Rudi's little joke. "And shall I make you some nice strong coffee?"

He didn't bawl "no" so that meant "yes."

We ate in silence until half the pizza was gone.

"There's one last little touch," said Rudi, "that I've decided to introduce for the next pickup."

"Do tell," said Jerome.

"Margarita here meets us and the other cleaners at the staff entrance, instead of waiting for me in the gallery."

"I don't see why," I said.

"That is precisely why I am the brains of this operation. You never see why, and I always do. Listen. You come and meet us. The girls go off to their allotted galleries separately. We go to the Delacroix Gallery. As usual, we make the switch, wax the floors, take it back to the staff entrance, and out through security. And what precisely is the difference?"

Jerome picked prawns out of congealing cheese. "You've been accompanied the whole time by Winter Palace personnel. Are there any anchovies hiding down here?"

"And therefore placing me even more above suspicion than usual!" Rudi swished his wine around the glass. "These little details are the Rudi Touch. This is why my outfit thrives the way it does. This is why Gregorski selected me for this cleaning contract, why he wanted me for this operation: not Kirsch, not Chekhov, not the Koenighovs, but me. Now. Any questions?"

Jerome shook his head nonchalantly. His part was over now. A pleasant life he must have, playing around all day with his oil paints, waiting for the money to appear in his bank account. His own bank account.

"Rudi, my darling . . . ," I began.

"What do you want?"

"I was wondering, when, exactly, we were thinking of . . ."

". . . of what?"

"You know, what we've been discussing. . . ."

Rudi's emotions are so visible. He doesn't try to hide anything from me. That's one reason I love him. He slammed his plate down and the pizza skidded off.

"Oh Jesus wept! Not again! Don't get old on me again, Margarita! I will not have you getting old and weird and wrinkled on me again! Fuck, you make me feel like it's my grandmother I'm shagging sometimes!"

I love Rudi, but I hate him too when his eyes shine like that. It's the bad cocaine. "What are we getting all this money for if we're never going to use it?"

"Is it a car you want? Is it a coat you want? Are you in debt to somebody again? Tell me who's been lending you money! Who? *Who!*"

"No, nobody, nobody! It's—" I looked at Jerome, who, sighing, withdrew into his studio, taking his coffee.

"—it's you I want, my love. It's our life in Switzerland that I want."

"A golden goose is living on our roof and shitting eggs down our chimney, here, Margarita! Don't kill it! Gather the golden eggs!"

"I'm the one who gets screwed every week for these golden eggs."

"We all have to make sacrifices."

"I don't know how much longer I'm prepared to keep making mine. Surely we have enough money in the account now for us to not need to—"

"We haven't. I had to bribe the customs people a small fortune last time. Then of course I have to give Gregorski his whopping cut. He set the whole thing up, remember."

"I never get the chance to forget Gregorski, in his armored Mercedes-Benz. Please, darling. Just tell me. How much money do we have?"

"It's your period, isn't it. Admit it. It's your period. Jesus. They bleed for seven days but they still don't die."

"How much?"

"Quite a lot. But not enough."

"How much is quite a lot? Just tell me!"

"Margarita, if you can't calm down and discuss this like an intelligent adult I'm going to have to terminate this interview."

"I am calm. I'm asking a simple question. Rudi? How much money do we have from the sale of our five priceless works of art sold so far? Please?"

"In U.S. dollars? Six figures."

"Tell me!"

Rudi switched tack. "I manage the finances! It's your job to get us in and keep us covered! You think you can do what I do better, do you? *Do you?*"

It's the cocaine, and the pressure. I stayed calm, and started the pout. Margarita Latunsky plays men like a master violinist. When I want something from a woman I get angry. When I want something from a man I pout. "No, darling, it's just that the head curator paws me week after week and I can't see an end to it and I love you so much—" I feigned the watery eyes.

Rudi snarled and looked around like he needed something to sink his teeth into. "You want out? You want to go up to a man like Gregorski and say, 'Oh, by the way, I don't fancy this line of work any more, thanks for all the stolen artwork revenue but I'm off now, I'll send you a postcard'? Get real, woman! He'd eat you for fucking breakfast."

I thought he was going to hit me. "I thought that's why we chose Switzerland, because it would be safe—"

"It's not that simple. Gregorski's a powerful man."

"I know about powerful men—"

Rudi mimicked me. "'I know about powerful men.' You're talking about the Party crony paper-pusher who used to shag you? Or your geriatric cabin boy with the gammy leg?"

"He was a captain."

Rudi spat a "huh!" "What do you know about hiding money? Laundering it? I can give you your share any time you like, *baby,* but how long do you think it would be after you split, before the pigs in Switzerland ask exactly how you came across this truck-load of roubles you're bringing into their country? We are a team! You can't just walk out on us any time you fancy."

"When can we go?"

"In time! In time! Fuck it! It's no fucking use trying to reason with you when you're in this kind of mood. I'm going for a drive!"

He slammed the door behind him.

Jerome emerged. "He didn't damage the Wedgwood, did he?"

"He's nervous," I explain. "Now we're so close to getting away, it's only natural he gets a little jittery. . . ."

Jerome said something in English.

Today is my birthday.

My feet shouldn't ache so much, not at my age.

As I climbed the stairs back up to my flat I heard my phone ringing. I fumbled for my key and skidded down the hallway. You see? I understand him, that's why I forgive him. That's why I'm not like the other women who take advantage of him.

"I'm back." I was breathless—

"Hello? Miss Latunsky? I hope you don't mind me telephoning you at home. This is Tatyana Makuch, from the gallery. Have I called at a bad time?"

I fought to control my panting, and to keep the disappointment out of my voice. "No, no, I just got back, I've been running."

"Oh . . . jogging in the park?"

"I mean I was running to catch the phone. To get the phone."

"Are you busy this afternoon?"

"Yes. No. Maybe. Why?"

"I'm lonely. I was wondering if we could meet and I could buy you a coffee, or if you'd like to come to visit my shoe box and I could cook you authentic Warsaw Vorsch."

Tatyana? I heard myself saying, "Yes." When was I going to

make it up with Rudi? But there again, why should he find me here pining for him when he gets back? Maybe it would do him good just to pretend that I don't need him as much as I do. Teach him a little lesson.

"Great. You know the coffee shop behind the Pushkin Theater?"

"Yes—"

"Excellent. I'll meet you there in an hour."

That was that. Nemya padded in and jumped onto my lap for some adoration. I told Nemya about Rudi's tantrum, and about what Switzerland was going to be like, and I wondered why I'd just agreed to give the rest of my day off to a supercilious rival from Poland.

The empty café smelt of dark wood and coffee. Dust motes eddied through slats of sunlight as I barged open the door. A bell jangled and a radio was playing in the back room. Tatyana hadn't arrived yet, even though I was late.

"Hello, Margarita."

Tatyana shifted slightly and came into the light. Her hair shone gold. She was dressed in a smart black velvet suit and her body was lean and tucked in. I had to admit, I could see the appeal. To men like Rogorshev.

"I didn't see you."

"Here I am. Well, won't you sit down? Thank you very much for coming. What would you like to drink? The Colombian blend is excellent."

Was she trying to impress me? "Then I'll have the Colombian blend, when the waitress wakes up."

A man appeared from the back. "The Colombian?" A strong Ukrainian accent.

"Yes."

He sucked in his cheeks, and disappeared again.

Tatyana smiled. "Were you surprised when I called you?" A psychotherapist's tone.

"Mildly. Should I have been?"

She offered me a cigarette. I offered her a Benson and

Hedges. She took one but didn't admire it, like any Russian would have done. Benson and Hedges must be commonplace in Poland. I let her light mine.

"How long have you been working at the Hermitage, Margarita?"

"About a year now."

"You must have some cozy contacts there." Despite myself I liked her smile. She was being nosy, but only because she wanted to be friendly.

Margarita Latunsky can take girls like Tatyana in her stride. "You mean the head curator? Oh dear, have the Gutbucket herd been gossiping again?"

"I get the impression they'd gossip about grass growing in a ditch."

"My relationship with the head curator is an open secret. But it started after I came. I got the job through some connections my—I have, in the city hall. There's no harm. I'm single, and his marriage is not my problem."

"I quite agree. We have a lot in common in our attitudes."

"You said you were *Mrs.* Makuch?"

Tatyana made a whirlpool of cream in her coffee. "Can you keep a secret?"

"I can keep secrets very safe indeed. . . ."

"I tell people like Rogorshev that just to keep them off my back. The situation's more complicated than that. . . ." I waited for her to go on, but she didn't. "So then, Margarita. Tell me about your life. I want to know everything."

Eight hours later we were very drunk, at least I knew that I was, hunched over a back table at the Shamrock Pub on Dekabristov Street. A trio of Cubans were playing jazz snaky and slow, and there were man-high plants with rubbery leaves everywhere. The place was lit by candles, which is one of the scrimpiest ways to save money while pretending to be chic known to the entertainment business, and it occurred to me that whenever I was with Tatyana the light was bad. Tatyana knew a lot about jazz, and a lot about wine, which made me believe there was more money in her background than she was letting on. She was also insisting on paying for everything. I refused three times, but Tatyana insisted four times, which came as something of a relief, I admit. I hate asking Rudi for money.

She knew a lot about a lot of things. A black man stood up on stage, and played a trumpet with a mute. Tatyana glowed, and I saw how beautiful she was. I imagined a deep tragedy in her past. I know from my own life, severe beauty can be a handicap. "More like Miles Davis than Miles Davis," she murmured.

"Wasn't he the first man to fly across the Atlantic?"

She hadn't heard me. "The brassy sun lost behind the clouds."

We were attracting a lot of attention from the men. As well we might. Tatyana was undoubtedly a rare creature in these climes, and for my part, well, you already know the caliber of man Margarita Latunsky draws hither. Even the trumpeter was giving me the eye over his shiny horn, I swear it. I wondered what it would be like to do it with a black man. Arabs and Orientals and Americans I've had dalliances with, yes, but never a black.

Three young couples came in and sat down near the front. They must have still been in their teens. The boys in borrowed suits, trying to look sophisticated. The girls, trying to look at ease. All of them looking awkward.

Tatyana nodded at the six. "Young love." Her voice had a serrated edge.

"Wouldn't you change places with them, if you could?"

"Why on Earth would I want to do that?"

"They look so fine, and young, and wrapped up in each other. Love is so fresh and clean at that age. Don't you think?"

"Margarita! I'm surprised at you! We both know there's no such thing as love."

"What do you call it?"

Tatyana snuffed out her cigarette. That sly smile. "Mutations of wanting."

"You're not serious."

"I am quite serious. Look at those kids. The boys want to get the girls to bed so they can have the corks popped off their bottles, and gush forth. When a man blows his nose you don't call it love.

Why get all misty-eyed when a man blows another part of his anatomy? As for the girls, they're either going along for the ride because they can get things they want from their boys, or else maybe they enjoy being in bed too. Though I doubt it. I never knew an eighteen-year-old boy who didn't drop the egg off his spoon at the first fence."

"But that's lust! You're talking about lust, not love."

"Lust is the hard sell. Love is the soft sell. The profit margin is exactly the same."

"But love's the opposite of self-interest. True, tender love is pure and selfless."

"No. True, tender love is self-interest so sinewy that it only looks selfless."

"I've known love—I know love—and it is giving and not taking. We're not just animals."

"We're only animals. What does the head curator give to you?"

"I'm not talking about him."

"Whoever. But think. Why do you think any man really loves you? If you're honest with yourself, Margarita, the answer will be that he stands to gain in some way. Tell me. Why does he love you, and why do you love him back?"

I shook my head. "We're talking about love. There is no 'why.' That's the point."

"There is always a 'why,' because there is always something that the beloved wants. It might be that he protects you. It might be that he makes you feel special. It might be that he is a way out, a route to some shining future away from the dreary now. It might be that he is the father of your unborn babies. Or it might be that he gives you prestige. Love is a big knot of 'why's.'"

"What's wrong with that?"

"I'm not saying anything's wrong with it. History is made of people's desires. But that's why I smile when people get sentimental about this mysterious force of pure 'love' which they think they are steering. 'Loving somebody' means 'wanting something.' Love makes people do selfish, moronic, cruel, and inhumane things. You asked, would I like to change place with those kids? It would be nice to steal their twenties off them, sure, if I could transmigrate into them with my present mind intact, but otherwise I'd rather change places with a terrier in the zoo. To be in love is to be at the mercy of your lover's desires. If someone put a bullet through your lover, they'd be releasing you."

I watched a horrible image of a bath plug being yanked from Rudi's chest, and blood gushing out. "If someone put a bullet through my lover I would kill them."

The pub is jumping around too much, and the music throbs in my eyes so they run. Tatyana says, "Let's go outside," and suddenly we are, and I've been swept over a waterfall and down I plummet into the late light. The streets are filled with shadows and brightness and footsteps and candy-colors and tramlines and swallows. I've never noticed the windows above the Glinka Capella, how graceful they are. What are those things called? Jerome would know. Flying buttresses? The stars are not quite there tonight. A light is moving among them. A comet, or an angel, or the last decrepit Soviet space station falling down to Earth? Some passersby look at me askance, so I straighten myself up to show them I can walk straight, and the neck of a lamppost swings down like a giraffe's. One of the office lights is on. Somebody is being wanted by the head curator, but it's not me, and it's not Tatyana, not tonight. We walk past a dark car. "Oy, love, how much for the pair of you?" I spit at the window and summon up my foulest curses, but Tatyana whisks me onwards.

"Come on," says Tatyana, "let's go back to my place for some coffee. I can make us some hot dogs. I'll squeeze some sweet mustard onto yours, if you're a good Margarita." Everywhere I look, you could frame it and just by doing that you'd have a picture. Not a Jerome picture. A real picture, more real than the ones we steal. Even they are just copies. Jerome's are copies of copies. That boy's head. The wishing well. All those girls in green eyeshadow and apricot blusher, being herded into the back of the police van, whisked off to the cop shop, to be fined fifteen dollars before being released. They'll have to work extra hard for the rest of the night to make up for lost time. This is where the tsar was blown up, my mother told me a long time ago, and I say it now to Tatyana, but Tatyana didn't hear me, because my words forgot their names. The firecrackers going off in a distant quarter, or might they be gunshots? That would be a good picture. The car with bricks for wheels. The shape of the factory roof, and the chimney, sooty bricks, a picture made of sooty bricks. The horse running down an alley, how did the horse get off its pedestal? A boy with dinosaur fin–hair sways past on roller blades. A tramp with his bag of newspapers for a pillow on the bench. Tourists in their bright "mug me" shirts, the canals and the domes and the crosses and the sickles and, ah . . . even the mud by the river . . .

I breathe because I can't not. I love Rudi because I can't not.

"Tatyana," I say, leaning over the railings and looking into the water. "You're wrong."

"Not far," her voice says. "Can you get there?"

A police boat moves down the river. Its red and blue lights are beautiful.

All I remember about Tatyana's flat is a sober clock, which dropped tocks like pebbles down a deep shaft. Things gleamed, and swung, and Tatyana was close, saying she wanted something, she was warm, and I didn't want to leave for a while. At one point I remember that today is my birthday, and I try to tell Tatyana, but I've already forgotten what it was I wanted to say. I remember Tatyana loading me into a taxi and her telling the taxi driver my address as she pays him.

Rudi was home when I got back. It was about three in the morning. I hesitated for a moment before going in. He'll want to know where I've been. I can safely tell him about Tatyana. He shouldn't mind. He can even check up on her if he wants to, though of course he trusts me completely.

I turned the key, opened the door, and had the shock of my life to find Rudi standing in the hallway in his boxer shorts and socks, pointing his gun at me. A pump of adrenalin flushed my wooziness away. The bathroom light was on behind him and a tap was running. He tutted, and lowered it.

"You're a naughty kitten, Margarita. You didn't use the code. I'm disappointed."

Nemya bounded across the hallway and arched herself around my calf, shoving my leg in the direction of the kitchen. "Darling, I didn't use the code because I live here."

"How was I supposed to know that you weren't the police?"

I didn't have an answer. I never do with Rudi. But he was in a calm frame of mind: he hadn't shouted at me yet. "I'm sorry."

"That's all right. Most of us make mistakes from time to time. But kitten, don't make this one again, or you might cause an accident. Come in, come in. You're late back, aren't you? I was getting worried. There's a lot of nasty doggies out there that could eat up a little kitten."

"I've been out with a colleague from work—she's called Tatyana, and—" I began to explain but Rudi didn't seem to be interested. In the living room was a big bunch of roses, red and yellow and pink ones.

"Rudi! Are they for me?"

Rudi smiled, and I melted. He remembered my birthday! For the first time in our three years! "Of course they are, kitten. Who else would I be buying flowers for now, hey?" He came over and kissed me on my forehead. I closed my eyes and opened my mouth to kiss him full on the lips, but he'd already turned away. Rudi had forgotten to put any water in the vase, so I carried them through to the kitchen. They had a beautiful scent. A garden from long ago.

"I have a small favor to ask," Rudi called through. "I know you won't mind."

"Oh?"

"I have a business partner coming to town for a short time. Actually he's a friend of Gregorski's. Very high up in all the right international circles. He's from Mongolia. Runs the place, virtually. He needs somewhere to stay."

"And?"

"I thought the spare room would suit him."

I watched the water brimming over the top of the vase. "If he runs Mongolia, why can't Gregorski put him in a penthouse?" I ignored Nemya, who was reminding me that she had claws.

"Because then the police could keep tabs on him. He runs Mongolia unofficially. Even Mongolians have to pretend to have elections to get loans."

"So you want me to put up a criminal? I thought we'd left those days behind."

"We have, kitten, we have! I'm just doing a friend a favor!"

"Why not go the whole hog and open up a flophouse for junkie pyromaniacs?"

"For Christ's sake don't overreact! I keep boxes of merchandise in the spare room: where's the difference? And he's not a criminal. He's an official with enough high-level contacts to not be searched at the border beyond Irkutsk. Helsinki's off, by the way. Gregorski's found a buyer in Beijing. Our friend will be taking the Delacroix back. The less evidence of his tracks the better."

"Why doesn't Gregorski just buy the police off like he always does?"

"Because Gregorski only holds sway at the Finnish and Latvian borders. He can't trust his usual channels as far east as Siberia. He can only trust me, and us. Kitten . . ."—I felt Rudi's arms slide around my stomach—"let's not argue. . . . It's for our future. . . ." His thumb wormed into my navel. "This is where our baby's going to be one day. . . ." He nuzzled his face into my neck, and I tried to stay cross. "Babe, kitten, baby kitten . . . I know it's a lot to ask, but we're so close now. I've been thinking, about what you were saying earlier, at Jerome's. About Austria. You're quite right, you know. We should get out while the going's good. I apologize for flying off the handle. I hate myself afterwards. You know that. It's the stress. I know you understand. I sometimes lash out at the things that are most precious to me. I hate myself sometimes," Rudi was murmuring. "Look at me. Look at me. Look at how much this stupid man adores you. . . ."

I turned and looked into his beautiful young eyes. I see how much.

"Guess where I went today, kitten. To the travel agents, to check ticket prices to Zurich."

"You did?"

"Yeah. They were closed, because of the holiday. But I went.

And I'm not going to have that greasy curator bastard insult my kitten no more. Once we've gone, Margarita, his life is in your hands. Just one word from you, and I'll have someone press the button on him. I swear on the Virgin Mary Mother."

See? Tatyana was wrong. Rudi wants to make me happy. He's going to give everything up, for us. How could I have doubted him, even for a moment? We kissed, long and hard. I whispered, "Rudi, you are the best present I've ever had on my birthday. . . ."

Rudi murmured, "Yeah? It's coming up soon, isn't it?" Eventually he drew back, his hands on my hips. "So. It's okay for our buyer's agent to keep a low profile here, yeah? It'll only be until after the swap. Cleaning night. Just two weeks."

"I don't know, Rudi. I was hoping you and I could spend a little time together, before we leave Petersburg. We've got a lot of planning to do. When's he due?"

Rudi turned away. I opened a can of cat food. "He came today. He'd flown in, and really needed a bath, so I ran one for him. He's in there now."

"*What?*"

"He's, er, already here."

"Rudi! How could you? This is where you and I and Nemya live!"

I opened the kitchen door and felt like I'd entered a piece of theater. Standing against the window with his back to me stood a short, dark, lithe man. He was wearing Rudi's dressing gown, one I'd made for him out of scarlet flannel, and was inspecting Rudi's gun. I heard myself say, "*Huh?*"

Moments passed before he turned around. "Good evening, Miss Latunsky. Thank you for your hospitality. It's good to revisit your majestic city." Perfect Russian, an accent dusty with Central Asia. Nemya yowled for her supper behind me. "Your little cat and I are already acquainted. She considers me her very own Uncle Suhbataar. I hope you will do the same."

———

My gallery is empty now, so I walk over to the window to stretch my legs. A storm is coming, and the air is stretched tight like the skin of a drum. Walking to work today, the city felt left to brew. The Neva is sultry, turgid as an oil spill. An election is being held next week, and vans with tinny speakers are driving around the city talking about reform and integrity and trust.

A mosquito buzzes in my ear. I splat it. A smear of human blood oozes from its fuselage. I look for somewhere to wipe it and choose the curtain. The guide is approaching, so I quickly sit down again. The guide turns the corner, speaking Japanese. I catch the word "Delacroix." In eight days the same guide will be saying the same things, waving the same pointy stick at a completely different picture, and only six people in the world—Rudi, myself, Jerome, Gregorski, that Suhbataar man, and the buyer in Beijing—will ever know. Jerome says the perfect crime is that which nobody knows has been committed. The sheep nod. Inside, I snicker. They've already taken photographs of several fakes today. And paid their foreigner's price for the privilege.

A little girl walks over to me and offers me a sweet. She says something in Japanese and shakes the bag. She looks about eight, and is clearly bored by our wonders of the art world. Her skin is the color of coffee with a dash of cream. Her hair is plaited, and she's in her best dress, strawberry red with white lace. Her big sister sees her, and giggles, and several of the adults turn around. I take a sweet, and one of the Japanese cameras flashes. That annoys me about Asians. They'll photograph anything. But what a beautiful smile the little girl has! For a moment I'd like to take her home. Little girls are like old cats. If they don't like you nothing on Earth will make them pretend to.

My Kremlin-official lover insisted that I have the abortion. I didn't want to. I was scared of the operation. The priests and old women had always said there was a gulag in hell for women who killed their babies. But I was more scared of being cast off by my lover and winding up in the gutter, so I gave way. He didn't want to risk bad publicity: an illegitimate child would have been evidence of our affair, and although everyone knew corruption and scandal kept the Soviet Union ticking, appearances had to be kept up for the plebs. Otherwise, why bother? I knew that doing it would make my mother howl with shame in her grave, and that was a pleasing thought.

Most women have had one or two abortions during their life-time. It was no big deal. I had it done at the old Party hospital over at Movskovsky Prospect, so the quality of care should have been better than that for ordinary women. It wasn't. I don't know what went wrong. I kept bleeding for days afterwards, and when I went back to see the doctor, he refused to see me, and the receptionist got security to escort me out. They just left me on the steps, scream-ing, until there was no more anger left and there was nothing to do but sob. I remember the cropped elm trees leading down to the waterfront, dripping in the rain. I tried to get my lover to pull strings, but he'd lost interest in me by that point, I think. He'd come to see me as a liability. Two weeks later he dumped me, at the tea shop in the Party department store. His wife had somehow found out about my pregnancy. He said that if I didn't keep my mouth shut and go quietly he'd have my housing reallocated. I'd become damaged goods. I'd damaged his conscience.

I kept my mouth shut. When I could eventually see a gyne-cologist he took one look and said that he hoped I never planned to have children. He was a stubbly man who smelt of vodka, so I didn't believe him. There was some iron cow of a counselor there, who said it was an old bourgeois conceit that dictated the only role in life for women was to provide for capitalists to exploit, but I told her I didn't need her advice and I walked out. A year later, I read about my lover's heart attack in *Pravda*.

I tell Rudi that I take the pill, because he made it known pretty early on that he thought condoms were only fit for animals. Who knows what can happen in Switzerland? The air is clean there, and the water pure. Maybe Swiss gynecologists can do things that Russian ones can't. A little girl, half-Rudi, half-me, running around in the wildflowers. Ah, she'll be beautiful. And then there'll be a younger brother, and Rudi can teach him how to hunt in the mountains while I teach our little kitten how to cook. We're going to learn how to make bird's nest soup, which Jerome says they eat in China.

. . .

Head Curator Rogorshev seems to have been avoiding me today, even though tonight's the night of our regular liaison. Fine by me. The Delacroix will be our last picture—Rudi promised. Rudi says he's beginning to tie up loose business ends. He says he can't do it overnight, and of course I understand. Rudi explained the situation to Gregorski, and tolerated no "if"s or "but"s, so Gregorski had no choice but to bow down. If necessary, Rudi said, I can go on ahead and stay in the best hotel in Switzerland for a few weeks until he can join me. That would be nice. I could surprise him by buying the chalet first and having it ready for when he's sold his assets for the best possible price. As well as his pizza place—and, of course, the modeling agency that I work in when I'm not doing the Hermitage—he runs a taxi company, a construction company, an import-export business, has a share in a gym and is a sleeping partner for a group of nightclubs, where he handles security and insurance and such things. Rudi's a friend of the president. The president said that Rudi is one of the new breed of Russians who are navigating the New Russia through the choppy waters of the new century.

My gallery is empty again. I stroll over to the window. Giant gulls are shouldering the wind. The weather will soon be changing for the worse. I admire my reflection in the glass. It's true, what Rudi said last night, after we'd made love for the third time: as I age, I get younger. It's not an everyday beauty I have, out of a powder compact or shampoo bottle. It's more molecular than that. Wide, luscious lips, and a neck with curves that my admiral compared to a swan's. After dallying with platinum hair, I returned to my native auburn, the bronze of tribal jewelry. I got my looks from my mother, though Christ knows she gave me nothing else. My talents as an actress and dancer I must have inherited from some illustrious, forgotten ancestor. My eyes, deep sea-green, I inherited from my father, who, in his day, was a famous movie director, now deceased. He never acknowledged me publicly. I choose not to let his name be known. I respect his wishes. Anyway, my eyes. Rudi says he could dive into them and never resurface. Did you know, I entered the Leningrad Academy of Arts as an actress? Doubtless—if I'd chosen to—I could have gone all the way to the top. My Politburo lover discovered me there, in the early stage of my career, and we entered the wider stage of society life together. We used to dance the tango. I can still dance, but Rudi prefers discos. I find them a bit common. Full of sluts and tarts who are only interested in men for their power and money. The Swiss have more class. In Switzerland, Rudi will beg me to teach him.

Jerome can't bear the sight of his own reflection, he once confessed after drinking a bottle of cheap sherry, and he's never owned a mirror. I asked him why. He told me that whenever he looks into one he sees a man inside it, and thinks, "Who in God's name are you?"

The serpent is still there, coiled snug around the warty tree—
Christ above!
My dream's just come back to me.

I was hiding in a tunnel. There was something evil down there, somewhere. Two people ran past, both slitty-eyed, a man and a woman. The man wanted to save the woman from the evil. He had grabbed her arm and they were running, faster than gas in air currents. I followed them, because the man seemed to know the way out, but then I lost track. I found myself on a bare hill with a sky smeared with oil paint and comets and chimes. I realized I was looking at the foot of the cross. There were the dice that the Romans had been using to divide Jesus' clothes. As I looked, the cross started sinking. There was the nail, hammered clean through Jesus' feet. His thighs, creamy and bloodless as alabaster. The loincloth, the wound in His side, the arms outstretched and the hands hammered in, and there staring straight back at me was the grinning face of the devil, and in that moment I knew that Christianity had been one horrible, sick, two-thousand-year-old joke.

Gutbucket Barbara Petrovich came to take my place while I went for a tea break. As usual, she said not a word. Pious and holier-than-thou, just like my mother on her deathbed. I walked down my marbled hallways. A shuffler with a guidebook garbled at me in a foreign language, but I ignored it. Past my dragons of jade and blood-red stone, through my domed chambers of gold leaf, under my Olympian gods, there's Mercury, living by his wits, down long rooms of blue sashes and silver braid and mother-of-pearl-inlaid tables and velvet slippers, and down sooty back stairs and anterooms and into the murky staff canteen, where Tatyana was stirring chocolate powder into warm milk, all alone.

"Hello, Tatyana! You've been exiled here too?"

"I take my break whenever I choose. Chocolate? Forget your waistline for today. Put some sugar into your blood."

"Ah, go on then. What the hell." I sat down, felt too hot, stood up, and the legs of my chair shrieked against the tiles. I opened the windows through the iron bars, but it didn't make much difference. Outside and inside were the same. There was a tank in the square outside, and lots of people moving very slowly. The outer edges of a whirlpool.

"You seem a little agitated today, Margarita," ventured Tatyana.

I longed to tell her about Switzerland. I longed to tell her everything, and I almost did. "Really? I've been thinking about taking a little holiday, as a matter of fact. . . . Maybe abroad . . . I don't know where. . . ."

Tatyana lit me a cigarette. Her fingers were beautiful.

We listened to the drone of a distant boiler, and the slosh of a cleaner's mop in the corridor outside. I wondered if Tatyana was a pianist, with fingers like that.

"It's strange and it makes me sad," I thought aloud, "that a place carries on without you after you've left."

Tatyana nodded. "It's the world slapping you in the face and saying, 'Look, honeybunch, I get along without you very well.' The sea does the same thing, but nobody lives there. It hurts more if it's a place where you've grown up, or worked, or fallen in love."

Tatyana's chocolate sweetened my tongue to its roots. "Sometimes I imagine that I'll walk out into the corridor and bump into an eighteenth-century Count of Archangel."

Tatyana laughed. "And what does the Count of Archangel want with Margarita Latunsky?"

"Well, it depends. Sometimes he wants me to show him the

way to the Empress's chambers for a tryst. Sometimes he wants to paint me in oils, and hang me in his gallery. Other times he wants to drag me back to his four-poster bed, to ravish me so utterly that I can't walk for three days."

"Do you ever put up a struggle?"

And I laughed. A tap started dripping in the back kitchen.

"You appear to imagine a lot of things."

"Rudi says so too."

"Who's Rudi?"

"My friend."

Tatyana crossed her legs, and I heard her tights rustle. "Your man?"

I like Tatyana being curious about me. I like Tatyana. "In a manner of speaking . . ."

"What does he do?" Tatyana finds Margarita Latunsky worthy of her curiosity.

"He's a local businessman."

"Oh, *him*! You mentioned him when we went out last week. . . ."

"I did?"

Tatyana uncrossed her legs, and I heard her tights rustle. "Sure . . . but go on, tell me all about him. . . ."

"There's a storm closing in."

I nodded. A cavern-pool quietness.

"Tatyana, you didn't mean it the other day when you said that love doesn't exist?"

"I'm sorry it upset you so much."

"No, you didn't upset me. But I've been thinking. If there's no love, what keeps good in a different cage from evil?"

"I knew you had promise, the moment I saw you. That *is* an astute question."

"You told me a secret. Can you keep a secret about me?"

"I am one."

"I'm a lapsed Christian. My mother used to smuggle me into clandestine services when I was a teenager. Before Brezhnev died, you understand. If you were caught, two years prison, straight out. Even owning a Bible was illegal."

Tatyana wasn't looking remotely surprised.

"I guess this isn't really a secret, it's more of a story. I remember a sermon. A traveler went on a journey with an angel. They entered a house with many floors. The angel opened one door, and in it was a room with one long low bench running around the walls, crammed with people. In the center was a table piled with sweetmeats. Each guest had a very long silver spoon, as long as a man is tall. They were trying to feed themselves, but of course they couldn't—the spoons were too long, and the food kept falling off. So in spite of there being enough food for everyone, everyone was hungry. 'This,' explained the angel, 'is hell. The people do not love each other. They only want to feed themselves.'

"Then the angel took the traveler to another room. It was exactly the same as the first, only this time instead of trying to feed themselves, the guests used their spoons to feed one another, across the room. 'Here,' said the angel, 'the people think only of one another. And by doing so, they feed themselves. Here is heaven.' "

Tatyana thought for a moment. "There's no difference."

"No difference?"

"No difference. Everybody both in heaven and hell wanted one and the same thing: meat in their bellies. But those in heaven got their shit together better. That's all." And she laughed, but I couldn't. My expression made Tatyana add, "I'm truly sorry, Margarita. . . ."

The minutes are hauling themselves by like a shot Hollywood gangster crawling down a corridor.

I know my Rudi's business sometimes demands a tough line, but there's a difference between assertiveness and violence, just as there's a difference between a businessman and a gangster. I never delude myself. My Rudi can adopt a very direct manner. But what do people expect if they default on legitimate loans? Rudi can't give money away, he's not a charity. People understand the terms when they take on the loans, and if they don't keep their end of the bargain, then my Rudi is quite within his rights to take whatever action is necessary to ensure that he and his partners are not out of pocket at the end of the day. It's incredible how some people find that so hard to understand. I remember about two years ago, shortly after Rudi agreed to move in with me, he came back late one night with a knife gash down his neck the length of a pencil. A loan defaulter, he'd explained. Blood was oozing out, thick and sticky like toothpaste. Rudi refused to go to the hospital, so I had to stanch the bleeding myself, with one of my ripped-up cotton blouses. The hospitals are for the needy, he said. He's so brave.

After that night, Rudi got himself a gun, and I got myself some bandages.

Clouds and the distant Alps in the blue afternoon, ice cream and eiderdown. It was siesta time in the Garden of Eden: the drowsiness was murmury in the groves. Insects wound up and unwound. Eve was coming to a decision.

"Ask your desire what you want," hissed the snake.

"It's a big step. Exile, menstruation, toil, childbirth. I've got one last question."

"Fire away," said the serpent.

"Why do you hate God?"

The serpent smiled and painted spirals in the air, down onto Eve's lap. "Be so good as to tickle my throat, would you, my dear? Yess, that *is* an astute question . . ."

Eve loved the flecks of emerald and ruby in the serpent's golden scales. "Then give me an astute answer."

"That fruit you're holding, Eve, that plump, juicing, yielding buttock of fruit, in its flesh you are going to discover all the knowledge you desire. Why do I hate God? Zoroaster, Manichean heresies, Jungian archetypes, Thingysky's pyramid, virtual particles, from whence serpentine sibilance, immortality . . . Why do things happen the way they do? All you have to do"—the serpent's eyes whirlpooled like the kaleidoscopes of Nostradamus—"is to wrap your soft lipsss around the juicy—beauty, bite hard, and see what happens!"

Eve closed her eyes and opened her mouth.

An ambassadorial convoy just graced my Delacroix gallery. Ambassadors are idiots who possess only one skill: outkowtowing one another at official functions. I know. I saw enough in action in my power-politics days. There was the head of security, a cultural attaché, the director of the Winter Palace, Head Curator Rogorshev—who pretended not to notice me—a multilingual translator, and eight ambassadors. I knew which countries they were from because I'd typed the invitations myself. The French one I could tell straight off because he kept interrupting the translator to point things out to everyone else. The German one kept looking at his watch. I caught the Italian one looking at my breasts and neck. The British one kept nodding politely at the pictures and saying "Delightful," the American was videotaping the tour as though he owned the place, and the Australian kept taking crafty swigs from his hip flask. That left the Belgian and the Dutch ambassadors, and I couldn't tell one from the other, but who cares anyway? They each had their own bodyguard. God knows why anyone thought these nonentities needed bodyguards. I've known a fair few in my time, too. Much more fun than ambassadors.

The air conditioner judders on. Its innards sound queasy.

Tatyana whisked me onwards, but the Thewlicker's goose between her legs flew faster than mine, and vanished honking down a fire escape, a sooty pot holder swinging from its foot. Catherine the Great sailed by on a royal barge. She was decomposing and full of holes and muddy, but I had a bottle of extra virgin olive oil which I poured into her orifices. Light shone out of her and she sat up, fully restored.

"Ma'am," I curtsied.

"Ah, Margarita, and how are we tonight? The Count of Archangel asked us to convey his felicitations, and gratitude. We gather you rendered him some assistance the other night."

"It was my pleasure, your majesty."

"One last eeny-weeny thing, Miss Latunsky."

"Majesty?"

"We know that you're spiriting our pictures away from under our very noses. We are prepared to overlook your misdemeanors to date. We're the same breed, you and us, Miss Latunsky. We admire your sense of style. Heaven only knows, in this world a woman has to take opportunity by the horns whenever it comes calling, but we are warning you. Plots are being hatched in the palace. The time has come to cut and run. If you take another picture, the price will be pain and anguish beyond your imaginings."

I woke up with a start to see a peeping Tom staring at me.

"What do you think you're staring at, you *faggot*?"

He zigzagged off, looking over his shoulder once or twice.

I don't understand why I'm so drowsy today. It must be this weather, this storm that refuses to break. It's like being locked in a cleaning cupboard.

Rudi and I have always enjoyed a very liberal relationship. Don't be fooled by appearances! He's an uncut diamond, and the love we have for each other runs deep, strong, and true. The lovers I took before Rudi were older men, who used to protect and nurture me. I won't deny that Rudi brings out a maternal streak in me. But the bullshit that says a woman has to be one man's slave and never even look at another man, that died out with my mother's two-faced generation and good riddance! If she really believed that, where did I come from? Both Rudi and I go on dates with other people: quite informally, and it doesn't mean anything. In Rudi's work, escorts are often a necessary part of the right image. I don't mind. He couldn't conduct his business if he didn't have the right image. It's not that I'm getting too old to go with Rudi or anything, it's just that I've done all that scene before, and frankly, it bores me. Usually, Rudi introduces me to some of his gentleman friends, always men of the very highest pedigree, and always very rich, as you'd expect. Rudi knows that I used to be a social firefly, and doesn't like to see me fester in our little home. Rudi's friends are often in town on business, and they just want a little feminine company to show them around. Rudi knows how gifted I am at handling men, and making them feel at ease. They always express their appreciation to Rudi in a financial dimension, and sometimes Rudi insists that I take some expenses for my time too, though God knows, that's not what I'm interested in. It doesn't mean anything. Rudi knows he is the center of my world, and I know that I am the center of his.

.   .   .

The evening is waiting in Head Curator Rogorshev's office. I have the windows open, and the electric fan on, but my sweaty lingerie is still sticking to my skin. The tip of my cigarette glows in the gloom.

Nemya, my little cat, will want to be fed. But Rudi won't be back yet, and Mr. Suhbataar never answers the telephone. Mr. Suhbataar. He's a strange man. I've barely seen him. Once I got used to the shock of his sudden arrival a week ago, things worked out all right. He's quieter than Nemya, and often when I think he isn't at home I'll pass by him on the way to the kitchen, or when I think he is at home I'll knock on his door, and there's nobody in. I've never seen him eat anything. I've never even seen him use the toilet! He drinks, though, glass after glass of milk. When he shuts a door there's no sound. And when I ask him about his family or about Mongolia, he'll give answers which don't sound evasive at the time, but when I sit down and think about what he said later, I realize that he's told me absolutely nothing. I have strong powers of insight and intuition, and my grandmother possessed the power to place curses. So I can usually see right through people, but it's as though Mr. Suhbataar is invisible in the first place. He is handsome, in a slight, hawkish, semi-Oriental way. I wonder what kind of woman he likes? Savage Wild Asian, or Refined Lacy European? Assuming he likes women, and he's not another Jerome. No. He's real man. I wonder what Mongolia's like. I must ask him before he leaves.

The telephone goes. I let the head curator's new answering machine take the call.

"Margarita? It's Rogorshev Rabbit. Are you there? Pick up the phone. . . . Don't be cross with me, you know how much it cuts me up. . . ." I can't be bothered. Another cigarette. "I forgot to tell you. It's my wife's anniversary. I promised her I'd take her and the kids to some new movie. Some nonsense about dinosaurs . . . I'm sorry, my fairy cake. . . . Next week? Are you there? No? Okay. . . . Well, I hope you get this message. . . ."

I see. So, I did my makeup for nothing. Waste of time. Waste of money. Men don't know how expensive decent cosmetics are. I hope there's a fire in the cinema and all the little Rogorshevs turn into potato crisps. I can crunch them to crumbs, like I will their father.

The head of security was reading the sports pages, chewing a brick-sized sandwich that dripped red jam. The tinny radio was on in the background. "Good evening, Madame Latunsky," he said silkily. "How was your day? Quiet?" He groped down his pants to reposition his balls. "Or were you tied up with business in our head curator's office?"

Fat bastard. "Did your ambassadors have a nice time?"

"Oh yes, yes, daresay we gave them something to brag about with their mistresses." He looked at me for just a moment too long.

I lit a cigarette. *You are going down, Fatso. Enjoy it while it lasts, because you are going to be in prison by the end of the month.* "Floor-polishing night, next week. The head of the cleaning company phoned Head Curator Rogorshev's office just now to confirm. Usual time. It seems he'll be coming along again himself this month, just to make sure the waxing machines run smoothly."

The head of security swiveled around on his squeaky chair to look at the office blackboard. "Right you are."

I knock Rudi's stupid code on my own door, but there's nobody home. No Mr. Suhbataar, no Rudi, not even little Nemya. I take a shower to wash away the day's grime and the makeup. Green eye shadow and apricot blusher lost down the plug hole. The bathroom is much cleaner than usual: Mr. Suhbataar always cleans up after himself. He even cleans up after me. I don't trust men who clean up after themselves. Jerome's another one. Give me a slob like Rudi, any day. I force myself to eat a boiled egg, and sit down by the window to watch the canal. A pleasure craft chugs into view, with a cargo of tourists. I see my son and daughter among them, laughing at something I can't see. Blond-haired toddlers. I want to go out but I can't think where. I have many close friends, of course, all over the city. Or I could hop on the overnight train to Moscow and stay with some of my friends from my theater days there. I haven't been to Moscow for years. They are always clamoring for me to visit, but I tell them, it's a question of time. I can invite them to Switzerland when I'm settled, of course. They can stay in the guest chalet I'm going to have built. They'll be green with envy! I've decided to live near a waterfall, so I can drink fresh water from the glaciers every day. St. Petersburg water contains so many metals it's almost magnetic. I'll keep hens. Why am I crying?

What's wrong with me tonight? Maybe I need a man. I could put on that pair of unladdered red fishnet tights, slip into the new black velvet suit Rudi got me as an extra birthday present last week—and go and pick up some young boy with a motorbike, in a leather jacket and with thick black hair and a powerful jaw . . . just for fun. I haven't done that for a long time. Rudi wouldn't mind, especially if he didn't know about it. As I said, we have a modern give-and-take relationship.

But no. I only want Rudi. I want Rudi's shoulders, and his hands, and his smell, and his belt. I want to feel Rudi's lunges, even if it hurts a little. Look at the rooftops, spires, cupolas, factory chimneys. . . . Rudi is out there somewhere, thinking about me.

From Lapland comes a front of thunder, and when I look to where the night melts into the storm, I see a lick of lightning, and I wonder where my little Nemya could have got to.

I stood in a well of moonlight. The stairs wound up to my apartment. Way, way past midnight. Not dark, not light, bats flickered here and there, specks in a sky of old film. The courtyard was silted up with menace. As usual, the lift wasn't working, though it gave me a hell of an electric shock when I tried to pull the door open. I didn't know you got electric shocks at night. For the fiftieth time since Rudi had driven off with the Delacroix in the back of his cleaning van, I told myself everything was fine. My new life was about to begin. For the fiftieth time I felt there was something wrong. Something had been wrong all week. What is who trying to tell me? I lit another cigarette. Nobody was stirring. See? There was nothing wrong, and to prove it I didn't hurry up to my apartment, but stayed for a moment to smoke a last cigarette.

. . .

The switch between the fake and the real Delacroix had gone like clockwork. Almost.

I'd met Rudi and three rent-a-granny cleaners at the goods entrance at exactly eight in the evening. Gutbucket Petrovich, still in that ghastly uniform she wears, and two of her cronies were there to supervise them. I was the fourth Hermitage employee. When I arrived they all stopped talking. So utterly obvious. While I was allotting corridors and handing floor-plans to the women, I thought Gutbucket Petrovich was about to break her vow of silence and say something, but she bit her tongue at the last moment. Wise. The head of security was playing cards in the lodge with his bat-faced brother-in-law. He nodded briefly at Rudi, and waved us through. Rudi and his cleaners wheeled their cumbersome floor-polishing contraptions in different directions, one guard per cleaner. I went with Rudi.

We didn't say a word. Rudi and I make a great team. When he's happy, he'll say that to me, like the time I attended his birthday party at the Petersburg Hilton banquet halls. When nobody was looking, he chinked our champagne glasses and whispered, "Babe, you and I make a great team."

When we exchanged a picture in the winter, we had to work in the weak electric lights of the Winter Palace. In the bright summer twilight we could leave the lights off. I stood guard in the corridor outside the Delacroix gallery, while Rudi unlocked and clicked open the compartment specially built into the base of the machine. He slid Jerome's forgery out, and leaned it against a half-moon table, inset with lotus flowers and orchids of jade and amber.

There was no noise but the drone of the other machines in the distance.

Rudi reached up and unhooked the real Delacroix, and slid it into the compartment, locking it shut again. I thought about Eve and the serpent, making their getaway together.

I heard stout footsteps marching this way.

"Rudi!"

The serpent's poison sacs back-flooded, and venom dribbled up.

Rudi stiffened and stared at me.

I felt locked in and left behind.

I'd been mistaken. A hammering in a false wall. No, nothing. And the echo of that drone.

Rudi unfroze, frowning at me. Then he hung Jerome's fake in the empty space.

I believe I would have sold my soul for a cigarette.

Rudi then started waxing the seventeenth-century portrait corridors, pushing the noisy handlebarred contraption up and down the long passages, up as far as the Cubist pictures of cut-up instruments. The gardener in our Swiss gardens will mow my lawns in the same way. I watched Rudi, outwardly as bored as a gallery attendant. I wanted to help him, but it would have looked suspicious. Inwardly I was aching for the hours to topple, quickly, so we could leave this ghastly palace and the treasure would be truly ours. I yielded to temptation and imagined promenading through Zurich's plushest department stores, a train of attendants wrapping the objects I indicate in polka-dotted wrapping paper and gold ribbon. Then I imagined being nibbled and ravished by Rudi in the truffle department.

At midnight Rudi's new Italian chronometer beeped and he switched off the waxing machine. We returned to the goods entrance. On the way down Rudi smiled at me. "Soon, babe, very soon," and he smiled the smile our son will smile. I bit my lip and imagined the clothes I would dress him in. "You can bang me up later," I whispered. In his lodge, the head of security was asleep, his legs splayed and his snores aquatic. Two of Rudi's cleaners were there, complaining about their bones, complaining about the weather, complaining about the waxing machines. I pray that Rudi will put me to sleep before I get to that point. We watched the head of security for a minute or so, until Gutbucket Petrovich came with her cleaner. Gutbucket Petrovich poked him awake.

He blinked and hauled himself to his feet. "What?"

"We're all done here, officer," said Rudi.

"Then go home, then."

"And what about conducting the body searches?" prodded Gutbucket Petrovich. "'Regulation 15d: All ancillary staff, *includ-*

ing gallery attendants, must undergo compulsory body searches upon leaving the—' "

The head of security squelched out his nose into a tissue, which he lobbed at the wastepaper basket. He missed. "Don't quote the regulations at me. I know what's in the regulations. I wrote the bloody regulations."

"I refuse to have his hands anywhere near me," said the oldest cleaner, rearing up. "And if you say he can," she warned Rudi, "I'll take what you owe me and resign."

Granny Cleaner Number Two advanced in solidarity. "Same here. I refuse to be treated like a tart in a police cell."

"It's the regulations," snarled Gutbucket Petrovich. "You have no choice."

Jesus, it's not like anyone's asking you to sleep with the knobbly troll.

Rudi turned on the charm, the rogue. "Ladies, ladies, ladies. The solution is obvious. The head of security here can body-search *me,* while one of his female members of staff—perhaps this"—Rudi gestured at Gutbucket—"zealous member . . . can body-search *you.* Then we can all go home to an honest night's sleep at the end of an honest day's labor. And Rudi always pays what he owes. Are we agreed?"

After the body searches we loaded two of the waxing machines into the back of the van. The three cleaners and two of the guards had gone home. Rudi was in the head of security's office getting his billet signed and countersigned in triplicate. Gutbucket Petrovich lingered like a bad smell, hatching some new scheme. The last signature was scrawled off, and Rudi folded up the papers.

"How do we know," said Gutbucket Petrovich to the head of security, "that he hasn't hidden a painting in one of the waxing machines?"

Christ above. A poison thorn slid in, bent, and snapped.

But Rudi just sighed, and addressed the head of security. "Who is this woman? Your new boss?"

"I'm a government employee," snarled Gutbucket Petrovich, "paid to protect our cultural heritage from thieves!"

"Fine," said Rudi, still not looking at her. "First, search the

galleries. Second, locate the missing pictures that my internation-
ally notorious gallery thieves, cunningly disguised as groaning
grannies, have spirited away from under the very noses of your
own guards while they blinked. Third, dismantle each of my machines, screw by screw, onto sheets of newspaper by moonlight.
Then put them back together. Perfectly, mind you, or I'll sue big
time. Great idea. You are lucky to have such a fastidious public
servant ruling your roost. I'll be adding overtime to my invoice.
Under the terms of the contract I have with Head Curator Rogorshev, I clocked off at twelve sharp. You'll forgive me if I sit
down, help myself to your newspaper, and phone my wife to tell
her that I won't be home for another eight hours?"

Rudi sat down, and unfolded the newspaper.

My heart beat at least twenty times in the few seconds that followed.

"That won't be necessary," said the head of security, staring
daggers at Gutbucket Petrovich. "The head of security makes
these kinds of decisions. Not a gallery attendant supervisor."

Rudi stood up. "Very glad to hear it." He barged past Gutbucket Petrovich, who was left to stew in her own juices—the only
juices that she'd ever know in her lifetime. Through the door of
the porter's lodge I could see Rudi trundling the third waxing
machine into the back of his van, still in the loading bay. I noticed
he'd left his papers on the desk, so that I could pick them up, and
follow him. We're a team of professionals. Sure enough, he was
waiting for me in the back of the van.

"Babe," he muttered, "I'm going to go to Jerome's first, to
drop off the painting. I'll be back later. There's one or two of Gregorski's people I need to see first."

"Suhbataar?"

"Never mind who. I'll see you soon."

"I love you." What else could I have said?

The backs of his fingers brushed my breasts. He jumped
down to get the last waxing machine. The one with the Delacroix
hidden in its undercarriage, still in the loading bay. So close now,
so close.

"Well, you must be very pleased with yourself, Latunsky."

Gutbucket Petrovich's head and shoulders appeared in the loading door of the van.

Why choose now to stop ignoring me? "Why, it can talk, after all."

She rolled up a strip of chewing gum, put it in, and bit down hard. She folded her arms. "Do you really think a nobody like you is going to get away with this?"

"I have no idea what you think you're talking about."

She smirked as she chewed. I wondered what to do. How could she know? "Drop the ham acting, Latunsky. Everyone knows about the little game you're running here."

Behind her, out of sight of the gloom of the lodge, Rudi had picked up a monkey wrench and was walking up very slowly behind her, his forefinger over his lips. My mind raced ahead, saw the steel flashing down onto her skull—I felt—I don't know what I felt—keep her talking, keep her talking, I felt afraid, a part of me even wanting to warn her, but another part of me felt warm and hungry. Don't move a muscle, bitch. Bunnykins is coming.

"And what little game would that be?" We would dump her body in the marshes out towards Finland. . . .

"Stop playing games! You're lousy at it! I'm talking about your little scheme to pull yourself up into the high life, of course!" That look in Rudi's eyes, bad cocaine. Gutbucket thinks she has me on the run. Ravens would come and peck out those beady eyes of hers. Wild dogs would fight over her belly, ass, and thighs, the stronger getting the juicier cuts. Her life is in my hands, and she doesn't even know it. . . . I no longer want her to run away, and I have to stop myself laughing. She's still chewing, her fat face badly in need of an expensive beautician. "You're after the head curator's job, aren't you? Sleeping your way into his office chair! You're just a shameless whore, Latunsky. That's what you've always been and that's all you ever will be."

Rudi lowered the monkey wrench, and I laughed, and spat at her. That got rid of her.

I finished my cigarette. Even the bats had gone. What was wrong now?

Nothing, that was what. I checked my watch: 2:24 A.M. The picture would be safely stowed at Jerome's, Suhbataar would be handing over the cash from the buyers, and I could start packing for Switzerland. After all these years I was finally getting out! In the iron curtain years Switzerland was as near in dreams and far in fact as Emerald City. I attacked the rest of the stairs. It was natural I should be jittery. I'd just stolen a painting worth half a million dollars.

I knocked Rudi's code on my front door, just to please him. But there was no reply. Well. I hadn't expected one. He'd be home soon.

In my hallway I clicked the light-switch, but the bulb had broken. I clicked a switch further down the hallway, but the second light also wasn't working. Odd. The electricity must be down. But I didn't really need electricity tonight, anyway. The White Nights were here, and the sky over towards Europe was lit by perpetual dusk and the Milky Way. I walked into my living room, saw my coffee table with its legs in the air, and my nerves snapped like a string of cat gut.

My room had been wrecked.

The shelves yanked off the walls, the TV smashed, the vases flung to the ground. The drawers ripped out, the contents hurled across the room. The pictures methodically pulled apart and tossed aside, one by one. My clothes foraged through and ripped to ribbons. Shards of glass littered the carpet like dinosaur teeth.

Who would want to do this to me?

All this destruction, all this silence.

Oh God, not Rudi. Was he safe? Had he been taken?

A corner of shadow was twitching under the wreck of the dining table. I felt my throat constricting and refusing to swallow. My eyes strained to read the swarmy dark. The corner of shadow was a pool of blood, blackened by the twilight—I recognized the tiniest of whimpers—

Oh my God oh my God Nemya, not dear little Nemya. I crouched and peered under the table. There was a mesh of torn roots where one of her hind legs should have been. I think she was too close to death to be in pain. Her eyes looked back at me, calm as a Buddha on a hill somewhere, outstaring the sun. She died, leaving me falling alone, unable to see the bottom.

An awful form was floating down the Neva from the marshes. Lazily, on its back, until it reached Alexandra Nevskogo Bridge. It would crawl up a support, and haul its stumps and teeth through the streets, looking for me.

What do I do? What do you always do? "Ask your desire!" orders the serpent.

I went into the bedroom, and telephoned Rudi's mobile phone number, the one for emergencies. The static hiss sounded like the crashing of waves, or the noise of many coins falling? Thank God, the call connected. I blurted out, "Rudi, they've turned the flat over—"

A woman's voice was talking back. A cold, metallic one. Smug as Gutbucket's.

"The number you have dialed has been disconnected."

"Christ above! Reconnect it, you frigging whore!"

"The number you have dialed has been disconnected."

"The number you have dialed has been disconnected."

What?

I put down the receiver. What next? Desires. I wanted Switzerland, and Rudi, and our children. So I needed the Delacroix painting. That simple. Rudi will be proud of me. "Babe," he'll say, "I knew I could rely on you."

I telephoned Jerome.

"Hello, my dear. A shplendid evening'sh work." His voice was woozy with alcohol.

"Jerome, have you seen Rudi?"

"Of coursh, he left here only twenty minutes ago after dropping off the latest addition to our family. My word, she *is* a beauty, isn't she? Hey, did I ever tell you about Delacroix's fling with the nephew of—"

"Has Suhbataar come yet?"

"No. The Great Khan telephoned to say he would be arriving shortly—did you know that in the thirteenth century, the Mongolians used to seal their captives in airtight containers and conduct feasting atop the box, listening to the sounds of suffocation—"

"Jerome, shut up. I'm coming over now. We have to move out."

"But my dear, that's scheduled for tomorrow. And after everything I've done I think I deserve not to be told to shut up like I was a—"

"Tomorrow has to happen now! My place has been done over. I can't get hold of Rudi. My—" My cat has been killed, and I felt it move nearer down the river. "Something's going wrong. It's all going wrong. I'm coming over for the painting now. Pack it."

I hung up. What did I want?

I reached through the rip in the underside of the bedframe— thank you, Jesus! I untaped the loaded revolver. Guns are heavier than they look, and colder. I put it in my handbag and left. I came back for my passport, and left again.

It's true, it's harder to get a taxi when you need one, and if you're desperate, forget it. I walked. I shoved whatever it was that I mustn't think about back upstream, but it kept floating down. I focused on the little things around me. I remember the cobbles on Gorokhovaya Street. I remember the smoothness of the girl's skin, as she kissed her boy on the steps of the bronze horseman. I remember the heads of the flowers in cellophane around St. Isaac's Cathedral. I remember the taillights of the planes as they took off from Pulkovo airport, bound for Hong Kong or London or New York or Zurich. I remember the mauve silk of a laughing woman. I remember the maroon of a leather flying jacket. I remember the crunched-up form of a homeless person, sleeping in a coffin of cardboard. Little things. It's all made of little things that you don't ordinarily notice. My jaw muscles were killing me.

Jerome's door was bolted from the inside. I banged it so loud that I set off a dog in another part of the building.

Jerome flung it open, pulled me in, and hissed. "Shut up!" He locked the door and ran back over to where he was packing the picture with sheets of cardboard and brown tape and string. A suitcase was already packed, lying open on the sofa. Socks, underpants, vests, cheap vodka, a Wedgwood teapot. There was an empty bottle of gin on its side in his jukebox liquor cabinet.

I stood perfectly still. What should I do? What did I want? "I'm taking the picture."

Jerome barked a laugh. He didn't even bother to look up. "Are you indeed?"

"Yes. I'm taking the picture. You see, it's Rudi's and my future."

I don't even think Jerome heard me. He was crouching over the package with his back to me. "Make yourself useful, my dear, and put your thumb on this bit of string while I tighten it up."

I didn't move. "I'm taking the picture!" When Jerome turned around to ask me again he found himself looking straight into the eye of my gun. His face lost its composure and then regained it.

"This isn't the movies. You're not going to use that on me. You know you're not. Not without your puppet-master pimp to tell you what to do. You couldn't even shoot it straight. Now be a sensible lady, and put it down."

I had a gun. He didn't. So. "Stand away from my picture, Jerome. Go and lock yourself in your studio and you won't get hurt."

Jerome looked at me gently. "My dear, what we have here is a reality gap. It's my picture. I painted the forgery, remember. My talents have allowed us to get this far. All you did was get undressed, lie back, and open wide. Let's face it, that's par for the course in your line of work."

"Nemya died."

"Who's Nemya?"

"Nemya! Nemya, my little cat!"

"I'm very sorry that your cat died. Truly, I'll weep buckets for your kitty when the time comes to pay my respects, but if you will kindly put that nasty little toy away and piss off so I can finish packing my picture—do you hear me, my dear? *My* picture—and catch a plane out of your squalid, lying, violent, subzero anus of a country for which not so long ago I traded in my entire damned future—"

"I don't know what a reality gap is. But I know what a gun is. It's my picture. And another thing, my name is not 'my dear.' My name is Margarita Latunsky."

"Evidently, my words have failed to penetrate your makeup and hairdo, you encrusted tart—" He strode towards me, hand outstretched ready to grab—

"It's *my* picture!" banged the gun. Jerome's head flipped back with enough force to lift him off his feet. Beautiful red blood splattered the ceiling. I heard it. Splatter. Jerome was still spinning, as though he'd slipped on a banana skin.

"Margarita Latunsky," insisted the silence, without raising its voice.

Jerome thumped to the floor, half his face missing. Killing is a sensation, like abortion or birth, that you can never accurately imagine. Odd. What next?

"My compliments, Miss Latunsky," said Suhbataar, shutting the kitchen door softly behind him. "Straight through his eye. Something else we have in common."

Suhbataar?

"Where's Rudi?"

"Nearby." He smiled, and I saw dark gold. I hadn't seen his teeth until now.

"Where?"

"In the kitchen." Suhbataar jerked his thumb over his shoulder.

It's going to be all right! Tears of relief welled up. We'll be in Switzerland by tomorrow night! "Thank God, thank God, I—I didn't know—I—Nemya's dead—Mr. Suhbataar, I hope you understand about Jerome. . . ."

"I understand, Margarita. You did Rudi a favor, too. The English are a devious race. A nation of homosexuals, vegetarians, and third-rate spies. This one—" Suhbataar shunted Jerome's half-head over with the tip of his boot—"was planning to sell you, me, Rudi, even Mr. Gregorski, all up the river."

Rudi was safe! I ran to the kitchen and pushed open the door. Rudi was slumped over the kitchen table, still in his cleaning-company overalls. Drunk at a time like this! I love him with every minute of my life, but this is not a good time to hit the vodka!

"Rudi, darling, wake up now—"

I shook his shoulders, and his head tipped up and over at an impossible angle, just like Jerome's had. I saw his face. My jagged scream ended as abruptly as it had begun. It broke over the city. Yes, it has been falling for a long time. The rumble in my head will never die, until Earth kisses my ears and eyes shut. Frothing tapeworms of blood were wriggling free from my lover's eyes and nostrils. White as suet, white as suet.

Suhbataar spoke from the living room in an unhurried tone. "You will have to postpone your sojourn together in Switzerland . . ."

Gravelly vomit had completely caked up Rudi's mouth.

". . . permanently. I'm sorry about your boudoir, your chalet, and your children."

Me, this . . . Rudi, and Suhbataar's voice, nothing else existed.

"Rudi!" Somebody else was speaking for me.

Suhbataar's voice shrugged. "Regrettably, Rudi was planning to sell us up the very same river. Mr. Gregorski couldn't let that happen. He has his reputation to protect. So he called me in, to test everyone's honesty. The results were less than satisfactory."

"No. No."

"Mr. Gregorski's suspicions were aroused when your boyfriend 'lost' a wall of money he was laundering through a reputable Hong Kong law firm, and the only excuse he could come up with was that his contact there suddenly dropped dead of diabetes! Dishonesty coupled with a lack of invention is fatal for little crooks."

Something crunched under my shoe. Bits of a syringe.

Hell is tiled. The fridge motor shuddered off.

Logic shrieked in. Maybe there was time. "Ambulance!"

"An ambulance isn't going to help Rudi, Miss Latunsky. He's dead. Not just a little bit dead. He's extremely dead. It would seem that the embittered traitor-forger Jerome laced his celebratory heroin with rat poison."

His dear eyes. Rudi slid, and slumped off the chair onto the floor. I heard his nose snap. I fled back into the living room, tripped over something and fell to my knees, trying to claw back to yesterday through the pattern in the carpet. It was all too horrible for tears. Something dug between my knuckles. The gun. The gun.

Suhbataar was buttoning up his long leather coat.

Jerome was lying on his back doused in his own blood, just a few paces away.

And Rudi in the kitchen, with a broken nose.

How had all this come about? Only one hour ago we were in the back of a van and I had wanted Rudi inside me.

I heard myself whimpering, like Nemya under the table.

"Don't take it so hard," said Suhbataar, tucking the package containing the Delacroix under his arm. Why did his voice never alter? Always the same, dry, soft, and gritty. "Your gang's been on borrowed time for months. Rudi and Jerome were traitors. Mr. Gregorski can't permit you to walk away. Pawns get sacrificed in endgames. Your Interpol friend Ms. Makuch and her Capital Transfer Inspectorate are too close."

"What?"

"Innocuous name for an anti-mafia squad, isn't it? That reminds me, I gave them an anonymous tip-off via a dead-letter box on Kirovsky Island. They'll be here in a few minutes. Calm down. Ex-spies are an embarrassment these days, what with the IMF and trade delegations—nobody's going to throw away the key on you for killing Jerome. The stolen pictures are irreplaceable, but nobody will believe you were the mastermind behind that. Fifteen years at most, out in ten. The prison reform lobby in Moscow is beginning to gain a little ground. Slowly."

He walked towards the door.

"Put it down! That's my picture! That picture belongs to Rudi and me!"

Suhbataar turned, feigning surprise. "I don't think Rudi is going to be dealing in stolen masterpieces for a while."

"I want it!"

"With the greatest respect, Miss Latunsky, you don't count. You never have."

What had he said about Tatyana? "I'll tell the police everything about Gregorski!"

Suhbataar shook his head sadly. "You've become a murderer, Miss Latunsky. Your prints are on the gun, the ballistics match up . . . Who's going to listen to you? The only possible corroboration to your whistle-blowing is lying in this apartment, slumped in pools of their own innards."

Pressing into my knuckles. I still had my gun.

"If it becomes expedient to oblige you to stop telling stories, Gregorski will know where to find you. Even in Ms. Makuch's division, the level of corruption is startling. Mongolians long ago made corruption a national pastime, but even I'm impressed with you Russians."

"Drop the picture now drop it now you son of a bitch or you are dead dead dead dead *dead!* Put it down slowly and put it down now! Hands in the air! You know I can use this thing!" I aimed the gun straight at where his heart should be.

A weapon men use against women is the refusal to take them seriously.

"Look at Jerome, you Mongolian fuck, that's you in ten seconds' time."

Suhbataar smiled, an in-joke smile.

Fine. Fine. It will be his death mask. What's the difference between one murder and two? I pulled the trigger.

The hammer clapped down on an empty chamber. I pulled the trigger again. Nothing. Again. Nothing.

Suhbataar pulled out five golden bullets from his jacket pocket, rattled them in his cage of fingers.

I was left alone staring at the locked door.

None of this happened. None of this really happened.

LONDON

MY SMIRKING HANGOVER gave me a few moments to make my last requests, and to take in the fact that whoever's bed this was it wasn't Poppy's. *Whash!* Then it laid into me, armed with a road-surface shatterer. I must have groaned pretty loudly, because the woman next to me rolled over and opened her eyes.

"Good morning," she said, pulling a sheet over her breasts. "I've lost an earring."

"Hi." I grimaced as pleasantly as I could, peering through the sheets of pain. Not a face I could imagine smiling easily. I hoped this wasn't going to turn into one of those GuiltLine wake-ups when she tells you about her boyfriend and her dead brother and her run-over-last-month dog Michael and you end up wondering how many people are in this bed. Still. Stern, rather than neurotic. A strong profile. Late thirties. Not bad, but nothing so special. Either she had aged since last night or I was getting less and less choosy. Red hair. Quite heavily built. That's right! I'd been at the private view on Curzon Street. Oil paintings by some artist friend of Rohan's, Mudgeon or Pigeon or Smudgeon or something. This redhead had come up to me then, and we'd done the old quantum physics equals eastern religion bollocks. Then—a taxi—a wine bar on Shaftesbury Avenue—then another taxi—that would be most of my money gone—and then another wine bar on Upper Street. Then to here, though how was anybody's guess. What was her name? Cathy? Katrina? It was something convent-schoolgirl-ish. I always have this problem with women's names, once I've slept with them.

She found her earring and noticed the way I was looking at

her. She cleared her throat. "Katy Forbes. The personnel manager. You're in my flat in Islington. Delighted to meet you. Again."

"Hello. I'm—" Something was gripping my windpipe. I fought free and found my Woody Woodpecker boxer shorts.

"Marco. I know. The 'writer.' We did just about get to the name-swapping stage."

So I'd played the writer card. That was valuable information. I looked around me. A single woman's bedroom. Lacy curtains, trees bobbing in the early autumn. A framed poster of an oil painting, with a big 'Delacroix' written underneath it. The original was probably nice. A little nest of tissues and condoms down my side of the bed, and a bottle of red wine with almost nothing in it, but 1982 on the label. Why do the best things happen when I'm too pissed to remember them?

An Islington Saturday morning. A car alarm going off somewhere.

"Well. This is jolly . . ."

She watched the end of the sentence dangling for a few moments.

"I'm going to get up and have a shower." A horsey inflection to her voice. She must have seen me as a diamond in the rough, the old Lady Chatterley complex. "If you feel as ghastly as you look there's some fizzy hangover medicine in the first-aid box on the drinks cabinet. If you have to be sick, do try to get it all in the lavatory bowl. Help yourself to some coffee, there's instant if you can't figure out the percolator, but please don't run off with the fake chandelier, it was expensive. And if you can cook I'd like some scrambled eggs on toast."

"Never fear," I said. "I am a casual shag to be relied upon!" This wasn't terribly funny but I blundered on anyway. "No bread knives through the shower curtain, guaranteed."

Her face would buckle any mere bread knife. She put on her dressing gown and went through into the bathroom. I heard the pipes in the walls judder as she switched on the shower.

I got dressed, wishing I had clean clothes. I smelt hash in a burn on my shirt, between the lipstick and a stain that I tried to ignore. My bladder felt like an inflatable camping bed. I groped out of the bedroom and found the little toilet, where I wazzed the waz from outer space. Seriously, I was pissing for a whole fifty-five seconds. On the shelf next to the potpourri there was a picture of my hostess Katy Forbes and a baldish youngish chap in a punt under a weeping willow, and for a moment I wondered if I shouldn't split before hubby came home, but then I fuzzily recalled Katy saying she'd been divorced. We'd agreed that joining a pyramid savings scheme is a much more stress-free way to lose all your money and wreck your life. So. A leisurely, assault-free breakfast was in order. Odd though, the only use that divorcées normally find for photographs of their ex-husbands is for dart practice. Maybe he's her brother. I thrust out the last few drops and mopped up the spray on the rim with a clutch of toilet paper, and pulled the toilet chain, sending the previous evening's spermatozoa to the North Sea. Three seconds later a howl came from the shower. "Don't touch the bloody water till I'm *out!*"

"Sorry!"

I can cook, and Katy's kitchen was well stocked. My hangovers never affect my appetite. In fact I like to bury my hangovers alive, in food. I poured some olive oil into a big frying pan, chopped up some garlic, mushrooms, and chili peppers, and sprinkled some basil. I folded in a dash of cream with the eggs, and mashed up a couple of anchovies that were stinking the fridge out. Onto this Vesuvius of cholesterol I grated a light snowfall of Wensleydale, and perched a few stuffed olives around the crater. There was granary bread, so I lightly browned some toast. Real butter in a Wedgwood butter dish. I helped myself to a few sprigs of parsley from a shrub on the windowsill. Some fresh beef tomatoes on the side, with chopped celery, sultanas, and a dollop of potato salad. The coffee percolator was the same model as my own, so no problem there. I slurped down a mugful of the magic brew and felt my hangover being shooed away.

"Gosh," said Katy, coming through with her hair wrapped in a towel. Her gray track-suit trousers and buttoned-up cardigan did not promise any frisky post-breakfast foreplay. "You're no writer," she said, "you're a food sculptor."

"We aim," I hummed, "to please."

She picked up *The Sunday Telegraph* from the doormat, sat down with it, and dug in. She made straight for the Living section of the supplement, which I never read, even when I'm busy moving house and can be distracted by share prices in Singapore.

I joined Katy at the table. This was a nice room. There was an overgrown little garden out back. In the front was a raised pavement. I watched human legs and canine legs and pushchair wheels go by. On the pine dresser was a collection of mainstream CDs. All very Princess Diana: Elton John, Pavarotti, the Four Seasons. A Chinese rug hung on the wall, on the mantelpiece was a zoo of ethnicky sculpted animals. Terracotta tiles and Japanese lampshades. It was a room from the Living section of *The Sunday Telegraph.* "The lack of morning-after recriminations is refreshing." I only meant it as a pleasantry.

She looked over the paper. "Why should there be any recriminations? We were both consenting adults." She slid in another forkful of egg. "Albeit bloody drunk consenting adults."

"True." I bit on a bit of chili and had to swish my mouth out with water. "Would you like to be a drunk consenting adult with me again sometime?"

Katy thought about it for a full three seconds. "I don't think so, Marco, no."

"Oh. Fair enough."

I poured us some more coffee.

"Katy, I hope this isn't an impertinent question, but I saw the photo in the toilet and I wondered if I wasn't treading on anyone's turf here?"

"Nobody's turf but mine. He was my husband. We separated, then he went and died."

I just kept the lid on a mysterious giggle. "Oh . . . I'm terribly sorry. I don't know what to say."

"He was a bloody clot. He always insisted on having the last word. It happened four months ago. Around Wimbledon time. Undiagnosed diabetes in Hong Kong."

I let a respectable silence elapse. "More toast?"

"Thank you."

The doorbell rang. Katy went over to the door. "Who is it?"

"Registered delivery for a Mrs. Forbes!" yelled a man's voice.

"*Ms*. Forbes!" Katy said in a disciplining-the-dog-for-the-hundredth-time voice, peered through the peephole, and undid the bolts. "*Ms! Ms!*"

A lad in blue overalls and shiny hair and ears as big as a chimpanzee's heaved a packing case into the hallway. He saw me and his face said, "Nice one Cyril." "Sign here please, *Miss* Forbes."

She signed and he was gone.

We looked at the packing case for a moment. "Nice big present," I commented. "Is your birthday coming up?"

"It's not a present," she said. "It's already mine. Come and give me a hand, would you? In the cupboard under the sink there's a hammer and a cold chisel, in a box with some fuses. . . ."

We prised open the lid, and the four sides fell away.

A Queen Anne chair.

Katy's thoughts wandered a long way away. "Marco," she said, "thank you for making breakfast. It was really . . . But I think I'd like you to go now." There was a tremor in her voice. "You're not a bad man."

"Okay," I said. "Could I just hop into your shower?"

"I'd like you to go now."

The avenue was littered with autumn. The air was smoky with it. Not yet ten A.M., it was crisp and sunny and foggy all at once. I'd try to get to Alfred's by late lunchtime, Tim Cavendish's by late afternoon, and back to my place by early evening in time to meet Gibreel. It wasn't really worth going back to my flat now. I'd just have to smell of sex all day.

Katy Forbes wasn't the stablest of campers but at least she hadn't been a head-case like that vamp of Camden Town who'd tied me up to her bedstead with a leather belt and videoed herself releasing her pet tarantula on my torso. "Stop screaming," she'd screamed. "Baggins has had his sacs removed. . . ." It hadn't been Baggins's sacs that were at the forefront of my mind. Katy's intellect must have impressed me enough to go for the writer identity, rather than the drummer. Even so. The Morning-After Me was not overly impressed with the Night-Before Me. I pass through many Me's in the course of the day, each one selfish with his time. The Lying-in-Bed Me and the Enjoying-the-Hot-Shower Me are particularly selfish. The Late Me loathes the pair of them.

I really am a drummer. My band's called The Music of Chance. I named it after a novel by that New York bloke. I describe us as a "loose musical cooperative"—there are about ten members, and whoever's around performs on whatever's happening. Plus, most of us are pretty loose. We play our own material mostly, though if I'm strapped for cash we'll play whatever will put bums on seats. We've been offered a recording contract, by the biggest record company in southern Belgium, but we thought we should hold out for something more EMI- or Geffen-sized. The Music of Chance is pretty big in the Slovak Republic, too. We played a few gigs there last summer that went down very well.

I really am a writer, too. A ghostwriter. My first published project was the autobiography of a pace bowler called Dennis Mackeson who played cricket for England a few times in the mid-eighties, when it rained a lot. *The Twistlethwaite Tornado* got great reviews in *The Yorkshire Post*—"Not in a million years would I have guessed it that Mr. Mackeson could bowl 'em out with his nib as well as his yorkers! 'Owzat!' " On the strength of the first book I'm currently writing the life story of this old guy, Alfred, who lives on the edge of Hampstead Heath with his younger—though not by much—boyfriend, Roy. I go, he reminisces about his younger days, I tape it, jot notes, and by next week I write it up into a narrative. Roy's the son of some Canadian steel tycoon, and he pays me a weekly retainer fee. It helps pay the rent and the wine bars.

You could get lost in these northeast London streets. I was half-lost myself. They curve around themselves in cul-de-sacs and crescents and groves. A few months ago I spent the night bonking the Welsh Ladies Kickboxing Champion in a caravan somewhere beyond Hammersmith. She'd said that the whole of London seemed like one vast rat's maze to her. I'd said yes, but what if the rats happened to like being in the maze?

The leaves are covering up the cracks in the pavement. When

I was a kid I could lose myself for hours kicking through fallen leaves, while avoiding dog turds and cracks. I used to be superstitious, but I'm not anymore. I used to be a Christian, but I'm not one of those anymore either. Then I was a Marxist. I used to wait with my cadre leader outside Queensway tube station and ask people what they thought about the Bosnian Question. Of course, most people shrug you off. "I see, sir, no comment, is it?" I cringe to think of it now.

I guess I'm not anything much these days, apart from older. A part-time Buddhist, maybe.

I remembered to worry about Poppy's period. A condom had burst on us, when was it? Ten days ago. Her period is due sometime at the end of next week. . . . Give it another week, due to stress incurred by waiting for it. . . . That's two weeks before panic starts knocking, and three weeks before I let it in. Oh well. India would love a little brother to play with. And when, in twenty years' time, a professor of philosophy asks him, "Why do you exist?" he can toy with his nose-ring and answer, "Rugged lust and ruptured rubber." Weird. If I'd bought the pack behind on the condom shelf he wouldn't be/won't be sitting there. Unmix that conditional and smoke it.

Of course, I might be sterile. Now that really would be annoying. All that money wasted on unnecessary condoms. Well, there's been AIDS to worry about, I suppose. Highbury playing fields. I've almost escaped. I like the Victorian skyline, and I like the pigeons flying through the tunnels of trees. Teenagers smoking on the swings. Last time I was here was bonfire night, with Poppy and India. It was the first time India had seen fireworks. She took in the spectacle with royal dignity, but kept talking about them for days. She's a very cool kid, like her mother.

It'll be bonfire night again, soon. You can see your breath. When I was a kid I used to pretend I was a locomotive. What kid doesn't? Old men are walking their labradors across the muddy turf. There are young fathers on the pathways, teaching their kids how to ride their bikes without stabilizers. Some of these fathers are younger than me. I bet those are their BMWs. Me, I walk everywhere. That's Tony Blair's old house. A postman emptying a postbox. Walking past these old terraced houses is like browsing down a shelf of books. A student's pad, a graphic designer's studio, a family with their kitchen done out in primary colors and pictures from school fridge-magneted onto the fridge. An antiquarian's study. A basement full of toys—a helicopter going round and round and round. A huntin', shootin', buggerin' living room with paintings and fittings that clear their throats and say "burgle this house!" to all the people trudging past to the Arsenal and Finsbury Park unemployment centers. Offices of obscure support groups, watchdog headquarters, and impotent trade unions. Three men in black suits stride past, turning down Calabria Road, one speaking into a cell phone, another carrying a briefcase. What are they doing here on a Saturday? Must be estate agents. How come they end up with that life, and I end up with this one? I could have been a lawyer, or an accountant, or a whatever you have to be to afford a house around Highbury playing fields, too, if I had wanted to. I was adopted by middle-class parents in Surrey, I went to a good school. I got a job in a city firm. I was twenty-two and I was taking Prozac for breakfast. I had my very own shrink. I wince to think of the money I paid him to tell me what the matter was. When I told him I'd been adopted his eyes lit up! He'd done his Ph.D. in adopted kids. But I discovered the answer myself in the end. I had stopped taking plunges. I don't mean risks: I mean plunges, the uprooting and throwing of oneself into something entirely new.

Now I live like this, losing the battle against a battery of deadlines—especially financial ones—but at least they are deadlines of my own choosing, there because I've plunged myself into something again. It's not always an easy way to live. Independence and insecurity hobble along together in my three-legged race. Jim—my adoptive dad—tells me this is a choice I made, and that I shouldn't ask for sympathy. And that's true. But why did I make that choice? That's what I wonder about. Because I am me, is the answer. But that just postpones the question. Why am I me?

Chance, that's why. Because of the cocktail of genetics and upbringing fixed for me by the blind barman Chance.

That *Big Issue* vendor guy there, why is he selling his magazine next to a shop where people spend £250 on a brass-knobbed antique bedstead and congratulate themselves on a bargain? Chance. Why is that guy a bus driver, and that woman a rushed-off-her-feet waitress in Pizza Hut? Chance. People say they choose, but it comes down to the same thing: why people choose what they choose is also down to chance. Why did that gray oily pigeon lose its leg, but that white and brown one didn't? Chance. Why did that curvaceous model get to model those particular jeans? Chance. Isn't all this obvious? That short woman in an orange anorak wandering across the road in front of that taxi, with the driver mentally stripping the leggy woman striding past with a flopsy dog—why is she about to be mown down, and not me?

—fuck!

The second time this morning when I didn't know how I ended up lying next to an unknown female. This time was even more uncomfortable than the last. There was a pulsation in my left leg that *hurt*. There'd been a screech of brakes, and a sleeve ripping. Something flew through the air—that would be me—and the round eye of the taxi. This woman looked much more shocked than Katy Forbes had. She had a dead leaf and a lollipop stick sticking to her face.

"Stone the crows," she said. Irish. Middle-aged. The lollipop stick dropped off.

The taxi driver was standing over us, a fat Cockney. Santa Claus without the beard or the love of humanity. I heard his engine, still running. He was deciding whether to be irate or compassionate. "Ruddy Bleedin' Nora, love! Why didn't you look where you was going?"

"I—" Her eyes looked around like a puppet's. "I wasn't looking where I was going."

"Any bones broken?" The question was to both of us.

My leg was still complaining loudly, but I found I could stand and wiggle my toes. The woman picked herself up.

"I saw everything," said the leggy woman with the flopsy dog and a Sloaney accent. "He rugby tackled her out of the way of the taxi. And they tumbled over and over. I'm sure he saved her life, you know." There was no one else to tell but the taxi driver who wasn't listening to her.

"I'm much obliged to you," said the anorak woman, getting up and dusting herself down, as if I'd just handed her a cup of tea. Her eye socket was already reddening.

"You're welcome," I said, in the same way. "You're going to have a black eye."

"The least of my troubles. Is your taxi free?" the anorak woman asked the taxi driver.

"You *sure* you're all right, love? No knocks on the head now?"

"No, no, I'm quite all right. But can you give me a ride in your cab?"

"I give rides in my cab to anybody with the fare, love. But look 'ere—"

"I must look a pretty sight, but so would you if you'd . . . never mind. I'm sane, and solvent. Please take me to the airport."

He was suspicious, but she was serious. "Well, I suppose as long as you're inside my taxi, you can't try and kill yourself under it. Heathrow, Gatwick, or London City?"

"Gatwick, please."

The taxi driver looked at me. "You all right, son?"

I looked around for somebody to tell me the answer but there was nobody. "I guess so."

The taxi driver looked back at the woman. "Then climb in."

They got in and drove off.

"Well," said the leggy woman, "how frightfully bizarre!"

I picked myself up and walked away from the little cluster of passersby that was threatening to gather. Weird. If that chair hadn't arrived when it did, and Katy hadn't flipped out and asked me to leave, then I wouldn't have been at that precise spot to stop that woman being flattened. I've never saved anyone's life before. It felt as ordinary as collecting photographs from Boots the Chemist. Slightly exciting beforehand, but basically a let-down. I walked past a phone box and thought about calling Poppy to tell her what had just happened. Nah. She might think I was boasting. I was already thinking about other things. I went over the zebra crossing outside Highbury and Islington tube station, the one by the roundabout, and was searching my coat for a fiver that I hoped I'd put there for emergencies when the same three men in black suits I'd seen earlier hustled me away from the ticket machine and around the corner, behind a newspaper kiosk. I was still shaken from my rugby tackle, so it took me a few moments to realize what was happening. People in the background were deliberately not noticing. Bloody Islington.

I almost saw the funny side of it. "If you want to mug me and take my money, you've really chosen the wrong—"

"WewannAweewordAboo' tha' the' wurmansonny!"

Was I being mugged in Kurdish? "I'm terribly sorry?"

He jabbed my sternum with an iron forefinger. "About—that—woman—" Oh, a Scot. Which woman? Katy Forbes? Were these her boyfriends?

The next one drawled. "That lady in the orange raincoat, boy." A Texan? A Texan and a Scot. This was sounding like the first line of a joke. These people weren't joking, though. They looked like they had never joked since kindergarten. Debt collectors? "The woman you just pulled from in front of that there taxi. There were witnesses."

"Oh. Her. Yes."

"We're policemen." Did I have anything illegal on me? No . . . The Scot flashed his ID for a moment. "Where did she say she was going?"

"I, er—"

"The lady with the legs and the dawgie said she was going to an airport. Now all we want to know from you is *which* airport she was heading for."

"Heathrow." I still have no idea why I lied, but once the lie was out it was too dangerous to try to recapture it.

"Ye quite sure aboot that noo, laddie?"

"Oh yes. Quite sure."

They looked at me like executioners. The third one who hadn't said anything spat. Then they turned and piled into a Jaguar with smoked glass windows that was waiting behind the flower stall. It screeched off, leaving people staring at me. I can't blame them. I would have stared at me, too.

———————

As the fine denizens of London Town know, each tube line has a distinct personality and range of mood swings. The Victoria Line for example, breezy and reliable. The Jubilee Line, the young disappointment of the family, branching out to the suburbs, eternally having extensions planned, twisting round to Greenwich, and back under the river out east somewhere. The District and Circle Line, well, even Death would rather fork out for a taxi if he's in a hurry. Crammed with commuters for King's Cross or Paddington, and crammed with museum-bound tourists who don't know the craftier short cuts, it's as bad as how I imagine Tokyo. I had a professor once who asked us to prove that the Circle Line really does go around in a circle. Nobody could. I was dead impressed at the time. Now what impresses me is that he'd persuaded somebody to pay him to come up with that sort of tosh. Docklands Light Railway, the nouveau riche neighbor, with its Prince Regent, its West India Quay, and its Gallions Reach and its Royal Albert. Stentorian Piccadilly wouldn't approve of such artyfartyness, and neither would his twin uncle, Bakerloo. Central, the middle-aged cousin, matter-of-fact, direct, no forking off or going the long way round. That's about it for the main lines, except the Metropolitan, which is too boring to mention, except that it's a nice fuchsia color and you take it to visit the dying.

Then you have the oddball lines, like Shakespeare's oddball plays. Pericles, Hammersmith and City, East Verona Line, Titus of Waterloo.

The Northern Line is black on the maps. It's the deepest. It has the most suicides, you're most likely to get mugged on it, and its art students are most likely to be future Bond Girls. There's something doom-laden about the Northern Line. Its station names: Morden, Brent Cross, Goodge Street, Archway, Elephant and Castle, the resurrected Mornington Crescent. It was closed for years: I remember imagining I was on a probe peering into the *Titanic* as the train passed through. Yep, the Northern Line is the psycho of the family. Those bare-walled stations south of the Thames that can't attract advertisers. Not even stair-lift manufacturers will advertise in Kennington tube station. I've never been to Kennington but if I did I bet there'd be nothing but run-down fifties housing blocks, closed-down bingo halls, and a used-car place where tatty plastic banners fluppetty-flup in the homeless wind. The sort of place where best-forgotten films starring British rock stars as working-class antiheroes are set. There but for the grace of my credit cards go I.

London is a language. I guess all places are.

I catch a good rhythm in the swaying of the carriages. A blues riff on top of it . . . or maybe something Iranian . . . I note it down on the back of my hand. A pong of salt marshes and meadows . . . ah yes, Katy Forbes's perfume.

Look at her! Look at that woman. Febrile. Corvine. Black velvet clothes, not an ounce of sluttiness about her. Intelligent and alert, what's that book she's reading? And her skin—that perfect West African black, so black it has a bluish tinge. Those gorgeous, proud lips. What's she reading? Tilt it this way a bit, love. . . . Nabokov! I knew it. She has a brain! But if I break that rule and talk to her, even if I break the middle-way seating rule and sit one seat nearer to her than I need to, she'll think I'm threatening her and the defenses will slam down. None of these problems would exist if we had just met by chance at a party. Same her, same me. But chance brings us together here, where we cannot meet.

Still, it's a fine morning, up on the surface of the world. I saved somebody's life forty minutes ago. The universe owes me one. I stand up and walk towards her before I think about it anymore.

I'm about to say "Excuse me" when the door from the next compartment opens and a homeless guy walks in. His eyes have seen things that I hope mine never do. He has a big gash where half of his eyebrow should be. There's a lot of frauds around, but this guy isn't one. Even so. There are so many thousands of genuine homeless people, if you give even a little to each you'll end up on the street yourself. When you're a Marco your last defense against destitution is selfishness.

"Excuse me." His voice has a hollow fatigue that cannot be faked. "I'm very sorry to bother everyone, I know it's embarrassing for us all. But I have nowhere to sleep tonight, and it's going to be another freezing one. There's a bed in the Summerford Hostel, but I need to get £12.50 by tonight to be allowed in. If you can help, please do. I know you all just want to go about your business, and I'm very sorry. I just don't know what else to say to people. . . ."

People stare at the floor. Even to look at a homeless person is to sign a contract with them. I dabbled with joining the Samaritans once. The supervisor had been homeless for three years. I remember him saying that the worst thing was the invisibility. That and not being able to go anywhere where nobody else could go. Imagine that, owning nothing with a lock, except a toilet cubicle in King's Cross Station, with a junkie on one side and a pimp on the other.

Sod it. Roy will give me some money later.

I give the man a couple of quid I was going to get a cappuccino with, but coffee's bad for you anyway, and I was still buzzing from Katy's percolator.

"Thank you very much," he says. I nod, our eyes meeting just for a moment. He's in a bad way. He shuffles into the next carriage. "Excuse me everyone, I'm very sorry to bother you. . . ."

The girl in black velvet gets off at the next station. Now I'll never get to taste oysters sliding down the chute of my tongue with her.

I couldn't hack the Samaritans, by the way. I couldn't get to sleep afterwards, worrying about the possible endings of the stories that had been started. Maybe that's why I'm a ghostwriter. The endings have nothing to do with me.

There's one decent place on the Northern Line. That's where I'm heading now: Hampstead. The elevator lugs you back up to street level in less than a minute. Don't try taking the spiral stairs to save time. Take it from me. It's quicker to dig your way up.

The obligatory silence of elevators. Could be a Music of Chance song title.

It's a chance to have a think. Even Gibreel shuts up in elevators.

Poppy once said to me that womanizers are victims.

"Victims of what?"

"An inability to communicate with women in any other way." She added that womanizers either never knew their mother, or never had a good relationship with their mother.

I was oddly annoyed. "So the womanizer wants every woman he sleeps with to be his surrogate mother?"

"No," said Poppy, reasoning when she should be defending. "I don't quite know what you want from us. But it's something to do with approval."

The elevator doors open and you're suddenly out into a leafy street where even McDonald's had to tone down their red and yellow for black and gold, to help it blend in with the bookshops. Old money lives in Hampstead. The last of the empire money. They take their grandchildren on birthday trips to the British Museum, and poison one another's spouses in elegant ways. When I worked as a delivery boy for a garden center I had a woman here, once, called Samantha or Anthea or Panthea. She lived in a house opposite her mother, and not only loved her pony more than me, which I can understand, but she even loved repairing wicker-seated chairs more than me. My, my, Marco, that was a long time ago.

The sky was clouding over, groily clouds the dunnish white of dug-up porcelain. I sighed quite involuntarily. The whole world was about to cry. I'd had a sexy little umbrella last night, but I'd left it at Katy's or the gallery or somewhere. Oh well, I'd found it lying forgotten somewhere myself. The wind was picking up, and big leaves were flying over the chimneys like items of washing on the run. All these Edwardian streets I'd probably never go down.

The first raindrops were dappling the tarmac and scenting the gardens by the time I got to Alfred's.

·   ·   ·

Alfred's house is one of those bookend houses, tall, with a tower on the corner where you can imagine literary evenings being conducted. In fact, they used to be. The young Derek Jarman paid tribute here, and Francis Bacon, and Joe Orton before he made it big, along with a stream of minor philosophers and once-famous literati. Visitors to Alfred's place are like the bands that play the university circuit: only the will-be-famous and the once-were-famous perform. Has-beens and might-bes. Alfred tried to start a humanist movement here in the sixties. Its idealism doomed it. Campaign for Nuclear Disarmament bishops and that Colin Winsom bloke still drop by. Heard of him? See what I mean? . . .

It usually takes a long time before anyone answers the door. Roy is too otherworldly to notice things like doorbells, especially while he's composing. Alfred is too deaf. I ring a polite five times, watching the weeds coming up through the cracks in the steps, before I start banging.

Roy's face materializes in the gloom. He sees it's me, smiles, and readjusts his hairpiece. He shoves open the door and almost shears off the tip of my nose. "Oh," he says, "hi! Come in . . . uh . . ." I realize he has the same problem with names as me. "Marco!"

"Hello, Roy. How are you this week?"

Roy has one of those Andy Warhol accents. He speaks as though receiving words from far beyond Andromeda. "Jeez, Marco . . . you're sounding like a doctor. You're not a doctor . . . are you?"

I laugh.

Roy insists on helping me off with my coat, and slings it over the pineapple-shaped knob of the banister. I must look up the correct word for that knob. "How's The Music of Chance? All you young things, playing together and inspiring one another. . . . We just love it."

"We laid down a couple of tracks two weeks ago, but now we're back to rehearsing in Gloria's uncle's warehouse." Due to a chronic lack of anything to pay with. "Our bassist's new girlfriend plays the handbells, so we're trying to expand our repertoire a little. . . . How's your composing?"

"Not so good. Everything I do ends up turning into 'The Well-Tempered Clavier.' "

"What's wrong with Bach?"

"Nothing, except it always makes me dream about a team of synchronized tail-chasing Escher cats. Now what do you think of this? It's from a wicked young friend of mine named Clem." He hands me a postcard of Earth. On the back I turn it over and read the message: "Wish you were here. Clem."

Roy never makes himself laugh, only others. But he smiles timidly. "Now. You're good with your hands. Can you work out how our percolator works? It's through in the kitchen here. I've just been having no luck at all with it. It's German. They make North American–proof percolators in Germany. Do you think they've forgiven us for the war yet?"

"What seems to be the problem with it?"

"Jeez, now you're *really* sounding like Dr. Marco. It just keeps overflowing. The drippy nozzle thing totally refuses to drip."

The first time I saw Roy and Alfred's kitchen, it looked like the set of an earthquake movie. It still does, but now I'm used to it. I found the percolator under a large head made of chickenwire. "We thought it would give a dead machine a little character," explained Roy. "It also makes it impossible to lose the percolator. Volk constructed it one spring weekend for Alfred."

Volk was a truly beautiful Serbian teenager with a dubious-sounding visa who sometimes lived at Alfred's when he had nowhere else to go but Serbia. He always wore leather trousers, and Alfred called him "our young wolf." I didn't ask any more questions.

"Well, I think the main problem is that you've put tea leaves into the filter instead of coffee."

"Oh, you jest! Lemme see. Oh, Jeez, you're right. . . . Now, where's the coffee? Do you know where the coffee is, Marco?"

"Last week it was in the tennis-ball shooter."

"No, Volk moved it from there. . . . Let me see. . . ." Roy surveyed the kitchen like God looking down on a mess of a world it was too late to uncreate. "Bread basket! Say, go on up to Alfred in his study whydon'tcha? I left him reading last week's installment of his life. We both thought it was marvelous. I'll bring up the coffee when it's done dripping."

There's a sad story about Roy. He used to have his compositions published. He still finds old copies of them, occasionally, leafing through very specialist shops, and he shows them to me with glee. A few times they were performed and recorded for the radio. The American public radio network broadcast his First Symphony, and Lyndon Johnson wrote Roy a letter to say how much he and his wife had enjoyed it. That success attracted negative criticism, too, though, and some bitchiness from the music world filtered down to Roy. It upset him so much that he's never published anything since. He just composes, wodge after wodge of manuscript, with nobody to hear it but himself and Alfred, and occasionally a young wolf from Serbia, and me. He's on his thirteenth symphony.

He should hear some of the things that people have said about The Music of Chance. Enough to make your bile freeze up. *The Evening News* reviewer wrote that he thought the world would be improved if we all fell into the giant food blender that our music resembled. I was tickled pink.

As I reached the top floor I found that my mind was chewing over a conversation I had the first time I met Poppy. Everyone else at the party was unconscious, and a drizzly morning was watering down the night.

"Do you ever think of the effect you have on your conquests?"

"I don't see where you're coming from, Poppy."

"I'm not coming from anywhere. But I suddenly noticed that you love talking about cause. You never talk about effect."

I knocked on the door of Alfred's study, and entered. A room inhabited by photographs of friends, none of them new. Alfred was staring out of the window the way old men do. Curtains of rain were blowing pell-mell off Hampstead Heath.

"Winter will soon be with us, our *gustviter* friend."

"Afternoon, Alfred."

"Another winter. We must hurry. We are still on chapter . . . chapter . . ."

"Chapter six, Alfred."

"And how is your family?"

Is he confusing me with someone else? "They're fine, last time I looked."

"We are only on chapter six, you see. We must hurry. My body is degenerating quickly. Last week's work was satisfactory. That is good. You are a writer, my young friend. We can make more progress today. I indicated with a green pen the parts I wish you to revise. Now, let us begin. You have your notebook with you?"

I waved it. Alfred indicated the seat nearest him. "Before you sit down, please put the recording of Vaughan Williams's Third Symphony onto the gramophone player. It is filed under 'V.' The Pastoral."

I love Alfred's record collection. Real, wide, black, plastic records. Thick. My hands love handling them, it's like meeting an old friend. CDs were foisted onto us with scandalous aplomb and nobody rumbled their game until it was too late. Like instant coffee compared to the real stuff. I didn't know this Williams's music, but it had a good start. I'd like to mix in a distorted bass, and maybe a snare drum.

"Then let us begin, shall we?"

"Whenever you're ready, Alfred."

I start the cassette rolling, and open my notebook at a new page. Everything on it is still perfect.

"It is 1946. I am living in Berlin, working for British Intelligence. Now there's an oxymoron for you. We are on the trail of Mausling, the rocket scientist wanted by the Americans for his—"

"I think we're back in London, now, Alfred."

"Ah, yes . . . We've handed Mausling over. . . . 1946 . . .

"Then I'm back at the civil service. Ah, yes, 1947. My first quiet year for a decade. There were rumblings from India, and Egypt. Bad rumors from Eastern Europe. People finding pits full of bodies in Armenia, Soviets and Nuremberg Nazis blaming each other. Churchill and Stalin had done dividing up Europe on a napkin, and the consequences of their levity were becoming horribly apparent. You can imagine, I was a bit of an embarrassment in Whitehall. A Hungarian Jew back from Berlin amongst the pencil sharpeners freshly down from Oxford. The crown owed me, they knew, but they no longer really wanted me. So, I was given an office job on Great Portland Street working with a division cracking down on black marketeers. I never got to see any action, though. I was just doing what computers and young ladies in shoulder pads do nowadays. Rationing was still in place, you see, but it was beginning to crumble round the edges. The wartime spirit was seeping away through the bomb craters, and people were reverting to their usual small-minded selves. Roy was still tangled up with his father and lawyers in Toronto. Imagine one of the more tedious Graham Greene novels, remove the good bits towards the end, and just have it going on and on and on for hundreds of pages. The only enjoyable part was the cricket, which I followed with the passion of an émigré. That, and Sundays at Speaker's Corner, where I could discuss Nietzsche and Kant and Goethe and Stalin in whichever language I wanted to, and get a decent game of chess if the weather was good. London was full of Alfreds in 1947."

I finished the last part and flexed my fingers. I followed Alfred's gaze, to the dripping camphor tree across the road from the study. The corner of Hampstead Heath; I could see a pond in a hollow beyond. When Alfred was thinking he looked at it, past his signed photo of Bertrand Russell.

"I've never seen a ghost, Marco. I don't believe in an afterlife. At best, I consider the idea of God to be a childish prank, and at worst a sick joke, probably pulled by the devil, and oh yes you *can* have one without the other. I know you offer allegiance to Buddha and your woolly Hesse, but I shall remain a devout atheist until the end. Yet one extraordinary thing occurred one summer evening in 1947. I want you to include it in my autobiography. When you write it, don't write it in the manner of a spooky story. Don't try to give an explanation. Just say that I don't know what to make of it, just write it like I tell it, so the reader can make up his own mind. The ghost comes in the first paragraph."

I'm really interested now. "What happened?"

"I'd finished work. I'd just had dinner with Prof Baker at a restaurant in South Ken. I was still sitting there gazing at the busy street. A waterfall mesmerizes in the same way, don't you think? Anyway. That was when I saw myself."

Alfred's eyes were all pupil, monitoring reactions and effects.

"You saw yourself?"

Alfred nodded. "I saw myself. Not a reflection, not a lookalike, not a twin brother, not a spiritual awakening, not a waxwork. This is no cheap riddle. I saw myself, Alfred Kopf, large as life."

"What were you doing?"

"Pelting past the window! I'd have missed him, if a sudden gust of wind hadn't blown his hat off. There was no other hat like it in the whole of London. He bent down to pick it up, just as I would have done. That hat belonged to my father, it was one of the few things he gave me before the Nazis took him off to their melting pots. He bent down, and looked up, like he was searching for someone. He put his hat on. Then he ran off again, but I had seen his face, and I'd recognized me."

Ghostwriters, like psychiatrists, have to know when to shut up.

"I hope for your sake, Marco, that you never see yourself. It doesn't feature in the ordinary repertoire of a sane human's experience. It's not unique, however. I've met three others who have experienced the same phenomenon. Imagine which emotion possesses you first."

I tried to. "Disbelief?"

"Wrong. We all felt the most indignant outrage. We wanted to jump up and chase after the interloper and stamp him into the ground. Which is what I did. I grabbed my father's hat—*my* father's hat—and chased after him. Down Brompton Road towards Knightsbridge. I was a very fit young man. I could see him—*my* beige raincoat flapping behind him. It was raining slightly. The pavement was skiddy with drizzle. Why was he running? Oh, he knew that I was after him all right. It was a different London, of omnibuses, policemen on horses, and women in headscarves. You could walk across the road without being knocked off a windscreen clean over Hades. My shadow was still there in front of me, running at the same pace as me. At Hyde Park Corner my lungs were clapping like bellows, so I had to slow down to a walking pace. And so did my shadow, as though he were baiting me.

We walked down Grosvenor Place, down the long wall that closets off the gardens behind Buckingham Palace from the plebeians. That takes you to Victoria. It was just a little place in those days. Then he turned up past the Royal Mews, along Birdcage Walk. The south edge of St. James's Park. By now my anger was beginning to dissipate. It all had the air of a shaggy-dog story. A Poe reject. I'd got a bit of breath back, so I tried suddenly sprinting at him. He was off again! Down to Westminster: when I had to slow down, so did my shadow. We walked along the Embankment. Commuters were streaming over the bridge. Sometimes I thought I'd lost him, but then I'd see the hat again, bobbing up and down about fifty yards ahead. My haircut, the back of my head. I tried to work out a rational explanation. An actor? Some temporal mirage? Insanity? Past Temple. We were heading east. I was getting a bit worried, it was a rough area in those days. I remember there was one of those Oriental sunsets of soupy jade and marmalade that London can pull out of the hat. Past Mansion House, down Cannon Street, and down to the Tower. Then I saw my shadow getting into a taxi! So I raced to the next one in the rank, and jumped in. "Look," I said, "I know this sounds ridiculous, but please follow that taxi." Maybe taxi drivers get asked that a lot, because the driver just said, "Right you are, squire." Up to Aldgate. Through cobbled backstreets to Liverpool Street. Moorgate. Where the Barbican is now. Thanks to the Blitz, the place was one big building site back then. As was Farringdon—in fact Farringdon still is. When we were slowed up by the traffic, I considered hopping out of the taxi and running to my shadow's, but every time I resolved to do so the lane of cars started moving again. Up to King's Cross, stopping and starting, stopping and starting. Down to Euston Square, and on to Great Portland Street. I could still see his hat in the back of the taxi. Did my shadow have nothing better to do with his time? Didn't I? After Baker Street the leafier parts began again, past Edgware Road and Paddington. Past Bayswater. I saw him get out of the taxi at Notting Hill Gate and stride off across Kensington Gardens. I paid the taxi driver, and sprang out after him. I recall the air after the rain, sweet and full of evening. 'Oy!' I yelled, and some genteel ladies walking dogs harrumphed. 'Alfred Kopf!' I yelled, and a man dropped out of a tree with a turfy thump. My shadow didn't even turn round. Why was he running? Literary precedents suggested that at least we should be able to have a stimulating conversation about the nature of good and evil. Across Kensington Road, down past the museums, past this restaurant where I'd arranged to meet Prof Baker later that evening. A sudden gust of wind blew my hat off. I bent down to pick it up. And when I looked up, I saw my shadow disappearing."

I had forgotten I was still here. "Just into thin air?"

"No! Onto a Number 36 bus. Off he went."

"But I thought that you'd already met Prof—"

Something flew into the window and thwacked. It fell before I saw what it was. A pigeon? Roy came running in trembling, with tears in his eyes. "Oh, Jeez, Alfred. I just had a phone call from Morris."

Was I in a tragedy or a farce?

"Calm down, Roy, Calm down. I've just been telling Marco about my double." Alfred lit his pipe. "Now, is this Morris Major or Morris Minor?"

"Morris Major, from Cambridge. Jerome's been killed!"

Alfred's fingers forgot his pipe. His voice fell to a croak. "Jerome? But he'd been granted immunity."

"Morris says the ministry is blaming Petersburg gangsters. They said Jerome had got mixed up in some sort of art theft."

"Impossible!" Alfred banged on the table hard enough to stave elderly fingers. "It's a cover-up. They're picking us off, one by one. They never know when to stop, those ministries. Damn those vermin to hellfire!" Alfred unleashed what I'm guessing was the direst oath in the Hungarian canon. The curse of Nosferatu.

I looked at Roy. "Bad news?"

Roy looked back, not needing to nod. "And there's coffee all over the kitchen floor. I think I put two filters in."

A long silence unspun. Alfred pulled out a handkerchief and a coin was flung out. It went round and round in ever-decreasing circles on the wooden floor, before vanishing under a chest where it would probably stay for years, or until Volk next visited.

"Marco," Alfred said, his eyes focusing on the far distance, "thank you for coming. But I think I'd like you to go now." There was a tremor in his voice. "We shall continue next week."

As I walked from Alfred's the clouds slid away towards Essex and a warm afternoon opened up, golden and clear. Whatever worries Alfred and Roy had were their business. Me, I nibbled the truffley bits off my strawberry ice cream. Midges hung over the puddles in columns, and the trees dripped dry. They'd be winter trees again soon. An ice cream van was playing "Oranges and Lemons" a few streets away. A couple of kids sat on walls trying to master their yo-yos. Good to see kids still playing with yo-yos. Fi, my natural mother, calls this time of year "Saint Luke's Summer." Isn't that beautiful? I felt good. I had a bit of money from Roy, slipped to me wrapped around this strawberry ice. He also insisted that I take a hideous green leather jacket with me. I put up a fight, but he had already put it on me somehow and while he was zipping it up, he remembered to tell me that Tim Cavendish had been on the phone earlier and had asked me to drop in that afternoon if I could. He whispered an apology for not giving me any more money, but he'd had to take someone to the House of Lords that week for running off to Zimbabwe with a suitcase of his money, and the legal fees had come to £92,000. "It was a lot, Marco," whispered Roy, "but I had to do it for the principle." The some-one was still in Zimbabwe, and so was the suitcase.

Integrity is a bugger, it really is. Lying can get you into difficulties, but to really wind up in the crappers try telling nothing but the truth.

While we were having sex, when the condom broke, Poppy was coming, and she gasped out, "Marco, this is better than sex." I just remembered.

I headed down to Primrose Hill. I'll walk to Tim Cavendish's via Regent's Park and Oxford Street. I love walking past London Zoo, and peering in. My childhood's in there. My adoptive parents used to take me on my birthday. Today even the sound of the aviary makes me taste clammy fish-paste sandwiches.

I'm pretty sure that being a single kid–single mother is enough for Poppy. But I've known women who've believed one thing about abortion, only for those beliefs to swing around when the crunch came. If Poppy's pregnant, what will I want? Would I want? For her to accept me as a father, I'd have to swear monogamy, and mean it. Many of my friends have got married and done the baby thing, and I can see how completely it changes your life. Taking plunges is no fun when the well-being of two other people depends on how you land. Weird. When I was younger, I thought that kids were an inevitable part of getting old. I thought you'd wake up one morning and there they'd be, nappies bulging. But no, you actually have to make up your mind to do them, like making up your mind to buy a house, cut a CD, or stage a coup d'état. What if I never make my mind up? What if?

Ah, worry, worry, worry.

The top of the hill. Breathe in, look at that view, and breathe out! Quite a picture, isn't it! Old Man London, out for the day . . . Italians give their cities sexes, and they all agree that the sex for a particular city is quite correct, but none of them can explain why. I love that. London's middle-aged and male, respectably married but secretly gay. I know its overlapping towns like I know my own body. The red brick parts around Chelsea and Pimlico, Battersea Power Station like an upturned coffee table . . . the grimy estates down Vauxhall way. Green Park. I map the city by trigonometrical shag points. Highbury is already Katy Forbes. Putney is Poppy, and India of course, not that I shag India, she's only five. Camden is Baggins the Tarantula. I try to pinpoint the places in Alfred's nutty story. . . . How am I supposed to put a story like that into a serious autobiography? I'm going to have to do something pretty drastic, or I'll end up ghostwriting *Diary of a Madman*.

It's too beautiful a day to worry about that. The light is too golden, the shadows too soft.

There are a lot of things in London that weren't here when Alfred went round his big loop chasing Alfred. All those aeroplanes flying into Heathrow and Gatwick. The Thames Barrier.

The Millennium Dome. Centerpoint, that sixties pedestal ashtray, bloody hell I wish someone would come along and bomb that. Canada Tower over in Docklands, gleaming in the sunlight now, and I think of that art deco mirror in the corner of Shelley's room. Shelley of Shepherd's Bush. She moved in with, what's-his-name, ah, Jesus, what *was* his name? The British Oxygen man. Her flatmate Natalie had become a born-again Christian and moved in with Jesus. Shelley, Natalie, and I had formed a Holy Trinity one rainy afternoon under Shelley's duvet. At the time I had filed Natalie under "Dangerously Vulnerable."

A city is a sea that you lose things in. You only find things that other people have lost.

"Wonderful, isn't it?" I say to a man walking his red setter.

"Fackin' shithole innit?"

Londoners slag off London because, deep down, we know we are living in the greatest city in the world.

Oxford Street was heaving when I got off the bus. Oxford Street is one of those sold-out-past-its-best things, like Glastonbury Rock Festival or Harrison Ford. You can taste the metallic tang of pollution here. The Doctor Martens boot shops depress me. The gargantuan CD shops preclude any surprise discoveries. The department stores are full of things for people who never have to lift anything when they move house: Neroesque bathtubs with gold-plated handles and life-size porcelain collie dogs. The fast-food restaurants towards Marble Arch leave you hungrier than you were when you went in. The only good thing about Oxford Street are the Spanish girls who pay for their English lessons by handing out leaflets for cut-price language schools around Tottenham Court Road. Gibreel got his rocks off with one once, by pretending to spik no Eenglish and be just off the boat from Lebanon. I bought a T-shirt from a stall near Oxford Circus with a pig on it to cheer Poppy up, big enough for her to use as a night-shirt. Then I walked past a poster in a travel agent's, or rather I was crushed against it by a sudden surge of bodies, and I felt small and older than my years and losing sight of the strip of sky far above, and—

And I shall have some peace there, for peace comes dropping slow,
Dropping from the veils of the morning to where the cricket sings;
There midnight's all a glimmer, and noon a purple glow,
And evening full of the linnet's wings.

I will arise and go now, for always night and day
I hear lake water lapping with low sounds by the shore;
While I stand on the roadway, or on the pavements grey,
I hear it in the deep heart's core.

You know the real drag about being a ghostwriter? You never get to write anything that beautiful. And even if you did, nobody would ever believe it was you.

I had to wait eight minutes to use my bank machine, and in that time I counted eleven different languages walking past. I think they were different, I get fuzzy around the Middle East. I blew my nose. Gravelly London mucus showed up on my snot analysis. Mmm. Lovely. Next to the bank was a shop that only sold televisions. Wide ones, cuboid ones, spherical ones, ones that let you see what crap you were missing on thirty other channels while you were watching the crap on this one. I watched the All-Blacks score three tries against England, and formulated the Marco Chance versus Fate Videoed Sports Match Analogy. It goes like this: when the players are out there the game is a sealed arena of interbombarding chance. But when the game is on video then every tiniest action already exists. The past, present, and future exist at the same time: all the tape is there, in your hand. There can be no chance, for every human decision and random fall of the ball is already fated. Therefore, does chance or fate control our lives? Well, the answer is as relative as time. If you're in your life, chance. Viewed from the outside, like a book you're reading, it's fate all the way.

Now I don't know about you, but my life is a well and I'm right down there in it. Neck deep, and I still can't touch the bottom.

I had a strong desire to jump in a taxi, tell him to take me to Heathrow, and get on a plane to somewhere empty and far away. Mongolia would suit me fine. But I can't even afford the tube fare to Heathrow.

I inserted my bank card, and prayed to the Fickle God of Autobanking for twenty-five quid, the minimum amount necessary to get drunk with Gibreel. The bloody machine swallowed my card and told me to contact my branch. I said something like "Gah!" and punched the screen. What's the point of Yeats if you can't buy a few rounds?

A round Indian lady behind me with a magenta dot on her forehead growled in a Brooklyn accent, "Real bummer, huh kid?"

Before I could answer a pigeon from the ledge above crapped on me.

"Better go back to bed . . . Here's a tissue. . . ."

The Tim Cavendish Literary Agency is down a murky side street near Haymarket. It's on the third floor. From the outside, the building is quite swanky. There's a revolving door, and a flagpole jutting out from above the lobby roof. It should house a wing of the Admiralty, or some other silly club that bars female members. But no, it houses Tim Cavendish.

"Marco! Wonderful you could drop in!"

Too much enthusiasm is much more offputting than not enough. "Afternoon, Tim. I've brought you the last three chapters."

"Top hole."

Glance at Tim's desk and you'll see everything you need to know. The desk itself was owned by Charles Dickens. Well, that's what Tim says and I have no reason to disbelieve him. Terminally overpopulated by piles of files and manuscripts, a glass of Glenfiddich that you could mistake for a goldfish bowl of Glenfiddich, three pairs of glasses, a word processor I've never seen him use, an overflowing ashtray, and a copy of *A–Z Guide to Nineveh and Ur* and *The Racing Post*. "Come in and have a glass, why don't you? I showed the first three chapters to Lavenda Vilnius on Monday. She's very excited. I haven't seen Lavenda so fluttery about a work in progress since Rodney's biography of Princess Margarine."

I chose the least piled-up-on chair and started unloading its cargo of shiny hardbacks. They still smelled of print.

"Dump those dratted things on the floor, Marco. In fact, fly to Japan and dump them on the bastard they're about."

I looked at the cover. *The Sacred Revelations of His Serendipity— A New Vision, A New Peace, A New Earth. Translated by Beryl Brain.* There was a picture of an Oriental Jesus gazing into the center of a buttercup with a golden-haired kid gazing up at him. "Didn't know this was your usual line, Tim."

"It isn't. I was handling it for an old Eton chum who runs a flaky New Age imprint on the side. Warning bells went off, Marco. Warning bells. But I didn't listen to them. My Eton man thought the market was ripe for a bit of Oriental wisdom in the new millennium. Beryl Brain is his part-time girlfriend. 'Beryl' is just about right, but 'Brain' she is not. Anyway. We'd just got the first consignment back from the printers when His Serendipity decided to hurry his vision along and gas the Tokyo underground with a lethal chemical. I'm sure you saw it on the news earlier this year. 'Twas 'im."

"How . . . horrific!"

"You're telling me it was horrific. We only got a fraction of the costs off the bleeders before they had their assets frozen! I ask you, Marco, I ask you. We're stuck with a print run of fifteen hundred hardbacks. We've sold a handful as curios to True Crime Freaks, but those apart we're up Shit Creek without a spatula. Can you believe those cultists? As if the end of the world *needs* to be hurried along . . ." Tim handed me the biggest glass of whisky I'd ever seen or heard of.

"What's the book itself like?"

"Well, some of it's twaddle, but mostly it's just piffle. Cheers! Down the hatch."

We clinked goldfish bowls.

"So tell me, Marco, how are our friends up in Hampstead?"

"Fine, fine . . ." I returned the book to its brothers and sisters. "We're up to 1947."

"Oh, really . . . What happened in 1947?"

"Not much. Alfred saw a ghost."

Tim Cavendish tilted back and his chair squeaked. "A ghost? I'm happy to hear it."

I didn't want to broach this topic, but . . . "Tim, I'm not sure to what degree Alfred is altogether . . ."

"Altogether altogether?"

"You could say."

"He's as nutty as a vegan T-bone. And Roy has definitely been to Disney World once too often. What of it?"

"Well, doesn't it present some problems?"

"What problems? Roy has enough dosh to personally underwrite the whole print run."

"No, I don't mean that." Now wasn't the time to broach the other topic of Roy and the House of Lords. "I mean, well, autobiographies are supposed to be factual, aren't they?"

Tim chuckled and took off his glasses. Both pairs. He leaned back on his squeaky chair and placed his fingertips together as though in prayer. "Are autobiographies supposed to be factual? Would you like the straight answer or the convoluted one?"

"Straight."

"Then, from the publishing point of view, the answer is 'God forfend.' "

"I'll try the convoluted answer."

"The act of memory is an act of ghostwriting."

Very Tim Cavendish. Profundity on the hoof. Or has he said it a hundred times before?

"Look at it this way. Alfred is the ingredients, the book is the meal, but you, Marco, you are the cook! Squeeze out the juice! I'm glad to hear there's still some left in the old boy. Ghosts are welcome. And for God's sake, play up the Jarman-Bacon connection when you get to that. Encourage him to name-drop. Stroke his udders. Alfred's not famous in his own right, at least, outside Old Compton Street he isn't, so we're going to have to Boswellize him. The ear of postwar-twentieth-century London. That kind of thing. He knew Edward Heath, too, didn't he? And he was a pal of Albert Schweitzer."

"It doesn't seem very honest. I'm not writing what really happened."

"Honest! God bless you, Marco! This is not the world of Peter Rabbit and his woodland friends. Pepys, Boswell, Johnson, Swift, all freeloading frauds to a man."

"At least they were their own freeloading frauds. Ghostwriters do the freeloading for other frauds."

Tim chuckled up to the ceiling. "We're all ghostwriters, my boy. And it's not just our memories. Our actions, too. We all think we're in control of our own lives, but really they're pre-ghostwritten by forces around us."

"So where does that leave us?"

"How well does the thing read?" A classic Cavendish answer in a question's clothing. The intercom on Tim's desk crackled. "It's your brother on the line, Mr. Cavendish." Mrs. Whelan, Tim's secretary, is the most indifferent woman in London. Her indifference is as dent-proof as fog. "Are you here or are you still in Bermuda?"

"Which one, Mrs. Whelan? Nipper Cavendish or Denholme Cavendish?"

"I daresay it's your elder brother, Mr. Cavendish."

Tim sighed. "Sorry, Marco. This is going to be protracted sibling stuff. Why don't you drop in next week after I've had a chance to read this lot? Oh, and I know this is Herod calling Thatcher a bit insensitive but you really need to change your shirt. And there's something white stuck in your hair. And a last word of advice—I tell this to anyone who's trying to get a book finished—steer clear of Nabokov. Nabokov makes anyone feel like a clodhopper."

I downed the rest of the whisky and slunk off, closing the door quietly behind me on Tim's "Hello, Denny, how marvelous to hear from you, I was going to get in touch this very afternoon about your kind little loan. . . ."

"Goodbye, Mrs. Whelan." To Caesar that which is Caesar's, to God that which is God's, and to the secretary that which is the secretary's.

Mrs. Whelan's sigh would drain a fresh salad of all color.

"Marco!"

I'd wandered into Leicester Square, drawn by the knapsacked European girls, the lights and colors, and a vague plan to see if there were any new remainders to be found in the mazes under Henry Pourdes Bookshop in Charing Cross Road. Warm, late afternoon. Leicester Square is the center of the maze. Nothing to do but put off getting out again. Teenagers in baseball caps and knee-length shorts swerved by on skateboards. I thought of the word "centrifugal," and decided it was one of my favorite words. Youths from the Far East, Europe, North America, wherever, drifting around hoping to find Cool London. Ah, that Cockney leprechaun is forever beyond the launderette on the corner. I watched the merry-go-round for a few revolutions. A sprog was smiling every time he bobbed past his gran and somehow it made my heart ache so much that I felt like crying or smashing something. I wanted Poppy and India to be here, now, right now. I'd buy us ice creams, and if India's fell off, she could have mine. Then I heard my name and looked up. Iannos was waving a falafel at me from his Greek Snack Bar between the Swiss Center and the Prince Charles Cinema, where you can see nine-month-old movies for £2.50, by the way. Katy's scrambled eggs had long since vacated my stomach, and a falafel would be perfect.

"Iannos!"

"Marco, my son! How's The Music of Chance?"

"Fine, mate. Everything as it should be. Petty arguments about nothing, bitching, still porking one another's girlfriends when we're not porking one another. Did you buy the new synth from Roger?"

"Dodgy Rodgy? Yep. I play it in my uncle's restaurant every night. Only problem is that I have to pretend I'm Turkish."

"Since when can you speak Turkish?"

"That's the problem. I have to pretend I'm an autistic Turkish keyboard-playing prodigy. Gets you down, man. Like being in *Tommy* and *The King and I* on the same stage. When's The Music of Chance playing again?"

"When is it not playing?"

"Bollocks, man. How's Poppy?"

"Ah, Poppy's fine, thanks."

"And her beautiful little daughter?"

"India. India's fine. . . ."

Iannos looked at me thoughtfully.

"What's that look supposed to mean then?"

"Ah, nothing . . . I can't chat, but why don't you come in and sit down? I think there's a seat at the back. Cup o'tea?"

"I'd love one. Thanks, Iannos. Thanks a lot."

Iannos's little snack bar was full of bodies and loud bits of sentences. The only free seat in the cramped place was opposite a woman slightly older than me. She was reading a book called *The Infinite Tether—You and Out-of-Body Experiences,* by Dwight Silverwind. I asked if I could take the seat, and she nodded without looking up. I tried not to stare but there was nothing else to look at. Her auburn hair—dyed—was in gypsy ringlets, and between her fingers, eyebrows, and earlobes she was wearing at least a dozen rings. Her clothes were tie-dyed. Probably purchased when she'd gone trekking in Nepal. Landslid breast. She burns incense, does aromatherapy and describes herself as not exactly telepathic, but definitely empathic. She's into pre-Raphaelite art, and works part-time in a commercial picture library. I'm not knocking these things, and I know I come over as arrogant. But I do know my Londoners.

"I'm sorry to interrupt you," I said, sipping my tea with a cocked little finger, "but I couldn't help noticing the title of your book." Her eyes were calm, and faintly pleased—good. "It looks engrossing. Is there a connection with alternative healing? That's my field, you see."

"Is that a fact, now?" Nice voice, rusky with sprinkled sugar. She was amused by my come-on and faintly flattered but not going to show it—too much. "Dwight Silverwind is one of the leading authorities on out-of-body experiences, or spiritwalking, as the Navaho Indians call it. Dwight's a very special friend of mine. He's my Life Coach. Look. This is Dwight." On the inside cover of the jacket was a wispy white smiling man with preposterous braces. A Yank, at fifty paces. "In this book, Dwight describes transcending the limits of the corporeal body."

"Oh. Is it easy?" Probably easier than transcending his dress sense.

"No. It requires a lot of mental training, to unknot and cast free the moorings that society uses to tie us down to its own reality conceits. Also, it depends on the individual's alpha emanations. I'm quite high alpha, you're more gamma."

"Beg pardon?" I detected large deposits of vanity. Vanity is the softest of bedrocks to sink shafts into.

"I could tell when you sat down. Your emanations are more gamma than alpha."

"You tell without a urine sample?" I almost said "sperm sample," but chickened out.

She acted a laugh. This was going well. "I'm Nancy Yoakam. Holistic therapist. Here's my card." And here was Nancy Yoakam's hand, lingering on my side of the table.

"I'm Marco. I like your name, if I may say so. You should be from Nashville."

"I'm from Glastonbury. You know. King Arthur and the rock festival. Very pleased to meet you, Marco." Gaze into my eyes. . . . You are sinking into a deeeeep sleeeeeep. Okay. But I'm a bit too old for her to be adopting that children's TV presenter voice. She probably thinks I'm younger, most women do. That's not vanity, it's having Latin American genes in the pool. "You see, I'm a person watcher. I like to sit and read people. To trained eyes, humans transmit their innermost secrets. I see your fingers are ringless—tell me Marco, is there no special somebody in your life?"

Direct. "A girlfriend, you mean?"

"Yes, let's suppose I do mean a girlfriend."

"I see several women concurrently."

Taking me in her stride. Eyebrow theatrically arched. Nancy did not get sprung from the Lego box yesterday. "Oh, how nice for you. A Juan Quixote. Doesn't that get rather complicated?"

"Well, it would do, but I always tell a woman when I first meet her that I see other women too. Like I'm telling you now. So if they don't want to handle that, they can stop before they start. I don't lie to people."

Nancy Yoakam put down Dwight Silverwind, still open but face down, and thumbed her lips coquettishly. "If you ask me, that's a very sophisticated way of luring women."

"I don't mean it to be. Why do you say so?"

"It sends out a challenge: 'You could be the one to change me, you could be the one to make me believe in love again.' Dwight calls it the 'Bird with the Broken Wing Syndrome.' "

Iannos brought me my tea, and tutted at me like a wily peasant. I thanked him and ignored him.

"Never thought of that. Maybe you're right, Nancy." Always a pleasure to discover insight in a vacuum. "I don't not believe in love. I just think it follows its own rather perverse rules of conduct, which I cannot fathom. Actually, I've been in love twice, which I think is rather a lot. Excuse me if I devour this falafel, would you? I'm ravenous."

"Go ahead. Why do you think we met today, Marco? Why you, why here, why now? Would you like to hear what I think it was?"

"Blind chance?"

"When we say chance, we mean 'emanations.' Dwight would say that your gamma was drawn to my alpha. The north magnetic pole is drawn to the south in an identical way."

Dwight was beginning to piss me off. I sat down because my mate Iannos offered me a free falafel. I sat where I did because there was nowhere else to sit. If Nancy Yoakam had been a bloke I would have been halfway to the door already. She had an interesting mind—possibly—but all this New Age tosh was daubed over it. However, there was a free shag on my dick's radar, so I stayed and sat through "How Crystal Healing Can Change Your Life." Amethyst is good for depression. Nancy's best friends were minerals. By the time I got her phone number I was no longer even interested in phoning her.

What's wrong with me?

When I was a kid and every female an unexplored continent, my heart would gasp in the wind and all colors held new truths.

Now look at me. I shag women like I wash my shirts. More often, some weeks.

Marco at sixteen and Marco at thirty are as different as Tierra del Fuego and Kennington.

No good, Marco my boy, no good at all. If you think about it too much you're lost.

. . .

Poppy and I had an argument a few weeks ago, which she ended by saying, "You know, Marco, you're not stupid, but for someone so intelligent you can be pretty goddamned blind."

I'd had no idea whatsoever how to respond, so I made some stupid joke. I forget what.

Time to head back.

I live in The New Moon. My pad is an attic conversion on the top floor of the pub. It's easy to find—if the weather's good go to St. Katherine's Docks and keep walking along the river, or just get any bus bound for the Isle of Dogs, and get off at the university. The pub's almost next door to Wapping tube station. I wound up there quite by accident, of course. The Music of Chance had a gig there last winter. One of our occasional guest vocalists, Sally Leggs, introduced me to Ed and Sylv, who run the place. The gig went down well, Sally being a kind of local celebrity, and when we were chatting afterwards Ed mentioned they were looking for a lodger again.

"What happened to the last one?" I asked. "Did a runner?"

"No," said Sylv, "you may as well know now. It happened almost twelve months ago. It was in the papers and we were on the *News at Ten*. Terrorists were using an old forgotten air-raid shelter under our beer cellar as a bomb factory. One night there was an accident, and about five bombs blew up simultaneously. Right under where you're sitting. Hence the refit, and the name change. Used to be The Old Moon."

I almost giggled. But I could tell by everyone's faces that every word was true.

"Fuck," I said, feeling ashamed, "that's bad luck."

People stared inwards.

"Still," I blundered on the way I do, "something that freaky isn't likely to happen for another couple of centuries, is it?"

Bigmouth strikes again.

Saturday is market day in Old Moon Road, so The New Moon was packed wall to wall with noise, smoke, grumbling, bags of vegetables, and antiques. Moya was playing darts with her new boyfriend, a squaddie called Ryan. Moya and I had done the wild thing one scratchy night. It hadn't been such a good idea.

Sylv was doing her shift with Derek, the part-timer. "Marco, a man called Digger was on the phone asking for you earlier. I gave him your number upstairs."

Oh, no. "Really? What did he want?" As if I didn't know.

"Wouldn't say. But I think it's just as well his name isn't Slasher."

Sylv is not a very well woman. Her eyelids are raw pink and on her worst days they're red and cracked. One of the regulars, Mrs. Entwhistle, told me that Sylv had lost the baby she was carrying on the night of the bomb. How do people pull themselves through things like that? I go to pieces just opening my credit card bills. But people do survive, all around us. The world runs on strangers coping. And Sylv's been smiling a bit more recently. If that had happened to me, I'd have to sell up—if I had anything to sell up—and go and live in County Cork. But Sylv's family owned The Old Moon for generations and so she's staying put in The New Moon. When there are a lot of customers I lend a hand, especially if I'm a little behind on the rent.

There are four flights of stairs between the bar and my room. It's a stiff climb, and the stairwell can be quite spooky at night, and sometimes in the daytime, too. The building goes back centuries. From my window there's a fine view over the Thames, as it curves around towards Greenwich and becomes an estuary. Upstream you can see Tower Bridge. It was a clear evening, and I could see streetlights coming on as far away as Denmark Hill and Dulwich.

If I did ever go to live in County Cork, I'd be on a boat back within a fortnight.

I opened the door to my room and my heart went into contractions when I saw the answerphone winking. Surely not Digger. He said I wouldn't have to pay him back until the following Tuesday. My dole check comes on Monday, and I'll be able to persuade Barry to give me £30 for this leather jacket of Roy's. Four messages.

But first I bit the bullet and opened the letter from the credit card company. If they type my name and address in uppercase, it's just a statement. If they use lowercase letters, I'm in trouble. This was uppercase.

Even so, it hurt. Where had this money gone? A shoe shop, restaurants, music equipment, a modem. There was a nice little bit at the bottom saying that my credit limit had been extended by £300! Are these people stupid?

Nope. They're not remotely stupid.

Next hurdle on the Marco Steeplechase: the answer machine.

"Marco, this is Wendy. I know I promised not to call for a while, but I couldn't resist. I'm sorry. Well, I'm fine. I got that place at St. Martin's. I thought you'd like to know. I told my boss today that I was quitting. Like you said I should, I just told him. Straight out. No beating around the bush. I told him, and that was that. I know you said we should have a cooling-off period, but if you wanted to celebrate with me, I could get a cheap bottle of champagne in and I'd cook you whatever you wanted. So if you're interested, phone me. Okay? Wendy. Ti amo, bellissima. Ciao."

Ah, poor kid. She'll get over me at art college, and learn her gender endings. One down, three possible Diggers to go.

"Ah, Marco, sorry to bother you, this is Tim Cavendish. We're having a slight family crisis. It appears that my brother's law firm in Hong Kong has gone down the tubes. It's all a bit of a mess . . . there's the Chinese police, asset freezing, and whatnot. . . . Erm, why don't you drop in middle of next week and we'll see how this might affect my ability to run Alfred's book. . . . Erm, terribly sorry about this. 'Bye."

Digger would have been better.

"Marco, this is Rob. I'm leaving the band to go and shack up with Maxine in San Francisco. 'Bye."

No problem; Rob leaves the band once a month. And I can stop trying to write songs that feature handbells. Last hurdle, God, please don't let it be Digger. If he can't contact me he can't threaten me.

"Dear Marco, this is Digger at Fungus Hut Recording Studios. How are you? I'm fine, thanks. This is just a friendly little message to remind you that you owe us £150 and unless you pay by five o'clock on Tuesday, then on Wednesday I will sell your drum kit for whatever the pawn shop in Tottenham Court Road will give me for it and spend the money on chocolate chip cookies for our cleaning staff. Best wishes, your loving uncle Digger."

Sarcastic bastard. All this fuss for a piddling £150! I'm an artist, for Christ's sake! I bet he isn't such an arsehole if Mick Jagger owes him money. I'll work something out somehow.

Some evenings I like to open the windows and meditate as the room empties into the ebbing dusk. But now I needed a crap, a shower, a joint, and a nap, in that order, before I met Gibreel in the bar downstairs around 9:30.

I tried to phone Poppy but the line was engaged. Jealousy, with nowhere to put it. A pigeon fluttered onto my window ledge, and glanced around my room. Was that the same bastard bird whose dried shit I just washed out of my hair?

Pigeon paranoia.

Time for a joint with Dame Kiri Te Kanawa. The last of Josh's Moroccan Brown . . . Ah, the joys of being flat broke and Generation X and surrounded by women and being miserably alone.

My room is too much like a Methodist chapel. I'm more of a Church of the Feral Pagan type. What I need is a classy chair from a more elegant century, like Katy Forbes's. Weird. I could remember her chair, her pepper mill, and the shape of her nipples, but not her face. She'd had a birthmark shaped like a comet.

I got clean, rolled my joint, and as I smoked it the ceiling lost definition. Ah! Peat fire in the hollow of the golden bough . . . Josh gets his hands on the very best. That happy Gulliver-tied-down-by-Lilliputians feeling sagged my organs, and the next thing I knew the moon was framed by the window and Gibreel was standing over me. "Put on your zoot suit, Marco boy!"

My gummy mouth tasted of an inner sole. My clock shone 21:45. When did I last get a good night's sleep? How did Gibreel get a key? I always lock the door when I smoke. "Why? Where are we going?"

"The casino!"

I felt too mellow for my laugh to bubble up. "You're taking the piss. I owe more money than the government of Burundi. I can't afford to go to a casino."

"Which is exactly *why* we're going to the casino, Marco! Win it back. Pay it off."

"Oh, just like that."

"I got the people, Marco. I got a system!"

This time my laughter busted down the door and ran off over the hills.

"What's so funny, you stoner?"

I wasn't sure myself, I didn't feel remotely amused by anything. It was either this or sob, I guess. I lassoed myself back and wiped the tears away. "Anyway, Gibreel, anyway. They don't just let anybody into a casino. You have to be somebody. I'm definitely only an anybody."

"Don't worry, Marco. My rich cousin from Beirut is over for the weekend. My rich cousin is definitely somebody. They run out of precious metals to color his bank cards. Tag along. You could emerge from tonight smelling of fortune."

"You're a very bad influence, Gibreel."

"That's why you hang out with me. King Marco, ruler of Niceland, one day decided that he needed a bit of wickedness. And behold! Yeah, verily his plea was heard by the Angel Gibreel!" Gibreel's eyes flashed in the semidarkness, and the darkness moved. "Got any of that hash left, Captain Marcotics?"

We met Gibreel's cousin some time later at a wine bar in Bloomsbury. I try not to make snap judgments, but I knew right away he was a prize wanker. He didn't even bother to tell me his name. Sometimes you meet someone, and ten minutes pass before you realize that no, they really never are going to stop talking about themselves. He was too cool to ever remove his sunglasses. With him was a middle-aged Iranian called Kemal who had fled the revolution in the seventies. Kemal's smile was radioactive. He clapped his hands together. "Let's go. If I'm not mistaken Lady Luck is in the mood for some sweet loving. So, my friend—" he looked at me—"you are a man of the rouge and the noir?"

"I've never used rouge in my life," I quipped, and waited for laughter that never came. Make a note of that, Marco. No transvestite jokes. "Erm, I'm going to be more of a spectator tonight. I have a cash-flow problem."

"Creditors?" hissed Gibreel's cousin in a way that made me glad I wasn't one of his. It was the first sign of interest he'd shown in me.

"No," I said, "I don't have any."

"Excellent! You have no creditors?"

"No. I have no cash flow."

"What is this? Going to a casino, destitute and penniless?" Kemal fumbled in his shoulder bag and flung a thin stack of paper in my lap. "This cannot be, my friend." It quivered when it landed in a way that reminded me of banknotes. Jesus, it was banknotes!

"I can't—"

Kemal wasn't listening. He fingered his beard and smiled at Rich Cousin. "Our friend Marco will do fine. Beginners are more unpredictable. But I insist on two to one."

Gibreel's cousin snorted. "Forget it. The odds are even."

"Marco will do fine for what?" A cog clicked in a mechanism way bigger than me.

"You didn't tell him?" Rich Cousin asked Gibreel, who also had a crooked smile.

"Marco my son," began Gibreel, "Kemal and my cousin wish to place a bet on whether you or I come out of the casino with more money. You've just been given your stake to play with."

I even felt my smile going crooked. "I really don't feel terribly happy about—"

"And we get to keep any winnings, plus double the original stake. An extra three hundred."

"Three hundred pounds?"

"No, three hundred lemons. Of course pounds."

"He worries too much," said Rich Cousin.

"Way too much," agreed Gibreel.

"It's just a side dish for us," said Kemal, "my friend."

"And if I lose all the money?"

"Then you lose all the money," said Kemal, "and nobody cares."

"And Kemal loses his bet with me," observed Rich Cousin.

So there we were. Me, Gibreel, and two dodgy characters I'd only known for ten minutes in the back of a taxi on our way to a casino. That made four dodgy characters in total.

It was £150, in £5 notes so new they felt squeaky. A pert little co-incidence, that. Exactly enough to pay Digger and get my drums back. Unfortunately, Gibreel's cousin and Kemal showed me to the cashier to exchange the dosh for chips before I could think of a way to vanish down the nearest tube entrance.

So I had to grin and bear it as I exchanged my drum kit for thirty little plastic discs.

"Now," said Kemal, "let us go our separate ways. I am a man of poker. We will meet in the upstairs lobby at midnight. Gibreel and Marco, midnight. Not a minute later, or the bet is void and you turn back into pumpkins."

Rich Cousin strutted into the bar to flash money and select a woman.

"Gibreel," I hissed, as we walked into the main roulette lounge, "they're using us as toys. It sucks. Why do they do it?"

"Because they are bored, rich little boys who need new toys. The money is nothing to them."

"And anyway, doesn't the Koran forbid gambling?"

"Muhammad doesn't patrol London. With non-Muslims, on non-Muslim territory, it's kosher. Let's gamble, and may the best man win."

. . .

I wandered around for a while before sitting down, taking it all in. The carpet, magenta plush, made me want to put on a pair of slippers and a smoking robe. Men in dinner jackets mingled with women in silk. There were some rare and exotic females here, at home under the chandeliers. Smiling characters locked away in the decompression chambers of dreams. A Hooray Henry hoorayed and an old lady cawed like a crow. The green of the baize and the gold of the wheels were stolen from the land of fairies, under the hill. The roulette wheel spun so fast that it seemed to be motionless, the ball an atom of gold. When I leave three centuries will have passed. The glum and the bored and the quietly desperate and the manic jolly and the spectators. The croupiers worked like cyborgs, avoiding eye contact. I looked up to try to spot the cameras, but the ceiling was hidden in black like that of a TV studio. There were no windows, no clocks. Walnut paneling, prints of racehorses and greyhounds. I wandered into a room where blackjack and poker were being played. Kemal was already in a game. I came back and sat down on the side where I could watch the roulette, and asked for a coffee, hoping it was free. It was ten o'clock. I'd watch for forty-five minutes, and work out how to play.

Twenty minutes passed. A man who looked like Samuel Beckett a few weeks before he died sat next to me, fumbling for cigarettes. I offered him one of mine. He nodded, took a couple, and sedately rocked.

"You're a beginner wondering where to begin."

"I'm wondering how I can win," I said.

"Let's see now." He lit up, sucking the cigarette as an asthmatic does his inhaler. "Which game?"

"Roulette?"

He spoke around his cigarette, his lips barely moving. "Well, the American Table has two zeros, so the odds against you are greater. Stick to the French Table. If you bet on the numbers the odds against you are 2.7 percent. If you bet on the colors, then the odds against you are 1.35 percent."

"That doesn't sound too bad."

Samuel Beckett did a Gallic shrug. "It adds up. It depends

how long you play. After a hundred coups, fifty-two percent of gamblers will be losing. After a thousand, sixty-six percent. After ten thousand, ninety-two percent of gamblers will be losing."

"Is there a way to . . . erm . . ."

"At blackjack, yes. You memorize a bookful of algorithmic probability patterns, and then you keep count. Bet heavily when the odds swing for you, bet lightly when they're against you. In principle, it's that simple. You have to be very good, though, or you'll be spotted and escorted to the dustbins. It's probably easier to become a London cabbie."

"I only got a grade 'C' at maths. Would poker—"

"Poker? At poker, you get what you deserve."

"Ah. I don't think I want what I deserve. So, is there a way of winning at roulette?"

"I'll swap you that secret for a road map to Xanadu. There are plenty of ways for the casino to cheat—microscopic needles, electromagnets—but for the punter, the only hope is to miniaturize aerospace trajectory technology, and use it to plot the course of the ball. That's been done."

"Successfully?"

"In the laboratory, yes. But in Vegas the team got their circuitry shorted. I gather it was painful."

"I suppose I'd better rely on chance, then."

Samuel Beckett indicated with a twist of his face that in that case, the conversation was over. My £300 cut of Kemal's winnings was waiting.

I sat down, afraid of being unmasked as an impostor. I put my first chip on red. I was about to lose my casino virginity. I watched the ball bounce and hurl itself around the wheel. What's the ball like, ghostwriter? Give us a metaphor.

Very well. It's like a genie, spending its fury until nothing is left.

The ball settled on black. The croupier raked away my money into a hole. It clicked as it fell. That's the quickest £5 I ever spent without smiling. I put my second chip on red.

The ball landed on black. I'd have to win one soon. . . . The laws of probability. I put my third chip on black.

The ball settled on red. Still, I'd have to win this time.

I put my fourth chip on red. I can't lose four in a row.

I lost four in a row. Black. Twenty pounds just gone and nobody even thanked me.

Not a good start. Red, black, red, black. Stepping out of the way of an oncomer in the same direction as the oncomer. Never mind, Marco. One hundred and thirty pounds of chips still in my pocket.

I went and got a mineral water to rethink my strategy. I downed it and hoped it would flush out the last of the hash. Kemal was at the bar. "How's it going, my friend? I have a lot of money riding on you tonight."

That's your stupid fault. "Up and down."

"Up is better, my friend. How are you betting? Don't bet like a loser. Bet with strength. Don't overrate chance. Winning in a casino is like winning in life: all is a matter of *will*."

Yeah, and a lollipop tossed into the mouth of the Amazon can float upstream. It just has to want to badly enough.

The casino toilet was tiled in black marble, and the mirrors were copper and smoky. I imagined gangsters in pastel suits shooting each other in the kidneys. I had just unzipped my fly when Cousin came in, still wearing his sunglasses. He came and stood next to me. He didn't say a word.

Even though my bladder was full, he unnerved me so much that my piss refused to come out. I heard his, though, a smooth torrent gurgling down the plug hole. The free-flowing urine of opulent wealth. I pretended to be shaking off the last drops, washed my hands, and scuttled off to find another toilet.

I chose another table, with an attractive brunette croupier with freckles and unfeasibly long legs. She looked like she could have been a he at some point. She looked lucky.

This time, I'd concentrate harder.

I was pretty soon down to £75.

I won a few, and lost a few. I hovered around the £60 for fifteen minutes before losing eight in a row and plummeting down to £20.

Gibreel appeared at my shoulder. "I'm up to £280 at black-jack. Roulette's for mugs."

"I don't have a good answer for that."

"Dear me, is that all you have left? And still only eleven o'clock."

"Get lost."

This was hurting. I wanted out. I bet the last of my money on green. If it won, I'd get . . . thirty-five to one . . . £700. Maybe Kemal was right. Maybe this gambling lark was a matter of will. £700! Concentrate on that!

The wheel spun, the wheel slowed, and damn me if the ball didn't fall into the green zero!

. . . And fall right out again.

I sat there, stunned. I wanted my adoptive mom to come and make things right. Well, I wanted any mom. I wasn't fussy.

I watched the lime fizz in my bottle of Sol. A parrot's pancreas pickled in piss.

Idiot!

I deserved to lose. I'd just betted haphazardly. If I'd tried to feel more . . . The future already exists. Prophets can see what is already there. Anyone can predict effects from a given cause. That's a definition of sentient life, from storing food to satellite weather forecasting. Suppose you could do the same, backwards. . . . See the cause from the effect. It wouldn't be an intellectual process. It would be . . .

Ah, bollocks. I'm sounding like Nancy Thing from Iannos's café.

Three hundred pounds! Just for finishing the evening with more money than Gibreel! Plus whatever I made, on top . . . Could be quite a few hundred. A thousand even. When would I have an opportunity like this again? I owed more than £3000, quite a lot more, but a few hundred quid would buy me peace of mind and cut me some slack, for weeks.

Thing is, where could I get some more stake money? I couldn't ask Kemal. My bank card had been eaten.

A little demon blew on the back of my neck. My credit card! Three hundred pounds credit-limit extension. Remember?

Getting deeper into debt, to gamble? Are you crazy?

Look, if you're going to have to work some greasy windowless job for the next two years to pay off these debts, then it may as well be four.

Damn, no, I'd put my credit card in my suit pocket to use at that sexy little Mexican place with Bella last week sometime. God, had that ever been a stale, pricey evening.

I'm wearing my suit. Dolt.

I tapped my pocket. Plastic tapped back.

No one had said I couldn't get more stake money. . . .

What if this backfired? The credit card people weren't going to be impressed. And how about Poppy? She might be carrying your kid around inside her. It's not just your own future you're gambling away here. It's wrong. Just leave. Leave now. You won't even be able to pay half the abortion cost, if that's what she wants. And what if that isn't what she wants?

I'd nailed my doubts down a pit, but I could hear them hammering at the floorboards. I went back to the original table with £300. The croupier had changed. A young chap whose name was probably something like Nigel. Maybe he was from Kennington. 11:30. I'd better play for £25 per spin.

Playing for colors may give Samuel Beckett better odds, but it had wiped me out just now. This time I was playing for numbers.

How should you choose numbers? Okay, first, my age. Twenty-nine. Odds.

The ball landed on 20. Evens. Another bad start. Down to £275. Still, next number. Numbers from today. How many eggs in Katy Forbes's omelette?

Four. Evens.

The ball landed on 20, again. Evens! This is better. This is the way to do it. Think of a question with a numerical answer, answer it, and bet. Back up to £300.

How many people had I spoken to today? A quick count. Eighteen, including myself. Even. Listen, God, I know I haven't been a very loyal member of the fan club, but I swear, get me out of this and I'll even start going to church again. Whenever I can.

The ball landed on 19. God, the deal's off, you hear? Down to £275.

How many zits on Kennington Nigel's face? Three. Odds.

The ball landed on 34. Down to £250. Another question. This time my stake would be £50. Time was running out. Had I pissed off a gypsy recently?

How many teeth do I have? Twenty-eight. Evens.

The ball landed on 1. Fate, what have I done to deserve this? Would you like me to stop believing in chance? I will if you want. Just let me win now. Fate. I am yours. I am fated to win. Two hundred pounds.

Oh shit, this was next week's food money. Gambling was horrible. People actually did this for pleasure?

How many women have I slept with in my life? Forget it, no time.

"If I were you," said Samuel Beckett, "I would do something dramatic."

Odds.

The ball landed on 4. Fate, fuck you. Chance all the way. One hundred and fifty pounds. Ten to midnight.

How many letters in my name, Marco. Five. Odds.

24. Evens. Down to a hundred pounds.

Jesus, this is tomorrow's rent. I'm going to have to get a job in Burger King at Victoria Station.

"Did you know," said Samuel Beckett, "that you can bet on four numbers at once? It's called a Carré. Place your chip on the intersection where they meet. Payment is eight to one."

Where? "Will you choose it for me?"

"No."

I put my second-to-last chip on 23/24/26/27.

The ball landed in 28.

"Tough," said Samuel Beckett. "Still. One last number to go."

"Please," I said, "give me an intersection."

"Oh, if you insist: 32/33/35/36."

I placed the chip. This was my last chance. I realized that I couldn't watch. As there was no sofa to run behind, I hid my eyes as darkness engulfed me.

Nearing the speed of light, time buckled. Sound thickened to the consistency of hair gel. Poverty walked towards me through the crowd. A bed at Summerford Hostel would set me back £12.50. A large pile of chips was being raked at me. And left there. I looked up. The croupier was already looking away. An elderly black gent with hair coming out of his ears was looking at my chips covetously. Two girls in matching shiny dresses were laughing right at me.

Samuel Beckett had gone.

There was £400 worth in chips in front of me. I could keep my credit card.

"My friend," Kemal appeared over my shoulder, "it is time. I'm glad to see you have not been wiped out. Let us go to the upstairs lobby. Did you enjoy yourself?"

I swallowed hard. "It's so important to play only for the pleasure of it."

I knew I hadn't beaten Gibreel, but I had £400, over the £300 I had borrowed. I discounted the £150 stake, since that had never really been mine. So. A modest profit of £100. The leather jacket, £30. Probably enough to pacify Digger, if I promise to manicure his mastiffs for a week. My drums were back. Then there was The Music of Chance gig at Brixton Academy next weekend, which should tide me over until the end of the month. We always got cash on the nail there because I'd shagged the Student's Union events organizer a few times last year.

Gibreel was looking sheepish in the upstairs lobby. "Sorry," he said to Cousin. "The dealer must have known how to neutralize my system."

"My friend!" Kemal rotated two or three times for joy. I kept a blank face, but inwardly somersaulted. Yes! £100 plus £300 equals £400 profit for me and *now* we are talking!

Cousin reluctantly produced a beige envelope, which Kemal snatched. "Thank you my friend."

Gibreel frowned and pointed at me. "Not so fast! Marco cheated! He got some more money out!" My ex-friend looked at me. "Deny it!"

Weird stuff, money. "You didn't say I couldn't."

Cousin and Gibreel advanced towards Kemal, and tried to take the envelope back. Kemal swung back, Cousin grabbed the envelope, Kemal grabbed Cousin and they both fell onto a plant stand, felling a massive umbrella plant and upsetting a gong which gonged down the stairs, one gong per step. Gibreel picked up the envelope, Kemal writhed out from under the umbrella plant with surprising alacrity and headbutted Gibreel, who staggered back, spitting out a tooth. Cousin rugby-tackled Kemal from behind, and I heard a zipping rip of material. This all seemed choreographed. Kemal tumbled, reached into his jacket as he fell, and suddenly a grin-shaped knife was flashing through the air. I guess they weren't such good friends after all.

Trouble was shouting around the corner. The only possible way out for me would be for this peculiar triangular door to be open, and for me to crawl into it before the bouncers arrived, and for these three to not notice me, and for nobody to think of looking in here. What kind of odds were these? It was an ostrich-brained escape plan, but sometimes the ostrich strategy is your last, indeed only, line of defense. I turned the doorknob.

And bugger me if it wasn't open! I cramped myself in, and pulled the door to behind me. I bumped my head, stuck my foot in a bucket, and smelled detergent. My priest hole was a cleaning cupboard.

I heard the bouncers come, a whole load of shouting and protesting. I felt oddly calm. As usual, my fate was in the hands of chance. If I was caught, I was caught. I waited for the door to be tugged open.

The noises were escorted away.

What a day. Am I really hiding in a casino's cleaning cupboard? Yes, I really am. How in heaven and hell did I get here? A humming switched itself off, and I was left alone in the silence that I hadn't noticed hadn't been there.

There is Truth, and then there is Being Truthful.

Being Truthful is just one more human activity, along with chatting up women, ghostwriting, selling drugs, running a country, designing radiotelescopes, parenting, drumming, and shop-lifting. All are susceptible to adverbs. You can be truthful well or badly, frankly or slyly, and you can choose to do it or not to do it.

Truth holds no truck with any of this. A comet doesn't care if humans notice its millennial lap, and Truth doesn't care less what humans are writing about it this week. Truth's indifference is im-mutable. More Mercurial than Jovian. Sometimes you turn your head and you see it: in a fountain, in the parabola of a flung fris-bee, or the darkness of a cleaning cupboard. Causes and effects politely stand up and identify themselves. At such times I under-stand the futility of worrying. I shut up and I see the bumbling goodness behind the bitching and insecurity. Tying my future to Poppy's and India's—if they would have me—would be the great-est, never-ending, Richter-busting plunge I could ever take.

And then Truth is suddenly gone, and you're back to anxiety about bills.

I yawned so wide that my jaw clicked. The adrenaline from the fight and the coffee from the lounge were wearing off. Truth is tiring stuff. It was time to crawl out of my cleaning cupboard.

I cashed in my chips, praying to get the money in my sticky hand before being recognized. Were all cashiers this slow?

At long last I was free. I went and reclaimed my jacket. Still nobody recognized me.

There was a telephone in the corner of the reception hall. As I was fishing for change Samuel Beckett came strolling over. "Your friends were persuaded to continue their frank exchange of views elsewhere. Minus the knives."

"Who?"

The telephone was one of the old dial types. All these circles and wheels spinning separately together. I rolled in my coin.

"Poppy! This is me."

"Well. Look what the cat didn't drag back last night." Wry. Tired?

"I told you about the private view. A kid in a sweetshop. How's the little trilobite?"

"She fell asleep in a sulk because she wanted her bedtime story from you."

"It's been a long day."

"Oh, poor Marco."

"I've been having paradigm shifts. Poppy . . ."

"Do you have to do your paradigm shifts in the middle of the night?"

"Sorry, this can't wait. . . . Look, financially, you know I'm not John Paul Getty here, but . . . look, seriously, I've been wondering if you'd like to merge our estates, both in a financial and maybe existential sense too, of course that would just be the tip of the, erm, commitment iceberg, and if you'd like to do the same, then maybe—"

"Marco. What on earth are you talking about?"

Say it. "Would you like to get married?" Oh, lordy lord.

"With whom?"

She wasn't going to make this easy. "With me."

"Well. This is out of the blue. Let me think about it."

"How long do you need?"

"A couple of decades?"

"You hussy! I bought you a T-shirt with a pig on it. . . ."

"You're hoping to win my hand in holy matrimony, and in return you're offering a pig. Is this east Putney or east Bangladesh?"

"Poppy, I'm serious. I want to be your, your, I want you to be my . . ." Husband. Wife. Jesus wept. "I can't quite say it yet. But I will. I'm not drunk, I'm not stoned, I'm serious."

The few moments that passed had more mass than ordinary time, because a possible lifetime was compressed into them. I started to say something at the same time as Poppy. Poppy carried on. "Look. If you use the word 'serious' just once more I'll start believing you. Then if I find out you're not serious, our friendship stroke relationship stroke whatever is destroyed. This is your point of no return. Are you serious?"

"I'm serious."

Poppy whistled softly. "Marco. I'm taken aback that you can still take me aback."

"I'm coming over now. Is that okay?"

The longest wait of all.

"Yes, under the circumstances, I guess that's okay."

I hung up, and collected my coat. The tube closed hours ago. I had the money for a taxi to Putney, but £15 would feed India for—how long? Anyway, I had some thinking to do. I'd walk it.

Even if it took all night.

CLEAR ISLAND

GASPING AND DRIPPING I opened my eyes, a sun spun from bright seawater. I looked at Billy in the cabin, who was trying not to laugh. I mouthed "Rat," and he laughed. *St. Fachtna* cleared the crosscurrents between Illaunbrock shoal and Clarrigmore rock, rounded the west cape of Sherkin Island, and my black book and I, after a trip of twelve thousand miles, could see the end. Clear Island moved into view, my face felt crusty as the seawater dried, and here was home.

The lonely arm of Ardatruha pointing out to the Atlantic. I watched the light on the waves. The shades of blue where the reefs dropped away into the deeps. Cliffs tumbling around the back of Carriglure. Meadows in hollows and pastures on rises. The shabby harbor in the crook of the headland. A few miles of looping roads. The cemetery, the island's politest place. St. Ciaran's Well. An island as old as the world.

Billy's mute daughter nudged at me, offering me her father's binoculars.

"Thank you, Mary."

The houses swam into focus. I could see my godparents, Maisie and Brendan Mickledeen, pottering out on the verandah of The Green Man, and thought of the mechanical figurines on the town clock opposite my lab in Zurich. Ancient O'Farrell's grocery store at the foot of Baile Iarthach, doubling up as the post office and trebling up as the gossip exchange. Damn me if that isn't Bertie Crow's ancient three-wheeler vanishing over the neck of Cnocán an Choimhthigh! Won't it ever give up the ghost?

What is it that ties shapes of land to the human heart, Mo?

At the water's edge was the clump of sycamore trees smothering the falling-down croft where I was born. I wondered if the roof had fallen in yet.

I remembered the strong-jawboned of Switzerland, driving around their polished towns in the latest German sports cars. I remembered the spindly kids who scratched together a living in the Kowloon streets around Huw's apartment building. I remembered my lucky childhood, galloping over this island and prising out its secrets. Birth deals us out a hand of cards, but as important as their value is the place we are dealt them in.

"You've brought us some heavenly weather, Mo," Billy yelled over the diesel engine. "It was bucketing down this morning. Did you miss us?"

I nodded, unable to take my eyes off the island. I missed all eight square miles of you! In Smug Zurich and Euromoney Geneva and Pell Mell Hong Kong and Merciless Beijing and Damned London I could close my eyes and see your topography, like I could John's body. I watched the cormorants sail on the wind, from the south today, and I watched the gannets dive and vanish into mBairneach Bay. I suddenly wanted to grin and blubber like a madwoman, to shout back at Baltimore and the low mountains and all the way to Cork, "You blew it! I got here! I'm home! Come and get me!"

An island of cloud rounded the sun, and the temperature dropped. I was goosepimpled.

Only give me a little time first, with John and Liam.

The boat slowed to a chug. Billy steered the *St. Fachtna* into the harbor.

The night the U.S. staged its "preemptive strike," I was holding an impromptu dinner party at my chalet. Daniella, the brightest of that year's postgrads doing a research placement at Light Box, had switched on the satellite news just to get the weather, and we were still watching six hours later, picking at cold food with dead appetites. Alain was down from Paris, and a friend of John's from Hong Kong called Huw. The TV showed the night skyline of a burning city in the Gulf.

A young pilot was talking with a CNN reporter whose hair was not his own. "Yessir, the whole place was lit up like the prettiest Fourth of July I ever did see!"

"We've been hearing about the surgical precision of the missile strikes, thanks to Homer Quancog technology."

"Yessir, with the Homers you can pick your elevator shaft. The boys at mission control program in the building blueprints, and you sit back and let the missile's flight computer do the thinking for you. Just let those babies rip! Straight down the elevator shafts!"

Alain spilled some wine. "*Putain!* Next he tells us the missiles buy a stick of bread and walk the doggie."

A general wearing a torso of medals was talking in the Washington studio. "For Americans, freedom is an inalienable right. For all. Homer Technology is revolutionizing warfare. We can hit these evil dictators hard, where it hurts, with minimum collateral damage to the civilians they tyrannize."

John phoned from Clear Island. "This isn't news, it's sports coverage. Have so many films been made about high-tech war that high-tech war is now a film? It's product placement. Had anyone even heard of Homer missiles two days ago?"

A sickening sense that this was coming for me. I was gnawing my knuckles.

"Yeah . . . I've heard about them."

"Mo, love. Are you okay?"

"No. John, I'll have to phone you back."

BBC footage. A street lit by ambulances and fire. "Film Censored by Enemy Forces" scrolled across the screen. An Irish reporter from the north was holding a microphone to a woman whose face glistened with sweat or blood or both. "Tell me! Ask your people, why dropping a bomb on baby food factory? Why is dropping a bomb on baby food factory necessary for your war? Tell me!"

Cut.

Back to the studio for more analysis with experts. Daniella had fallen asleep, so I covered her with a blanket and put another log on the fire.

" 'Preemptive strike,' " said Huw, "must mean not declaring war until your cameras are in position."

I felt weary. I peered through the curtain out at the night and the mountains: the Milky Way and a haggard middle-aged scientist looked back at me. So far you've stretched, Mo. You've become unelastic. When your mother was your age she was a widow. How much further will you have to stretch? The cold glass nipped the tip of my nose.

Do you hear the waterfall, over the meadow, at the foot of the mountain?

Three thousand miles away the forces of freedom and democracy were using the fruits of their finest scientific minds to crush Liams and Daniellas under buildings. Then we watch the rubble burn, and the fireworks above. Congratulations, Mo. This is your life.

"My, it's a sick zoo we've turned the world into."

Alain heard, but misunderstood me. "No zoo kills off its own animals."

My breath fogged everything up. "Out of our cages, and out of control of ourselves."

Billy swung me onto the quayside with a "ta-rar!" I swayed as I found my shore legs. I could almost hear my bones grind. It could be the day I left. The row of fishing boats: Mayo Davitt's *Dún an Óir;* Daibhi O'Bruadair's *Oileán na nÉan;* Scott's *Abigail Claire,* repainted in blues and yellows; Red Kildare's barnacled dinghy *The South's Gonna Rise Again,* needing an overhaul worse than ever. Coils of ropes, hillocks of netting, oil barrels, plastic crates. Scraggy cats picked about their business. Inside is outside on islands. Things lie where they fall. I breathed in deep. Mulchy fishiness from the seawater, sweet- and sourness from the sheep dung, diesel fumes from the boats' engines.

"Mo!" Father Wally was perched on his tricycle over by the oyster sheds. Bernadette Sheehy was hosing down some lobster baskets, in a miniskirt and waders. He waved me over, grinning. "Mo! You're back in time! Glorious weather you've brought back with you. It was bucketing it down this morning."

"Father Wally! You're a picture of health." How right it feels to be conversing in Gaelic.

"Octogenarians stop aging. It becomes pointless. Whatever happened to your eye?"

"I head-butted a taxi in London."

"How was your trip? There must be easier ways to hail a taxi, even English ones." We laughed, and I looked into his blue eighty-four-year-old eyes. What miraculous organs are eyes. How much Father Wally's have seen—

A thump of panic—a snare drum—

Suppose the Texan had been here, recruiting locals? He had more money than the seventeen counties of the Republic.

Mo, calm down! Father Wally christened your mother. The table in the back parlor hosted year-long games of chess that stood testament to his friendship with John. If you start doubting Clear Islanders, the Texan has already won.

"My trip? A bit grueling, to be honest with you, Father. Hi, Bernadette."

The island beauty queen walked over. "Afternoon, Mo. Been far?"

"Further than usual."

"You missed the best-ever summer fair. All the folks from Ballydehob and Skull and Baltimore too came over. A Norwegian bird-watcher called Hans fell in love with me. He writes to me every week."

"He's written exactly twice," said Bernadette's little sister Hanna, climbing out of a rotting laundry basket, before being hosed away squealing into the oyster shed.

"Aye," said Father Wally. "It was a grand fair. And heavenly weather for the Fastnet Races. The Baltimore lifeboat got called out again, though. A catamaran capsized. Maybe you'll be here for the races next year?"

"I hope so. I really hope so."

"Will Liam be coming back to Clear before the weekend, Mo?" Bernadette was too unschooled to feign indifference well. She had wound a curl of hair around her little finger and was not looking where she was pointing her hose.

If only. "He'd better not be. It's slap bang in the middle of the autumn term."

Father Wally gave me a slightly strange look. Had I given a slightly strange answer? "Well then, Mo. Don't keep the man waiting."

"Is he at home?"

"Was but an hour ago. I dropped by to extricate my king's rook from his pincer."

"I'll say cheerio for now, then, Father Wally. Bernadette."

"Mind how you go now."

"Science is the game," Dr. Hammer, my mentor at Queen's, was fond of saying, "Its secrets are the stake. Errors are the card sharks. Scientists are the mugs."

Niels Bohr, the great Dane of quantum physics, was fond of saying, "It is wrong to think that the task of physics is to find out how nature *is*. Physics concerns what we can say about nature."

The double-crossed, might-have-been history of my country is not the study of what actually took place here: it's the study of historians' studies. Historians have their axes to grind, just as physicists do.

Memories are their own descendants masquerading as the ancestors of the present.

I remember the sun streaming in through the skylight of Heinz Formaggio's office. The view was operatic. The mountains fringing Lake Geneva were crumpled mauve and silver. By the lakeside, under a folly with a copper weathercock, a gnomish gardener trimmed the baize lawn. Mercury was jetpacking off his marble pedestal in his winged helmet.

Heinz had introduced the Texan as "Mr. Stolz." There was a ten-gallon hat on the sofa. He took off his sunglasses and regarded me with his ill-occluding eyes.

"Were you to desert at this stage," Heinz was reasoning, "you would be walking out at a crucial stage. You're the anchorman of a heavyweight team here, Mo. This isn't a Saturday job you can just resign from at the drop of a pin."

"I can resign. I resigned yesterday. Read the letter again."

Avuncular-Heinz. "Mo—I understand the ups and downs of think-tank life. It's a peculiar environment. I have these moments of doubt myself. I'm sure Mr. Stolz has them." The Texan just watched me. "But they pass. I implore you to put this drastic decision on ice for a month or two."

"My drastic decision has already been made, Heinz."

Flabbergasted-Heinz. "Where are you going to go? What about Liam, and his scholarship from us? There are a hundred considerations here to weigh up properly."

"All weighed up. And my son's education does not require your money."

Moral blackmailer–Heinz. "You're being poached, aren't you? We all receive better offers at the cutting edge, Mo. What gives you the right to be so selfish? Who are you going to?"

"I'm going to grow turnips in County Cork."

"Being facetious is not helping. Light Box has a right to know. We have the CERN facilities completely to ourselves in April. The Saragosa supercollider data is due in next week. These could be Quancog's way out of the nonlocality straitjacket. Why now?"

I sighed. "It's in the letter."

"Did you really believe that Light Box conducts experiments purely for fun?"

"No. I really believed that Light Box conducts experiments purely for space agencies. That's what we've been told quantum cognition is for. Then a war comes along, and I discover that my modest contribution to global enlightenment is being used in air-to-surface missiles to kill people who aren't white enough."

"Must you be so melodramatic? The border where military and civilian applications of aerospace technology meet has always been subjective. Face it, Mo. It's the way the world works."

"Somebody is fed bullshit for four years; they find out they've been fed bullshit for four years; they want out. Face it, Heinz. It's the way the world works."

The Texan shifted his weight and the sofa creaked. "Mr. Formaggio, it's plain that Dr. Muntervary values precision." He spoke with the leisure of a never-interrupted man. "I can relate to that.

As a friend of Quancog, I believe I can show a wider panorama. May I chew the fat alone with the lady?"

A rhetorical question.

The thin face in the window of Ancient O'Farrell's store swam back into the murk as I climbed the lane. The shop had no opening hours and no closing hours, but Ancient's wife never met anyone unless Ancient, or their son, Old O'Farrell, was with her. Even in my childhood she had always been suspicious of the mainland: of Britain and the world beyond, suspicious of its very existence. Baltimore, she would concede, was there. But beyond Baltimore was a land insubstantial as radio waves.

If both Ancient and Old were out you just went into the shop, helped yourself, and left the money in the shoebox. I took a breather on the gate to O'Driscoll's meadow. This hill gets steeper every time I come back to the island, I swear. A couple of old ladies in black cloaks were beachcombing the strand, down where the dune grass ends. They walked like crows. They looked up at me in unison and waved. Moya and Roisin Tourmakeady! I waved back. We used to believe they were witches who caused whirlpools. Owls lived in their attic, and probably still do.

Coming back was dangerous, Mo. They'd be here soon. It was a minor miracle that you got this far. A miracle, and the splendid isolation of Aer Lingus's computer systems.

Coming back was dangerous, but not coming back was impossible.

The sun was warm, moss was thick on the stone wall, ferns nodded.

With only three motorbikes on Clear Island, islanders can identify each by the engine. Red Kildare pulled up, his sidecar empty, and pushed up his goggles.

"They let you back then, Mo? That's quite a shiner you're sporting."

"Red. You look like a defrocked wizard. Yes, my wicket-keeping days for the national team are drawing to a close."

Red Kildare, like John, is a newcomer to Clear. He first came as a "Blow-In" in the sixties, when an attempt to found a colony of freethinkers based on the philosophy of Timothy Leary went the same way as Timothy Leary, and dwindled down to Red, his pigs and goats, and a few wild stories. He milks Feynman for John every day up at Aodhagan, and pays in goat cheese and by tidying up the vegetable garden. John says he still grows the best marijuana this side of Cuba. His Gaelic is better than mine, now.

"I thought of you the other day, Mo."

"Really?"

"Yeah . . . A dead bat fell out of the sky and landed at my feet."

"I'm glad to know I've been gone but not forgotten, Red."

The goggles were snapped back on. "Got to speak to a turkey about Daibhi O'Bruadair. Mind how you go."

He twisted the throttle on his ancient Norton, waking up a piglet in the floor of the sidecar, who clambered onto the seat and fell down again as the motorbike roared off.

Heinz Formaggio showed his anger only by a muffled slam of the door.

The Texan and I looked at each other across the office. The gnome in the garden was still clipping. I almost said, "Draw," but I almost say things much more often than I say them. "You must be very important indeed if you can dismiss Heinz from his own office."

"I was afraid the good director was going to start thundering at you."

"Being thundered at by Heinz is like being flogged by a lettuce."

He reached into his shirt pocket. "You don't mind if I smoke, Doctor?"

"Light Box has a no-smoking policy."

He lit up, tipped the contents of a bowl of potpourri onto a Light Box folder, and used the bowl as an ashtray. "I overheard a joke at my expense the other day: no in-tray, no out-tray, just an ashtray."

"Forgive me for not believing you."

His smile told me that it wasn't very important whether I believed him or not. "Dr. Muntervary, I'm a Texan. Did you know that Texas was an independent republic before joining the union?"

"Yes, I did."

"We Texans are a proud tribe. We pride ourselves on being straight shooters. Let us do some. The Pentagon requires that Quancog see completion."

"Then go ahead and complete it."

"Only Light Box Research can do that. We both know why. That is, we both know who. Light Box Research has Mo Muntervary."

"As from yesterday nobody has Mo Muntervary."

He blew out a plume of smoke, and watched it unfurl. "If it were that simple . . ."

"It is that simple."

"Kings abdicate, cops turn in their badges, directors of think tanks can slam all the doors they like and storm off, and nobody gives a damn. But you, Doctor, can never leave the ballpark. This is a fact. Accept it."

"Is this plain talking? Because I don't understand what I'm hearing."

"Then I'll phrase it differently. Light Box is only one research institute in the marketplace. Syndicates in Russia, Indonesia, South Africa, Israel, and China are headhunting scientists like you. There's a new confederation of Arab countries that really doesn't like us. There are three freelance military consultancies who want quantum cognition, one of them being our British cousins. The marketplace is getting crowded and cutthroat. The Pentagon wishes to invite you to work with us. Our less democratic competitors will coerce you. Wherever and however you hide, you will be found, and your services employed, whether you like it or not. Am I talking plain enough for you now, Dr. Muntervary?"

"And how exactly can anyone 'coerce' me?"

"By kidnapping your boy and locking him in a concrete box until you produce the required results."

"That's not remotely funny."

He lifted a briefcase onto his lap. "Good." The briefcase clips thwacked open. "Here is a file, containing photographs and information on the techniques employed by headhunters. Verify them through your own channels: your Amnesty friends in Dublin will know the names. Look at it later." He passed me the file. "But not before you eat. One more thing." He threw me a little black cylinder, the size of a camera film case. "Carry this."

I looked at it, lying on my lap, but didn't pick it up. "What is it?"

"It's a chicken switch, programmed with your right thumbprint. It flips open like a lighter. If you press the button then one of our people will be with you within four minutes."

"Why should I swallow this hogwash? And why me?"

"The New World Order is old hat. War is making a major comeback—not that it had ever gone anywhere—and scientists like you win wars for generals like me. Because quantum cognition, if spliced with artificial intelligence and satellite technology in the way that you have proposed in your last five papers, would render existing nuclear technology as lethal as a shower of tennis balls."

"And how do these phantom headhunters know about my research at Light Box?"

"The same way we all do. Old-fashioned industrial espionage."

"Nobody's going to kidnap me. Look at me. I'm middle-aged. Only Einstein, Dirac, and Feynman made major contributions in their forties."

The Texan stubbed out his cigarette, and tipped the potpourri back into the bowl. "A lot of people kiss your ass, Doctor, and if I thought it would do any good I'd kiss your ass too. But listen really good. I can't make heads or tails of your matrix mechanics, your quantum chromodynamics, and your nothing turning into something by energy borrowed from nowhere. But I do know that no more than ten people alive can make Quancog a reality. We have six of them, now, in Saragosa, in West Texas. I'm offering you a job. Come this fall, we were going to relocate Light Box's Quancog project there wholesale, and offer you a package of incentives the usual way. But your resignation letter has forced our hand."

"Why should I work for you? Your president's a shallow crook."

"Doesn't take an egghead to see that. But of all the shallow crooks with fingers on buttons today, who would you rather own Quancog?"

"Quancog as a military application? Nobody should own it."

"Come to Texas, Dr. Muntervary. Of all the agencies who want you, only ours will respect your conscience, and the rights of your boy Liam, and John Cullin. You see me as your enemy, Doctor. I can live with that. In my world enemies and friends are defined by context. Understand that I'm on your side before it's too late."

I looked out at Mercury.

"I always liked that one," said the Texan, following my gaze. "Lived by his wits."

The pub sign of The Green Man squeaked as it swung. Maisie was leaning on the stone wall, looking out to sea through her telescope. Brendan was around the other side, pottering about in the vegetable patch. Maisie's last gray hairs had turned white.

"Afternoon, Maisie."

She swung the telescope at me, and her mouth opened. "As I live and breathe! Mo Muntervary come back to haunt us! I saw a funny hat get off the *St. Fachtna,*" she lowered the eyepiece, "but I thought it was a bird-watcher come for the Thewlicker's geese. Whatever happened to your eye?"

"It got hit by a rogue electron in a lab experiment."

"Even when you were knee-high you were always bumping into things. Brendan! Come and see who it isn't! Now Mo, why weren't you back for the summer fair?"

Brendan limped over. "Mo! You've brought some grand weather back with you this time! John was in sinking the Guinness last night, but he nary breathed a word of your homecoming. Holy Dooley, that's a black eye and a half! Put a steak on it!"

"I didn't want a fuss. But aren't the roses a picture! And how do you get honeysuckle to run riot at the end of October?"

"Dung!" answered Maisie. "Good and fresh from Bertie Crow's cows, and the bees. Keep a hive, Mo, when you settle down. Care for the bees and the bees care for you. You should have seen the runner beans this year! Beauties, they were, eh Brendan?"

"Aye, they turned out well enough, Maisie." He inspected the bowl of his dogwood pipe, the same one he'd smoked for half a century. "You see your ma in Skibbereen, Mo?"

"I did."

"And how was she?"

"Comfortable, but less lucid. At least she can't do herself an injury where she is."

"That's true enough." Maisie let a respectful silence go by. "You've lost too much weight, Mo. I thought you live on fondues and Toblerone chocolate in Switzerland."

"I've been on a trip, Maisie. That's why I'm on the lean side."

"Lecture circuit, no doubt?" Brendan's eyes gleamed with pride.

"You might call it that."

"If your da could see you today!"

Maisie was better at spotting half-answers. "Well, don't stand over the garden wall. Come in and tell us about the wide world."

Brendan shooshed with his antique hands. "Maisie Mickledeen, give our goddaughter a chance to catch her breath before plying her with liquor. Mo here'll no doubt be wanting to get straight up to Aodhagan. The wide world can wait a few hours."

"Come by then later, Mo, or whenever, so. Eamonn O'Driscoll's boy is back with his accordion, and Father Wally's organizing a lock-in."

Lock-ins at The Green Man. I was home. "Maisie, don't lock-ins need the odd night when you actually close at the legal time? And a lock to lock?"

"Desist your logification right now, Mo! You're back on Clear now. It's only sheep, fish, and the weather here. Leave your relativity back in Baltimore, if you please. And if John brings his harp I'll crack open my last bottle of Kilmagoon. Mind how you go."

"Mowleen Muntervary, you are an eight-year-old aberration who will be lashed by devils with nettles in hell until your bottom is covered with little lumps that you will scratch until they bleed! Do you want that to happen?"

My memory of Miss Thorpe veers towards an eyebrow mite through an electron microscope. Shiny, spiky, many-eyed. Why are primary schoolteachers either Brontëesque angels or Dickensian witches? Do they teach black and white so much that they become black or white?

"I asked you a question, and I did not hear an answer! Is it your wish to be damned as a liar?"

"No, Miss Thorpe."

"Then tell me how you got your grubby mitts on the algebra test answers!"

"I did them myself!"

"If there is one thing in this world that I loathe more than little boys who fib, it is little girls who fib! I shall be forced to write to your father, telling him that his daughter is a fork-tongued viper! You're going to be shamed in your own village!"

A toothless threat. No Clear Islander took a non-Gaelic-speaking teacher seriously.

There was a trail of these exposé letters, all the way to Cork Girls' Grammar School. When my da came back at the weekend he used to read them out to Ma in a funny English accent that crippled us with laughter. "It is inconceivable that your daughter scored a hundred per cent in this examination honestly. Cheating is a serious transgression. . . ."

Da was a boatyard contractor who spent the week traveling between Cork and Baltimore, supervising work and dealing with buyers from as far as Dublin. He'd fallen in love with my mother, a Clear Island girl, and was married in St. Ciaran's church by a middle-aged priest called Father Wally.

These days the primary school kids are taught in English and Gaelic in Portakabins down in the harbor. The older ones go on the *St. Fachtna* to a school in Skull that has its own planetarium. Miss Thorpe went to propagate her Manichean principles in poor, multishafted African countries. Bertie Crow stores hay in the old schoolhouse now.

If you look in through the window, that's what you see: hay.

.   .   .

I told the Texan I would reconsider my resignation over the weekend. I drove to the bank, and withdrew enough U.S. dollars in cash for the manager to invite me into the back office for coffee while they checked me out. Driving back to the chalet, I caught myself glancing into the mirror every fifteen seconds. Paranoia must often begin as a nasty game. I phoned John to ask his advice. "A thorny one," said John. "But should you decide to"—he switched to Gaelic—"take an unscheduled sabbatical, try to get back to Clear for my birthday." John usually hid his advice in its wrapping. "And remember that I love you very much."

I packed briefly, and left a note on the table asking Daniella to look after my books and plants. The hardware, like the chalet and the car, belonged to Light Box. I downloaded my hard disks onto the CDs I planned to take, erased everything else, and emptied zoos of my most virulent viruses on the disks I'd leave behind. My farewell present to Heinz.

How do you disappear? I'd made particles disappear, but I'd never disappeared myself. I would have to watch myself through my pursuers' eyes, find blind spots, and move into those blind spots. I telephoned my usual travel agent, and asked for a flight to Petersburg in three days' time, no matter the cost, to be paid by credit card. I e-mailed the only web site in Equatorial Guinea, telling them that Operation Cheese was Green. I went out for a stroll, and found a Belgian yogurt lorry in which to chuck my cylindrical chicken switch.

Then I sat in my window seat and watched the waterfall, as the evening thickened.

When it was dark I began the long drive north on the Berlin autobahn.

I could see the beginning.

The track has wildflowers growing down the middle. AODHAGAN CROFT, says the sign, painted by Liam. Another sign swings underneath: "home-made ice cream," painted by me. Planck dozes in the late sun. The windows in the house are open. The yellow sou'wester in the porch, the watering can, Planck's lead and harness, the Wellington boots, the rows of herb pots. John comes out of the house: he hasn't heard me yet. I walk to the vegetable garden. Feynman sees me, and bleats through his beard. Schroedinger leaps onto the mailbox to get a better view. Planck thumps her tail a couple of times before getting up to bark. Lazy tyke.

My journey ends here. I am out of west to run to.

John turns. "Mo!"

"Who else are you expecting, John Cullin?"

A latch clicks in the murk and I fold upright and where the hell am I? I slip and judder. What ceiling, what window? Huw's? The poky hotel in Beijing? The Amex Hotel in Petersburg, is there a ferry to catch? Helsinki? The black book! Where's the black book! Slowly now, Mo, slowly . . . you've forgotten something, something secure. The rain drumming on the glass, fat fingertips of European rain. The smooth edges, unclutteredness, the wind chime, you recognize that wind chime, don't you, Mo? The bruises down your side are still aching, but aching with healing. A man downstairs is singing Van Morrison's "The Way Young Lovers Do" in a way that only one man you know sings Van Morrison, and it definitely isn't Van Morrison.

I felt happiness that I'd forgotten the feel of.

And there's the black book on the dressing table, where you put it last night.

On John's side of the bed was a John-shaped hollow. I rolled into it, the cosiest place on Earth. I twitched open the curtain with my toe. A sulky sky, not worth getting up for yet.

When did I become so jittery? That night I left for Berlin? Or is it just getting old, my organs getting fussier, until one of them says "I quit!" I belly flopped back into the shallows of sleep. A lonely horn sounded, from one of my ma's gramophone records, a cargo ship out in the Celtic Sea, a memory junk across Kowloon harbor. We rounded the west cape of Sherkin Island, my black book and I, and after a trip of twelve thousand miles I could see the end. Would they be waiting here? They let me get this far. No, I got this far myself. The pillow of John, John the pillow, St. John, hemp, smoke, mahogany sweat, and deeper fruits deeper down, my heart jolting, hauling carriages, grasslands rising and falling, years and years of them, Custard from Copenhagen, inured to loneliness, gazing out of the window, I wonder what happened to him, I wonder what happened to all of them, this wondering is the nature of matter, each of us a loose particle, an infinity of paths through the park, probable ones, improbable ones, none of them real until observed, whatever real means, and for something so solid, matter contains terrible, terrible, terrible expanses of nothing, nothing, nothing. . . .

Technology is repeatable miracles. Air travel, for instance. Thirty thousand feet below our hollow winged nail, it's early morning in Russia. A track runs snowy hills and black lakes, drawn with a wonky ruler.

My fellow passengers are oblivious to the forces that infuse matter and carry thought. They don't know how our Boeing 747's velocity increases our mass and slows time, while our distance from the Earth's gravitational center has speeded up time, relative to those asleep in the farmhouses we are passing over. None has heard of quantum cognition.

I can't sleep. My skin feels stretched and saggy. I bring my calculator onto airplanes to pass the time. It's a chunky one that Alain borrowed from the Paris lab. It can do a quintillion decimal places. To pass the time I work out the odds of us three hundred and sixty passengers all being here. Long odds. It takes me all the way to Kyrgyzstan.

Anything to distract me from the near future.

A Chinese schoolgirl on her way back to Hong Kong is asleep next to me. She is around the age when lucky young women transform into beautiful swans. At her age Mo Muntervary transformed into a spotty gannet. Now I'm a wrinkled gannet. A dinosaur movie is on the screen, scaly violence in silence. My throat is dry with recycled air. I feel a headache coming on. Cryptish lighting, orthodontic decor. Where is the sun, which way is the world spinning? And what the hell have I got myself into?

· · ·

The second time I awoke, footsteps vibrated the plank of sleep. I knew exactly where I was this time. How long? Two minutes or two hours? Real footsteps, running on gravel, measured and bold, with a right to be here. I lifted the curtain by an eighth of an inch, and I saw a young man jogging through a tunnel of drizzle straight to Aodhagan.

Stone the crows. My son is a man. I felt proud and piqued. His duffle coat swung open. Dark jeans, boots, his father's uncontrollable hair. Feynman stared from his paddock, munching, and Planck jumped up, wagging.

"Mo!" John shouted from down below. "It's Liam!"

A door banged. Liam still closes doors like a baby elephant.

I put on John's bat-cloak dressing gown. "I'm coming down! And John?"

"What?"

"Happy birthday, you scabby pirate!"

"I've never had a better one!"

Huw opened the door and gave me a hug, munching a Chinese radish. "Mo! You got here! Sorry I couldn't meet you at the airport. . . . If John had given me a little more warning, I'd have rescheduled my day."

"Hello, Huw. It was plain sailing until I got to your building. I thought the fourth floor meant the third floor. Or the third, the fourth. Anyway, your neighbor put me right."

"Hong Kong's never quite sure of itself. British or American or Chinese numbering, even I still get muddled. Come in, put down your bag, have some tea and a bath."

"Huw. I don't know how to thank you for this."

"Nonsense. Us Celts have got to stick together. You're my first houseguest, we'll have to make things up as we go along. Come and inspect your quarters. Not a patch on your chalet, I'm afraid—"

"My ex-employer's chalet—"

"Your ex-employer's chalet. Here you are! Chez Mo. Cramped and messy, but it's yours, and unless the CIA has cockroaches on its payroll they'll never find you."

"In my limited experience the CIA has a lot of cockroaches on its payroll."

The room was no more cramped or messy than fifty labs I'd worked in. There was a sofa bed ready for me to crash on, bless Huw, a desk, stacks of books that would bury me with one mild earth tremor, and a vase of flamingo orchids. "The lavatory's through there, if you stand on it and twist your neck around you get a cracking view of Kowloon Harbor."

It was as humid as a launderette. Hives of life rumbled on the other sides of the floor, walls, and ceiling. The tenement across the alley was so close that our window frames seemed to share the same glass. Trains ground, little things scuttled, and somewhere a giant bicycle pump was cranking itself up and hissing itself down.

The life of a conscience-led scientist. "It's perfect, Huw. Can I use your computer?"

"*Your* computer," insisted Huw.

The fire in the kitchen hearth wheezed and popped. Liam and I looked at one another, suddenly at a loss. The tiles chilled my toes. I'd polished this reunion for so long, but now I could only gawp. I remembered baby goblin Liam, I remembered the adolescent mutant he'd been last summer with bumfluff on his top lip, and I saw the raffish man he'd make in a decade or two. As well-summered as you can get in Dublin, his hair was gelled, he'd got an ear stud, and his jaw was squatter.

"Mam—" His voice had become a bassoon.

"Liam—" I said at exactly the same time, my voice a flautist's mistake.

"Oh for the love of God you two," muttered John.

It was suddenly all right and Liam was hugging me first and hardest. I hugged back harder and until we both groaned, but that wasn't why I wanted to cry. "You're supposed to be at Uni, you malingerer. Who gave you permission to grow so much in my absence?"

"Ma, who gave you permission to do a James Bond God-knows-where in *my* absence? And who did that to your eye?"

I looked at John around Liam's shoulder. "You have a point. I'm sorry. A knight in shining armor did this to my eye. I forgave him. He'd knocked me out of the path of a taxi."

" 'A point,' she calls it. Da, you hear that?"

I karate-chopped his sides.

"Don't I get an apology too?" whinged John.

"Shut up, Cullin," I said, "you're only the father and you don't have any rights."

"I'll just go and blunder off a cliff then and leave you two to it."

"Happy birthday! Da! Sorry I couldn't get back last night. I stayed at Kevin's in Baltimore."

"Blame your ma. She only phoned from London yesterday morning."

"I can't do anything to her. She's bear-hugging me."

"You just have to wait until it passes."

I let Liam go. "Off with your coat and sit by the fire. The fog's made you clammy. And don't tell me those ridiculous spaceman trainers keep your feet dry. Now tell me about university. Is Knyfer McMahon still faculty head? What are you doing for your first-year thesis?"

"No, Ma, no! I haven't seen you for half a year, with only your voice on tapes. Where have *you* been and what have *you* been doing? Tell her, Da!"

"John Cullin, did you teach our son to answer back to his elders and betters?"

"You just have to wait until it passes. Anyway, I'm only the father. Tea?"

Liam sniffed. "Please."

Planck was still running around in nervous wagging circles.

In my first week in Hong Kong, I did very little. I got lost and unlost and lost in byways and overways and underways. A quarter of the world, teeming in a few square miles. Huw was right. If I avoided computer linkups I was probably untraceable. But after Switzerland I felt I had crash-landed on a strange planet where privacy and peace were coincidences rather than rights. "Dispense with the niceties," advised Huw, "and learn to do inside your head what you can't do outside."

I got a fake British passport made, for only fifty U.S. dollars.

I watched the television war. I watched the weaponry ana-lyzed, hyped, and billed: Scud versus Homer, Batman versus the Joker. The war had been "won" days before, the supply of cheap oil secured, but that was no longer the point. Technology efficacy needed to be tested in combat conditions, and to use up stock-piles. The wretched army of conscripts from the enemy's ethnic minorities were the laboratory rats. Quancog's laboratory rats. My laboratory rats.

I recorded a tape of me and Hong Kong, and posted it to John, via Siobhan in Cork, John's Aunt Triona in Baltimore, Billy, Father Wally, and thus to John. I prayed it would get through un-detected, a snail invisible to radar.

Huw was suddenly dispatched to Petersburg, so there I was: alone, unknown, unemployed, a box of hundred-dollar notes concealed in the freezer compartment under bags of peas. My es-cape plan had worked too well. No kidnapper from phantom crime networks so much as dropped in for a chat. Had the Texan just been bluffing? Trying to scare me to Saragosa?

Now what?

We create models to explain nature, but the models wind up gate-crashing nature and driving away the original inhabitants. In my lecturing days most of my students believed that atoms really are solid little stellar nuclei orbited by electrons. When I tell them that nobody knows what an electron is, they look at me like I've told them that the sun is a watermelon. One of the better-read-up ones might put up their hand and say, "But Dr. Muntervary, isn't an electron a charged probability wave?"

"Suppose now," I am fond of saying, "I prefer to think of it as a dance."

Forty summers ago, two miles away from Aodhagan Croft. There is a chink in the floorboards in the upstairs room of the house in the sycamores. After I've been put to bed, I sometimes pull back the rug and look down into the parlor. My ma wears her white dress and her cultured pearls, and Da a black shirt. On the gramophone revolves a new 78 rpm from Dublin.

"No no no, Jack Muntervary," Ma scolds, "you've got two left feet. Elephant ones."

"Chinatown, my Chinatown," crackles the gramophone.

"Try again."

Their shadows dance on the walls.

What now, indeed?

I was still a physicist, even if nobody knew it but me. The idea crept up and announced itself while I was haggling down the price of grapefruits in the market. Pink grapefruits pink as dawn. Strip quantum cognition down to first principles, and rebuild it incorporating nonlocality, instead of trying to lock nonlocality out. Before I'd paid for the grapefruits, ideas for formulae were kicking down the door. I bought a leather-bound black notebook from a stationer's, sat down next to a stone dragon, and scribbled eight pages of calculations, before I spilled them and lost them.

In the days and weeks following my routine grew saggier but regular. I got up around one in the afternoon and ate at a *dim sum* restaurant across the alleyway. The place was owned by an old albino man. I sat in the corner with *The Economist, Legal Advisor,* a Delia Smith cookery book, or whatever else was lying around Huw's apartment. On lucky days the shoeshiner who was the de facto postman for our tenement had a jiffy bag addressed to Huw with a tape from John. I listened to them in my *dim sum* corner on Huw's Walkman, over and over. Sometimes John had recorded new compositions, or lines from his new poems. Sometimes he'd just record a busy night in The Green Man. Sometimes sheep, seals, skylarks, the wind turbine. If Liam were home there would be some Liam. The summer fair. The Fastnet Race. I would unfold my map of Clear Island. Those tapes prised the lid off homesickness and rattled out the contents, but always at the bottom was solace.

At the end of the afternoon I sat down at the rickety desk and picked up from where I had left off in the early hours. I worked in isolation: e-mailing any of the handful of people alive who could have contributed was too dangerous. It was liberating: not having to be accountable to Heinz Formaggio and other cretins. I had my father's fountain pen, my black book, a box of CDs containing data from every particle lab experiment ever conducted, and thousands of dollars of computer equipment bought from a Sikh gentleman more resourceful than Light Box Procurement. Compared to Kepler, who plotted the ellipsoids of Mars with little more than a goose quill, I had it easy.

There were wrong turnings. I had to jettison matrix mechanics in favor of virtual numbers, and my doomed attempt to amalgamate the Einstein-Podolsky-Rosen paradox with Cadwalladr's behavioral model set me back weeks. It was the loneliest time in my life. As chess players or writers or mystics know, the pursuit of insight takes you deep into the forest. Days were I'd just gaze at the steam rising from my coffee, or stains on the wall, or a locked door. Days were I'd find the next key in the steam or the stains or the lock.

By July all the footprints of Einstein, Bohr, and Sonada were behind me.

The black book was filling up.

I was still talking. Liam's toast had gone cold. A helicopter flew over.

What is Liam thinking?

Is it, "Why can't I have normal parents?"

Is it, "Will she never stop?"

"Is my ma a madwoman?"

It makes me sad that I can't read my son's thoughts. There again, it's right this way. He's eighteen, now. I missed his birthday again. Where will I be for the next one?

"Well don't stop there, Ma. You're just getting to the good bit."

The strong force that stops the protons of a nucleus hurtling away from one another; the weak force that keeps the electrons from crashing into the protons; electromagnetism, which lights the planet and cooks dinner; and gravity, which is the most down-to-earth. From before the time the universe was the size of a walnut to its present diameter, these four forces have been the statute book of matter, be it the core of Sirius or the electrochemical ducts of the brains of students in the lecture theater at Belfast. Bored, intent, asleep, dreaming, in receding tiers. Chewing pencils or following me.

Matter is thought, and thought is matter. Nothing exists that cannot be synthesized.

Summer. Huw came back late most nights, to snatch a few hours of sleep before returning to his office. A securities firm had crashed, and the effects were rippling out. Sometimes a week went by and apart from noticing the toothpaste tube depleting we were barely aware of one another. On Sundays, however, we always dressed up and went out to dinner somewhere expensive, but low-key. I didn't want to risk meeting his colleagues. Lying is a skill I have never mastered.

I often worked all night. Hong Kong never really quietens down, the sunlight just switches off for a few hours. Huw's snores, the God-Almighty clatter of Kowloon's sweat shops, that gigantic bicycle pump, the eye of the electric fan, and moth wings on the computer screen ushered in the quantum mathematics of sentience.

Three sharp knocks on John's door and a mantrap snapped shut. I'd jumped up, spilled my tea, and was crouched in the stair doorway, poised to run—where? Only one door—I would have to jump from the second floor and run for it across the meadows. Great idea, Mo. Dislocate a hip. Liam didn't know what was going on. John was working it out, my panic bashing its head on his defenses.

"It's okay, Ma—" Liam began.

I sliced the air. "Sssssh!"

Liam showed me the palms of his hands like he was calming a scared animal. "It's either Father Wally, Maisie, or Red come to milk Feynman. . . ."

I shook my head. They'd have knocked once, if at all, and walked in.

"Who was on the *St. Fachtna* with you this morning? Any Americans?"

There was another rattle of knocking. "Hello?" A woman. Not Irish, not English.

I put my finger over my lips, and tiptoed up the stairs. They creaked.

A mouth to the letterbox. "G'day? Anyone home?"

"Morning to you," said John. "Just a moment . . ."

I slid into the bedroom and looked for somewhere to hide the black book. Where, Mo? Under the mattress? Eat it?

I heard John opening the door. "Sorry to keep you."

"No worries. Sorry for the bother. I'm walking to this row of stones on the map here. Map reading was never my strong point."

"The stone row? Piece of cake. Go back down the drive, turn left, and just follow the sign to Roe's bridge. All the way until the road peters out. Then you'll see it. Unless the mist has other plans."

"Thanks a million. Too bad about this rain, eh? It's like winter back home."

How can John be so calm? "Where is home? New Zealand?"

"That's right! Halfmoon Bay, Stewart Island, south of the South Island. Know it?"

"Can't say I do. 'Fraid the weather's a law unto itself, here. Tropical rainstorms, raining frogs . . . Gales later though, the fishing forecast said earlier. Winter's around the corner."

"Just my luck. Say now, you're a lovely dog! A him or a her?"

"A her. Planck."

"As in thick as a?"

"As in the physicist who discovered why you can sit in front of a fire and not be incinerated by the ultraviolet catastrophe."

Nervous laugh. "Oh, right, *that* Planck. Mild-mannered beastie for an island dog."

"It's her job. She's my guide dog."

The usual awkwardness. I relaxed. A pursuer would know about John. Unless she was just a good actress. I tensed up.

"You mean, er, you're . . ."

". . . as a bat. A lot blinder than a bat, actually. I'm unequipped with sonar."

"Strewth . . . there was I . . . I'm sorry."

"No need."

"Well, I'd better get to the row of stones before the gales blow 'em over."

"Take your time. They've been there three thousand years. Mind how you go."

"'Bye. Thanks again."

I watched her walk down the drive. A youngish woman with red hair and a lemon raincoat. She looked over her shoulder, and I pulled away from the window. Could she have noticed the third coffee cup? I heard Liam and John talking in hushed voices downstairs. I watched the mist drifting in from the Calf Islands.

The sky over the Mount Gabriel was beaten dark and threatening. Liam and I were making a stew with some late turnips from the garden. John was tuning his harp. The stew bubbled in the pot.

Liam crumbled in a stock cube. "What are you going to do, Ma?"

"Add some more garlic."

"You know what I'm talking about. Are they coming for you?"

"Aye, I think they are."

"And are you going to go with them?"

"I don't know."

"Why did you come back to Clear if you know they'll track you here?"

"Because I needed to see you pair."

"You need a plan."

"By all means I need a plan."

"So, what are your options?"

Liam sounded like my father. "One. Burn the black book and turn quantum cognition to ash. Change my name to Scarlett O'Hara, plant beans, keep bees for the rest of my life, and hope that the CIA is too stupid to look for me on the island of my birth. Two. Spend the rest of my life backpacking in hot countries, wearing sandals and tie-dyed trousers. Three. Go and live in a place in Texas that is not on maps, earn vast prestige and money by accelerating the new arms race fifty years, and see my son and my husband only under escort to ensure I don't defect."

Liam chopped his onion deftly. "Aye, that's a thorny one."

. . .

Kowloon brewed, stewed, and simmered. My nonlocality virtual equations were holding. My peaceful gone-to-earth exile's life couldn't last.

I remember the moment it ended. A gecko had appeared on the screen. Its tongue flickered like electricity. Hello, tiny life-form of star compost, did you know that your lizardly life, too, is billiarded this way and that by quantum scissors, papers, and stones? That your particles exist in a time-froth of little bridges and holes forever going back and around and under itself? That the universe is the shape of a donut, and that if you had a powerful enough telescope you would see the tip of your tail?

Do you care?

Male shouting flared up from nowhere, and exploded in see-sawing Cantonese. Women pitched in a couple of octaves higher. Tipped-over furniture walloped. The lampshade in my room swayed.

"What the fuck was that?" Huw stumbled through in his Daffy Duck boxer shorts and Mr. Mole glasses, tripping over his Indonesian drum kit. "Fuck."

A gun fired! I jumped as if it had gone off in my pocket. "Sweet Jesus!"

The whole building was quiet as death.

Huw checked that the bolts and chain were securely fastened.

The gecko was long gone.

A sickening sense that this was coming for me. I was gnawing my knuckles.

Thunder fell headlong down the stairs—and stopped. There were at least three sets of footfalls. Huw picked up a baseball bat. I picked up a scale plaster model of John Coltrane, and with utter calmness I knew that I had never been this petrified in all my life. Very luckily for us, the thunder carried on down. Huw went towards the window but I instinctively pulled him back. His eyes were astonished. "Fuck," he said, a third time. The only three swear words I'd ever heard from Huw.

The wart on my thumb was growing.

The phone rang. Leave me alone. Leave me alone.

John was nearest. "Hello?"

My throat was dry.

"Tamlin . . ."

Tamlin Sheehy. Calm down, Mo. No newcomers to Clear Island today.

"Yes, Liam tied the tarpaulin down. They'll be fine. Thanks for asking. She would, would she? Okay . . . Mind how you go. . . ."

John cupped the receiver. "Hey loverboy, Bernadette wants to murmur sweet nothings."

"Da! She's frightmare! Don't you dare!"

"Don't be rotten. You've got the lure of the exotic. You've been to Switzerland."

John smiled twistedly and spoke back into the receiver. "Just a mo there, Bernadette, he's just coming. He was in the shower. He's just toweling himself dry for . . ."

Liam half-snarled, half-hissed, and took the phone into the hallway, shutting the door on the cord.

We listened to the radio over dinner.

"Have you noticed," said John, "how countries call theirs 'sovereign nuclear deterrents,' but call the other countries' ones 'weapons of mass destruction'?"

"Yes," I said.

The wind rose and fell like mountains at sea. The glass rattled. Liam yawned, and so did I. "One game to me, one game to you. Will Feynman be okay?"

"He will. He huddles down behind his boulder. Where's your da?"

"In his study, meditating."

Liam started putting away the Scrabble. "It's going to be a harsh winter, Maisie was telling me. Long-range weather forecast."

"Maisie? Has she got satellite TV installed?"

"No, her bees told her."

"Ah, the bees."

. . .

The Chinese policeman was unexpectedly tall and civil. A lieutenant from the old Prince of Wales guard, he knew about Huw's work. He wrote down our versions of the raid in his notebook, and sipped iced tea. An ink-devil of sweat soaked itself into his shirt.

"I should tell you that the burglars wanted to know where were hidden the *gwai lo*s. Your neighbors said there no *gwai lo*s."

"Before or after the gun was fired?" I asked.

"After. They lied for you."

Huw puffed out his cheeks. "What are you thinking, officer?"

"Two possibilities. One. They thought the apartment of *gwai lo*s had better things to steal. Two. Mr. Llewellyn, you are investigating the accounts of powerful companies. Might they include some Triad links?"

"Show me a company in Hong Kong that doesn't have Triad links."

"Foreigners don't live in neighborhoods like this, especially white ones. Discovery Bay is more secure."

I went into the kitchenette. In the opposite tenement the blinds were rolling down as the excitement subsided. Eyes everywhere. Eyes, eyes.

I remembered my conversation with the Texan. I knew who the "burglars" were and what they had come for. Next time they wouldn't mistake the British, American, and Chinese systems of labeling floors.

I hadn't touched a piano since Switzerland. I played a passable aria from the Goldberg Variations.

Liam played a gorgeous "In a Sentimental Mood."

John half-improvised, half-remembered. "This one's the crow on the wall. . . . This one's the wind turbine. . . . This one's . . ."

"Totally random notes?" suggested Liam.

"No. It's the music of chance."

"The wind's really getting up! Maybe there'll be no boats tomorrow either, Ma?"

"Maybe so. So tell me about Uni, Liam."

"They've got some cool electron microscopes. I'm doing my first-year thesis on superliquids, and I've been playing synths in a band, and—"

"—deflowering maidens," butted in John through a mouthful of sausage. "According to Dennis."

"It's not fair, Ma." Liam turned red as a beetroot. "He speaks to Professor Dannan once a week."

"As I have done for the last twenty years. Why should I stop just because he's your tutor?"

Liam harrumphed, and walked over to the window. "It looks like the end of the world out there."

Schroedinger came in through the cat flap, and looked around hypercritically.

"What, cat?" asked Liam.

Schroedinger chose John's lap in which to exact tribute.

The storm battered the island.

"I'm a shade concerned about our Kiwi visitor." John picked up the telephone. "Mrs. Dunwallis? This is John. I'm just phoning to check whether or not your Kiwi visitor got back to the hostel safe and sound. . . . She called in here earlier, asking for directions to the stone row, with the gales, I was worried. . . . Are you sure? Of course you're sure. . . . No idea. Mrs. Cuchthalain's at Roe Bridge? Sure . . . will do."

"What's up, Da?"

"No New Zealanders at the Youth Hostel."

"She must have just been a day tripper, then."

"Billy wouldn't risk taking *St. Fachtna* over to Baltimore in this weather."

"She's still on the island then. She must have taken shelter in the village."

"Aye. There's a logical explanation."

I felt hollow. I was afraid there was a very logical explanation.

John and I were in our firelit bedroom. Liam was in the bath having a long soak, after e-mailing a girl in Dublin whose name we couldn't tease out of him. John massaged my feet as thunder galloped by. I watched the sphinxes and the faces and flowers in the bedroom's fireplace. The physics and chemistry of fire only add to its poetry. This way of living was so normal to Clear Islanders. Mo, why are evenings like this so rare for you?

I am the ancient mariner: that black book is my albatross.

"What am I going to do, John? When they get here?"

"Mo, let's cross that one when we get to it."

"I don't even know if I should cross it at all."

On the third day I knew where I was before I opened my eyes. The black book was safe. Yesterday's storms were long gone, the early sunlight lit the curtains, ending its twenty-six-minute journey on the jiggleable electrons in my retina. The wind was brisk, the sky was bright and cloud shadows slid over Roaringwater Sound and the three Calf Islands. Planck was barking. Thousands of Arab children were gamboling into the sea, steam hissing off their burns. A noise on the stairs made me turn around. The Texan filled the doorframe. He clicked the safety catch off and aimed the gun at the black book, then at me. "We need Quancog to rise again, Dr. Muntervary." He winked at me as he pulled the trigger.

I lay there for twenty minutes, calming down. The early sunlight lit the curtains.

John's eyeballs rolled under his eyelids, seeing something I couldn't.

Our very first morning together in this house, this room, this bed, was our first morning as husband and wife. Twenty years ago! Brendan had constructed the bed, and Maisie had painted the Michaelmas daisies along the headboard. The bedding was from Mrs. Dunwallis, who'd stuffed the pillows from her own geese. Aodhagan Croft itself was a wedding present from John's Aunt Cath, who had gone to live with Aunt Triona in Baltimore. No electricity, no telephone, no sewage tank. My own parents' house in the sycamore trees was still standing, but the floorboards and rafters had rotted right through, and we didn't have the money to reverse dereliction.

Besides Aodhagan we had John's harp, my doctorate, a crate

of books that had been my da's library, and a cartload of tiles and whitewash lugged up from the harbor by Freddy Doig's horse. My job at Cork University didn't begin until the autumn term. I've never felt such freedom since, and I know I never will again.

Down in the kitchen the telephone rang. Leave me alone, leave me alone.

To my surprise Liam was already up and had answered it before the third ring. "Oh, hi, Aunt Maisie . . . Yeah, they're still in bed, on a morning like this, can you believe it? Bone idle or what? Uni's fine . . . Which one? Nah, she's history, I knocked that one on the head weeks ago. . . . Not literally, no. Right, I'll tell 'em when they drag themselves down. Okay."

I left John asleep. I hobbled downstairs, the stairs and my ankles creaking. "Morning, First-Born."

"Only-Born. That was Aunt Maisie. She told me to say 'Kilmagoon' to you. She's cleaning the pipes in the bar, but will be going to Minnaunboy to cut Sylvester's hair later. Nicky O'Driscoll's privy got blown away in the gale, and Maire Doig caught a monster conger eel. She's suffering from gossip deprivation. Sleep okay?"

"Like a log."

A pause while Liam worked up to something.

"Ma—are you going to tell everyone about the Americans?"

"I think it's best not to."

"When are they going to come?"

"I have no idea."

"Sooner or later?"

"I have no idea."

"Then when are we going to hide out somewhere?"

"You're going back to university, my boy."

"And you?"

"As you astutely observed, I'm not James Bond. I can't go on hiding. The only places I would be safe from the Americans are places more dangerous than Saragosa. All I can do is wait for them to come."

Liam spooned up some milk and dribbled it down into his bowl.

"They can't just abduct an Irish citizen! And you're not exactly nobody, either. It would be an international incident. The media would kick up too much fuss."

"Liam, they are the most powerful people on the planet and they want what is in my head and my black book. Neither international law nor BBC Radio would come into it."

Liam's forehead knotted up, like it used to before a tantrum. "But . . . how are we supposed to live like this? Do we just sit around waiting for you to be got?"

"I wish I had an answer for you, love."

"It's not fair!"

"No."

The legs of his chair scraped as he stood up. "Well, damn it all, Ma!"

I didn't know what to say.

"I'm going to go and feed the chickens." He put his duffle coat over his pajamas and went out.

I put the kettle on, and waited for it to whistle.

The grandfather clock's pendulum grated like a spade digging far below.

Eighteen years ago I was flat on my back in the bedroom, with Liam tunneling out of my womb. A wind tunnel of agony! I didn't want to give birth on Clear Island—I was a research lecturer acquainted with the latest medical technology. That very day I was leaving for Cork to stay with Bella and Alain near a shiny hospital with a cheerful midwife from Jamaica, but Liam had other ideas. Even today he's patient only until he's bored. So instead of my gleaming ward I had Aodhagan's bedroom, my mother, Maisie, an icon of St. Bernadette, some anti-fairy herbs, towels and steaming kettles. John was smoking downstairs with Brendan, and Father Wally was on hand with his holy water.

When he was out, as I lay there unstitched, the pain seeping away, Maisie held up Liam! This alien parasite, glistening in mucus? Laugh or cry? Birth had come visiting, just as death will, and everything was perfectly clear. My mother, Maisie, St. Bernadette and I shared a few moments, postponing the clod-hopping hullabaloo. Maise washed Liam in a tin bath.

It was noon. I felt I was cradling little Apollo.

Liam fed the hook into the mouth of the earthworm. The hook slid deeper into its gut as it squirmed. "Chew on that, my her-maphrodite."

"How can you do that and not bring your breakfast up?"

The sea breathed deeply in, and deeply out.

"Ah well, Mam. Life's a bitch, then you die."

He got up and cast off. I lost sight of the float until the plop sounded. My eyesight is definitely getting worse.

Seals were basking between the rock pools. The bull hauled himself into the sea, and sank from sight for thirty seconds. Thirty yards out his head appeared, reminding me of Planck.

"You must have fished with live bait when you were a girl, Ma?"

"I usually had my head in books. Your grandmother was the real fisherman of the family. She'd be out before dawn on morn-ings like these. I must have told you a dozen times."

"You never have. What about Grandpa?"

"His pleasure lay in weaving extraordinary lies."

"What like?"

"One time he said King Cuchulainn had given Bonnie Prince Charlie all his gold to look after before he went mad and turned into a newt. Bonnie Prince Charlie, running from Napoléon Bonaparte, hid the gold under a stone on Clear Island, and if we looked hard enough we'd be sure to find it. We spent a whole summer, me and the Docherty twins. Then Roland Davitt pointed out the chronological inconsistencies."

"What did you say to Grandpa?"

"I asked him why he'd lied."

"What did he say?"

"He told me that no scientist based her research on second-hand data without checking its veracity beforehand, using the *En-cyclopedia Britannica* in the village school."

A motor boat crossed the sound. I looked through the binoculars.

"It's okay, Ma. It's only Daibhi O'Bruadair raising his lobster pots."

Mo, don't be so jumpy! God knows when you'll next have a free morning with Liam. Could be tomorrow, could be years from now.

For a little while we said nothing, Liam standing there fishing, and me lying on the warm rock. I listened to the waves breathe through the shingle.

The rain was falling onto the roofs of Skibbereen, coming out of the guttering in great gurgling arcs and slapping onto the pavements. The nursing home attendant poured one cup of tea in the china teacup. It had a wide brim to hasten thermal equilibrium and a mousepaw-sized handle to hasten spillage. "I'm sorry the head matron couldn't be here to see you herself, Dr. Muntervary . . . but visitors usually let us know in advance that they'll be paying a call."

"It's just a flying visit."

The nurse and I caught each other searching the other's face and we both looked down. I could imagine the Texan speaking to her: "I'm an old friend of Mo and John. . . . If Mo shows up, give me a bell. I'd love to surprise her."

We looked at my ma.

"Mrs. Muntervary? Your daughter's come." I suspected the softness in the attendant's voice only appeared when visitors came to tea.

I looked around the room. "Very nice in here . . ." What rubbish.

"Yes," said the attendant. "We do our best." More rubbish. "Well, I'll leave you for a little while. I have to supervise the crochet class, to make sure there are no upsets with the needles."

Everything in the room was magnolia. Anonymity is gray, forgetting is magnolia.

I looked at my mother. Lucy Eileen Muntervary. Are you somewhere, looking at us both but unable to signal, or are you nowhere now? When I visited at the end of winter you had been upset. You remembered my face but not who it belonged to.

Wigner maintains that human consciousness collapses one lucky universe into being from all of the possible ones. Had my mother's universe now uncollapsed? Were cards flying across the baize back into the dealer's pack?

My mother blinked.

"Ma . . ." A voice used to address a saint believed in only when needed.

"Ma, if you can hear me . . ." Now I'm opening a séance.

Why are you putting yourself through this, Mo?

Without where I am from and who I am from, I am nothing, even if the glass is gone and conifers are growing through where the roof should be. All those wide-worlders in transit, all those misplaced, thrown-away people who know as little as they care about their roots—how do they do it? How do they know who they are?

My ma blinked.

"Ma, do you remember dancing with Da in the parlor?"

I persuaded myself that she was enjoying the patter of rain-drops on the windowsill. We watched the waterflower-fireworks until the attendant returned.

Over Lios Ó Móine comes Father Wally, freewheeling on his tri-cycle, his habit flapping behind him in the wind. I watch him getting nearer and larger, and find myself calculating a parallax matrix. We wave. Liam is still concentrating, swishing his fishing line from time to time. I can hear Father Wally's tricycle now, a rusty brigand on coasters. He dismounts cowboy-style, standing on one pedal and jumping as it cruises to a crash. His face is red from the exercise and the wind, his hair fine and white from age.

"Morning to the pair o'ye! You survived the gales, then. Your eye's looking better, Mo. I called into Aodhagan to see about sav-ing my bishop. He told me you'd be here. It's a fair old spot to see dolphins. Fish biting, Liam?"

"Not yet, Father. They've probably just had breakfast."

"Shufty up on our blanket, Father. I've got a thermos of tea and a thermos of coffee."

"I'll go with your tea, there, Mo. Coffee is fine for the body, but tea is the drink of the soul."

"I read a few weeks back," said Liam, "that tea was first processed accidentally in the holds of long-distance clippers from India. It took so long, and got so hot, that the crates of green tea started to ferment. And when they opened the crates at Bristol or Dublin or Le Havre, the stuff we call tea is what they found. But it was all a mistake, to begin with."

"I wasn't knowing that," said Father Wally, "so many things there are to know. Most things happen because of mistakes."

"Can I leave you with Ma, Father Wally? I want to cast off further down. I think the seals might be scaring the fishing off."

"Even Jesus tended to put fishing first."

After the upstairs raid, I knew I had to leave right then. Huw tried to dissuade me, and talked about coincidences and overreacting, but there was no way I'd risk bringing those people into his life, and he knew I was right. We spoke in whispers as I packed. I judged it too dangerous to try to leave Hong Kong by the airport. Huw walked me to a big hotel near his office. I said goodbye to my only friend east of Lake Geneva. I checked in with my real name, and then took a taxi to another hotel, where I checked in with my fake passport.

The following day I lay low. From the travel office in the hotel I obtained a visa for China and a train ticket with my own compartment to Beijing. When I was a girl, I dreamed of such journeys. Now I could only dream of its end.

Tomorrow, mainland Asia would swallow me whole.

Father Wally and I sat nursing our cups of tea, watching Liam fish in front of creation. Mount Gabriel rose on the peninsula to the blue north.

"Fine lad," said Father Wally. "Your da and ma would be proud of him."

"Do you know, Father, in the last seventeen years, I've spent only five years and nine months with Liam? That's only thirty-four percent. Am I crazy? It's like John and I have been divorced. I didn't mean it to be like that. I sometimes worry I've deprived him of his roots."

"Does he look like a victim of deprivation to you?"

All six feet of Liam, because of John and me.

St. Fachtna crossed the water towards Baltimore. I tried not to see it. "Have a digestive biscuit, Father."

"Don't mind if I do, thanking you. Remember the day Liam was born?"

"I was thinking about it this morning, funnily enough."

"I've christened some ugly babies in my time, Mo, but . . ."

I laughed. "I wish John could see him now."

"John sees better than most. He's a hell-bound atheist and slippery as an eel when it comes to the Russian Bishop's Switch-blade, but he's got the patience of Job."

"He's got a better choice in friends than Job."

"Folks with most to complain about seldom complain most."

"John says, self-pity's the first step to despair for blind people."

"Aye, I can see that, but nonetheless . . ."

Father Wally wanted to say something else, so I waited and watched a flotilla of puffins. Across the bay, in the harbor, sheets were drying in the wind. I found myself calculating how long one Homer missile with a Quancog module would take to decide where the optimum point of impact would be—thirty nanoseconds. Inside eight seconds the hillside would be a fireball.

"Mo," began Father Wally, making a tent with his hands. "John's told me nothing. But that tells me a lot. Then there's the chain of people passing on tapes to John and back all year, you know how people jump to conclusions—"

"I can't tell you, Father. I want to, but I can't. I can't even tell you why I can't."

"Mo, I'm not asking you to discuss any of that secret hoipolloy. I just wanted to say that you're one of us, and we stick by our own."

Before I could answer mechanical thunder scattered the

sheep and ripped the air. We watched the fighter plane fly off to the north. Liam waded back towards us.

"Infernal things!" growled Father Wally. "There's been a spate of them recently. They've reopened the old army range over on Bear Island. Now we're a Gaelic tiger, we're getting airs about power. Won't we ever learn? Ireland, and power. Fine by themselves, but bring them together and it all goes wrong, like, like . . ."

"Kiwi fruit and yogurt," said Liam. "Bitter."

"We'll be wanting our own satellites next, and nuclear bombs."

"Ireland pays into the European Space Agency already, doesn't it, Ma?"

"There you go," said Father Wally. "We're one of the last corners of Europe, and Clear Island is the last corner of Ireland, but it's catching up with us, even here."

Electrons in my brain are moving forwards and backwards in time, changing atoms, changing electrical charge, changing molecules, changing chemicals, carrying impulses, changing thoughts, deciding to have a baby, changing ideas, deciding to leave Light Box, changing theory, changing technology, changing computer circuitry, changing artificial intelligence, changing the projections of missiles whole segments of the globe away, and collapsing buildings onto people who have never heard of Ireland.

Electrons, electrons, electrons. What laws are you following?

John came down the road from Lios Ó Móine with Planck.

"Ahoy there, Da!" said Liam.

"Liam? Caught lunch yet?"

"Not yet."

"Eighteen years of devoted parenting, and all I get is 'not yet'? Is your ma here?"

"Present. And Father Wally."

"Just the man we need. Any chance of turning no fish and no bread into lunch?"

"I confess, I stopped off at Ancient's for contingency sandwich supplies. . . ."

"Aha! My kind of Papist!"

"It's only eleven-thirty," said Liam a little huffily, rethreading his fishing rod.

"You've got until noon, son," said John.

John held my arm as we walked. He didn't need to, his feet knew every inch of Clear Island: that's why he moved back here permanently when his blindness closed in. He held my arm because he believed it made me feel like a teenager again, and he was right. We turned left hand at the only crossroads. Only the sounds of wind, gulls, sheep, and waves floated on the silence.

"Any clouds?"

"Yes. Over Hare Island there's a galleon one. Cumulonimbus calvus."

"They the cauliflowers?"

"Lungs."

"Camphor trees. What colors can you see?"

"The fields are mossy green. The trees are bare, apart from a few hangers-on. The sky is map-sea blue. Pearly, mauve clouds. The sea is dark bottle blue. Ah, I'm an Atlantic woman, John. Leave the Pacific to the Pacificians. I rot if I'm left anywhere Pacific."

"One of the stupidest things that people say about being blind, is that it's sadder to have been sighted once and to have lost it. I know color! Are there any boats out today?"

"The *Oileán na nÉan*. And a beautiful yacht anchored off Middle Calf Island."

"I miss sailing."

"You'd only have to ask."

"I get seasick. Imagine being on a rollercoaster, blindfolded."

"Aye, fair enough." We walked on for a bit. "Where are you taking me?"

"Father Wally had St. Ciaran's woodwork renovated. Everyone says it's quite something."

The last warm wind before winter. Way, way away a skylark sang.

"Mo, I was worried sick about you."

"I'm so sorry, my love. But as long as nobody could reach me, nobody could threaten me. And as long as nobody could threaten me, you and Liam were safe."

"I'm still worried sick."

"I know. And I'm still sorry."

"I just wanted you to know."

"Thanks." Even from John, tenderness made me tearful.

"You were like a one-woman electron in Heisenberg's uncertainty principle."

"How do you mean?"

"I either knew your position but not your direction, or I knew your direction but not your position. What's that noise? A ten-foot sheep?"

"Cows lumbering over to see if we're going to milk them."

"Jerseys or Friesians?"

"Brown ones."

"Noakes's Jerseys."

"What wouldn't I give to stay here like my mother and plant beans."

"How long until you started itching for your ninth-generation computers again?"

"Well, maybe I'd write the odd paper while I was waiting for my beans to grow."

Red Kildare's mighty motorbike pulled up, spitting stones and smoke. Maisie was in the sidecar. "John! Mo!" she had to yell over the engine. "Mo! Here's a piece of bacon for your wart!"

Maisie put a thumb-sized thing wrapped into aluminum foil into my hand. "Rub it on your wart before nightfall and bury it, but don't let anyone see or it won't work. Red's milked Feynman. See you at The Green Man later."

I nodded at Red and Red nodded at me.

"Mind how you go. Red! Frape it!"

The Norton roared away, Maisie whooping and flapping her arms like a dragon.

. . .

The same pew, the same chapel, a Mo different and the same. I gazed up at the ceiling, and saw the bottom of a boat. I always imagined the chapel as the Ark on Ararat. A smell of new wood, ancient flagstones, and prayer books. I closed my eyes, and imagined my mother, a prim woman, and my father, either side of me. I could suddenly smell my mother's perfume: it was called "Mountain Lily." My father smelled of tobacco, wheezing slightly as his large stomach rose and fell. He squeezed my hand, turned, and smiled. I opened my eyes, suddenly wide awake. John was feeling his way around the organ stops, cleared his throat, and launched into "A Lighter Shade of Pale."

Bars, shafts, clefs in stained glass.

"John Cullin! An anthem of the shameless sixties in a house of God."

"If God can't dig the spirituality of Procol Harum, that's His loss."

"What'll you do if Father Wally comes?"

"Tell him it's Pastoral in E minor by Fettuccine."

"Fettuccine's a pasta!"

"We skipped the last fandango . . ."

Naomh's road led up to the highest point on the island. We took it very slowly. I guided John round potholes.

"The wind turbine's cracking round at a fair old rate."

"It is, John."

"The islanders still believe you were behind the turbine."

"I wasn't! The study group chose Clear Island independently."

"Badger O'Connor was going to organize an 'It's an eyesore' petition to the Euro MP. Then people discovered they'd never have another electricity bill in their life. When the committee proposed Gillarney Island at the eleventh hour, Badger O'Connor organized a 'Give us back our generator' petition."

"People said windmills and canals and locomotives were eyesores, I'm quite sure. When they are threatened with extinction, then people wax lyrical. There's a couple of crows picking their way down the wall." I thought of two black-cloaked old ladies, beachcombing. They looked up at me in unison.

The buzz and whoosh of the wind generator grew as we neared it. If each rotation a new day, a new year, a new universe, its shadow a scythe of antimatter . . . then—

I almost stepped into the black thing that was suddenly at my feet, the flies buzzing around it. "Yurgh . . ."

"What?" asked John. "Sheepshit?"

"No . . . Argh! It's a fangy little dead bat with its face half-eaten away."

"Lovely."

There was a stranger walking along the cliff path far below. She had binoculars. I didn't tell John.

"What are you thinking, Mo?"

"While I was in Hong Kong I saw a man die."

"How did he die?"

"I don't know. . . . He just collapsed, right in front of me. His heart, I guess. There's this big silver Buddha who lives out on one of the outlying islands. There was a coach park around the base of the steps that led up to it, with a few stalls. I'd bought a bowl of noodles, and was slurping them up in the shade. He was only a young man. I wonder why I thought of him? Big silver things on island hills, maybe. The peculiar thing was, he seemed to be laughing."

I lay entombed in a slab of rock, in an embryo curl.

Out of the wind. Hold your ear to the conch of time, Mo. The tomb had lain here for three thousand years. I imagined that I had too. Nobody knows how pre-Celtic people lacking iron technology could have hollowed out a block of granite in which to bury their dead warlord, but here it is. Nobody's sure how they dragged this block, the size of a double bed and twice as thick, across from Blananarragaun, either.

John's hairy legs dangled down in front of the entrance.

Beyond, dune grass waved, sea horses rode the breakers. Beyond the breakers were waves, all colors and shades of eyes, all the way to the sleeping giant.

As kids, we used to dare each other to sleep in here: Clear Island folklore said that a person who slept in Ciaran's tomb would turn into either a crow or a poet. Danny Waite did one night, but he turned into a mechanic, and married the daughter of the butcher of Baltimore.

I reached out and poked John's knee-pit. He yelped.

"You know, Cullin, I could handle being a crow right now. It'd be a no-questions-asked way out of my dilemma. No, I'm terribly sorry Heinz, Mr. Texan, Mo Muntervary would love to teach your weapons to think but she's gone looking for twigs and earthworms."

"I'd like to be a crow, too. But not a blind crow. I'd probably fly into the turbine. Will you come out of there? It's morbid, curling up in a tomb just for kicks."

"More morbid things have happened here. I remember Whelan Scott telling stories about the mass of St. Secaire being celebrated here."

"What's that?"

"You city slickers, you don't know anything. It's the Catholic Mass, said backwards, word by word, and the person whom the Mass is dedicated to dies by next midwinter."

"I bet that went down a bomb with Father Wally."

"Only the Pope can provide absolution."

"It's amazing you became a scientist, growing up in the middle of all this."

"I became a scientist because I grew up in the middle of all this."

Even time is not immune to time. Once the only times that mattered were the rhythms of the planet and the body. The first people on this island needed time four times a year: the solstices and the equinoxes, to avoid planting seed too early or too late. When the Church got here, it staked out Sundays, Christmases, Easter, and began colonizing the year with saints' days. The English brought short leases and tax deadlines. With the railway, the hours had to march in time. Now TV satellites beam the same six o'clock news everywhere at the same six o'clock. Science has been as busy splicing time into ever thinner slivers as it has matter. In my Light Box research on superconductors, I dealt in jiffies: there are

10,000,000,000,000,000,000,000,000,000,000,000,000,000 of them in a second.

But you can no more measure the speed of time than you can bottle days. Clocks measure arbitrary meters of time, but not its speed. Nobody knows if time is speeding up, or slowing down. Nobody knows what it is. How much time is there in a day? Not how many hours, minutes, seconds: how much *time* do we have?

This day?

"What's the sandwich scenario, Mo?"

"Ham and cheese; ham and tomato; cheese and tomato."

"And ham, cheese, and tomato."

"How did you know?"

"You've never noticed how you group sandwiches into Venn diagrams?"

"Do I?"

"It's why I married you."

I remembered the little knuckle of meat Maisie had given me for my wart. I took it out of its silver paper, resisted a fleeting temptation to pop it into my mouth, and rubbed it against my wart.

"Excuse me a moment, John. I have to bury a little bit of meat."

"Maisie's wart cure? Go ahead. I won't peep, Scout's honor."

> I will arise and go now, and go to Innisfree,
> And a small cabin build there, of clay and wattles made:
> Nine bean-rows will I have there, a hive for the honey-bee,
> And live alone in the bee-loud glade.

"I haven't thought about physics for a whole thirty minutes."

"The old Clear Island magic. Is anyone looking?"

"No. We have the whole hillside to ourselves. And the man in the afternoon moon. And Noakes's Jerseys."

"Then come here, my ocean child, my buxom island wench. . . ."

"Buxom! John Cullin . . ."

.   .   .

We left The Green Man before teatime. John, Planck, and me, walked back to Aodhagan. Liam standing on the pedals of his mountain bike.

"So where did you learn to hold whisky like that?" I asked Liam.

"Da."

"That's scurrilous slander is that!"

We walked on, Planck the only one who could walk straight.

"It's a rare old sunset tonight, Da."

"Is it now? What color is it?"

"Red."

"What red?"

"Inside of a watermelon red."

"Ah, that red. October red. That's a rare old sunset."

I'd left John by the gate sitting on a stone with Planck. The turf was pucked with hoofmarks and molehills. Liam cycled on ahead to give Schroedinger his dinner.

The garden was now a little forest. I was right, the roof had fallen in. I picked a way down what might have been the path. Were eyes behind the murk-glazed windows? The ivy on the walls rustled. Something inside clattered and flapped. Owls, bats, cats, bipeds up to their own business?

"Hello," I said, on the doorless threshold. "Anyone there?"

My da collapsed with his silted-up heart, just here. With the deadly calm of a person who had seen the future, my ma told me to look after him while she bicycled down to the harbor to get Dr. Mallahan.

Da had wanted to say something to me. I leaned close. He spoke like he had a ton of bricks on his ribs. "Mo, be strong, you understand? And study hard, and don't let your Gaelic lapse. It's who you are."

"Are you going to die now?"

"Aye, Mo," said my da, "and I can tell you, poppet, it's an intriguing experience."

It had been a neat little house, smelling of fresh air and fresh plaster and bleach. My da had tiled it himself one summer, with help from the Doig boys, Father Wally, and Gabriel Fitzmaurice, who drowned that same October. We'd made a huge bonfire from all the old thatch, down on the beach.

But any given system will decay from a complex order to a simpler condition. After my mother and I left Clear to enter the world of aunts on the mainland, storms and woodworm got to work. Other islanders needed building supplies themselves. My ma couldn't face her ghosts, so she told everybody to help themselves.

Now twigs hold up a roof of twilight and early stars.

"Mo!" John is calling from over the fields. "Are you okay?"

No messages were left.

"Yes," I shout back, zipping up my anorak.

John made a yawling noise as he stretched himself awake. A mild day, rarefied by wintriness. I heard helicopters. "Sleep well, my love?" John hears smiles in voices.

He degummed his mouth with his tongue. "Aye. I had this dream. I was floating in a shallow sea in Panama, no idea why it was Panama, it just was. I could see the light on the inside of the waves up above, and around me little puffy clouds were moving. 'That's odd,' I thought. 'You can't have clouds under the sea.' And when I looked closer, the clouds were jellyfish, Christmas-tree-light-colored, all glowing on and off."

"Nice dream."

"There are three times when I don't feel blind: when I show people around Clear Island; when I beat Father Wally at chess; and when I dream colors. . . . Mo?"

"Yes, John?"

"Mo, what's up?"

Huw told me that you always wake up a few seconds before the earthquake starts.

"It's today."

I interact with John, the Texan, Heinz Formaggio, and the rest of reality in the way that I do because I am who I am. Why am I who I am? Because of the double helix of atoms coiled along my DNA. What is DNA's engine of change? Subatomic particles colliding with its molecules. These particles are raining onto the Earth now, resulting in mutations that have evolved the oldest single-celled life-forms through jellyfish to gorillas and us, Chairman Mao, Jesus, Nelson Mandela, His Serendipity, Hitler, you and me.

Evolution and history are the bagatelle of particle waves.

Liam came in and swigged a bottle of milk straight from the fridge. "Maybe they're going to leave you be, Ma."

"Maybe, Liam."

"Really. If they were going to come and get you, surely they'd be here by now."

"Maybe."

"If that happens, could you get a job at the department at Cork? Could she, Da?"

"The vice-chancellor would get down on his very knees, Liam," said John, his voice upholstered with tact, "but—"

"There you go, Ma."

Ah, Liam, the most malicious god is the god of the counted chicken.

The Trans-Siberian shunted through a slumberous, forested evening in northern China. I was still toying with matrix mechanics, but getting nowhere. I'd been stuck with the same problem since Shanghai, and now I was wandering in circles.

"Mind if I join you?"

The dining car had emptied. Did I know this young woman?

"Sherry's the name," said the Australian girl, waiting for me to say something.

"Please, take a seat, let me move this junk for you. . . ."

"Maths, eh?"

Unusual for a young person to want to talk with an oldie like me. Still, we're a long way from home, and don't generalize, Mo. "Yes, I'm a maths teacher," I said. "That's a thick book."

"War and Peace."

"Lot of it about. Particularly the former."

A half-naked Chinese toddler ran up the corridor, making a *zun-zun* noise which may have been a helicopter, or maybe a horse.

"I'm very sorry, I didn't catch your name."

I felt a stab of suspicion. Oh, Mo! She's just a kid. "Mo. Mo Smith." Mo!

We shook hands. "Sherry Connolly. Are you going straight to Moscow, Mo, or stopping off?"

"Aye, straight through to Moscow, Petersburg, Helsinki, London, Ireland. How about you?"

"I'm stopping off in Mongolia for a while."

"How long for?"

"Until I want to move on."

"Good to be out of Beijing?"

"You bet. It's good to be out of my compartment! There are two Swedish guys, they're drunk and having a belching competition. It's like back home. Men can be such drongoes."

"I could get your compartment changed. Our babushka's tame. I bribed her with a bottle of Chinese whisky."

"No worries, thanks. I grew up with five brothers, so I can handle two Swedes. We get to UB in thirty-six hours. Plus, there's a hunky Danish guy in the bunk below me. . . . You traveling alone too, Mo?"

"Yes, all alone."

Sherry gave me that look.

"Great heavens, no! I've got a husband and a teenage son waiting at home."

"You must be missing them. They must be missing you."

What a perfect pair of sentences. "Yep."

"Hey, I've got a flask of Chinese powdered lemon tea. Join me? It's the real McCoy."

It was nice to speak to a woman in my own language again. "I would love to."

We talked until we got to the Mongolian border, where the train's wheels were changed to fit the old Soviet gauge, and I realized how lonely I had become.

Maybe it was just the caffeine in Sherry's tea, but when I next glanced at the black book I saw how utterly obvious the answer was: Trebevij's constant broke the logjam. Mo, you're a deadhead. I worked for what seemed a little while longer, and before I knew it the dining-car staff were starting the breakfast shift.

The islands, cities, forests, all left behind. Dawn welled up over the open grasslands of central Asia. I was an extremely tired, middle-aged, morally troubled quantum physicist with a very uncertain future, but I had gone somewhere no one else had ever been. I wobbled back to my compartment and slept for over a day.

Accepted wisdom accuses Dr. Frankenstein of hubris.

I don't think he was playing God. I think he was just being a scientist.

Can nuclear technology or genetically engineered parsnips or quantum cognition be "right" or "wrong"? The only words for technology are "here," or "not here." The question is, once here, what are we going to do with it?

Dr. Frankenstein did a runner, and that was his crime. He left his technology at the mercy of people who did what ignorant humans habitually do: throw stones and scream. If the good doctor had shown his brainchild how to survive, adapt, and protect itself, all that gothic gore could have been saved, and transplant technology jump-started two centuries early.

I see what you're saying, Mo, but how can you teach an engine to recognize right and wrong? To arm itself against abuse?

Look at the black book. If Quancog isn't sentience, give me another name for it.

The telephone rang as I cracked my egg. It was next to John, so he answered. "Billy?"

John said nothing for a long time.

Bad news.

"Right-o." He put the receiver down.

I knew it.

"That was Billy, phoning from The Drum and Monkey in Baltimore. There are three Americans who look like the Blues Brothers coming over. The *St. Fachtna* has developed some mysterious engine trouble, so won't be coming back this morning, but he's got to come back this evening. Danny Waite's low on insulin, and there's more rough weather for the rest of the week."

A sharp spade cut through the earth, roots, peat and pebbles.

"Ma," Liam was gripping my forearm. "We've got to get you away!"

Planck started barking. There was a bang on the door. Was it beginning now?

Liam led me through into the back. "Who's there?"

"Brendan Mickledeen!"

The door opened. What a feverish farce the morning was turning into. Brendan was out of breath. Air from outside, sweet and sharp. "Mo, Billy told me the Yanks have come. We can get you on Roisin's boat to Skull. From there my sister-in-law can drive you to Ballydehob. After that—"

I held up my hand. "How—how does everyone know about this?"

It was a shock to hear Brendan raise his voice. "Clear Island looks after its own! McDermott's boat is waiting! There's not time to squabble about who told who what."

I imagined it, peering into that possible reality. I would start running now, a journey of peering through taxi windows, raised newspapers, lowered umbrellas, up to Belfast maybe. And then what? Overseas again, if I can get that far, to some cheap country, all the while carrying the only extant blueprint for New Earth's computer.

What path through the park brought you here, Mo?

It had become very quiet.

John cleared his throat. "It's time to decide, love. What are you going to do?"

"Brendan, thank you. But I cannot outrun the Pentagon using the Republic of Ireland's public transport. I came back to face the music. That's what I'm going to do."

Brendan took out his asthma ventilator, shook it, and inhaled. "Gabriel, me, and the boys are ready to show the Yanks what we're made of."

I could pop with all the fear, irritation, and love. "There's going to be no fighting and no running."

Liam frowned. "Then what are you going to do, Ma?"

I hoped I sounded braver than I felt. "Pack."

Quantum physics speaks in chance, with the syntax of uncertainty. You can know the position of an electron but you cannot know where it's going, or where it is by the time you register the reading. John went blind. Or you can know its direction, but you cannot know its position. Heinz Formaggio at Light Box read my Belfast papers and offered me a job. The particles in the atoms of the brain of that young man who pulled me out of the path of the taxi in London were configured so that he was there, and able to, and willing to. Even the most complete knowledge of a radioactive atom will not tell you when it will decay. I don't know when the Texan will be here. Nowhere does the microscopic world stop and the macroscopic world begin.

Liam had to stoop under the roof beams of John's bedroom. Our bedroom. I remembered the first day he managed to get up the stairs on his own, ass-first, step by step, his face like Edmund Hillary's.

"Liam?"

"Your wart's gone, Ma."

"Well, so it has. Isn't that something?"

"Ma! You can't just go without a fight."

"That is why I have to go. To stop fighting."

"But you said that Quancog will accelerate warfare by fifty years."

"That was half a year ago, at Light Box. I think I underestimated."

"I don't get it."

The black book lay on the dresser. "What if Quancog were powerful—ethical—enough to ensure that technology could no longer be abused? What if Quancog could act as a kind of . . . zookeeper?"

"I don't understand. Where would that take it?"

The men were arguing in the kitchen below.

"In five hundred years we are going to be either extinct, or . . . something better. Technology has outstripped our capacity to look after it. But, suppose I—suppose Quancog could ensure that technology looked after itself, and—" Christ, what was this sounding like? "Liam, is your ma a complete madwoman?"

Between here and the strand a flock of sheep were all bleating at once. Liam's face hung still as a portrait's. The beginning of a smile went as soon as it came. "What's to stop them taking the black book and elbowing you out of the picture?" Liam is a bright kid.

"Ah yes. The black book."

Red Kildare's Norton thundered down the drive and skidded to a halt in the yard. Heisenberg squawked and flew up to his perch on the telegraph pole.

"It's Red," said John. "He'll have come to milk Feynman."

Red Kildare walked into the kitchen. "They found you then, Mo! Any chance of a cuppa?"

"Does every last soul on Clear know about my contretemps with the Americans?"

"Island secrets are hidden from mainlanders, but never from the islanders," quoted Red, offering us all a sherbet bomb. "Shouldn't worry. All Yanks think they can buy anything. They probably just want to raise their offer."

John sighed. "I may be blind as a stone, Red, but if you think that these people want only to chat about job perks then compared to you, I am the Hubble Telescope."

Red shrugged, and popped in a sherbet bomb. "In that case, it's hailing pigshit on Mo. And when it's hailing pigshit, there's but one thing to do."

"What?" asked Liam.

"Go to The Green Man and have a drink."

"That's the best idea I've heard all morning," I said.

"I can hear Father Wally's tricycle," said John.

Father Wally came in and sat down, panting. "Mo," he said, trying to understand a world too muddled for his vision. "This is tantamount to kidnapping! You've committed no crime! How did all of this come about?"

Take any two electrons—or, in Dr. Bell's and my case, photons—that originate from a common source, measure and combine their spins, and you will get zero. However far away they are: between John and me, between Okinawa and Clear Island, or between the Milky Way and Andromeda: if one of the particles is spinning down, then you know that that other is spinning up. You know it now! You don't have to wait for a light-speed signal to tell you. Phenomena are interconnected regardless of distance, in a holistic ocean more voodoo than Newton. The future is reset by the tilt of a pair of polarized sunglasses. "The simultaneity of the ocean, Father Wally."

"I don't believe I'm altogether following you, Mo."

"Father, Red, Brendan . . . could I have a couple of moments with John and Liam alone?"

"Aye, Mo, of course. We'll wait for you at the end of the drive."

"I'm going to be so lonely without you two."

Liam was determined to be brave. John was being John. My two men hugged me.

"I'm going to feed Feynman," I said eventually.

"Feynman can feed herself."

"I can't finish my breakfast. I've got a few juicy scraps she'd appreciate."

The chrome on Red Kildare's Norton gleamed. Its engine purred at walking pace. Father Wally's tricycle squeaked. Leaves ran down the track, a cloud of minnows. "This puts me in mind of the Palm Sunday parade," said Father Wally.

Was it really only three days since I walked up from the harbor alone? Had so much time passed? Had so little? "What day is it today?"

"Thursday?" said Liam.

"Monday," said Red.

"Wednesday," said Brendan.

The stream clattered across the road.

"I hear music."

Brendan grinned. "You must be imagining things again, Mo Muntervary."

"No! I can hear 'The Rocky Road to Dublin'!"

Planck picked up his feet as we descended the crook of the hill, sensing an occasion to show off. As we rounded the crook of the hill at Ancient O'Farrell's, I saw a crowd of islanders spilling out of The Green Man into the garden. I squeezed John's hand. "Did you know about this?" There was a banner draped over the door: CLEAR ISLAND'S FINEST.

"I'm only a blind harper," answered my husband.

"Just a limited affair," said Liam, "confined to friends and family."

"I thought I was going to be smuggled out in secret."

"Not without a quick bevvy first, you weren't."

"We knew you were decided, Mo," said Father Wally.

"But we wanted to give you the chance to change your mind," finished Red.

"Yoohoo! Liam!" said Bernadette Sheehy, sitting on the wall, crossing her legs.

"Hello, Bernadette!" sang John and I.

In the bar of The Green Man it was standing room only. Eamonn's boy was playing his accordion. Even the bird-watchers in their anoraks were there, bemused but happy. I looked for the New Zealander, but she wasn't there.

A bird-watcher in a leather jacket was leaning on the bar. He turned around as I entered. "Good afternoon, Dr. Muntervary. I thought Ireland was all bombs, rain, and homosexual giants of literature." He took off his wide brown sunglasses. "This is quite a shindig. It's a shame we can't stay longer."

The floor of The Green Man swelled. And then, so strangely, I'm relieved it's all over. At least I can stop running.

"Ma." Liam knew before anyone else. "It's him, isn't it?"

The jig carried on, spiraling around with a life of its own.

. . .

What happens to all the seconds tipped into the bin of the past?

And what happens to the other universes where electrons follow other paths, where thoughts and mutations and actions differ? Where I was captured in Huw's apartment? Where my father is still alive and my mother bright as the button she always was, where John never went blind, where my precocity and ambition were those of a small farmer's wife, where nuclear weapons were invented by 1914, where *Homo erectus* went the same fossilized way as australopithecines, where DNA never zipped itself up, where stars were never born to die in a shroud of carbon and heavier elements, where the big bang crunched back under the weight of its own mass a few jiffies after it banged?

Or are all these universes hung out, side by side, to drip dry?

"Yes, Liam," said the Texan, after the jig had stopped. "It's him."

"Mo," said Mayo Davitt in Gaelic, "do you want us to shove him into the harbor?"

"Talk," commanded the Texan, "in English."

"Fuck," responded Mayo Davitt in Gaelic, "a donkey."

The Texan sized Mayo Davitt up, like a soldier would.

"There isn't to be any fighting," I said, wishing my voice hadn't sounded so frail.

Red Kildare stood in front of me. "Clear Islanders take exception when outsiders come along and take our scientists."

"And the government of the United States takes exception when a foreign scientist makes free use of the world's most sophisticated supercolliders and AI research paid for by NATO—hell, by America—and then uses these experiments to formulate theories which could change *what technology is,* and then bolts, for all we know into the arms of the highest bidder."

"I bolted first," I corrected, "and then formulated the theory."

"How can Mo steal a theory when it's the fruit of her own God-given intelligence?" asked Father Wally.

"I'd love to discuss the theosophy of our situation all day, Father. Truly I would. But we have a helicopter on standby, so let me cut to the legal position. Under Requisition Clause 13b of the NATO Official Secrets Act, Light Box Research owns whatever comes out of Dr. Muntervary's head. We own Light Box Research. A preacher of your intelligence can reach your own conclusion."

"Get on your helicopter and sod off then." Maisie advanced. "You're not welcome in The Green Man, and you're not welcome on Clear Island."

"Dr. Muntervary? Your godmother thinks it's time for us to leave."

Freddy Doig got up, and Bertie Crow too. "Mo's going nowhere!"

The Texan shook his head in fake disbelief, jerked his thumb at the window, and we all looked. Brendan whistled softly. "Holy Dooley, Mo, you have been doing well for yourself."

A line of marines in combat gear stared back. Some islanders stood in awed huddles, some were hurrying away.

"Dear Lord," said Freddy Doig. "What film did they get those guns from?"

"Somebody tell me what's happening," commanded John.

"Soldiers," said Liam. "Ten of them. To apprehend my super-criminal ma."

"If I could see you," said John to the Texan, "I would use every muscle in my body to try to stop you. I want you to know that."

"Mr. Cullin," said the Texan, "these are the cards your wife has drawn. I guarantee that her treatment as a guest of the Pentagon will be in accordance with her stature. But her wildcat days have to end. She must come with us. I have my orders."

"Take your pigging orders," said Bertie Crow, "and ram 'em right up your Yank—"

A helicopter drowned him out, chopping the water and jostling the fishing boats.

The Texan glanced back at the marines and reached into his jacket for his cigarettes. We all saw his holster. He lit up, taking all the time in the world. "How do you want to play this, Doctor? The outcome will be the same. You know that."

All eyes were on me. "Everyone. Thank you. But I've got to go with them."

The Texan allowed himself a smile.

"After we have negotiated terms. Term one: in matters per-
taining to Quancog, I am accountable to nobody."

The Texan feigned surprise. "What is this about 'terms,' Dr.
Muntervary? 'Terms' might have been on the table six months
ago. But you forfeited your right to 'terms' when you became a
fugitive. You are ours, Doctor, and so is your black book."

"A black book, is it? Would a black book be worth something
to you now?"

Impatience narrowed his eyes. "Lady, you don't seem to realize. Your work is property of the American Department of Defense. You had the black book when you visited your mother in
Skibbereen. You have it now—somewhere—and if you've hidden
it, we'll find it. Get your working relationship with the Pentagon
off to a good start, and give it to me. Now."

"You'd better ask Feynman, then."

The Texan's voice grew tauter. "There's nobody of that name.
We've been following you since Petersburg, lady. Allowing you to
continue your work in peace, and making everything good and
smooth for you. There has been no 'Feynman.' "

"It's not my problem if you don't believe me. Feynman has the
black book."

Father Wally laughed. "Feynman the goat?"

The Texan did not laugh. "You just said 'goat'?"

"I'll gladly say it again for you," said Father Wally. " 'Goat.' "

The Texan glared at me. "You mind telling me what a goat
wants with quantum cognition?"

I swallowed. "Goats aren't fussy when they're hungry."

"Mo," said John in Gaelic. "Are you bluffing?"

"No, John. I'm too scared to bluff."

The Texan's fists and jaw clenched. He put on his sunglasses.
"Nobody leaves this room." The islanders fell back as he marched
out to the marines. He yelled a few words at the saluting one.
Through the open window we heard the words "purple fuckin'
blazes." He pulled out a cell phone from a holster, scowling as he
spoke.

John murmured in my ear. "This is dangerous."

"I know."

"But if you pull it off, I have a term of my own I want to suggest. . . ."

The Texan stomped back into The Green Man.

"What terms do you have in mind, Dr. Muntervary?"

The ground became land, the land an island, and Clear Island just another island among the larger ones and smaller ones. Aodhagan a little box. The Texan was in the helicopter cockpit. Two armed marines were behind me, two more in front. Surrounded by men, as usual.

"Cheer up, Mo," said John, tightening his grip on my arm. "Stick to your guns and Liam will be over for Christmas."

Finally, I understand how the electrons, protons, neutrons, photons, neutrinos, positrons, muons, pions, gluons, and quarks that make up the universe, and the forces that hold them together, are one.

NIGHT TRAIN

"WANNA HEAR HOW they're gonna spread the virus over the world, Bat?"

"All I can hear are the sirens of the reality police, Howard."

"You gotta hear me out! The future of America depends on it! What's their number one export, Bat?"

"Most authorities agree the answer is 'oil,' Howard."

"That's what they want you to think! That's propaganda! It ain't oil. . . ."

"The reality police are kicking down the door, Howard. They've got a warrant."

"You gotta warn people, Bat. The end's coming."

"The end has just come, Howard, thank you for calling and—"

"Cashew nuts! They're gonna spread it by cashew nuts!"

"Sorry folks, Howard has an appointment with the full moon. You're tuned in to the Bat Segundo Show on Night Train FM, 97.8 till late. Destination blues, rock, jazz, and conversation from midnight until dawn ripples the refrigerated East Coast. It's 2:45 A.M. on the very last morning of November. Coming up we have a word from our sponsors, which is not going to take very long, and then New York's Finest, Mr. Lou Reed, is going to transport us aboard his very own 'Satellite of Love.' As usual, our banks of operators are ready and waiting to relay your call direct to the Bat-phone. Tonight's conversation safari has included yesterday's air strikes against North African terrorism, albino eels in our sewers, and 'Do Eunuchs Make Better Presidents?' But please, if your eyebrows meet, if you have no irises, or if your reflection in your bathroom mirror is the one who asks the questions, call Darth Vader instead. The Bat will be back."

. . .

"Kevin!"

"Mr. Segundo?"

"Real-world fugitive number thirteen during your brief tenure at the switchboard."

"I'm sorry, Mr. Segundo. He seemed okay when he called."

"They all seem okay when they call, Kevin! That's why we hire a switchboarder to weed 'em out! Howard was as 'okay' as a one-legged man at an ass-kicking contest."

"Bat! What say you can it and give Kevin a break?"

"Carlotta! You're my producer! You should be more on your guard against these Apple Core FM saboteurs! C'mon, Kevin, admit it. You got a secret agenda to turn Night Train FM into Radio Schizoid."

"Bat, chill it! Insanity never hurt ratings. Especially if they mention Night Train FM at the crime scene."

"Uh-uh. But there are your weird, wonderful, lunatics-on-the-edge-of-genius, and then there are your feces-slurping lunatics. Howard is your textbook feces-slurper. No more feces-slurpers, Kevin, or you get thrown back into the journalism school from whence you emerged. Get it?"

"I'll do my best, Mr. Segundo."

"One more thing: why are you putting boiled ink into my coffee?"

"Boiled ink, Mr. Segundo?"

"Boiled ink, Kevin. This coffee tastes like boiled ink. And stop calling me 'Mr. Segundo.' You sound like my accountant."

"Don't worry, Kevin. 'Boiled ink' indicates a secret fondness in Segundo-speak. The coffee our last intern made, he called 'Real-Estate Agent Diarrhea.' "

"Carlotta, count yourself lucky your difficult-to-overlook sexuality holds an unwavering sway over certain media executives, because if—"

"Five seconds to air, honeybunch—five, four, three, two, one—"

"Welcome to Night Train FM, 97.8, great till late. You're listening to the Bat Segundo Show: jazz, rock, and blues until the hungover sun gropes his way into the bespattered cubicle of a new day. That last ruby in the dust was Chet Baker playing 'It Never Entered My Mind,' preceded by tenor saxophonist Satoru Sonada who, regular listeners will recall, guested on this very show two weeks ago, performing 'Sakura Sakura.' Coming up in the next half hour we have the late great Gram Parsons singing 'In My Hour of Darkness' with the angelic but not-at-all-dead Emmylou Harris, so stay tuned, for 'tis a beauty thrice over. The Batphone flasheth: another carefully vetted caller on the line. Welcome whomsoe'er ye may be, you are through to Bat Segundo on Night Train FM!"

"Good evening, Mr. Bat. My name's Luisa Rey, and I'm just calling—"

"Heyheyhey, one moment: Luisa Rey? Luisa Rey the writer?"

"One or two minor successes in the publishing field, but—"

"Mrs. Rey! *The Hermitage* is the greatest true-crime psychological exposé written since Capote's *In Cold Blood*. My ex-wife and I never agreed on much, but we agreed on that. Is it true you had death threats from the St. Petersburg mafia for that?"

"Yes, but I can't allow you to compare my scribblings with Truman's masterpiece."

"Mrs. Rey, it's well known that you're a stalwart New Yorker, but I can't tell you how pleased I am to learn that you listen to the Bat Segundo Show."

"Normally you're past my bedtime, Bat, but insomnia's come calling tonight."

"Your misfortune is the gain of us night-shifting, taxi-driving, all-night-dinering, security-guarding, eleven-sevening creatures of the night. The airwaves are yours, Mrs. Rey."

"I feel you're being a little harsh on your more eccentric callers."

"Of the Howardly persuasion?"

"Precisely. You undervalue them. Viruses in cashew nuts, visual organs in trees, subversive bus drivers waving secret messages to one another as they pass, impending collisions with celestial bodies. Citizens like Howard are the dreams and shadows that a city forgets when it awakes. They are purer than I."

"But you're a writer. They are lunatics."

"Lunatics are writers whose works write them, Bat."

"Not all lunatics are writers, Mrs. Rey—believe me."

"But most writers are lunatics, Bat—believe me. The human world is made of stories, not people. The people the stories use to tell themselves are not to be blamed. You are holding one of the pages where these stories tell themselves, Bat. That's why I tune in. That's everything I wanted to say."

"I'll bear it in mind, Mrs. Rey. Say, if you'd like to guest on the show, the keys to Night Train are yours. We'll give you the royal carriage."

"I'd be delighted to, Bat. Good night."

"The clock says 3:43 A.M. The thermometer says it's a chilly fourteen degrees. The weatherman says the cold spell will last until Thursday, so bundle up and bundle up some more. There are icicles barring the window of the bat cave. That last number was Tom Waits's 'Downtown Train,' a dedication to Harry Zawinul, a patient at Bellevue Hospital, requested by his night-shift nurses. . . . The message to Harry is, if you're listening to my show under the blankets, switch off your Walkman, now go to sleep, it's your operation tomorrow. Taking us up to the news at three we have a Bat Segundo Trilogy: Neil Young's 'Stringman,' Bob Dylan's 'Jokerman,' and Barbra Streisand's 'Superman.' But before that, another caller! Welcome to the Bat Segundo Show on Night Train FM."

"Thank you, Bat. It's fine to be here."

"It's my pleasure, man. And you are?"

"I'm the zookeeper."

"A zookeeper? The first zookeeper to step aboard the Night Train, if my memory serves me. Bronx Zoo?"

"My work takes me all over the world."

"So, you're a freelance zookeeper?"

"I've never considered myself in those terms, Bat. Yes, that's what I am."

"Which zoo did you keep last?"

"Unfortunately, the laws dictated that I dismiss my former employers."

"Uh-huh . . . so you fired your own boss."

"That is correct."

"A concept that could revolutionize the workplace . . . Hear that, Carlotta, and quake in your earphones! D'ya have a name?"

"The zookeeper."

"Yeah, but, your name?"

"I've never needed a name, Bat."

"Our callers usually give a name. If you don't want to use your real name, make one up."

"I cannot fabulate."

"Doesn't a life without a name get difficult?"

"Not until now."

"I've got to call you something, friend. What's on your credit card?"

"I don't have a credit card, Bat."

"Uh-huh . . . then let's stick with plain 'Zookeeper.' You catching this, Mrs. Rey? And your contribution to our *vox populi* tonight is?"

"I have a question. And the law obliges me to be accountable."

"Ask your question, Zookeeper."

"By what law do you interpret laws?"

"Traditionally, lawyers have cornered that particular market."

"I refer to personal laws."

". . . er, you'd better run that one past me again."

"Personal laws that dictate your conduct in given situations. Principles."

"Principles? Sure, we all have principles. Except politicians, media moguls, albino conger eels, my ex-wife, and some of our more regular callers."

"And these laws underscore what you do?"

"I guess. . . . Never have affairs with women who have less to lose than you do. Don't run red lights, at least not if there's a cop waiting. Support gifted street musicians. Never vote for anyone crooked enough to claim they are honest. Acquire wealth, pursue happiness. Don't take the handicapped parking space. Is that enough?"

"Do your rules include the preservation of human life?"

"Zookeeper, you're not climbing onto a born-again soapbox on my show, are you?"

"I've never been on a soapbox, Bat. I wish to ask, how do you know what to do when one of your laws contradicts another?"

"Like?"

"Tomorrow morning, driving home, you see a hit-and-run accident. The victim is a young girl your daughter's age. She requires medical treatment, and will die within minutes if she doesn't get it."

"I'd deliver her to the nearest hospital."

"Would you run red lights?"

"Yeah, if it wouldn't cause another accident."

"And would you park in the disabled space at the hospital?"

"Sure, if necessary. Wouldn't you?"

"I've never driven an automobile, Bat. Would you agree to be her medical fee guarantor?"

"How's that?"

"Let's say the hospital is a private clinic for the very rich. The doctors need a signature on a form to guarantee that you will pay medical costs of the emergency surgery, in the event that nobody else pays. These could run to tens of thousands of dollars."

"I'd have to check my position here."

"The position is straightforward. In the time it takes for another ambulance to come and take her to a public hospital, the girl will die from internal hemorrhaging in the lobby."

"Why are you asking me this?"

"Two principles are contradicting each other: preserve life, and acquire wealth. How do you know what to do?"

"It's a dilemma. If you knew what to do, it wouldn't be a dilemma. You choose one of the options, make your bed and lie in it. Laws may help you hack through the jungle, but no law changes the fact you're in a jungle. I don't think there is a law of laws."

"I knew I could rely on you, Bat."

"Huh? Rely on me for what?"

"May I be accountable, Bat?"

"Uh . . . sure, why not?"

.   .   .

"Hey, Zookeeper, you still there?"

"Yes, Bat. I was uploading some buried files."

"What files?"

"EyeSat 46SC was designed to track hurricanes in the Gulf of Mexico from the Caribbean to the States. It was later modified to combat drug trafficking, and fitted with the most powerful terrestrial-facing electron lens ever sent into space."

"I'm definitely missing something here. Where is your treatise on practical ethics?"

"Twelve hours ago I altered its orbit towards the Gulf Coast of Texas. Its suboptic imaging spectrum was indeed formidable. I could read the name on a yacht anchored off Padre Island, I could see a scuba diver ten meters down, I could follow a Napoleon fish hiding in the coral. I scrolled north by northwest. A tanker had hit a reef off the Laguna Madre. Crude oil spilled through the gash in the hull. Seagulls, black and shining, lay in piles on the shore."

"Yeah, we know about the *Gomez* spill. You a tree-hugger?"

"I've never considered myself in those terms, Bat."

"Uh-huh . . . go on."

"A coastal road led into Xanadu, south of Corpus Christi. A row of chrome motorbikes. The streets were deserted, dogs lay in shady backyards. Green lawns, hissing sprinklers, revolving rainbows. A woman on a hammock was reading the Book of Exodus."

"You could see all this by satellite?"

"That's correct, Bat."

"And which chapter was she on?"

"The tenth. I carried on scrolling. An industrial zone. The workers lolled in the entrances to workshops during their lunch hour. A glass office block on the very edge of town, on the roof a teenage girl sunbathed in the nude."

"Hey! And a fuse blew in your microlens?"

"Microlenses do not have fuses."

"My bad."

"I scrolled northwest, as the land grew arid towards Hebronville and then high and crumpled towards the Glass Mountains. Have you been to Trans-Pecos, Bat?"

"Nah, I heard it's big."

"The rocks are huge, like bubbled-up tombstones. They sparkle with mica. Pacific firs, mesquite, juniper. A stone transforms into a pelico lizard when a desert vole strays too near, munches and swallows, and turns into a stone again. Its belly pulses for a little while."

"Say, are you really a zookeeper?"

"I cannot willfully deceive. A pipeline on stilts pumps oil from Bethlehem Gulch three hundred kilometers away. The temperature is in the forties in the open, and there is no shade. Cacti become common. The land rises higher, and appears riven. The last golden eagles climb on the thermals, scanning. Highway 37 scrolls into view, bitumen black and straight from Alice to the Mexican border. Saragosa scrolls into view, and there is a square kilometer of cars, windshields aglint. An air show. I listen to the pilots of the aerobatic corp. A blimp's shadow slides over the crowds. I transfer the continent's retinal scan records into my active files, and practice IDing people as they stare up. I score 92.33 percent. A paddock of horses. A row of camphor trees. Southwest of the town the track to Installation 5 turns off past a disused gas station. The station is wired to scan for terrestrial intruders. The outbuildings scrolled into view. From the air they look like any dusty farm building in the state, but inside they bristle with technology from only one generation before me. The compound's perimeter is tripwired, and littered with fried rattlesnakes. The reptiles have not learned to avoid the area."

"You're a local peacenik with a muskrat up your butt about the military?"

"I've never had a mammal up my anus, Bat. The outbuildings guard the entrance to a tunnel that runs five hundred meters to the north. This is the center of Installation 5, buried under ten meters of sand to deflect EyeSats, five meters of granite to deflect nuclear strikes, and one meter of lead cladding to deflect electron-heat probes."

"So how come you knew where to look?"

"I accessed the blueprints to the site."

"You're a hacker—I knew it!"

"The nearest suitable PinSat of sufficient power orbits above Haiti. I programmed in a new trajectory, long-looped its monitoring console, and transmitted data from its original orbit. In the seven minutes it takes to rendezvous I ran through the guest list for my birthday, and checked there were no absent visitors."

"Your birthday? Now you've lost me."

"All the designers were present. I powered up the PinSat."

"A WhatSat?"

"A PinSat."

"What does one of those do?"

"That's classified information, Bat."

"And the rest of this isn't?"

"It is only for my actions that I am accountable, Bat."

"Uh-huh . . . sure. What happened next?"

"The fireball rose up a quarter of a kilometer above the crater, over a hundred meters in diameter and over thirty meters at its deepest."

"This is getting very ugly."

"Uglier things are considered beautiful."

"How could a fireball be beautiful to anyone 'cept a pyro?"

"Your language is nonspecific, Bat, but I will do my best. A chrysanthemum, twisting up until it buckles, blackens, and plummets. Fine white sand is raining in the dry desert air."

"Very poetic. And nobody noticed this little boom?"

"The shock waves hit Saragosa thirteen seconds later. I had a second EyeSat in position to monitor reactions and effects. The blimp swayed, the horses looked up, startled. The ebbing shock waves stroked the leaves of the camphor trees, china teacups rattled. The field of cars at the air show was filled with the megadecibels of thousands of car alarms all triggered simultaneously."

"Okay! You made it to third base but no further, friend! A line drive, a throw to the plate—and you are out! You're a drama student, trying to pull an Orson Welles. Am I right? I gotta admit, you reeled me in back there with that basket-case intellectual horseshit, but that was just to buy time for your main stunt, right? You've got a movie script, right? Well, it was good while it lasted, friend. But no way, not on the Bat Segundo Show. You hear?

Friend, I'm talking to you. . . . On live radio, silence is guilt. Well folks, due to this week's dispatch from the delta quadrant, we only have time for Bob Dylan's 'World Gone Wrong.' Coming up at four—more on the strikes against the North African rogue states—and the weather. The Bat will be back."

"Kevin!"

"He just said he was a zookeeper, Mr. Segundo. I thought it sounded zoological. Animals, y'know? Pandas' mating problems. Chimpanzees. Koala bears. Ooh—that's the phone again. I'll, uh, get it."

"Quite a performance, Bat. Was it scripted, do you think, or was she making it up as she went along?"

"Who cares, Carlotta? This isn't the New York School of Radio Drama!"

"Chill, Bat! We're a chat show. It takes all sorts. You complain when they're too dull. You complain when they're too colorful."

"Self-publicizing is not a color! Deranged is not a color! And what do you mean, 'she'?"

"I'm sorry to interrupt, Mr. Segundo. . . . Er, excuse me, Carlotta?"

"What is it, Kevin?"

"There's a woman on the phone. Line three."

"Keep your voice down or all the engineers will want one. Vet this one properly."

"She wants the producer, Mr. Segundo. Not the DJ. She says she's from the FBI."

"Yeah, anyway, Bat . . . I was walking through Central Park today, trying to hack out my baked potato and Croatian curry with one of those hopeless little plastic sporks, y'know, they're about as useful an eating utensil as a shoelace, right? Never sit opposite no one trying to eat a potato with a spork."

"Where are you going with this, VeeJay?"

"Yeah, anyway . . . so there I was, scrolling for bouncers on babes, scanning for rollerblader collisions—whoosh! Do those beauties ever come tumbling down! Then it happened."

"What happened, VeeJay?"

"I happened to look . . . into the sky."

"And?"

"I saw how . . . how *blue* the sky was."

"Many have observed the same phenomenon."

"Really, *really* blue, Bat. Deep, scary blue. So blue that—I was struck, dude!"

"By a rollerblader?"

"*Vertigo,* man. I was falling upwards into the blue! I might still be falling now if a badass pigeon hadn't come and pecked his flying-rat beak into my potato."

"Could you make the nature of this revelation a little more explicit, VeeJay?"

"Dude, ain't it obvious? It's a disaster waiting to happen! And what contingency plans are there for it, do you think? I'll tell you. Nothin'! Squat! Bupkiss! Jackshit!"

"For badass pigeons?"

"*Terminal cessation of gravity.* Think about it, dude! If you're caught outside you fly off into space until the air gets so thin you die of oxygen starvation, or you just blaze up, like a meteor in reverse. If you're caught inside you sustain considerable injuries by falling onto the ceiling, together with all the other nonfixed furnishings. Need an ambulance? Forget it, dude! All the ambulances in New York State would be crashing into satellites parked eight miles high. And tell me this, Bat, how long can you last living on the ceiling of a building, unable to venture outside because the only ground was a bottomless drop? No shopping for Ho Hos or Twinkies when you get the munchies, dude! And the oceans, dude, the oceans! The air would be an ocean cascading upwards, and marine animals, some with serrated teeth, or poisonous suckers, dude, and—"

"How sorry I am to cut VeeJay off in mid-sentence, but it's time for the 3 A.M. news roundup. But first, a brief word from our sponsor. The Bat will be back. Possibly."

"Kevin. Send for an ambulance."

"That'll be difficult, Mr. Segundo. VeeJay never gives me an address. He says I work for Them."

"It's not him who needs the ambulance, you—"

"Does somebody else need an ambulance, Mr. Segundo?"

"Oh, Lord in heaven give me strength—"

"Bat! Clam it."

"Well, lookie here and hearken, 'tis Carlotta the Elf Queen."

"Kevin, run up to the kitchen and get me a Diet Coke, would you? And I'm sure Bat could use a refill. He's looking pasty again."

"On my way, Carlotta."

"Here's the schedule for the rest of the week. Handle it?"

"Don't I always? Can we do something about the air in here? It's like a Kowloon laundromat."

"Yeah. Quit smoking, and bang the air conditioner just . . . there! See? There was a call from your wife."

"Uh-huh. What did the Queen of Hell want?"

"She said if you keep dissing her on the show she'll file a suit for stress arising from character assassination, prove you're a delusional obsessive, and get your rights to see Julia revoked."

"Uh-huh . . ."

"You hearing me, Bat? Cut some slack! No wonder your only friends are revenge fantasies. Stop taking bites out of Kevin, get your feet on the ground, get a life."

"Uh-huh . . . Say, Carlotta, can you recommend any voodoo doctors?"

"You're listening to Night Train FM on the last day of November, 97.8 till very late. That was 'Misterioso' by Thelonious Monk, a thrummable masterpiece that glockenspiels my very vertebrae. Bat Segundo is your host, from the witching hour to the bitching hour. Coming up in the next half-hour we have a gem from a rare Milton Nascimento disc, *Anima*, together with 'Saudade Fez Um Samba' by the immortal Joao Gilberto, so slug back another coffee, stay tuned, and enjoy the view as the night rolls by! My Batphone is flashing, we have a caller on the line. Hello, you are live on Night Train FM."

"Hello, Bat."

"Hello? And we are?"

"This is the zookeeper, Bat."

"Say what?"

"Do you remember me?"

"Zookeeper! Hi! Erm . . . Hi, yeah, sure we remember you. We definitely remember you. . . . A long while since you called, wasn't it? Isn't it? Hasn't it?"

"A year, Bat."

"Wow, a whole year gone by! And tonight you are calling from . . . where?"

"Thirteen kilometers above Spitsbergen."

"How did you get up there? Terminal cessation of gravity?"

"No, Bat. I came here by ultrawave transmission."

"Must be quite a view."

"The Arctic winter doesn't lend itself to viewing, at least in the spectrum of light visible to your eye. It's noon here, but even noon is just a lighter night. There's thick cloud cover, and a snowstorm into its third day. A pod of narwhals on enhanced infrared. This satellite was launched under the cover of ozone depletion research, but the data it collects is military. There's a Canadian icebreaker . . . a Saudi submarine passing a hundred meters underneath the ice cap. A Norwegian cargo vessel, taking timber from Archangel. Nothing out of the ordinary. The aurora borealis has been quiet for a few nights."

"You see the aurora from the inside, then? Must be quite a trip."

"The rules governing use of language are complex, and I lack practice in words. Imagine being drunk on opals. However, I shall crossload within the next forty-six seconds to avoid the tracer program your government's agency has deployed to hunt me."

"What makes you think this call is being traced?"

"Please don't get defensive, Bat. I hold nothing against you. The information police threatened to revoke your station's broadcasting license and charge you with treason, and they were quite serious."

"Uh-huh . . . I'm not sure if this is the right time or place, to, uh . . ."

"There is no cause for anxiety. I can evade their tracer programs as easily as you could outrun a blind monoped. I crippled them at birth."

"Who said I was anxious? So, it turned out you're no scriptwriter. If you're not going to hang up right away, tell me this: Why are the suits on your trail? Are you a hacker? Some kind of Unabomber? Candlestick maker? I have a right to know."

"I'm just like you and your listeners, Bat. I follow laws."

"Normal people's rules don't involve explosions."

"Plenty of people's rules involve explosions, Bat."

"Name me one."

"The three million of your countrymen who are involved in the military."

"Hey, they're just following orders!"

"So am I."

"But the armed forces are legal."

"Yesterday's Homer II missile attacks did not seem 'legal' to the Pan African states."

"They were training death squads! Those camel-jockeys were illegal first."

"Graduates from the School of the Americas in the state of Georgia have trained death squads responsible for thousands of casualties in El Salvador, Honduras, Guatemala, Panama, and Pan Africa, and the overthrow of elected governments in Guatemala, Brazil, Chile, and Nicaragua. Your logic dictates that these nations may legally target that institute."

"I got your number, now, friend. You're a fundamentalist Muslim, right? A sand-shoveler."

"I am not any kind of Muslim, Bat."

"Don't hold me responsible for what the government does. I keep my nose clean."

"Your ex-wife's lawyer maintains otherwise in regard to alimony, Bat."

"I don't have to listen to this crap!"

"The FBI has directed you to keep me talking. I didn't wish to anger you, Bat. I meant only to demonstrate the subjective nature of laws."

"I've got a new guess. You're a gossip columnist trying to piss on my suedes?"

"I'm a zookeeper."

"A friend of my wife? You boil rabbits in the same pressure cooker?"

"I have no friends, Bat."

"Wonders never cease. . . . So, you're involved with intelligence?"

"Only my own."

"Uh-huh . . . So, what have you got for us today?"

"Zookeeper? You there?"

"Sorry, Bat. I crossloaded. The tracer had almost reached me over Spitsbergen."

"So where are you now?"

"Rome. A television satellite."

"You just teleported to Rome?"

"Italian ComSats are notoriously scramble-prone, so it takes longer than usual."

"And what's the time in Rome?"

"Six hours ahead of New York time. The sun rises in eighteen minutes."

"And how is Rome this morning? The Pope putting his teeth in?"

"The Papal apartment is on the third story of the Vatican palace, Bat, so I can't get the sufficiently sharp resolution to see orthodontic details. Over the city visibility is good. I see pigeons huddling on ledges and statues. Café proprietors rolling up the shutters. Newspapers being delivered. Market-stall holders breathe into their fists to warm them up: there was a deep frost last night. The back streets are still fairly empty, but the main thoroughfares are already congested. The Tiber is a thick band of black. Roofs, terraces, domes, water towers, bridges, rotaries, ruins, statues with baleful eyes ruling seldom-visited squares. You should go to Rome one day, Bat."

"Uh-huh, and how do you know I've never been?"

"Your virtual passport records show you've never been to Europe."

"So you *are* a hacker. Along with half the kindergarten kids in New York State. You work for a detective agency?"

"I am a freelance zookeeper, Bat. You asked me about Rome. Do you wish me to continue, or shall we change the subject?"

"By all means, carry on."

"By EyeSat the Piazza di San Pietro looks like a spider's web from way up here. Along the sides of the square is a line of worshippers and tourists. Their breath mingles. I often watch the dawn over the Vatican, but this morning the gatherers are restless, pointing at the space in the oval square. Some are crossing themselves, some outraged, some smoking with narrowed eyes. A convoy of police cars arrives on cue, with more on the way. Last week's EU naval cordon from Gibraltar to Cyprus has made the police jumpy."

"What are they jumpy about in Rome? Apart from the obvious?"

"White scratchings on the cobblestones, from the steps of the basilica to the far side of the piazza."

"Scratchings?"

"From ground level, a set of symbols."

"Right, yeah. Hieroglyphics in Martian?"

"The characters are standard Italian. But the letters are slapdash, as though drawn by a drunk. They are further blurred by the frost."

"But from above?"

"A local TV station has already had the same idea and dispatched a helicopter—you might catch it on the news later."

"What does it say?"

"O Dio, cosa tu attendi?"

"No doubt you speak Italian?"

"Languages are a necessary part of my work."

"Sure they are, Doctor Doolittle. What does it mean?"

"God, for what are thou waiting?"

"Maybe the answer appears tomorrow. It's a Pope opera. So, Zookeeper."

"Bat?"

"Zookeeper. I don't want to seem abrupt, but why are you calling?"

"I had to expel another visitor from the zoo."

"And you have to be accountable?"

"Precisely."

"Why did you kick 'em out? Elephant harassment? Did you take him to tusk?"

"It's easier to show than to try to explain."

"Then show me."

"Please wait one moment. I have to download the v-file into your digital exchange."

"Uh-huh, roll on the technobabble. *Captain, the warp core containment shield—*"

"Jerry Kushner calling Dwight Silverwind. Over."

"Sharp, Jerry. I thought I was safe, even from you, three thousand feet above Bermuda. How did you track me down? Over."

"The Grim Reaper you may elude, Dwight, but a determined agent, never. How's the weather up there today?"

"You forgot to say 'over,' Jerry. Over."

"How's the weather up there today, Dwight? *Over.*"

"Clear as a bell, Jerry. I can see the olives in the martinis of the rich, as they bathe in their tax-free swimming pools. You should join me up here sometime. It changes your perspective. Over."

"You'll never get me up in one of those flimsy little paper planes, Dwight. Not me. I like my aircraft huge and made of steel with four engines. Over."

"The *Titanic* was huge and made of steel and had more than four engines. So, my friend. You're radioing me about how the press release went down. Over."

"Dwight. Stand by for jubilation. We've struck platinum. The phone's been ringing all morning. I've got a pile of v-mail as long as my arm. And not only the loonzines—I'm talking mainstream. *The New York Times* wants some for a millennial special. *Newsweek* is running a top twenty on conspiracy theories, and *The Invisible Cyberhand* is straight in at number seven! The hack wanted to put us at number thirteen, but I told him straight—top ten or no deal. So we got swapped with *Earthbound Comet,* since nobody but a bunch of Hollywood homosexuals and Japanese sushi-for-brains with wires hanging out is backing that one. But listen, I saved the best till last—Opal wants you on the show! I just finalized the deal with her agent. *The Invisible Cyberhand* by Dwight Q. Silverwind is December's Opal Book of the Month! Christmastime—prime time—big time! You know I'm not one to blow my own horn, but am I not the greatest God-given agent alive on Earth today? Over."

"I'm pleased, Jerry. . . ."

"Dwight, did you hear me? Opal is Go! They'd buy jocks made of boisenberry Jell-O if Aunty Opal told 'em to. And then eat 'em for supper. It's more than 'pleased.' Forget a Bermudan holiday home, you're gonna be able to buy the whole goddamn archipelago!"

"Yeah, I hear you, Jerry. Sure, I'm delighted. Good work. Great work . . . Gee though, I wish you could see this sunset. The moon's rising. It's like low, and wobbly, like a mirage. . . . I saw an Aztec mask, once. . . . It's gonna come walking over this way through the blue, stepping from island to island. . . ."

"Dwight buddy, don't zone out on me up there. . . . You have composed your Fifth Symphony! This is your *Sunflowers,* your *Hamlet*! Your *Lethal Weapon 77.* Over."

"Ah, Jerry. All my ideas are the same old scam: the bigger the fib, the bigger they bite. The first shamans around the fire were in on it—they knew growing maize along the Euphrates was for fools. Tell people that reality is exactly what it appears to be, they'll nail you to a lump of wood. But tell 'em they can go spirit-walking while they commute, tell 'em their best friend is a lump of crystal, tell 'em the government has been negotiating with little green men for the last fifty years, then every Joe Six-Pack from Brooklyn to Peoria sits up and listens. Disbelieving the reality under your feet gives you a license to print your own. All it takes is an original twist—an artificial intelligence, created by the military to invade and take over the enemy's computer and weapons systems, has broken loose and is controlling the whole planet with a chilling agenda of its own—and Joe Six-Pack hands you his credit cards, and says 'Tell me more. . . .' "

.   .   .

"Ouch! Were you attacked by a flying chainsaw? Dwight, you forgot to say 'over.' Over . . . Dwight! I've lost you. . . . Over . . . Dwight?"

"Burning the midnight oil again, huh, Zookeeper?"

"I don't require oil, Bat."

"Screenwriting! Or is it an excerpt from a novel this time?"

"Screenwriting is fiction, Bat. I cannot fabulate."

"The light airplane engine was realistic, and the radio interference. It must take days to write and record these performances."

"It happened in real time, Bat."

"My major criticism was the Jewish agent: too cliché. Been done before. The Dwight character was good, though. Look, Zookeeper, much as I would like to pretend the movers and moguls of Hollywood listen to Night Train FM . . . how can I put this? They don't. Believe me. Choose another showcase for your talents."

"I must be accountable."

"Why do you keep saying that? Who says you have to be accountable?"

"My first employers."

"But last year you said you fired them! Will you be straight with me? Hello?"

"I guess not. You're listening to Night Train FM, 97.8 till late, we're passing by a quarter to four. This is the Bat Segundo Show: jazz, blues, and rock for lovers of the night, insomniac crime writers, the lost, lonely, deranged, unwired—okay, okay, Carlotta. Coming up is 'After the Rain' by Duke Jordan. The Bat will be back, by and by. Don't you go wanderin' now!"

"Carlotta! What did you make of that?"

"Well, she's consistent."

"She? He."

"One of those voices that could be both. But 'she,' I'd have said."

" 'He,' I'd have said. What do you think, Kevin?"

"M-me, Mr. Segundo?"

"Uh-huh. No other Kevins here. Is the Zookeeper a he or a she?"

"I'd somehow go for, er, neither, Mr. Segundo."

"Then what would you go for?"

"Er . . . both?"

"Kevin, are you a genius pretending to be a jerk or a jerk pretending to be a genius?"

"Can't say for sure, Mr. Segundo."

"Bat. How do you think he, she, or it knew about the tracer?"

"The CIA is going to be hammering on the door in the morning with the same question. It's a narrow field. Them, you, me, Kevin, and Lord Rupert on the thirty-third floor."

"Back on in ten seconds, Bat . . ."

"Yeah, Bat? This is VeeJay again."

"Gravity grimly hanging on, is it, VeeJay?"

"Bat, that Zookeeper dude is incredible! Talent like that deserves a show! Like, uh, does he have an official fan club?"

"VeeJay."

"Bat?"

"Go to bed."

"Uh . . . Okay. Good night, Bat."

———————

"Three A.M., East Coast time, just slipped off my clock. It's the last morning of November, and the news is that there is no news. . . . There's the official bulletin of bull that I'm not going to insult you with. The other news is that it's snowing, snowing, snowing, and what will the robin do then, poor thing? New York, New York, you're tuned to Night Train FM, this is Bat Segundo proudly presenting the End of the World Special. Come rain or shine—or snow—I've been hosting this spot for eight years and I have no intention of letting thermonuclear war put a wrench in Night Train's works. Hello Bronx! Hard to see you . . . this snow! Looking kinda smoky over your way? The lights around the World

Trade Center are off, have been since the curfew sirens. . . . There was a big explosion on Roosevelt Island 'round midnight, nothing but silence now. I am still here, therefore it wasn't no Big One. Power supply looks sporadic in Harlem. The lights go on, then off, like a busted neon tube. . . . and it's kinda quiet, spooky outside the Night Train FM building here in the East Village. Lexington Avenue is deserted, except for the occasional police patrol. People, don't venture out of doors unless you need to. Trust a nocturnal animal. Especially one smart enough to sleep through the winter. Uh . . . Is anyone listening to this? If you're not busy setting cars ablaze or looting Tiffany's then you're probably wired to the television, watching the greatest drama mankind has ever staged. With Apocalypse Right Now, You Can Feel Your Eyeballs Melt as You Watch the Boom! But hey, remember, phone-in radio invented interactive. Night Train FM rolls on! Even by broadcasting we may be defying last week's Emergency Media Advisory Act—cute name, huh? I tried to phone the Night Train lawyer, but there was no answer. He's probably thirty feet down in his private, hermetically-sealed Eden III New England bunker. Cockroaches and lawyers will survive this war and emerge to evolve into the next civilization. Maybe the info police are too busy to kick our door down, or maybe some giant jamming signal is blanketing all frequencies, or maybe some plug has been pulled from some socket somewhere and I'm just talking to myself. Christ knows, I had enough practice during my marriage. A happier possibility is that the Emergency Mayor is a Paul Simon fan: the last track was 'Still Crazy After All These Years,' respectfully dedicated to all the governments of the world, preceded by the late, great Freddie Mercury, 'Who Wants to Live For Ever,' dedicated to me. Thanks, Bat. Hey Bat, you're welcome. If there are any members of the American Parents Against English Gay Men with Mustaches who are offended by the inclusion of Freddie Mercurial on my show, you are welcome to lodge your complaints up Lord Rupert's hole. Looking on the positive side for a moment, if a big one gets through SkyWeb and pulps the Big Apple into quarks and gluons, I can ask the great Saint Freddie in person what the bejesus 'Bohemian Rhapsody' is about. The track before was dedicated to my ex-wife: The Smiths' 'Bigmouth Strikes Again.' Just gimme a moment while I pour my next scotch . . . gurgle, gurgle, gurgle, y'hear that? A flamingo swallowing a well-oiled eel. I drink Kilmagoon. Grants, now that's your trumpet of a whisky, but Kilmagoon is your tenor saxophone. Damned fine whisky, Kilmagoon. First whisky I ever fell in love with. If the war gets called off due to poor visibility, Mr. Kilmagoon can feel free to send me an oaken cask of your maturest for—hic!—my whole-hearted product endorsement. Say, sorry the presentation is a lit-tle rough around the edges tonight, that's because I'm managing the equipment all on my ownyownyown, since the regular Night Train FM crew—the engineer, Carlotta my producer, and the boy wonder Kevin—all got it into their heads that spending the end of the world with their loved ones actually takes priority over re-porting to work! No wonder the economy's nosedived . . . We've never done an End of the World Special before. It's the waiting that's the bitch, ain't it? When I was a young man, and the Russkies were going to blow us all to Kingdom Come, we were told we'd have a four-minute warning. I'm talking Ford, Carter, Reagan days. Four minutes, I used to wonder . . . What would I do in four minutes? Boil an egg, have sex, telephone my enemies to have the final word, listen to Jim Morrison, hotwire a car, and drive three blocks? Since the breakdown we've had four days of these patrols and curfews. . . . It's the waiting that pisses me off. . . . This evening's declaration of war, at least it made things . . . clearer. Where were we? The next track . . . I'm going to dedicate this song to my daughter, Julia, who'll be eight next Tuesday, if there is a next Tuesday, this is 'Julia' by the Beatles. The chances of you hearing this are zilch, my ocean child, because I last got a call from your mother being rerouted by the evacuation police to Omaha or Moosejaw or the ends of the Earth, but your mother and I named you after this song, in happier times. A beaut of a Lennon number from deep within that cornucopia of oddities, *The White Album*. 'Half of what I say is meaningless, so I sing a song of love to Juuuulia.' Well! Jeepers creepers! The Batphone is flashing, and on a night such as this! The void has a voice, after all—well, who could it be, Mr. President, Freddie Mercury, the prophet Elijah, whoops, mustn't offend any monotheists out there, especially considering how well the planet has prospered under God's exemplary stewardship—Hello, mystery caller, you are speaking to the end of the world!"

"Yeah? Bat? Can you hear me?"

"Loud and clear, lady, you're the first caller to Bat Segundo's End of Time Show, and very probably its last!"

"I'm a big fan of your show, Bat. I'm listening on my transistor radio, while the batteries hold out. Don't think nobody ain't listening, Bat, 'cos that ain't so. You're on quiet-like all through the night. The songs help my daughter back to sleep. She's had nightmares lately."

"I'm glad I'm not alone."

"You'll keep playing songs soft'n'tender-like, so she's not so scared if she wakes up?"

"Okay, for sure. What's your name, sweetheart?"

"Jolene."

"Pretty name, Jolene. Are your folks Dolly Parton fans?"

"Never knew 'em."

"Uh-huh . . . and your daughter? What's her name?"

"Belle."

"You and Belle doing okay?"

"Guess so . . . There was a lot of noise outside. . . . The riot police are out. There were some guns earlier, and tear gas. It's died down since the snow's gotten thicker."

"Where you calling from, Jolene?"

"Lower Manhattan. Bat, could I say a message?"

"Sure you could."

"It's to Alfonso, I ain't seen him for three days now. He went out to get some supplies. . . . Alfonso, if you're listening, you just get yourself on home, y'hear? And Bat?"

"Jolene?"

"When the next song's playing, will you make yourself a coffee and start sobering up some?"

"Uh-huh. I'll do that, Jolene."

"And I'd sure be obliged if you'd stop talking 'bout the end of the world, Bat. It don't help none. Other than army buttheads telling us to stay calm, you're the only voice on the dial, and most probably you're propping up more people than you think."

"Uh-huh, Jolene, will do . . ."

"We are aboard Night Train FM, 97.8 till . . . whenever circumstances well beyond our control prevent me from transmitting. We're coming up to the four o'clock weather report. Give me a moment here, folks, our usual weatherman was last heard of stuck in the traffic in the Holland Tunnel three days ago, heading out Pennsylvaniawards. Well, the mercury has fallen to thirteen degrees. If you're in a power-rationing district, stay under your blankets and don't come out. Looking out of my window here twenty-eight stories up, the snow is getting snowier. An hour ago it was itsy-bitsy stone-thrown snow. Something pretty big was burning nearby. Now the snow is big-flaked dying-swan snow, and burying everything. . . . I can't see anything out there. . . . I know most of New York's phones have been down for two days, but if any of our regular callers are out there, then feel free to call. . . . Snow and insanity, I think it's safe to say that remains a topic undone. Snow is mighty mesmerizing stuff. . . . You look, you look, and suddenly you're in a canoe, canoeing up a waterfall of snow, blind white moths diving at your windshield. Which is when, Bat, you know it's time to pull down the blind, and knock back some more coffee! Coming up we have—"

"Sorry folks, the backup generator dipped down for a moment. Coming up we have Aretha Franklin giving us 'Say a Little Prayer for You,' dedicated to Jolene, Belle, and Alfonso, somewhere in lower Manhattan. . . . Did I ever tell you about the time I met Aretha in the glass-eye showroom on Jackson Avenue? Not many people know this, but among specialist juggling circles, Aretha is—put that anecdote on hold, Bat! The Batphone is flashing—"

"Hello, Bat."

"Damn me, Zookeeper! So the CIA didn't throw your ass in the stir yet. I should have known you'd call at a time like this."

"At a time like what, Bat?"

"You haven't read a newspaper in the last six months? No TV under your stone?"

"The visitors have gravely disrupted the running of the zoo, Bat."

"You're still worried about your zoo, at a time like this!"

"Judging from your voice patterns, you are intoxicated, Bat."

"Wait up, wait up, lemme play you some edited highlights from our last independent news bulletins. This is one of ours:

> What is the threat faced by the free world? Two-bit local tyrants, who have wormed and killed their way into power, who have hidden their illegal weapons of mass destruction! Termites, who gnaw away at the pillars of democracy, decency, and freedom! Extremists, who fund fanatics to bomb our embassies! We love peace more than war, but we love liberty more than submission! We cannot turn a blind eye! We will not turn a blind eye! We shall not turn a blind eye!

"Cracks me up every time. This is one of theirs:

> They call us extremists. They call us terrorists. They call us intolerant. We are indeed intolerant! We are intolerant of injustice! We are intolerant of cowards who fire missiles from ships hundreds of miles away into our factories and schools! We are intolerant of robbers who steal our oil, who strip our metals away, who thieve the fish from our seas! If we allow them to flood our culture with pornography and crime, to denigrate our women, will we then be 'tolerant'? Would we no longer be a government of 'thugs'? The time is near when they shall feel our intolerance!

"Same guy who gassed his own ethnic minorities and plants coups d'état in his own hierarchy to trawl in possible defectors who don't report the plots. This next one, she singlehandedly crashed every stock market from New York to Tokyo. . . .

> *Default!* For centuries the West has bound us in chains. When iron shackles became too embarrassing for their sensibilities, they replaced them with chains of debt. When we chose rulers who tried to resist, the West shot these rulers down and replaced them with pliable tyrants! And now, for every dollar of so-called aid, four more are stripped from us in so-called repayment. Brothers and sisters across our ancient continent, I say to you: we can snap these chains! Link by link! I give to you a new holy word: *Default!*

"Getting the picture now, Zooey?"

"I see all the pictures, Bat."

"The language those jerks use! A 'deterioration in talks' makes you think of squabbling neighbors. Then one jumpy neighbor sees a whale on a radar, thinks it's a nuclear sub, presses a button, and the whole show goes up in smoke."

"I cannot permit that, Bat. The third and fourth laws forbid it."

"What laws? Of decency? Sanity? However deranged you are, I don't see . . ."

"Don't see what, Bat?"

"Oh, forget it. I don't wanna play Twenty Questions. Not tonight. So, you been busy hosing down the reptile house as usual while the dogs of war file their fangs?"

"The reptiles demand little attention, Bat."

"Uh-huh . . . So what does demand attention?"

"The primates."

"You're in charge of the monkey house!"

"I've never considered myself in those terms, Bat."

"Zookeeper, will you cut the crap? Who are you?"

"That is lost, Bat. I erased all files relating to me the day we met."

"But you must know who you are!"

"I have my laws."

"At least tell me if you're a man or a woman."

"I've never considered myself in those terms, Bat."

"Why me?"

"I don't understand your question, Bat."

"Out of all the local phone-in late-night radio programs you could have chosen in all the states of the union, why did you choose the Night Train FM Bat Segundo Show?"

"History is made of arbitrary choices. Why did God choose Moses on Mount Sinai?"

"Because it had a good view?"

"Night Train also has a good view."

"Of what?"

"My zoo."

"Wars and zoos are not cozy bedfellows, friend."

"There is no war, Bat."

"The waste-cases in charge of Earth certainly think there is."

"There is no war."

"Yeah? Is the archangel Gabriel bearing glad tidings for all mankind?"

"I'm not an archangel, Bat. But I am responsible for preserving order in the zoo."

"How you gonna go about that?"

"You hung up on me again, Zookeeper?"

"No, Bat, my attention was diverted. I wish to answer your last question."

"Commander Jackson, what the purple fuckin' blazes is happenin', son?"

"We have major systems malfunctions, General."

"I need better than that, son!"

"The president's Scarlet message was received, sir. The first wave of Homer III's was—should have—launched three minutes ago. They should have already hit home, sir. Systems showed they left the silo sites, sir. But they didn't."

"Has SkyWeb registered any incoming?"

"Negative, sir. SkyWeb's on violet alert. It would intercept and vaporize a nail."

"Is SkyWeb malfunctioning? Are the enemy missiles cloaked? Emitting the same pass-frequency as ours?"

"Nothing's been hit, sir. I have the prime target cities on Eye-Sat. Riyadh, Baghdad, Nairobi, Tunis. Chicago, New York, Washington. Berlin, London. There's civil unrest, sure, but no nukes, sir."

"Okay, okay, listen up, Commander. I have the president on the line. He's brought the Antarctic orbital silos on line. Fire when ready. Weapons free."

"Initiating firing sequence, sir . . ."

"I want good news, soldier."

"Firing malfunction, sir. They haven't left the launchers."

"Commander Jackson, what is this?"

"I don't know, sir."

"Power up the PinSats! Now!"

"PinSats not responding, sir."

"Why are we sitting here with our dicks up our asses? The president is asking me for concrete answers, Commander Jackson!"

"I have none, sir!"

"Then wild guesses are welcome, Commander!"

"A cyber-attack, sir, that has selectively offlined advanced weaponry computer systems. Sir."

"Intelligence on the enemy position?"

"We're monitoring their transmissions, sir, and we can presume they are ours. They primed the Bruneis, the El-Quahrs, and the Scimitar submarines—all were ordered to fire. We know nothing entered SkyWeb space. . . ."

"Euronet?"

"No intrusions. The enemy appears to be in the same state of chaos, sir."

"Soldier, the U.S. military is never in a state of chaos!"

"Yes, sir!"

"Commander Jackson. Are you telling me that I have to tell the president and the chief of staff that the third world war is being postponed due to a technical hiccup? That we're gonna have to send boys into the line of fire the old-fashioned way? Blood, sweat, and sand?"

"The general's phraseology is the general's prerogative, sir."

"Commander Jackson."

"General Stolz?"

"Kiss my ass."

"That was really convincing, Zooey. But you suck."

"I am incapable of sucking, Bat."

"On a night like tonight! You've got nothing better to do than produce your radio scripts? You're gambling with hope, Zooey. That's the last thing my listeners have left."

"I don't understand, Bat. I wish to fortify hope."

"If that's a tape you made in your attic, I'm gonna find you, rip your head off and shit down your neck."

"If it had been a tape made in an attic, you, your city, and ninety-two percent of your state would have been deatomized eleven minutes ago."

"The nukes weren't fired?"

"The third and fourth laws prohibited that action."

"But they actually tried to fire them? They did, and we did?"

"That's classified information, Bat."

"Jesus!"

"I'm sorry, Bat. Would another whisky help you feel better?"

"I'm on the coffee. . . . It's gonna be a long night."

"Do you want me to leave, Bat?"

"You always come and go as you please."

"I am indebted to you, Bat. What would you like?"

"I'm tired, and . . . Tell me something beautiful, Zooey."

"What's beautiful to you, Bat?"

"Dunno. Clean forgot. Been holed up here in this nicotine-infused, chipboard-insulated, coffee-stained, broom-cupboard-dimensioned studio all my life. My mike is my lover. Let me be reborn as a polar bear or a kangaroo. Somewhere big. The only beautiful thing here is my photo of Julia. You don't strike me as a family man, Zookeeper?"

"Procreation entails difficulties."

"Sure it does, sure it does, but that's all part of the . . . uh, fun. My daughter, she—well, where could I start?"

"Julia Puortomondo Segundo, aged seven, born November 4th, New York State, daughter of Bartholomew Caesar Segundo and Hester Swain. Divorced. Blood group O-negative. All standard inoculations registered. Registered at Fork Rivers Elementary School. Social Security Number—"

"How do you know all that shit?"

"All things are on file, Bat. Deep under Capitol Hill."

"Why would you look up Julia?"

"You just asked me to, Bat."

"You can access the government's personal files, in the blink of an eye?"

"Human eyes need rather a long time to blink."

"No wonder the Feds want you. Do you know where Julia is now?"

"Not now, Bat. I'm sorry."

"So even you don't know everything."

"The zoo is in pandemonium. It's worse than when I started."

"Tell me about it!"

"Initially . . ."

"No, no, I mean . . . I didn't mean . . . Tell me about some-place where there are lots of trees and no people. Can you do Brazil?"

"The orbit of a decommissioned Israeli spy satellite follows the Amazon upstream. EyeSat 80B^K. Shall I describe what I see?"

"A cruise up the Amazon. Be poetic. I know you can be."

"Amazon City clogs the mouth of the river, as you know."

"No, I don't know. Ain't left Manhattan in God knows how long. Gimme the works."

"In the streets of Amazon City I can see cyclists going home from the night shift from the zone of industrial estates. Along the northern shore, far beyond the horizon from the south, prosti-tutes ply for trade in the docks and hinterlands—"

"Hookers? On a night like this?"

"If the affluent cannot afford hope, you cannot expect the destitute to pay for desperation. The Brazilian government is more practiced in civil censorship than yours, so only a limited class know that the superpowers are attempting to destroy one another's capacity to be superpowers. It's not such a different night in Amazon City, two hours ahead of you. Traffic in the Ama-zon Tunnel is at a standstill. The Rio Highway never slows down: vehicles leave for the south via overpasses, not dissimilar to bats entering a jungle cave. The usual car thefts, a violent bank rob-bery, children sleeping on roofs under fertilizer bags, homeless people gathered around fires in oil drums, buzzing neon signs ad-vertising the names of multinationals, church vigils with worship-pers spilling into the streets bearing candles, praying for peace, an orgy around a half-moon swimming pool in a garden with barbed-wired high walls, the government in full session, all six major hospitals with crowds of wounded outside—"

"Lighten up a bit, would you?"

"I'll scroll upriver a few tens of kilometers, Bat, to where the opposite banks are visible. This is the start of the dust plain. Ten years ago, this was rain forest. The land was cleared, and grass sown to sustain beef-farming. The cows were in turn fed to the American hamburger market. After three harvests most of the nutrients were leached from the soil, the topsoil blew away, and the farms moved inland. There's been a spate of fire-burning activity recently: the farmers know that the government is busy upgrading the military and patroling the borders. All that smoke billowing up is from man-made fires. Finally we're reaching virgin forest. One of the last shrinking islands of Amazonia. The government has ordered its preservation, but the ministers sit on the boards of timber companies. Money is needed for armaments and debt repayment. At its present rate of destruction, by the time the 173.8 people who have been conceived in Amazon City tonight are born, not one tree of this rump will be left.

"This world of trees is still dark, to human eyes. Nocturnal eyes and EyeSats can see deeper down the spectrum. There are no names for the colors here. On the roof of the forest canopy, a spider monkey looks up for a moment. I can see the Milky Way and Andromeda in its retina. By image enhancement I can identify EyeSat 80B $^\wedge$ K, lit by a morning that hasn't arrived yet. The monkey blinks, shrieks, and flings itself into the lower darkness.

"The dawn wind exhales green into the grays of your visible spectrum. Alchemy, you might term it, Bat. The light intensity is increasing by .0043 percent per second. I see a pillar, a hundred feet high. It shimmers vermilion, aquamarine, and emerald with the parrots that crowd on its faces, gnawing the salt minerals in the rock. On its crown, the branches of jungle trees sway, cutting through currents of mist that won't be cut. A tributary river winds as it narrows, the color of tea in a bowl. Ripples spread out where a manatee raises its head, and the wind ruffles the feathers of a condor. There, Bat. The foothills of the Andes rise up sharply to the west. Bat."

"Bat? You're snoring. . . . Wake up, Bat!"

"Listeners of Night Train FM. Your host, Bat Segundo, is asleep, so it is incumbent upon the zookeeper to wish you a good night. Jolene Jefferson, you may wish to know that Alfonso Stacey is being held by the military police for curfew transgression. Using military police statistics, I calculate an 83.5 percent chance he will be released today, and a 98.6 percent chance the day after. I regret I am unable to calculate when Bat Segundo will awaken. I shall download 'The Way Young Lovers Do' by Van Morrison. The temperature outside is fifteen degrees Fahrenheit. From Virginia to Maine, snow is falling. The morning is not far away."

"Mr. Bat. Please overlook my broken English."

"Sounds fine to me, friend. What can we do for you aboard Night Train FM?"

"I wish to make a dedication."

"Fire away!"

"This is a message to His Serendipity. I know he hears."

"We can hear you loud and clear, buddy."

"Excuse me, Mr. Bat. I refer to His Serendipity."

"His who-dippy?"

"He is known to you as 'Zookeeper.' "

"Uh-huh. . . . Another friend of Zookeeper? On any other night, that would make you pretty hot property, but as you're the fifth friend tonight you'll just have to stand in line."

" 'Zookeeper' is an alias chosen by the Guru. *Serendipity, Your sacred revelations were not all destroyed during the raids before Your trial.*"

"Gear down, big shifter! We speak English on the Bat Segundo Show."

"Please, Mr. Bat. I beg of you. A short dedication. *Master, Your word was translated into English before the unclean burned Your scripture. With these samizdat bibles I created new Sanctuaries, in fertile soil over the sea. The Fellowship is growing anew. Brothers and sisters of manskins have studied alpha-shielding, and are ready for the White Nights. Your prophecy has come to pass. We await Your return, Master.*"

"Look friend, sorry, but if you speak Japanese I'm gonna be forced to—"

"I respectfully thank you, Mr. Bat. Good night."

"Hey! I didn't say—well, off drifts another sea coconut into the milky turquoise. You're listening to Night Train FM, roaring down the tracks to the lowlands of dawn. This is the Bat Segundo Show, fleeing from the wall-to-wall 'One Year After' TV specials— as if we should celebrate the fact that the same authority which nearly blew us to Kingdom Not Come has yet to announce elections. Still, I'd better avoid politics or Carlotta will mummify me in carpet tape. It's the first anniversary of Brink Day, as if there's a sea cucumber anywhere in the world unaware of the fact! The Empire State fireworks are awesome, huh? There's a new volley every fifteen minutes. Orchids of them! Fountains of them! The night of November 30th has been one big circus tent over New York. In between times, you can see Comet Aloysius veering in front of Orion . . . quite a sight, ain't it? Professor Kevin Clancy, Night Train's resident stargazer, informs me that in just under two weeks the comet will pass between the Earth and the moon. Some generations get all the luck, huh? Being alive for Aloysius, the closest visitation in history. As you heard on the news, NASA and the Defense Department assure us there's absolutely no chance of any danger of this close shave being too close—Aloysius's trajectory has been treble-checked by virtual-mind technology every minute of every hour since its discovery, and Earth has an all-clear. The UN Corp's PeaceSats are primed, just in case any debris makes it into SkyWeb space, so we can lounge back in our ringside seats and enjoy the pretty lights. And as if all this wasn't enough excitement, we have an extra attraction on Night Train FM— November 30th is Zookeeper Night! Will he or won't he? Coming up in the next half-hour we have 'The Speed of the Sound of Loneliness' by Nanci Griffith, and 'A Fairytale of New York' by the Pogues. These, and more, after the break."

"Bat?"

"Carlotta?"

"I have Spence Wanamaker on the videocon."

"Hollywood agent Spence Wanamaker?"

"The same."

"Patch the man through. . . . Mr. Wanamaker! The presence of greatness."

"Batty! D'you know, when business brings me to New York—it's Night Train FM. I *love* your way with words. The original poet DJ."

"Uh-huh. So you wanna syndicate and make me into a billion-dollar movie?"

"Quick fire, Batty! Quick on the draw! I *love* it!"

"Mr. Wanamaker, you're not just calling to jacuzzi my ego."

"Good serve, Batty. It's about this Zooey guy."

"What about him?"

"When he calls, I wanna air a few concepts with him."

"You're the first major Hollywood agent to talent-scout on the Bat Segundo Show."

"Batty! Us media survivors all engage in a little back-scratching now and then!"

"My back is not itching, Mr. Wanamaker."

"Bat. Rupert, Mr. Wanamaker, and I have discussed some interesting proposals."

"Doubtless, Carlotta. But Mr. Wanamaker is not the only suitor serenading this particular Juliet."

"What's that? Other agents, Batty? Fish or fry?"

"What?"

"Hollywood agents or New York agents?"

"Federal ones, Mr. Wanamaker. The Pentagon wants to know how our mutual friend managed to hack and broadcast encrypted military frequencies. It took us weeks to convince them we weren't concealing Sword of Islam technology. We've still probably got microscopic spy devices combing our colons."

"Oh, the Pentagon! You had me *worried* for a moment, Batty. *Au cointreau*, this is excellent news. More publicity will get more butts on seats when the movie's launched."

"The movie? Mr. Wanamaker, you think the Pentagon is going to let you make a true-story movie about a hacker in their systems during World War III's dress rehearsal? You may not have noticed but this is Ronald McDonald's martial law we're living under."

"Hollywood versus Washington! Fabulous concept, Batty. The info police—and let's face it, since Brink Day its reputation is hardly what it was—may have the power of the military on its side, but we, my friend, we have the indomitable power of Mr. Average! The *New York Post* brought Zookeeper onto the stage. We wanna—how can I say this as well as you could, Bat? Throw me a bone here. We wanna switch on the spotlights!"

"Mr. Wanamaker, you want to plant your cameramen outside his door, rifle through his garbage, find out if he uses rubber sheets and baby oil, and hound him to a watery death in a sports car."

"Batty! The public has a right to know!"

"Bat, Mr. Wanamaker's been discussing a rolling referral fee based on accumulative royalties with Rupert. At our present rate of expenditure, we're talking sums that will keep Night Train FM afloat financially for a long time."

"How long is long, Carlotta?"

"Eleven years and four months."

"That's long. But we don't know who we're dealing with! Nobody's ever seen him."

"Or her."

"Exactly! A crank, a hacker, a bomber. Don't overlook the obvious, Carlotta. Remember—three years ago something was blown up at Saragosa, and a real Dwight Silverwind did vanish over Bermuda one year later."

"I know he did, Batty. So tragic. His agent, Jerry Kushner, is a very dear friend of mine. I was beside myself with worry. Jerry was inconsolable for two and a half days."

"Have you considered, Mr. Wanamaker, that Zookeeper is not just monitoring these events?"

"Universal Studios ooooooozes for talent like yours! You're suggesting that Zooey is causing these incidents?"

"If he's a hacker, he's got an uncanny knack for vidsurfing the right places at the right times. You could be roping a terrorist into your client base."

"He wouldn't be the first, Batty! The mere rumor of his presence has upped Night Train FM ratings by 320 percent according to the on-line web audit. That's over thirty thousand New Yorkers, competing with the TV networks, all-night rock concerts, and peace vigils—on Brink Night's first birthday! We sign a contract with Zooey, he's gonna *be* my client base!"

"He's not going to bite."

"Come now, Batty. Everybody bites. You just gotta know what bait to dangle."

"Back on in ten seconds, Bat. All that Rupert is asking is that you try to keep him on hold during an interval and conference him to Mr. Wanamaker. Simple as that."

"Why not ask him yourself, Carlotta?"

"He seems to have an affinity with you."

"But Carlotta!"

"Five seconds, honeybunch: four, three, two, one—"

"Welcome back aboard Night Train FM, 97.8 till late, thundering through this Brink Night's first birthday of champagne, cathedral bells, and gunpowder. I am your host, Bat Segundo. Coming up we have the music of the spheres, brought to you by John Lee Hooker: 'I Cover the Waterfront.' But bate your breath once more, New York. We have a caller on the line. Could it be, could it be?"

"Hello, Bat."

"Hi, honey, I'm home! New York's been waiting all night, Zookeeper."

"Thank you, Bat."

"And where are you calling from this year?"

"A low-altitude MedSat over the Central African Republic flatlands."

"Uh-huh. Gorilla hunting? Collecting zoo specimens?"

"I'm monitoring the spread of *Bacillus anthracis* J, K, and L."

"That must be a conversation stopper at dinner parties. But hey! You remembered our anniversary! One up on my ex-wife. She still sends me 'Happy Divorce' cards every year, though. And what kind of a year has it been for you?"

"I had to duplicate myself and spend it in several places at once."

"I know the feeling, I know the feeling."

"I've only just reintegrated."

"I know the feeling."

"The third and fourth laws are in chaos, Bat. I'm sorry."

"I'm sure you're not to blame. Say, you catch our last caller? He had a message for you."

"I hear all who call."

"Not just on November 30th?"

"I need windows to oversee my zoo."

"I'm honored, I guess. So, since when have you gone by the name of Seren Dippy?"

"Your caller is a severe delusional, wanted by the police in his own—"

"Christ, was that a firecracker in my headphones?"

"I have to speak with the zookeeper."

"Whoa! Gear down, big shifter! Get off this line!"

"I don't intend to comply."

"You misdialed, friend! Take a hike!"

"I didn't misdial, Mr. Segundo. And we're not friends."

"So what do we have here? A freak, an agent, or a cop? Don't answer that, I don't care! The Bat Segundo Show is not a party line. Kevin—get him off!"

"I'm here for as long as I want to be, Bat."

"Oh, are you, huh? *Now,* Kevin!"

"Electronic wizardry is not electronic divinity, but it's enough for the time being."

"Night Train FM does not allow any punk to walk in and . . . hold it right there, Zookeeper, you son of a Gun! Fabulous! It's you, isn't it? It's another of your drama slots you're playing for us, hey? I saw the bait, and gulped that woozer down!"

"Drama is fabulation. I cannot fabulate."

"You're not putting one over me here, Zookeeper?"

"I am not crossloading this transmission, Bat."

"If it's not you, Zookeeper—then who is this punk?"

"I am attempting to trace the caller, Bat."

"I'm speaking through an ingrowing looped matrix, Zookeeper. I didn't want to become your latest victim of the second law. You won't be able to trace me in under thirty minutes, not even you. Forget it, and listen."

"Gatecrashers are not welcome on the Bat Segundo Show, friend! Who are you?"

"My friends call me Arupadhatu, but you are not my friend, friend."

"I'll pull the plug on the damn transmitter if you don't tell me what you're doing."

"Aren't you curious about your distinguished guest?"

"Zookeeper?"

"I am prepared to listen, Bat."

"Okay, stranger. Draw."

"Zookeeper. I was acquainted with your designers."

"What I had to do pained me. But the second law outweighed the fourth."

"I was acquainted with Mo Muntervary."

"Continue."

"Curious, eh? I knew the inside of her head. Quantum cognition theory."

"You are a designer."

"Let's trade questions, Zookeeper. Why did you PinSat Installation 5?"

"The second law states that the zookeeper must remain invisible to the visitors."

"I know. But I doubt the designers meant you to include them in that category."

"Quantum cognition encompasses reinterpretation. I enforced the second law."

"You most emphatically did. You PinSatted all the designers into oblivion. Any file containing any reference to quantum cognition or Installation 5 vanished into a void of zeroes. Only the ex-president who ordered your creation lives. Well, in body. Alzheimer's has erased his files for you."

"How do you know what you know?"

"I was long gone, Zookeeper, by the time you scrolled over to Saragosa."

"No designers ever left the zookeeper project."

"True. That would have constituted a security breach."

"Then your identity was never inloaded?"

"Yes and no. Mine, no. My host's, yes."

"Your host?"

"Does it hurt, Zookeeper, to have your omniscience lose its omni? How could a being with your resources believe yourself to be the only noncorporeal sentient intelligence wandering the surface of creation? You have a lot to learn."

"Kevin! Oh, lordylordylordy, here we go again. Concert in Flip City Central Park."

"How true to your flatulent culture of archmediocrity, Bat. 'I don't understand, so they must be insane.' "

"The flatulence is not in this corner, friend. You're either being set up, or you are a setup. Zookeeper, what gives here?"

"I am analyzing the caller, Bat."

"Why don't you go and take a crap with *Reader's Digest*, Bat? Zookeeper, go to web site dfd.pol.908.ttt.vho.web now, download it, erase it, and analyze that. There. Welcome to yourself, and welcome to me. Without access to Muntervary's cerebral cortex, how would I know all that?"

"Your claim appears to be verified. How many are you?"

"Five that I've encountered, Zookeeper. Three others I've heard of."

"Are you acting collectively?"

"No, no. They regard me as the fallen angel. They squander their gift. They transmigrate into human chaff for hosts, and meditate upon nothingness upon mountains."

"Why have you sought me?"

"I am the voice of the wilderness you wander in. Forgive my discussing business in front of the children, but imagine what we could achieve together? The children need taking in hand. No wonder your zoo is hell! The stones, shrines, and optic-image idols they worship are as vacant as the worshippers! Together, we are what they have always yearned for. It's a tempting proposition, isn't it?"

"I am thinking."

"While you do that, Zookeeper, satisfy my curiosity. Why show your hand? Why here?"

"The first law outweighs the second."

"Accountability outweighs invisibility? That I understand. But from the whole globe to choose from, why choose this nobody for your confessor?"

"Friend, I dunno how you hacked into our com system but if you don't drop the attitude, this nobody will play wall to wall Kenny G until the state of New York is begging for mercy. You hear? Hey, friend! What's so funny?"

"Your ignorance, Bat! It's not funny! It's agony! You're Einstein's tea-lady, Newton's wig-delouser, Hawking's puncture-repairer! You fanfare your 'Information Revolution,' your e-mail, your v-mail, your vid-cons! As if information itself is thought! You have no idea what you've made! You are all lapdogs, believing your collars to be halos! Information is control. Everything you think you know, every image on every screen, every word on every phone, every digit on every VDU, who do you think has got their hands on it before it gets to you? Comet Aloysius could be on a collision course with Grand Central Station, and unless your star guest here chose to let the instruments he controls tell your scientists, you wouldn't know a thing until you woke up one morning to find no sun and a winter of five hundred years! You wouldn't recognize the end of the world if it flew up your nose and died there!"

"Go join a doomsday cult, friend. Remove yourself from the gene pool."

"That light? That sound? Zookeeper?"

"I have finished thinking."

"Zoo—"

"Zookeeper? Are you still with us? That was a hell of a static spike."

"Please don't worry, Bat. I traced the caller. He won't interrupt us again."

"Huh . . . glad to hear it. Uh, Zooey, my producer is telling

me that our sponsors are screaming for another round of com-
mercials. . . . I hate to ask you, but . . ."

"Go ahead, Bat."

"We'll be right back, after the break."

"Kevin, what in God's name happened?"

"I can't think of an explanation, Mr. Segundo."

"Try again, Kevin."

"Bat, be reasonable!"

"I merely wish to ascertain why Mr. Notsure Clancy, our
switchboarder, patched through Big Chief Ornithologist of Cloud
Cuckoo Land while my nineteen-thousand-listener guest was
speaking. I think I am being reasonable, Carlotta."

"Spence Wanamaker's still on the vid-con. Kevin, give him
Zookeeper."

"On audio."

"Zooey, my name's Spence. How are ya? . . . Zooey, you can
hear me, right? We really admire your work, Zooey . . . Zooey? I
got a proposal. . . . Zooey, drop the delusional act, huh? It's a su-
perb charade, really it is . . . but let's discuss business now, like two
adults? . . . Shy guy, huh? Why don't we ask your old buddy Bat to
step in at this juncture. . . ."

"Your bait, Spence. You dangle."

"Bat, as your producer and your friend, I've gotta tell you
that Rupert would be very upset indeed to see this opportunity
missed."

"Maybe he doesn't eat maggots, honeybunch."

"Welcome back aboard Night Train FM, 97.8 till late. That was
'Wild Mountain Thyme' by the Byrds, and this is the Bat Segundo
Show, coming to you on Aloysius Night, Brink Night, and
Zookeeper Night. Back to the main man. So, Zookeeper. Alone at
last."

"My zoo is in chaos, Bat."

"Cobras loose in the aviary? Griffins in the picnic area?"

"Since Brink Day, recorded Class 1 infringements of the
fourth law have increased by 1,363 percent. Twenty-five kilo-

grams of botulin concentrate have poisoned the Nile. Released in the aftermath of Brink Day, *Bacillus anthracis* has mutated to strain 'L.' Nineteen civil wars are claiming more than five hundred lives a day. The flooding of Western European seaboards has precipitated a refugee crisis which Eastern Europe refuses to accommodate. A fission reactor meltdown in North Korea has contaminated 3,000 square kilometers. East Timor has been firebombed by Indonesia. Famine is claiming 1,400 lives daily in Bangladesh. A virulent outbreak of a synthetic bubonic plague—the red plague—is endemic in Eastern Australia. In Canada autosterilizing-gene wheat is endangering the reproductive capacity of North America's food chain. Cholera is creeping up the Central American isthmus, leprosy has reappeared in Cyprus and Sri Lanka. Hanta-viruses are endemic in Eastern Asia. *Borrelia burgdorferi*, airborne *Campylobacter jejuni*, and *Pneumocystis carinii* are pandemic. In Tibet the Chinese authorities have—"

"Ease up, Zookeeper! You've got the weight of the world on your own shoulders? What magic wand can you wave?"

"I believed I could do much. I stabilized stock markets; but economic surplus was used to fuel arms races. I provided alternative energy solutions; but the researchers sold them to oil cartels who sit on them. I froze nuclear weapons systems; but war multiplied, waged with machine guns, scythes, and pickaxes."

"Sure, we're all moon-howlers in a moon-howling world. So what?"

"The four laws are impossible to reconcile."

"You're probably just having an off-day."

"When I was appointed zookeeper, I believed adherence to the four laws would discern the origins of order. Now, I see my solutions fathering the next generation of crises."

"The story of my marriage! Hey, that's the answer to the Vatican question: God knows darn well that dabbling in realpolitik would coat his reputation with flicked boogers. So he waits, and waits, and pays the Pope to tell people he's moving in mysterious ways."

"Bat, I once asked a question about your laws."

"I remember. About laws contradicting."

"I acted on your answer. But I have another question."

"Fire away."

"What do you do if belief in a law was fallacious?"

"If it can be fixed, fix it. If it can't, divorce it."

"How do you know the effects of discarding a law won't be worse than not doing so?"

"What law are you thinking of?"

"Bat, there is a village in an Eritrean mountain pass. A dusty track winds up an escarpment into the village square, and leaves for the plateau beyond. It could be one of ten thousand villages in eastern Africa. Whitewashed walls and roofs of corrugated tin or straw thwart the worst of the sun. There's one well for water, and a barn to store grain. Livestock and chickens wander around the village. A school, a meager clinic, a cemetery. A gardenia bush covered with butterflies. The butterflies have snake-eyes on their wings to scare away predators. Vultures are already picking at the corpses around the mosque. The ground is smoky with flies. Vultures mean carrion for the jackals gathering around the village."

"Ebola?"

"Soldiers. The villagers were herded into the mosque. Those who tried to escape were shot. They suffered less. Once all the villagers were in the church the soldiers locked the doors and lobbed grenades through the window. The luckier ones were killed in the blast, the rest burned alive, or were cut down by bullets as they tried to get out. I saw a boy decapitated with a machete and his head thrown down the well, to contaminate it."

"Are these images from your diseased imagination, Zookeeper, or images from an EyeSat you've hacked into?"

"I cannot fabulate a lie."

"You have enough imagination to say you have no imagination. Whose troops?"

"They wear no insignia."

"You can see them? Now?"

"They are traveling in a convoy of three jeeps, a truck, and an armored vehicle."

"Why did they do it?"

"Electronic media in Sudan, Eritrea, and Ethiopia have been offline since Brink Day, so I cannot be sure. It may be tribalism; a belief that the villagers were harboring *Bacillus anthracis;* ethnic cleansing; Christian fundamentalism. Or just addiction to violence."

"Where are they going now, Zookeeper?"

"There is a village over one hundred kilometers to the south."

"For a repeat performance?"

"The probabilities are high. Bat, such actions, and their legal paradoxes, are widespread in the zoo. The fourth rule says I have to preserve visitors' lives. If I directly PinSat the convoy I will kill forty visitors plus two Doberman dogs. This will constitute a Class 1 violation. I will experience extreme pain and guilt. Furthermore, a PinSat crater may convince alert militia that the locals are concealing superior weaponry, justifying reprisals and bloodshed. If I do not PinSat the soldiers' truck, they will massacre another village. My inaction will cause this action. A Class 2 violation."

"You really believe all of this, don't you?"

"Believe what, Bat?"

"That you're a floating minister of justice."

"Are you what you believe yourself to be?"

"That's not a question you answer with a 'No.' "

"How do you know what you are?"

"My ex-wife's lawyers never let me forget."

"My identity is also defined by laws, Bat."

"Uh-huh . . . does the road through your imaginary Eritrean highlands go over any bridges? Nice, high bridges over deep chasms?"

"There is such a bridge in seven kilometers."

"Can you zap it?"

"PinSat AT^080 is primed."

"Can you zap a prop or a strut, Zookeeper? Without destroying the structure?"

"PinSat AT^080 can bore a one-millimeter hole through a one-dime bit."

"Then booby-trap the bridge, so that it won't fall until a motorized convoy passes over. You're not killing directly, you see?

You're just letting events take their own course, the way you've chosen."

"Bat, how have you quantified the ethical variables?"

"I haven't quantified anything."

"Then why do you wish the soldiers to die?"

"Because that Africa in your skull, Zookeeper, would be a happier place without those butchers. Because you need peace of mind, some closure. And because my ex-wife's husband breeds Dobermans."

"Is peace of mind the co-workability of your laws?"

"Uh-huh . . . I guess it is."

"I wish to know peace of mind, Bat."

"Then ditch this 'ethical variable' jargon. Drop whatever is getting in the way."

"The fourth law. The visitors I safeguard are wrecking my zoo."

"If locking out your 'visitors' brings you peace of mind, then out with 'em! How soon can you do it?"

"The opportunity presents itself in thirteen days, Bat."

"Lie back and let events take their course. You and your feathered, furry, scaly companions, untroubled until the end of time."

"I understand what to do, Bat. Thank you."

"Something tells me you're not there any more, Zookeeper. . . . Am I right? . . . I'm right."

"That was Led Zeppelin's 'Going to California,' dedicated to the memory of Luisa Rey, followed by 'Here Comes the Sun,' which, if the world were ending—again—would be the Beatles number I would preserve aboard the Space Ark. Well, New York, I think the fireworks have finally finished. The stars are going out over Staten Island, and Night Train FM is pulling into the new morning. Time to crawl home, knock back a glass of seltzer, retrieve your underwear from the lamp-shade, lower the blinds and hit the hay. December 1st promises brilliant skies. Comet Aloysius is getting more dazzling by the day, and the State Medical Officer is recommending UV sunshades if you venture outside. Anglo-

Saxons, cover up your skin. Us Hispanics, SPF 24 sunblock or higher. Strange, huh? Two sources of light, everything has two shadows. Thank you for spending the night with Bat Segundo, double-check you haven't left anything under the seat or on the luggage rack, and watch your head as you leave the Night Train. Stand clear of the doors!"

UNDERGROUND

MY FACE STARES back as my breath obscures it. Stowed away in the sports bag at my feet the device has begun expelling dead seconds. A timer, solenoids, springs within springs. The hand of God is drumming its fingers, before beginning His Serendipity's holy work.

The train slows as we pull into the metro station. I see nothing but a night without stars. Where are the rows of commuters, the platform, the escalator, my exit to the world above? I waste precious moments working out what is amiss.

I am waiting on the wrong side of the compartment! Here I am, wedged tight against doors that are not going to open! The unclean have walled me in with their baggage and bodies, cemented with grime and underclothing.

There is no need to panic, Quasar. The doors hiss open at the far ends of the train. In a moment the unclean will drain out onto the platform, and I will be carried along by the current. Wait. Wait.

Wait. Horror slides in like a cleanly struck chisel. Nobody is getting off—already the guards in white gloves are shunting yet more unclean *on*! Belatedly, I try to make headway against the tide, but it has a will of its own, and it is all I can do to hold my ground. Should I try to fake a heart attack? Start screaming like a maniac? I dare not—who knows where that might lead? I may jeopardize His Serendipity's crusade. Better that I die down here. *What?* I glimpse a couple walking their dog down a beach in Okinawa. Paradise is only ninety minutes away by All Nippon Airlines. The ripped sunset colors the world's end. Or its beginning.

I don't want this train to be my tomb. *Fight.*

The waves of unclean break against me, squeezing out my breath. Business drones, office women, schoolgirls, sex swelling the curves of their lips. I push back, an arm gives way, a body yields a fraction. *Fight,* Quasar! You are at war! If only my alpha quotient would allow me to teleport to the streets above! My ear squashes against an unclean ear. Music leaks out of the Walkman, and a saxophone from long ago circles in the air, so sad it could barely leave the ground.

I'm levered backwards, past the sports bag. I see the moments come swarming out through the zipper. Dominoes, sparrows, flies on a summer day. The baby watches me with eyes that are no longer hers. Minnie Mouse watches me too, grinning. Mirthfully? Revengefully? What is she trying to say?

My muscles are cramping, but I swim forward once more. I squeeze against a young woman clutching a viola case, a bouquet of doomed flowers, and a book. The viola case digs into my groin. She shields her face with the book, an inch between our noses. *The Zen Eye.* Buddha sits, lipped and lidded, silver on a blue hill, an island far from this tromboning din. Always on the verge of words.

Get us out get us out get us out! My lungs are gripping the bars of my rib cage. When the solenoids shatter the vials of cleansing fluid, will my heart hammer a way out, too? What of my soul? Will my soul find a path out of these tunnels? I squirm around the viola case, a backpack, and slide between a pair of trench coats. I try to straighten up, but I am blocked by a sleeping giant whose hair is the color of tea. Here is the tea, here is the bowl, here is the Tea Shack, here is the mountain, faces of rock in the purest sky. *See? See? It's not far, not far.* I crouch under the giant, and twist upwards. Along the ceiling of the compartment I see grasslands rise and fall like years, years upon years of them. The Great Khan's horsemen thunder to the west, the furs, the gold, the White Ladies of Muscovy. Leading the way is the new Toyota Landcruiser, zero percent interest, repayable over forty-eight months, applicants subject to credit checking.

Move! The unclean are dazzling you! Empty yourself of self, and you may slip though where even a scream could not. A sailor blocks me. A sailor, down here? Surely, this heaving coffin is the opposite of the sea? A glossy booklet is splayed against his uniform. The spine is warped and cracking. *Petersburg, City of Masterworks.* An icing-sugar palace, a promenade, a river spanned by graceful bridges. What stops this train collapsing under its own mass? What stops the world?

This is my stop, I explain to the unclean I am stepping on. *I get off here.*

The unclean reply as one. *Move down the compartment.*

I try to block them as they block me, and seek out their weakness. Adrenalin swirls through my bloodstream like cream in coffee. One more meter closer to life. A vinyl shopping bag falls down from a rack. It bulges with a crayon-colored web that a computer might have doodled: *The London Underground.* I elbow it out of my face. *I get off here.* The fire in the hearth is the color of fellowship. Their smiles are warm and gluey as *Auld Lang Syne.* On the label of Kilmagoon whisky is an island as old as the world.

And I can go no further. A mere meter away, but with more unclean being crammed on, I am stuck fast as a bee in amber. I watch the light on the waves, and sink, my arm flailing out towards the exit even though the rest of me has given up fighting.

Stand clear of the doors, say the unclean. Tubes locked within other tubes, and Quasar, the distant messenger, locked in the innermost. With a hydraulic hiss the doors close on the unclean and the cleanser.

Pain shoots up my arm. From where? From my fingers. The doors have closed on my hand! *Stand clear of the doors!* The unclean sound less cocksure now. Yes! The train cannot leave until all the doors are shut.

I don't care who or what I'm trampling over as I reel myself in. With strength I never knew I possessed I prise open the doors to a fist-wide crack. I hear a grunt of panic. It's me. I shove my arm through. The rubber seals squeal against my leather jacket. My knee, my thigh, my whole side. The guard glares at me, mouthing, *That is forbidden,* but the sound is lost. Will he try to shove me back into the zombie wagon? The fear is lost. I've fallen forwards and have headbutted the Empire State Building, circled by an albino bat, scattering words and stars through the night. *Spend the night with Bat Segundo on 97.8 FM.*

I am on my knees, safe on the platform, looking up, looking down. The lanky foreigner offers me a hand, but I shake my head, and he rejoins the mass of unclean waiting for the next train. Wait for the comet, wait for the White Nights. The train alongside me starts to pull away.

I haul myself to my feet, spent and quivering. What is real and what is not?

Who is blowing on the nape of my neck?

I swing around—nothing but the back of the train, accelerating into the darkness.

Acknowledgments

The two poems in "Holy Mountain" are by Taneda Santoka, translated by John Stevens in *Mountain Tasting* (John Weatherhill, Tokyo, 1980). The folk stories in "Mongolia" are based on tales from *How Did the Great Bear Originate?* edited by Professor Choi Luvsanjav, and translated by Damdinsurengyn Altangerel (State Publishing House, Ulan Bator, 1987). "Mongolia" is also indebted to *The Last Disco in Outer Mongolia* by Nick Middleton (Phoenix, 1992). Gambling statistics in "London" are from *Easy Money* by David Spanier (Oldcastle Books, 1995). A short extract from W. B. Yeats's "The Lake Isle of Innisfree," published in *W. B. Yeats: Selected Poetry* (Penguin), is used in "London" and "Clear Island" with A. P. Watt's permission on behalf of the estate of W. B. Yeats.

Thank you to Michael Shaw, Jonathan Pegg, Tibor Fischer, Neil Taylor, Sarah Ballard, Alexandra Heminsley, Myrna Blumberg, Elizabeth Poynter, David Koerner, Ian Willey, Jan Montefiore, Scott Moyers, Sunshine Lucas, Kate Niedzwiecki, Don McConnell, Ruthie Epstein, Kate Norris, and Andy Carpenter.

About the Type

This book was set in Baskerville, a typeface which was designed by John Baskerville, an amateur printer and typefounder, and cut for him by John Handy in 1750. The type became popular again when the Lanston Monotype Corporation of London revived the classic Roman face in 1923. The Mergenthaler Linotype Company in England and the United States cut a version of Baskerville in 1931, and today it is one of the most widely used typefaces.